ROYAL
PALACES
OF FRANCE

ROYAL PALACES OF FRANCE

IAN DUNLOP

HAMISH HAMILTON
LONDON

To
DEIRDRE
with all my love

First published in Great Britain 1985
by Hamish Hamilton Ltd
Garden House 57–59 Long Acre London WC2E 9JZ

Copyright © 1985 by Ian Dunlop

Book design by Michael Brown

British Library Cataloguing in Publication Data

Dunlop, Ian, 1925 Aug. 19-
The royal palaces of France.
1. Palaces——France——History
I. Title
944   DC20
ISBN 0-241-11450-0

Typeset by MS Filmsetting Ltd, Frome
Printed and bound in Great Britain by
Billing & Sons Ltd, Worcester

Contents

Acknowledgements

I WOULD LIKE to thank the marquis de Breteuil, Président de la Demeure Historique; Monsieur Jean Feray, Inspecteur en chef des Monuments Historiques; Monsieur J. P. Samoyault, Conservateur en chef of Fontainebleau and Madame Samoyault; Monsieur Daniel Meyer, Conservateur of Versailles; Madame Bercé of the Direction de la Patrimoine and Mademoiselle Bacou of the Cabinet des Dessins of the Louvre for all their help; the princesse Napoléon Murat, the marquise de Ganay, the marquise de Brissac and the comte and comtesse Roland Lepic for their help and hospitality, and the princesse Maria Pia d'Orléans-Bragance, comtesse de Nicolay for her charming hospitality at Le Lude.

1
The Palais de la Cité

T HE TERM "Sainte-Chapelle" properly describes the chapel of a royal palace. The presence of the most famous Sainte-Chapelle of all on the Ile de la Cité, in the middle of Paris, correctly proclaims that this area, now mostly occupied by the Conciergerie and the Palais de Justice, was once the residence of the Kings of France. The chapel itself is the earliest and by far the most important survivor.

Apart from the Sainte-Chapelle, nothing can be seen today of the palace inhabited by Saint-Louis. His name has been wrongly attached to some of the remaining fragments, all of which can be dated to a period about forty years after his death. The first depiction that we have of the palace – the exquisite miniature by Pol de Limbourg in the *Très Riches Heures du duc de Berry* – shows it as it was after the important additions and reconstructions of Philippe le Bel.

All that the Romantic imagination could picture of an idealised Golden Middle Age breathes from that lovely portrait. It is as if the medieval sky was always as untroubled as the clear and cloudless azure of Pol de Limbourg's painting. The scene is idyllic – the juxtaposition of a proud and princely architecture with the simple, rustic charm of the surrounding country. In the background is the palace, an exciting medley of high-pitched roofs with correspondingly acute-angled gables and towers capped with pointed *poivrières*: in the foreground are the meadows; the peasants are scything the hay while their women rake it into little stooks beside the pollard willows which line the stream. It is a halcyon day, and it only needs a kingfisher to complete the picture.

But over this delightful scene must be superimposed another, more sinister. The harvesters are working on an island which can only be the Ile des Juifs, which in those days separated the Ile de la Cité from the Quai des Augustins. It was here, on 18 March, 1314, "at the hour of vespers", that the Grand Maître des Templiers, Jacques de Molay, and the Précepteur de la Normandie, Geoffroy de Charnay, were burned to death, their last agonies watched by Philippe le Bel and his Council from the parapets of the royal garden. According to the Chronicle of Guillaume de Nangis, "they were seen to support the flames with such indifference and calm, that the constancy of their death and of their latest denials were to all that witnessed it a subject of marvelling and of stupefaction". Jacques de Molay, who had asked for his hands to be left untied so that he could join them together in prayer, died professing the Christian faith, his eyes fixed to the last upon the towers of Notre-Dame.

Just this view, showing the great Cathedral rising above the southernmost extremities of the palace, is reproduced in a miniature by Jean Fouquet in the

I

Heures d'Etienne Chevalier. If this is set alongside the one in the *Très Riches Heures*, the two together provide the full panorama of the palace. A further illumination, coming from a less well-known source called the *Romuléon*, illustrated by Jean de Colombe in the late fifteenth century, shows a view so similar to that of Pol de Limbourg as to cause suspicion that it is a copy of his and therefore not an independent witness. It is quite clear, however, that the viewpoint from which Pol de Limbourg did his painting was the top of the Tour de Nesle; the angulation may be checked on early maps. It was the obvious vantage point to choose. Another artist working from the same spot would inevitably have drawn the palace from exactly the same angle. Jean de Colombe has included a number of details, mostly dormer windows, not shown in the earlier picture, and he either knew, or pretended to know, more about the architecture of the buildings directly in front of the Sainte-Chapelle.

These three pictures need to be related to the ground plan before we can begin to tread with a sure foot among the place-names of the palace. It is a fascinating task to build up the topography of the buildings from the often chance remarks contained in the official documents which have survived.

Running right across the picture is a battlemented wall. The right-hand section of this wall, we know, was sixteen feet high, for it was stipulated that houses built against it should not exceed this height. The other section must have been considerably lower. In 1296 there was very serious flooding and the Seine rose so high that one could pass over these walls "à batel pardessus les murs du vergier du Roy". This large enclosed area of trellises and trees was usually known as the "Verger du Roi" to distinguish it from the smaller "Jardin du Roi" within the complex of the palace.

On the left of Pol de Limbourg's miniature is a gatehouse or watergate which occupied the western extremity of this orchard. Jean de Colombe has brought it into the centre of his picture by a deliberate use of artist's licence. Known originally as the Salle de la Pointe, and later as the Maison des Etuves, this gatehouse was officially the Gardener's house, but contained, at least in 1428 when an inventory was made, the *étuves*. This word, which sometimes comes through into English as "stuffe", designated a sort of steam bath.

Behind this, at the left-hand end of the palace buildings, is a tall, distinguished-looking block with an impressive enfilade of buttresses and pinnacles. It was known sometimes as the Salle sur l'Eau – for it fronted the Seine on the northern side – and sometimes as the Salle sur les Jardins. It later acquired and retained the name of Salle Saint Louis. This was a correct attribution, for the building dated from his reign. It was originally outside the line of fortification as established by Philippe-Auguste. Part of the work of Philippe le Bel was to incorporate the Salle Saint Louis within the rest of the palace and to advance the curtain wall to this new boundary.

The building was flanked to the north by a tall, cylindrical tower with a blue slate roof which is just visible in the picture. This tower was crenellated and bore the name of "Tournelle de la Réformation" – an appellation which refers to the housing within it of the record office of the *Enquêteurs-Réformateurs-Généraux*. Only later did it acquire its present name of "Bon-bec". "Avoir bon bec" means to have the gift of the gab, but it is here used with a rather more grim interpretation – the readiness to talk which is the end

1 *Left:* From the *Mss Romuléon.* Seen from the Tour de Nesle. The artist has placed the Salle de la Pointe in the centre; it should be off left. The roundels on the wall are imaginary.

2 *Below:* Painting by Ian Dunlop, showing the whole palace from the west.

product of the torture chamber. It is not, however, until the year 1500 that the undercroft of this tower is first actually described as "la Chambre où l'on donne la question".

At right angles to the Salle Saint-Louis a long façade stretches across the broad end of the Verger du Roi. The first section of this façade was one of the covered galleries known at the time by the general term of Grandes Allées, but later specified as the Galerie des Peintres. These galleries formed a cloister which enclosed the Jardin du Roi. Climbing up the outside wall of the Galerie des Peintres was a covered staircase which connected the Salle Saint-Louis with the royal orchard.

To the right, or south, of the Galerie des Peintres, and set back between two rectangular pavilions, is the Logis du Roi. The two pavilions, the Tour Carré on the left and the Tour de la Librairie on the right, were originally joined by a massive curtain wall with a *chemin de ronde* carried on four deeply-recessed arches. These buildings all date from Louis VI, known familiarly as Louis le Gros.

Louis had occasion to strengthen the security of his Parisian palace. On 12 March, 1111, Robert, comte de Meulan took advantage of the King's absence to pay off an old score and attack Paris. He made himself master of the Ile de la Cité. Louis rushed to the defence of his capital and, finding the bridges down, was attempting to ford the Seine when one of Meulan's soldiers attacked him. Louis, however, was the doughtier warrior and felled his man, observing as he did so: "It is not only in chess that it is forbidden to take the King."

It may have been this experience that caused Louis to reinforce his position. In the next few years he built the *donjon* or Grosse Tour. This great cylinder of stone with its huge conical roof can be clearly seen in all depictions of the palace, rising high above and behind the royal lodgings.

The measurements of the tower are given on the plan of the Abbé Delagrive. The external diameter was 11.70 metres and the internal diameter 6 metres, which gives the walls the thickness, at ground floor level, of nearly 3 metres. These additions occasioned the comment of Jean de Jandum on the "inexpugnabiles muri" – the impregnable walls – of the old palace.

As with so many feudal buildings, what began as a fortress ended up as a prison. The Grosse Tour seems to have been set apart for prisoners of distinction. It acquired its later name of "Tour Montgoméry" from the incarceration here, in 1574, of the comte Gabriel de Montgoméry.

It was he who had accidently killed Henri II in a joust. Not trusting the justice of the Queen Dowager, Catherine de Medici, he took refuge in England, where he became a Protestant. During the wars of religion he returned to France and fought on the side of the Prince de Condé. After the siege of Domfront, he capitulated on the condition that he was granted a safe conduct, but the Catholics did not honour their word and he was taken a prisoner to Paris. Arraigned before the Parlement on the absurd charge of having plotted with Coligny the murder of Charles IX, he was put to the torture – *la question extraordinaire* – and was decapitated on the Place de la Grève. Montgoméry's last speech, in which dignity was married with wit, was aimed at the injustices of his age. "Count me companion in death with all

3 Jean Fouquet. The south end of the Palace with the towers of Notre-Dame.

those many people, simple according to this world's standards, old and young and mere girls, who in this same place have endured the fire and the sword."

The Tour Montgoméry was free-standing and set in the Petite Cour, an area surrounded on three sides by the palace buildings. West of this, and occupying the first bay of the building to the right of the Tour Carré, was the King's bedroom. Jean de Colombe has placed his Salle de la Pointe in front of this, but it shows clearly in Pol de Limbourg's painting, distinguished by its two Gothic windows, each of two lancets surmounted by a rose.

5

We know that Saint-Louis' Chambre aux Plaids was on the ground floor because the chronicler Guillaume de Saint-Pathus happens to record that, when the King's Council or Curia Regis was in session, the King is described as "descendu de sa chambre". His own room was therefore at first-floor level. This can be identified further from letters patent dated January 1329 which describes the Oratoire as "juxta cameram regiam" – "next to the King's room". This oratory, which looks from the ground plan like a little Gothic apse, projected into the Petite Cour towards the Tour Montgoméry. It is described in the *Chronique des Règnes de Jean II et Charles X* as "la Chapelle d'emprès la Chambre Verte". "La Chambre Verte", therefore, was another name for the King's room, which was no doubt hung with tapestry of *verdure*.

To the south east of the Tour Montgoméry, Saint Louis added the Sainte-Chapelle and the Galerie des Merciers connecting it with the main buildings, which stood, with the exception of the Salle Saint Louis and Tour Bonbec, within the curtain wall of Philippe-Auguste.

In the reign of Philippe le Bel a decisive change was made; the buildings ceased to function as a fortress: they became a palace.

Philippe le Bel, in the words of the *Grande Chronique*, gave orders to Enguerrand de Marigny to build a new palace "de merveilleuse et coustable oeuvre, le plus très-bel que nul en France oncques veist" – "of wonderful and costly work, the most truly beautiful that ever was seen in France". A rather more detailed account is to be found in the *Chronographia Regum Francorum*, which states that Philippe, "considering the antiquity and age of his Parisian palace", pulled it down and "caused another new one, together with all those edifices appertaining thereunto, to be built, of admirable workmanship and by artisans and workmen of the greatest knowledge and experience that could be sought out, and caused his own image and those of all his predecessors to be affixed to the inside of the wall".

This is a particularly interesting use of the word *palacium*. Philippe le Bel did not pull down the *palace*: he did pull down the Great Hall or Salle du Roi and replaced it with the famous Grand'Salle in which his own "image" or statue was indeed set up, together with those of his royal forbears. The word *palacium* here, therefore, means the Grand'Salle and, by extension, "all those edifices appertaining thereunto".

The word "palace", deriving from the Palatinum Hill in Rome, where the Emperors ultimately made their dwelling, has elaborated into three distinct meanings; we speak of Buckingham Palace, the Palace of Westminster and, more easily in French than in English, the Palais de Justice.

The word, which covers much the same ground as the word "court", applies to the building connected with the essential functions of the monarch – the making and administration of the Law. In the early middle ages the "palace" was wherever the King might happen to be. By the twelfth century this tended to be more and more in Paris. But, as the business of ruling became more elaborate and departmentalised, so the function of the monarch became delegated among different groups in different buildings – his own residence, the Parlement and the Law Courts. Each retained the title of "Palace". In the fifteenth century the Kings of France ceased to reside on the Ile de la Cité, but the palace continued in the other two thirds of its function. Charles V made his residence in the Hôtel de Saint Pol. It has since become more usual to apply the term *château* to such buildings as Versailles or the Tuileries and to reserve *palais* for buildings connected with the Law.

The conglomeration of buildings inherited by Philippe le Bel had originally been hemmed in on both its river fronts by a large number of private houses and mills, many of them belonging to the family of Etienne Marcel. Any expansion of the palace must have been either at the expense of these houses or by means of encroachment upon the Verger du Roi.

The former was the course adopted and the enterprise was started in 1293 and completed in 1313. Colonel Borelli de Serres has traced with great accuracy the process of these expropriations. The pretext was usually stated as being "pro ampliatione Palatii" – "for the amplification of the palace". Having got rid of these site restrictions, Philippe le Bel could now proceed with his enlargements.

The most important additions were those to the north of the Grosse Tour and the Sainte-Chapelle. These presented a long façade towards the Seine, in the centre of which were two great towers, known then as the Tournelle Criminelle and the Tournelle Civile. They both survive today but have become the Tour de César and the Tour d'Argent. Behind these towers, at right angles to the façade, was the Grand'Chambre, the meeting place between King and Parlement, later rebuilt by Louis XII, and at right angles to this, the famous Grand'Salle.

These buildings are shown to the left of Pol de Limbourg's miniature – the two towers being distinguished by their red-tiled roofs – the roof of the Grand'Chambre, with the Tour de l'Horloge rising behind it, and the twin gables and parallel roofs of the Grand'Salle.

The Grand'Salle – as it was usually spelt – was a huge double nave, seventy metres long and twenty-three across. It was reputedly the largest in Europe. Known also in contemporary documents as the Aula Parisiensis or the Grand Palais, it was the focal point of the royal and governmental buildings. It was built during the first fifteen years of the fourteenth century.

In 1292 the Maître Maçon du Roi was Jean de Cerenz, sometimes known as Jean d'Esserent. His name was still being mentioned in the accounts in 1303, so that he was probably the architect responsible for drawing up the plan of the Grand'Salle. In 1301 the name of Jean de Gisors, Maître Charpentier, makes its first appearance in the records, and it is reasonable to assume that it was he who mounted the two enormous timber ceilings. A third name needs to be mentioned – that of Evrard d'Orléans, Maître Peintre du Roi. This was the "Magister Evrardus de Aurelianis pictor" who received payment "de operis regalis palacii Parisiensis de tempore Philippi Pulchri". He is here called "pictor" – painter – but in the assessments for the *taille* of 1292 he is qualified as "imager", which means sculptor. The term *peintre* in fact often covered both these professions. His successor, François d'Orléans, was given the task of adding a statue of Charles VI to the effigies of the Kings in the Grand'Salle. It is highly likely that Evrard was responsible for the initial forty-two figures.

The two most conspicuous features of the Grand'Salle were these statues of the Kings of France and the famous marble table.

On the eight central pillars and on the responds which answered them on either side stood the Kings, gilded and polychromed. By the time that the Grand'Salle was burnt in 1618 there were fifty-eight of them, Henri III being the last to be represented. There was an old tradition that those who were portrayed holding their hands high had been princes of virtue and of valour, whereas those whose arms hung by their sides were those whose reigns had been undistinguished.

The table, made of a black, Alsatian marble, was at the west end of the room, nearest to the royal apartments. Mounted on a dais of three steps and made up of nine separate slabs of marble, it occupied nearly the whole width of the Grand'Salle. It served two main purposes: it was the high table at which the King and his peers would sit, and it was also the stage where the Court actors – the Clercs de la Basoche – performed their masques and mummeries.

In the third arch of the central arcade, opposite the entrance to the Grand'Chambre, stood the gilded figure of an immense stag – "cervus ingens deauratus". Corrozet, the author of a sixteenth-century book *Les Antiquités, histoires et singularités de Paris*, states that in 1388 the financial advisers of Charles VI, desiring to put by a reserve of bullion, "decided to make a stag of solid gold: and for their model was made the one in wood which is in the *Salle du Palais*". Only the head and shoulders, however, were ever cast in gold.

In front of the right-hand half of the Grand'Salle, Pol de Limbourg and Jean Colombe show the Tour Carré, dating from Louis le Gros, with the Gothic windows of the King's Room or Chambre Verte immediately to the right of that. Beneath the King's rooms were those of the Queen; her bedroom followed by the Chambre Blanche and Chambre aux Eaux Roses. These were on the ground floor, their windows opening onto a little garden, known as Les Jardins Moyens, which lay between them and the orchard.

Next to the Chambre Verte on the first floor was a room known as "la Chambre faicte de bois d'Irlande". Irish Oak was much in use in the great houses and palaces of England at that time because it was repellent to spiders and free, therefore, from cobwebs. Beyond this was a large but ill-lit room, the Chambre d'Apparat, where the King usually heard petitions. This opened into the royal Library which occupied the square tower at the southern end of the Logis du Roi. In 1368, Charles V transferred the books to the Louvre together with a number of benches and lecterns and "roues d'étude" – presumably some sort of revolving bookstand.

To the right of the Tour de la Librairie, Pol de Limbourg shows another *poivrière* with a red-tiled roof. This was called the "tournelle de la Reine Blanche".

To the right of the Tour de la Librairie, Pol de Limbourg merely shows three roofs of unequal height. Jean de Colombe includes the façades beneath them. The first block, with two important windows, was the room described in the inventory of 1428 as "la grant chambre appellée la Chambre de Monseigneur d'Orléans". Monseigneur d'Orléans was the brother of Charles VI.

The difference between the palace as it now stood and the odd miscellany of buildings which had borne that title before the days of Philippe le Bel was that, under the new system, the royal rooms were carefully insulated from those to which the public were admitted and where the legal business of the

State was carried on. Moreover, the building had ceased to be a fortress. Philippe-Auguste had been sufficiently confident in his dynasty to dispense with the practice of having his son crowned within his own lifetime. Philippe le Bel now felt secure enough to abandon fortification. "This conception," says Jean Gerout, "was singularly in advance of its time: in short, the palace of Philippe le Bel is a forerunner of the châteaux of the first period of the Renaissance."

Corrozet, writing as late as 1561, is profuse in his praise. "The said palace for the greatness of the same, for the disposition of its parts, towers, rooms, chambers, galleries, courts and gardens is esteemed the most durable and perfect building that is in France."

Of this royal house the two medieval miniaturists have given us a portrait which leaves little to be desired. Above all they show that sharply-indented skyline which was so dear to the medieval architect – the steady build-up of roofs at differing heights, with elegantly-framed dormers cutting patterns of white stone against their blue slopes; of towers capped with *poivrières* like delicately-sharpened pencils; of chimneys, pinnacles and gilded weather vanes that seem to pierce the sky.

High above the roofscape of the palace rises the upper storey of the Sainte-Chapelle, its western rose window lifted clear of the surrounding buildings.

The chapel had been designed in about 1241 to house the precious relic of the Crown of Thorns, purchased two years earlier from the Emperor of Byzantium Baudouin II, for 130,000 livres. The enormity of that sum may be calculated from the fact that the building of the Sainte-Chapelle itself cost only 40,000 livres.

Nothing could symbolise more dramatically the passionate desire of the medieval Christian to establish some physical contact and continuity with the events which lay at the roots of his religion than the architecture of this gigantic reliquary. Placed in the inner sanctuary of the royal palace and ringed round by the protective walls of its enclosure, it stood out by virtue of its imposing height and by the impressive richness of its decoration. Pol de Limbourg has stated this contrast categorically in his painting. Anyone given to reflexion could see from a glance at the Ile de la Cité that, just as the great towers of Notre-Dame asserted the supremacy of God in the mind of man, so the soaring pinnacles and gilded ornaments of the Sainte-Chapelle proclaimed the sovereignty of Christ in the heart of the King.

Whether consciously or unconsciously, Saint-Louis went one step further. In the additions which he made to the palace – the Salle sur l'Eau and the Galerie des Merciers – he made the royal buildings reflect, at a humbler level, the architecture of the chapel. The supremacy of God was fully recognised, but the authority of the King was derived from this supremacy and was given a similar architectural expression. The title "Rex Christianissimus" was already current; even the term "Imago Dei" was used of the King of France.

Gauthier de Cornut, Archbishop of Sens, claimed that the acquisition of the Crown of Thorns made it seem as if Christ had specially chosen France "for the more devout veneration of the triumph of his passion". There is often a note of national pride sounded in the great fanfare of the Gothic style, but in the thirteenth century that pride was still inseparable from the idea that France was God's chosen land, and it found its impersonation in the figure of the King, anointed with the Holy Oil divinely delivered for the baptism of Clovis, from whom his royalty derived.

At no time was this ideal more nearly realised than in the reign of Louis IX.

Curiously enough Voltaire was one of those who appreciated Louis both for his saintliness and for his statesmanship. "His piety, that of an anchorite, did not minimise his virtue as a King. His wisdom over money matters did not prevent him from being generous. ... He knew how to combine political ability with scrupulous justice and he is perhaps the only King to merit this praise." His wisdom over money matters certainly never prevented him from being generous where religious buildings were concerned, and for the Sainte-Chapelle he clearly did not count the cost. It is therefore one of the most perfect specimens of medieval architecture ever created.

A work of Gothic architecture should always be considered from the inside first. As Ruskin said, the exterior should be regarded as "the wrong side of the stuff, where we see how the threads go which make up the right, or inside pattern".

Following the formula of most royal chapels, the Sainte-Chapelle is of two storeys, the ground floor offering a place of worship for the household staff, the upper storey opening out of the royal apartments on the first floor and providing a chapel correspondingly more magnificent for the King and his courtiers. The *chapelle haute* is a lofty, vaulted chamber, with the proportions, almost, of a cathedral. To either side, the whole wall space is devoted to four enormous windows. Between these windows a cluster of colonnettes, the diameter of each proportioned to the amount of thrust which it receives, provides the only visible means by which the vault is upheld. The buttresses which form the necessary complement to this system cannot be seen through the rich translucence of the coloured glass. By this means the architect has created, as François Gebelin puts it, "une étonnante légerté où il a poussé jusqu'au bout le logique de la construction gothique en supprimant les murs"; "an astonishing lightness in which by the elimination of the walls he has pushed the principle of gothic construction to its logical conclusion". In this simple progression of vaulted canopies and fully-glazed interstices, the Gothic style achieved the ideal towards which it had all along been striving.

The external architecture also is a simple statement of the logic of Gothic construction – an alternation of windows and buttresses, the naked strength of the latter making possible the delicate refinement of the former. It would have been feasible to have slimmed down the buttresses of the apse since they receive a smaller share of the total thrust; the refusal of the architect to do this suggests a deliberate aesthetic effect which he did not want to diminish. The competent perfection of the architecture is only equalled by the inspired variety of the decoration.

"One would have said," writes Denise Jalabert, "that the artists of the Sainte-Chapelle wanted to bring together in this holy place so many leaves, so many fruits, so many flowers, so many birds and charming little creatures in order to glorify God and to give thanks to Him for all the wonders of Nature."

These carvings belong, for the most part, to the arcading which runs right round the chapel forming a *sousbassement* beneath the windows. In the third bay from the west, on either side, this arcading opens into a wide recess in which the King and the Queen originally had their stalls. These were just inside the choir screen which has long since been removed. The figures of angels over these two royal recesses are of a delicacy which relates them to contemporary ivory carving and to the work of the goldsmith. Stylistically they were in advance of their times and ushered in a new school of sculpture in which an elegant realism was the key note.

This is true also of the figures of the twelve Apostles who stand against the columns between the windows, becoming thus symbolically the "pillars of the Church". It is noticeable that the whole *sousbassement* of arcading in no way corresponds to the arcading of the windows. There is a strong horizontal division between the two with no vertical links apart from the columns which support the vaulting arches. The Apostles are so positioned against these columns as to rise head and shoulders above the horizontal division and, as it were, encroach upon the area of the windows.

These figures were removed during the Revolution when shelving was erected against the side walls and they suffered badly. Only six of those now replaced are the originals. Two were lost and four, too badly damaged to be replaced, are in the Musée de Cluny. These, having lost their polychroming, give a far better idea of the sculpture than those which are now in place. The artists show an astonishing skill, not only in the rendering of the heavy folds of a woollen garment, but also in the seemingly endless variety which they give to their drape. Often a pleasing contrast is achieved between the plain surfaces of the upper parts, where the garment lies flat against the torso, and the rich play of light and shade of the widening folds caused by the increasing fullness of the robes. The style has many similarities with that of the central figure of the Beau Dieu in the west portal of Amiens, but here it is more advanced, more refined.

The mention of Amiens brings us face to face with the question: who was the architect of the Sainte-Chapelle? The claims of Pierre de Montreuil have long held the field, but more recently Robert Branner has distinguished three architects where history had seen but one. Pierre de Montreuil, taking over from Jean de Chelles at Notre-Dame and building the Chapelle de la Vierge and refectory at Saint-Germain-des-Prés; the "Saint-Denis Master" who did much of the rebuilding of Saint-Denis and the Chapel at Saint-Germain-en-Laye; finally the builder of the Sainte-Chapelle whose style is much closer to the east end of Amiens and the choir at Tours than to any of the buildings just named. Branner therefore proposes Thomas de Cormont – the undoubted architect of the choir of Amiens – as the author of the Sainte-Chapelle.

A comparison between the windows of the two Saintes-Chapelles of Saint-Germain-en-Laye and Paris reveals the force of Branner's argument. Both architects used, for the side windows, the geometrical progression of two simple lancets supporting a rose, the whole contained within a further lancet: this complex lancet twinned with another, both of which support a larger rose, and the whole circumscribed within an outer containing arch. This gives a row of four simple lancets beneath the tracery. At Saint-Germain the narrower lights of the apse are treated in the same way as the side windows, but there is only room for two simple lancets and one rose. These two simple lancets are perforce much taller than those of the side windows. The break in rhythm is clearly apparent.

In the Sainte-Chapelle of Paris the architect has been at pains to procure as nearly uniform a height as possible for his simple lancets. He has increased the height of those in the side windows by reducing the size of the rose, and reduced the height of those in the apse windows where he has replaced the rose with a group of three trefoils – similar to those in the apsidal chapels of Amiens.

There is in fact a slight discrepancy in the height of the lancets, but to anyone looking down from the west end this discrepancy is almost impossible to detect. "Nobody," says Grodecki, "would ever notice it, so adroitly has it been 'camouflaged'." The "camouflage" derives from the fact that the first of the apse windows on either side are not visible until one has advanced a considerable way up the chapel. In this device we can see a Master Builder "fully conscious of all the effects of monumental perspective".

The Sainte-Chapelle could be said to represent Gothic architecture at its best and most typical. Nevertheless, it made its appeal to the more sophisticated taste of the eighteenth century. Sauveur-Jérôme Morand, who wrote the first important history of the building, is generous in his praise. "The piety of Saint-Louis has been most happily complemented in the industry of his architects: one might say that they have transcended the limitations of their own century, since this work still commands the admiration of the connoisseurs of today. It seems as if some more than human hand was at work in this superb monument."

The taste of the late eighteenth century was less hostile to Gothic architecture than is sometimes thought, but it was often arrogant enough to try and improve medieval buildings according to its own principles. One expression of this attitude was the frequency with which mural paintings were removed or concealed beneath a coat of whitewash.

We have today, as the inheritors of eighteenth-century taste as well as of medieval architecture, become accustomed to the naked, and often extremely beautiful stone. Its very plainness can show up effectively the "savante disposition des couleurs" of the stained glass. It can come as a shock to see the finely-chiselled stonework of the Sainte-Chapelle entirely covered with gilding and polychroming. Instead of allowing us to enjoy the contrast between stone and glass, the architect has tried to match the brilliant translucence of the glass with the flat pigment of painting on the stone.

This colouring is a nineteenth-century reconstruction, but great care was taken to find and to copy the survivals of the medieval painting. These were considerable enough to give the architect Lassus confidence that he was restoring the building to its original appearance. The overall effect is certainly that which was originally intended. It is difficult not to find it deplorable. As Louis Grodecki has said: "elle est banale dans ses motifs et assez grossière dans son exécution". It is a question of taste, but it is worth while comparing the Sainte-Chapelle with the choir of Tours Cathedral, of which it is almost a copy. At Tours the stone is left *au naturel* and we can appreciate its slender lines uncluttered and unbroken by meaningless bands of colour.

Certainly the polychroming was in accordance with medieval taste. The earliest known description of the Sainte-Chapelle, written in 1323 by Jean de Jandum, praises "les couleurs très choisies de ses peintures, les dorures précieuses de ses images, la pure translucence de ses vitraux". "The very choice colours of its paintings, the precious gilding of its statues, the pure translucence of its painted glass" which, together with "les ornements extraordinaires de ses châsses aux joyaux éclatants, donnent à cette maison de prière un tel degré de beauté qu'en y entrant on se croit ravi au ciel, et que l'on s'imagine avec raison être introduit dans une des plus belles demeures du paradis". "The more than ordinary ornament of its reliquaries sparkling with jewels, gives to this house of prayer such a degree of beauty that on entering one fancies oneself caught up into Heaven, and one could reasonably imagine oneself to have been introduced into one of the most beautiful mansions of Paradise."

In 1244 Pope Innocent IV referred to the excellence of Louis' construction in the words "opere superante materiam" – "the workmanship surpassing the material". These words are a quotation from Ovid's *Metamorphoses*, where they describe Vulcan's exquisitely-wrought doors for the palace of Apollo. There is an implied comparison between the architecture of the Sainte-Chapelle and the work of the goldsmith. Robert Branner has made the ingenious comparison between the interior of the Sainte-Chapelle and the exterior of a gilded and enamelled reliquary.

But in all this richness the "pure translucence of its painted glass" is by far the most important element. Six hundred and eighteen square metres of window have replaced the walls. Of these, some two thirds are the original thirteenth-century panels and one third a nineteenth-century reconstitution. This was carried out with so scrupulous a regard to the evidence relating to the missing portions and to the technical details of those parts which had survived that it is today almost impossible to distinguish the old from the new. This great work was achieved by the two glaziers Lusson and Steinheil, backed by the archaeological researches of François de Guilhermy. Together they effected a restoration of unusual accuracy and erudition and restored the windows of the Sainte-Chapelle to their original appearance.

This is all the more fortunate because, just as the architecture of the chapel comes at the very peak of the Gothic style, so its stained glass windows were made at the moment when that art had reached nearest to perfection.

The marvellous ensemble of the windows of Chartres, so much of which has so miraculously survived, had been completed in about 1240. The windows of the Sainte-Chapelle were finished some eight years later. The similarities are so numerous, and often so exact, between the designs formed by the ferramenta and by the background "mosaic" patterns, that it is difficult not to infer a continuity of craftsmen between Chartres and the Sainte-Chapelle. The last windows to be inserted at Chartres were those of the east end and it is in these that the greatest similarity is found. In particular the windows of Charlemagne and St. James, both in the north-east ambulatory of Chartres, recall the window of Genesis and that which combines the Prophecies of Isaiah with the Tree of Jesse on the north side of the Sainte-Chapelle.

The great height and narrowness of the lancets in the Sainte-Chapelle have imposed certain obvious restrictions upon the design, for each lancet is treated as a separate entity. Only at a later date did glaziers spread their compositions across the whole window, regardless of the interruption of the mullions.

It has to be said that the smallness of the scenes makes them impossible to "read" with the naked eye in the upper parts of the lancets. François Gebelin has tried to minimise this defect by insisting how the eye "se laisse ravir par la splendeur de l'ensemble sans vouloir analyser les détails" – "allows itself to be enhanted by the splendour of the overall colouring without wishing to analyse the details".

To someone with binoculars, however, these details add a whole new dimension to the general effect. The little scenes, simple to the point of naivety because their narrow limits impose simplicity, are boldly drawn and bursting with life. They reveal to us the iconography that the "splendour of the overall colouring" exists to glorify.

The central theme is announced in the central window. It is devoted to the Passion of Christ and one of the scenes of course depicts the crowning with thorns.

This little panel, towards the bottom on the right, demands our scrutiny. As one soldier performs the act of coronation, the others raise their hands in a gesture of identification. It is perhaps not over-fanciful to see in this a similarity with another scene, depicted in a miniature in the Bibliothèque Nationale of about 1260 of a coronation at Reims. It shows the moment when the Archbishop has just placed the crown upon the King's head and the Twelve Peers of France "uphold the crown" by raising their hands in a similar gesture. Saint Louis was well aware that many an earthly crown had been a crown of thorns.

It was Louis' custom to exhibit his precious relics in person, dressed in his royal robes, on Good Friday. For this purpose he mounted one of the little spiral staircases – only the northern one contains original woodwork – which gave access to the platform on which the reliquary stood. Most of the engravings show a little edicule, almost itself a miniature of the Sainte-Chapelle. This was made in 1632 by a goldsmith named Pijard. Within this stood the reliquary proper, described as an "ark of gilded bronze, in which was kept the Crown of Thorns, a large portion of the True Cross, phials purporting to contain Our Lord's blood, Our Lord's sweat and his mother's milk, besides a number of other relics, mostly relating to the Passion".

The True Cross was exhibited in the chapel during the night of Maundy Thursday for the benefit of the sick, with the result that the place was filled with invalids and epileptics. This practice continued until 1781 when it was abolished by Louis XVI on account of "the tumult, even the indecencies, which it occasioned".

A very close guard had to be kept on these sacred relics, and it was the responsibility of the Treasurer and the Canons to see that security was maintained. They had two Officiers du Guette, whose duty it was to sound a horn at evening when the gates were to be closed. Six men were kept on night watch, according to an Ordonnance of John I dated 6 March, 1363, "allans et venans toute nuit par icelle, tant pour la garde des saintes reliques, comme du lieu". "Coming and going all the night by that [the courtyard] both for the guarding of the holy relics and of the palace." Every two hours they were to knock on the doors of the chapel, in which a clerc, a chefcier and a sonneur slept every night, to enquire whether their services were needed. The "chefcier" was a personal assistant to the Treasurer.

The Sainte-Chapelle was provided with a Foundation consisting of a Treasurer – there was no Dean – and twelve Canons, together with a number of Chaplains which tended to increase with time, and the personnel of the Choir.

Their chief concern seems to have been to augment the revenues and preserve the privileges of their position. These included exemption from the jurisdiction of the Bishop of Paris, who was not even invited to the Consecration ceremony. A single example will show how jealously this immunity was guarded. In 1292, when Simon de Bucy, Bishop of Paris, officiated at the wedding of Henry of Luxembourg and Marguerite of Brabant in the Sainte-Chapelle, he actually had to put his seal upon a solemn *Acte* before the Treasurer, that in so doing he in no way prejudiced the independence of the chapel from his episcopal authority.

A considerable amount of attention was paid in the statutes to the sartorial distinctions of the Canons. In 1371, Charles V "seeing to his displeasure that other churches had almuces [fur scarves] similar to those of the Sainte-Chapelle", gave orders that these should wear almuces of badger fur and presented each of the Canons with his first one to serve as a model. Philippe le Bel had even forbidden the wearing of badger fur to the ordinary bourgeois, from which it must be inferred that it was regarded as a considerable sartorial distinction. But if the Canons were to be distinguished in their ceremonial robes, in their daily clothing they were strictly forbidden to follow the frivolities of fashion.

Charles VI, in a *règlement* of 18 July, 1401, required the Canons to be dressed "in simple habits, without superfluity in the sleeves, with 'honest' hoods and footwear". The word honest occurs frequently in this connection. In the statutes of 1303 they were forbidden to wear shoes with elongated toe-caps known as *poulaines*, "which are not pertinent to Churchmen, neither are they honest". Guillaume Paradin records that men wore shoes "with a long point in front, half a foot long; the richest wore them a foot long and princes two foot long which is the most absurd and ridiculous thing it would be possible to see". In 1365 Charles V tried to forbid the laity also from wearing *poulaines* as being "contre les bonnes moeurs et dérision de Dieu". It was not honest to distort the God-given shape of the human foot.

To be a Canon of the Sainte-Chapelle was a great honour and a likely prelude to preferment. Many of the most distinguished names of France – Montmorency, Brézé, Robertet, Longueil, Gouffier – are to be found in the records. In 1408, Jacques de Bourbon, who was, as his name implies, a relative of the King's, was installed as Treasurer at the age of fourteen. Objections were raised on the ground that it was laid down in the statutes that the Treasurer should be in priest's orders, but were overruled in view of his rank.

Alongside these illustrious names are many "d'une famille médiocre" who had risen by virtue of their ability. Sometimes they rose from the ranks of the musicians. Among these Nicolas Formé deserves a mention. He had been

4 *Right:* The Palace in the 17th century. In the foreground are the original gatehouses. Engraving by Boisseau.

5 *Below:* Viollet-le-Duc: The Sainte-Chapelle before restoration.

"sous-maître et compositeur" and had sung counter tenor "avec une justesse admirable". He was sometimes so overcome by the beauty of his own compositions that he fainted during their performance. Once at Saint-Germain he lost consciousness and fell backwards off the rostrum, and hurt himself so badly that the Queen, Marie de Medici, offered her own litter to take him to Paris.

The Canons' houses were grouped together on the south side of the Cour de la Sainte-Chapelle. They are shown in Jean Fouquet's miniature as a picturesque jumble of red-tiled roofs crowded within the containing wall where today runs the Quai des Orfèvres. On the right, at the junction of this wall and the Pont Saint-Michel, a sturdy tower marked the south-east corner of the royal domain.

From here to the Tour de l'Horloge stretched the eastern range of the palace buildings, which followed, with many irregularities, the line of the present Boulevard du Palais. It is shown in the foreground of Boisseau's engraving. On the left of this range was the Hôtel du Trésorier, reaching as far as the little church of Saint-Michel. Next to this the Porte Saint-Michel formed the secondary entrance to the palace. The main entrance, flanked by a pair of cone-capped *échaugettes*, was further to the right and gave access to the Cour du Mai.

Boisseau has depicted the palace from an angle diametrically opposite to that of Pol de Limbourg and Jean de Colombe – and indeed he shows the Tour de Nesle, from which they did their paintings, a tall, double tower in the background towards the left.

But Boisseau did his engraving in the late seventeenth century, after the extensive rebuilding necessitated by a disastrous fire in 1618. On the right, the

Grand'Salle has been replaced by the Salle des Pas Perdus, still built with a double roof. The tall building which links this with the Sainte-Chapelle retains, in its name of Galerie des Marchands, the memory of the Galerie des Merciers. To the left of the Sainte-Chapelle, Louis XII's beautiful Chambre des Comptes, with its triple pavilion roof, remains intact. In this miscellaneous ensemble the Sainte-Chapelle is beginning to look strange and out of place. It was built, as its name implies, to be the place of worship in the residence of the King. Now it had lost its raison d'être.

It was only gradually that this change had come about. In 1358 the palace had been the scene of a massacre which did not endear the building to the memory of Charles V. He was Dauphin – the first to bear the title – at the time, and at the age of nineteen was acting as Regent of France while his father, Jean le Bon, was a prisoner of the English. On 22 February, Etienne Marcel, Prévôt des Marchands, broke into the palace with a mob of some three thousand and murdered Robert de Clermont and Jean de Conflans in the presence of the Dauphin, whom he forced to don the red and blue bonnet of the insurgents.

When he became King, Charles V virtually abandoned the Palais de la Cité, making his residence in the Hôtel de Saint-Pol near the Bastille and turning his architectural attentions towards the Louvre and Vincennes.

Only the Grand'Salle, with the unrivalled accommodation which it offered, continued in occasional use. Victor Hugo, in his *Notre-Dame de Paris*, gives a picture of the Grand'Salle in his opening chapter. He had clearly read the *Journal d'un Bourgeois de Paris* and probably also the *Chronique d'Enguerrand de Monstrelet*. Between them they give a picture of overcrowding on great occasions of which Hugo has made good use.

They both describe the coronation of the English King Henry VI, aged nine, in Notre-Dame and of the banquet offered in the palace afterwards. They dined in the Grand'Salle with the King and his personal guests at the Marble Table, but the others had to take their chance among a huge crowd "who had come," says the Bourgeois de Paris, "les uns pour voir, les autres pour gourmander, les autres pour piller". "Some to look on, some to stuff themselves and some to steal." The guests were "so badly served that no one had any praise for it, for most of the meat had been cooked on Thursday [it was now Sunday] which seemed a very strange thing to the French".

It was the end. When, on 12 November, 1473, Charles VII regained his capital, he spent a token night at the Palais de la Cité. He never slept there again. Made over officially to the use of the Parlement, the palace was placed in the charge of its Concierge. In due course the building became known as the Conciergerie.

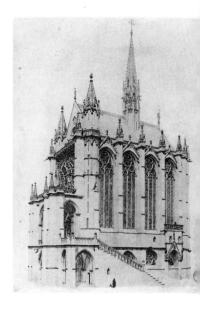

6 Viollet-le-Duc: The Sainte-Chapelle after restoration.

2

The Château de Vincennes

WITH THE DECLINE of the Palais de la Cité, the architectural interests of the Kings of France were transferred to the Louvre and to Vincennes. It is perhaps significant that these were both outside the confines of the city. It is true that they provided it with a defensive system, the one downstream guarding the river passage from the Vexin and the English territories beyond; the other upstream covering any possible threat from Burgundy. But it was not necessary for either of these fortresses to be the residence of the King. They may have been built not only to protect Paris but to intimidate it and to insulate the person of the King from the excesses of that over-excitable city.

Certain authors have been struck with the similarities between the genesis of Vincennes and that of Versailles. In each case there was a game-infested forest and a royal hunting lodge to attract attention to the site. In each case there was a desire on the part of the King to reside outside his capital. Finally, there seems to have been, in the mind of Charles V, a desire to set up a sort of royal town, where the leading figures of the government could have their habitation. Christine de Pisan, his earliest biographer, writes of it: "outside Paris the castel du Bois de Vincennes, *qui moult est notable et bel*, was intended to be an enclosed town and in it there would have been established fine manors, the houses of many lords and knights and others who enjoyed the greatest favour, and each would have been assured a lease for life, and the King wished it to be free of all [feudal] dues".

There is no evidence of any such houses having been built, but had the project been realised, Vincennes could indeed have been considered as the prototype for Versailles, and since it was here that Louis XIV first experienced the delights of building, it could have given him the ideas that he was later to elaborate.

The first official reference to a royal house here was in 1270, when it is called "regale manerium" – a royal manor. *Manoir*, in France, meant little more than a country house. Although a manoir might have been surrounded by a moat and built generally with an eye to self-protection, the word excludes the full paraphernalia of military defence. There were no such defences "in manerio regis apud Boscum Vincennarum". The word "boscum" – the *Bois* or forest – was the normal way of referring to the house. When Guillaume de Nagis describes Saint-Louis as taking leave of his wife and sleeping "aux Bois", it does not mean that they camped in the woods.

It was from here, on 12 June, 1248, that he took leave of his mother, Blanche de Castille, to go on his crusade to Damietta. It was to Vincennes that he returned in August 1254. It was from here that the greater part of his ordinances were dated. It was here, Joinville informs us, that he would sit administering justice beneath the foliage of an ancient oak. It was from here, in 1270, that he left for his final, fatal crusade.

It was equally popular with Saint Louis' immediate successors. Some of them were born here, all of them lived here, some of them died here. Vincennes was almost the family home of the House of Capet.

In 1334 Philippe VI decided to add to this unpretentious manor house a *donjon* or keep that would provide at the same time a residence more worthy of a King and a stronghold that was more or less impregnable. In 1337 work was interrupted by the war with England which was to last, on and off, for a hundred years, but in 1362 the work was resumed and a certain Jean Goupil was appointed treasurer "in opere turris novae apud nemus Vincennarum". He had a considerable work force to provide for – eight *tailleurs de pierre*, of whom the highest paid was one Guillaume d'Arondel, two hundred *maçons*, two hundred *compagnons* and one hundred *varlets*. In 1367 Charles V took up residence at Vincennes although two years' work was still to be done.

The keep which he built is more or less intact and offers a rare example of how a French King was lodged in the fourteenth century. It is surrounded by a curtain wall which supports a continuous *chemin de ronde* with alternate openings and arrow-slits. At each corner is placed a little turret or *échaugette*. On the west side of this outer fortification is a barbican or *châtelet* guarding the main entrance. It gives access to the keep proper, rising fifty-four metres above the level of the moat. To stand here and to look up at this mighty tower is to expose oneself to the full impact of the middle ages. Built for strength, it has perforce an austerity which is its only beauty.

The entrance to the keep is at first-floor level; a spiral staircase, with frequent openings towards the court, first led the visitor to this level within the *châtelet*. The central room of this outbuilding formed an appendage to the King's apartment and bore the name "L'Estude du Roy". From here the visitor crossed a narrow bridge, the far end of which was in the form of a drawbridge, which in turn gave access to the keep. This arrangement provided a high degree of security to the person of the king.

The plan of the building forms a square with strongly-projecting, cylindrical towers at each corner. These provide five principal rooms to each storey. From the north-west tower there is a small projection towards the north which afforded sanitary conveniences to each floor.

There are five storeys. At the bottom were the kitchens; the first and second floors formed the King's Apartment, the one above was affected to the royal children but also contained the Treasury; on the fourth floor were lodged the Officers of the Household and at the very top the soldiers slept as best they could, for much of the space was needed for storage of arms, clothing and munitions.

The architecture is simple and logical. A great central column, the spine of the whole structure, rises through each floor, supporting the vaults which divide the space naturally into four compartments.

The two floors occupied by the King's Apartment were served by a comfortably large staircase in the south-east tower, but from the third floor upwards this space is reserved for a further room and the staircase reduced to a narrow spiral contrived within the thickness of the wall.

The painting in these rooms is said to be original. That they were thus painted is beyond all doubt. We have in 1389 a payment to Jean d'Orléans "pour refaire et mettre à poinct de peinture l'ymaige de Monseigneur Saint Christophe qui est à l'entrée de notre petit chastel du boys de Vincennes, avec plusieurs autres choses qu'il faut ramender de peinture en notre chambre dudit lieu du Boys". "To repaint and put right the image of Saint Christopher which is over the entrance to our little fort in the Bois de Vincennes, with several other things where the painting needs renovation in our bedroom in the said place."

Thanks to the survival of the Comptes de l'Argenterie du Roy for 1387, it is possible to form some idea of the decoration and furnishing of the royal rooms.

The *Estude* or study in the *châtelet* had an oriental carpet, tapestry hangings with an arras over the door and a silver clock. The great coffers which stood against the wall were used also as seats, being provided with cushions. As well as a capacious fireplace, the room was provided with a *chauffe-mains* – a silver container which could be filled with glowing embers like a bedpan and used for warming one's hands.

In the Grande Salle on the first floor a huge fireplace occupied most of the north wall. To conserve the heat as much as possible, the web of the vaulting is panelled in chestnut – a wood largely repellent to insects – which has happily survived. The floor is of narrow bricks, which again are conservers of heat, over which was laid a deep pile carpet. The wall hangings and upholstery, known as the "chambre", were changed according to the season – winter, summer, Easter and All Saints. But the main ornament of the room was the dresser, of four tiers, richly garnished with gold and silver plate, with goblets of rock crystal and of tankards of jewelled enamel.

On the floor above, the "chambre haute" was the King's Bedroom. The bed, placed against the north wall, had a high dossier or *cheveciel*. The curtains of the bed were changed four times a year with the rest of the "chambre". From the centre there hung a sturdy band of cloth by means of which the King could hoist himself into a sitting position.

In the window recess towards the west, next to the chimney, was placed a large coffer which contained the library. They were mostly religious books, Missals, Psalters, Breviaries, Books of Hours, all exquisitely illuminated and bound in leather or ivory studded with precious stones. But among them were sixteen other books "délicieusement historiés".

Round the room were various coffers and cupboards, mostly filled with the richest silks and velvets from Europe or the Middle East, some of them embroidered with a crown surmounting the initials KK. Karolus, the Latin for Charles, was in those days usually spelt with a K.

Such was the keep which is so accurately depicted in the Heures d'Etienne

Chevalier by Jean Fouquet. The view is almost exactly the same as that which may be seen today from the windows of the Bibliothèque de l'Histoire de la Marine in what used to be the Queen's House. Every window, every opening remains the same. Only the battlements have gone, being replaced on the little corner turrets by conical roofs.

Another medieval illumination gives a remoter view from a clearance in the middle of the forest. The scene depicted is the *Hallali* – the kill at the conclusion of a boar hunt. The hounds are savaging their prostrated quarry, while one of the *valets de limier*, holding his hound on a short leash, is clearly in the last stages of exhaustion, whereas his opposite number can at least summon up the breath to sound his horn.

Over the treetops soar the clustered towers of the keep and to either side a group of large square castellated blocks stand up like the high-rise buildings of a modern skyline. These are the towers of the great curtain wall of Charles V, for it was he who determined to encircle both the manor house and the keep with the great girdle of towers which is the distinctive feature of Vincennes. There would be nothing distinctive about a curtain wall punctuated at regular intervals by towers, either round or square: it was the medieval formula for defence. But at Vincennes each tower was virtually a keep – a large block capable of housing a large number of people.

The only one of these blocks to survive in anything like its entirety is the Tour du Village, now the main entrance. The others were razed to the level of the curtain wall either by Napoleon in 1808 or by Louis XVIII in 1819.

It is really necessary to visit Vincennes even if it is only to gain a true impression of its immense size. The dimensions of the enclosure, taken from the inside of the moat, are 334 metres by 175, giving an area of six hectares, that is to say some fifteen acres. The height of the towers was originally 42 metres above the level of the enclosure and the depth of the moat 12 metres. The total masonry, therefore, of the towers was 54 metres above ground.

In January 1461, towards the end of the reign of Charles VII, ambassadors arrived at Vincennes from Florence and left an account of what they saw. "There were in all two immense fortresses" – presumably the keep and the Tour du Village – "and eight others, that is to say a total of ten." By "fortress", then, they must have meant each one of the large fortified blocks. These, they claimed, were each surrounded by a separate moat, but it is difficult to see how this could have been true. They contained "both in their upper and in their lower parts an infinity of lodgings, capable of receiving more than two thousand people".

The keep, "a fine palace", contained the most sumptuous interior that they had as yet seen, most particularly the Chambre du Roi, which was worked with gold and faced with panelling ("lavorata a oro et fasciata di legnano"). They much admired the great well which was sunk from the floor of the kitchens. Although the church was "in ruins", they found its remains "beautiful and as high as the roof".

The Sainte-Chapelle was not in ruins; it was merely unfinished. Its design dates from Charles V who laid the first stone in 1379, but he did not live to see the building progress much beyond the foundations. Charles VI continued the work, and in spite of the difficulties of his reign managed to raise the apse to

21

the height of the cornice, the nave to the spring of the window archivolts and the west front to the bottom of the rose window. Here, however, it had to be left, and it was in this state that it was seen by the Florentine ambassadors. Building was not resumed until the reign of François I, who stipulated that it was to be "very beautiful, very sumptuous and one that would last for ever". It was finally completed by his son, Henri II.

In 1853 Viollet-le-Duc was asked to make a report on the Sainte-Chapelle. "At first sight," he wrote, "the building presents a great unity, the artists of the Renaissance having, as far as it was possible, sought to retain the *ordonnance* of the building, and if it were not for the details of the sculpture and the degradation caused by rain and frost to the upper parts which were left open for a whole century, it would be difficult to find the places where the sixteenth century took over the construction". From the outside the salamanders on the parapet betray the patronage of François I, but from the inside, looking up at the vaults, it is astonishing to realise this was the work of Philibert de l'Orme – the builder of the strictly classical chapel at Anet.

Seen from the outside, the Sainte-Chapelle offers, as Viollet-le-Duc affirmed, "one of the most precious examples of the Gothic style in its period of decline". The fretted tracery of its narrow gables, which cut through the balustrades in typically flamboyant fashion; the contrast between the strong simplicity of the buttresses and the slender mullions of the great windows; the brittle encrustations of the pinnacles, seen against the huge expanse of roof, produce an impression of richness which is in no way reflected by the interior.

This defect was, of course, observed by Viollet-de-Duc, who drew attention to the fact that the columns set between the windows were originally adorned with figures of saints in niches of the most exquisite workmanship. "This ring of statues, as in the Sainte-Chapelle of Paris, formed the richest and most interesting feature of the decoration. Their destruction gives an appearance of nudity to the nave which contrasts with the richness of the exterior of the monuments."

To this must be added the furnishings of the chapel which were of an appropriately distinguished quality. There was, of course, a choir screen or *jubé*, with sculptured decorations by Jehan de la Gente; there were, too, choir stalls for the fifteen canons, their vicars, vicars choral, choirboys and all. These were carved by Francisque Scibec, whose name occurs so often in the accounts for Fontainebleau. Finally, there was the furniture proper to the ceremonies of the Order of Saint-Michel, which was transferred here from the Mont Saint-Michel for obvious reasons of commodity.

To right and left of the choir are side chapels provided for the King and Queen. Each had a fireplace in the back wall and was provided with a "squint", an oblique aperture in the wall through which the occupants could follow the liturgy. It is typical of the Gothic style that the chimneys which were necessitated by these fireplaces take their place undisguisedly among the pinnacles of the parapet.

In the fifteenth century Vincennes was for some time in the hands of the English. After the Battle of Agincourt, King Henry V married the Princess Catherine, youngest daughter of Charles VI, whose periodical insanity rendered him incapable of governing. By the Treaty of Troyes Henry became

7 The keep. Miniature by Jean Fouquet.

Regent of France and was recognised as heir to the throne. The Dauphin, however, the future Charles VII, continued to fight for his rights, but the English and the Burgundians were too strong an alliance for him. Nevertheless, in August 1422 he captured the important stronghold of La Charité-sur-Loire and was advancing on Cosne. Henry and the duc de Bourgogne set out to meet this threat, but at Melun Henry was struck down with dysentry – "un flux de ventre merveilleux" named by the chronicler Monstrelet "mal de Saint-Antoine". He was borne on a litter back to Vincennes, where he died, leaving a son still in his cradle to succeed to his two thrones. The Duke of Bedford was appointed Regent in France and the Duke of Exeter Regent in England.

The obsequies were performed in France. The King's body was boiled in the kitchens of Vincennes and then enclosed in a leaden coffin filled with aromatic herbs. A procession of two hundred and fifty torch bearers conducted the coffin to the Cathedral of Notre-Dame where it lay in state before being taken by ship to Westminster. It was left to Joan of Arc to restore the fortunes of the French monarchy.

During the fifteenth century the Château de Vincennes continued for some time to play an important part in the affairs of the Crown, but towards the end of the century it began to decline. The Loire Valley became the favourite residence of the King and another rôle was found for the old Fortress of the Bois.

A building that was designed for security can be made to function in two different ways. It can be used to keep people out or it can be used to keep people in. The transition from fortress to prison was easily achieved and this was the fate of a number of medieval castles when they became obsolete as fortresses. In the long intervals when Vincennes was not serving as a palace, it was used as a place of detention – chiefly for prisoners of exalted social position. It might have served no other purpose had not the Bourbons decided to bring it up to date as a palace.

It was Henri IV who first determined on such a course, but the dagger of Ravaillac prevented him from putting it into execution. His widow, however, Marie de Medici, took up the idea and on 17 August, 1610, the young Louis XIII laid the first stone of a building which was to occupy the site between the south-west tower and the keep. It was not a very imposing building – one room thick, one storey high with a tall roof and dormer windows.

In the other part of the palace distinguished prisoners came and went. The prince de Condé, the prince de Conti, the duc de Longueville, the Maréchal d'Ornano, the chevalier de Vendôme, the Cardinal de Retz – all were here at some period and some of them escaped. The most notable of these was the duc de Beaufort. The common feature to nearly all these escapes was the fact that on Sunday the entire garrison would be hearing Mass. When Condé was a prisoner it was stipulated that the Mass was to be said in French, lest, in the course of the liturgy, any communication might be made to him in Latin which the guards would not understand. Detention, however, was not severe. Anyone was allowed to bring his servants and, in the case of Condé, even his wife. The Cardinal de Retz kept rabbits on the roof.

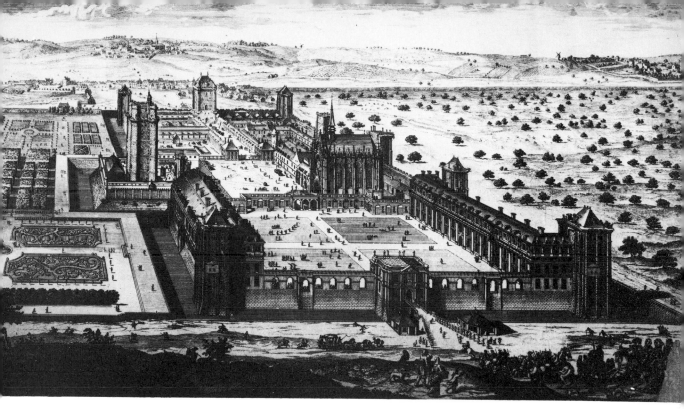

8 Aerial view from the south, after Louis XIV's additions. Engraving by Brissart.

These men were imprisoned because of the part they played in the uprising known as the Fronde. During the minority of Louis XIV Cardinal Mazarin became the virtual ruler of France and amassed an almost inconceivable fortune. Such a combination of power and wealth was certain to provoke opposition and intrigue.

In 1652 the Governor of Vincennes, Bouthillier de Chavigny, died and, on the advice of his secretary Colbert, Mazarin took the post for himself. A stronghold just outside Paris was a most attractive proposition, but in all the huge ensemble of Vincennes there was no building capable of satisfying his taste for grandeur. The architect Le Vau was chosen and invited to produce plans for rebuilding the Pavillon du Roi on far more grandiose lines.

The façades of Le Vau are deliberately austere. In his various projects – now in the Bibliothèque de la Ville de Paris – the richer, more sumptuous alternatives were set aside. To harmonise with the strong simplicity of the medieval towers, Le Vau made his buildings simple and strong.

These severe but dignified exteriors contained apartments in which the impressiveness of the proportions and the richness of the decorations combined to produce a royal style hitherto unknown in France. In some of the rooms the frescoes of the window embrasures have recently been revealed; in one the coved ceiling painted by Philippe de Champaigne and his pupil Dorigny has survived. But above all the restoration has recreated the original volumes. It was no doubt at Vincennes that Louis XIV dreamed of the magnificence later to be realised at Versailles.

The royal apartments only preceded by a year or two the oversumptuous ensemble of Vaux-le-Vicomte. It is with an imagination informed by Vaux-le-Vicomte and the Hôtel de Lauzun that we should reconstruct the vanished glories of Vincennes.

25

The royal lodgings were not only the first important commission of Le Vau; they provided Colbert with his first experience of supervising a building site. In a letter to Mazarin dated 21 May, 1658, he shows himself appalled by "the excessive cost of building". He took the matter into his own hands and spent a fortnight on the spot, checking, verifying, playing one contractor off against another. "I hope this diligence," he wrote, "will result in a considerable diminution of the cost".

The great work of Colbert in the re-organisation of France under Louis XIV has been recently assessed by Inez Murat. She has estimated that Louis spent some 60 million livres on building. "But the beauty of the buildings does not suffice to proclaim the intellectual and artistic primacy of France. The King and his Minister were to become aware of the necessity of a veritable policy of culture – a policy which was to be one of the most brilliant successes in our national history."

Louis XIV spent his honeymoon at Vincennes with his new Queen Marie-Thérèse. It was here also that he began his love affair with Louise de la Vallière. But Saint-Germain became the official seat of the Court until Versailles was ready to replace it. For fifty years Vincennes was abandoned.

On his death-bed, however, Louis said to the duc d'Orléans, who was to be Regent during the minority of Louis XV: "as soon as I am dead, have the King taken to Vincennes, where the air is good, until all the ceremonies are finished at Versailles and the château has been thoroughly cleaned, before you bring him back to Versailles, which is the residence I have destined for him".

So the young King went to Vincennes. "He is enjoying the best of health here," wrote Dangeau, "and becomes every day more agreeable both in mind and in manners." In 1722 he returned to Versailles. For a short period Vincennes was made over to Elizabeth d'Orléans, Dowager Queen of Spain, but when she left in 1726 the place was abandoned. It would probably have passed out of the mainstream of French history had it not become, in 1804, the scene of Napoleon's most discreditable action.

During the Consulate the garrison at Vincennes was under the command of a certain Harel. He had gained his position by denouncing to the police his fellow conspirators Ceracchi, Arena and Demerville for plotting against the life of Napoleon. It was a time when attempts of this sort seemed to be multiplying. Harel's lodgings were in Le Vau's gatehouse, the Port du Bois, probably because it was the only part of the château which was habitable. This man was to preside over the most flagrant act of injustice of the whole reign, the murder of the duc d'Enghien.

Louis-Antoine-Henri de Bourbon was the grandson of the prince de Condé, the commander of the émigré army. He was born at Chantilly in 1772. Naturally he had joined the army which his grandfather commanded. This army, however, was now disbanded and he was living at Ettenheim in the Grand Duchy of Baden. He had secretly married the princessè Charlotte de Rohan-Rochefort.

On 11 March, 1804, Napoleon sent instructions to General Ordener to proceed at once to Strasbourg, to cross the Rhine to Ettenheim and to secure the person of the duc d'Enghein. On 15 March, at five in the morning, the

9 Royal Hunt in the Bois de Vincennes. Painting by J. B. Martin.

Duke awoke to find his house surrounded by some two hundred soldiers. The doors were broken in and he was forced to accompany them over the frontier to Strasbourg.

On Sunday, 18 March he was woken at 1.30 in the morning and scarcely given time to dress. Orders had come from Paris. A carriage and six horses was waiting for them in the Place de l'Eglise. He was told that their destination was Paris. This was a matter of great relief, for he assumed that he would be able to have an interview with the First Consul. "A quarter of an hour with him," the Duke declared, "and all will be set to rights."

On arrival in Paris, however, the carriage went straight to the Ministère des Affaires Etrangères in the rue du Bac. It stood there for half an hour and he was not permitted to get out. From here he was taken to Vincennes, where he arrived at about 5.30 in the evening. It was Monday, 19 March.

He was conducted to an apartment in the Pavillon du Roi, which he thought he recognised; he had once been brought to Vincennes before the Revolution by the prince de Condé. He had no sense of impending disaster but offered Harel his word of honour that he would not try to escape if he could only be allowed to hunt in the Bois.

Outside in the courtyard troops were silently arriving from Paris. The garrison of Vincennes, apparently, was not to be trusted. The new troops were under the command of General Savary, aide-de-camp to Napoleon.

Seven officers had been summoned by order of Napoleon, and assembled in Harel's lodging. They were cited to judge "the çi-devant duc d'Enghien, accused of having borne arms against the Republic, of having been and still being in the pay of England, of taking part in conspiracies originating from this Power contrary to the security, both internal and external, of the Republic."

At about one in the morning the Duke was woken and told that he was to stand trial "for wishing to assassinate the First Consul". In his interrogation he flatly denied having ever even met the conspirators Pichegru or Dumouriez. Before he signed the procès-verbal he made a strong plea to be allowed to see Napoleon.

At about 2 a.m. he was taken into the next room and brought before the Commission. He had no one to defend him. One of the Commissioners proposed that his request for an audience should be forwarded immediately, but Savary intervened at once saying that such a course of action would be "inopportune". The Commission came to the unanimous verdict of guilty (one might well ask *of what*?) and signed a minute which "lui applique l'article . . . de la loi du . . . ainsi conçu . . . et en conséquence l'a condamné à la peine de mort". It was clearly the act of men who scarcely knew what they were doing.

Hullin, writing afterwards to exculpate himself, drew attention to the blanks left in the "first minute" which they had all signed. He stated that the "only correct minute" did not carry the order to execute the sentence immediately but merely stated that it was to be read to the prisoner. The execution, therefore, was carried out without the authority of the Commission.

Immediately after the "trial", Hullin sat down and began to write, at the unanimous request of the Commission, to the First Consul referring to him the prisoner's demand for an audience. As he wrote, a man who had been in the room throughout the proceedings, but whom Hullin would not name, came forward and asked what he was doing. On being told he said: "Your business is concluded; this is now my responsibility." Hullin avers that he took this to mean that the man accepted the responsibility of writing to the First Consul.

Meanwhile, in another part of the château, Savary and Harel were not waiting on events. A man was found and ordered to dig a grave in the moat near the south end of the Pavillon de La Reine. A firing squad was detailed to take up its position near the grave.

On the other side of the Cour Royale, in the Pavillon du Roi, the duc d'Enghien, still unaware of what was to be his fate, had been conducted back to his apartment by Lieutenant Noirot. Noirot and Enghien had met before the Revolution and were engaged in vivacious conversation. The conversation was interrupted by the arrival of Harel, holding a lantern. He told the Duke to follow him. Noirot, Brigadier Aufort and two gendarmes formed the escort. As one contemporary engraving quoted, "c'était pendant l'horreur d'une profonde nuit", and it was raining hard.

There was only one means of access to the moat and that was by taking a narrow spiral staircase in the tower known as the Tour de Calvin or Tour du Diable. The sight of this staircase awoke in the duc d'Enghien the first beginnings of suspicion. "Where are you taking me?" he asked. "If it is to bury me alive in a *cachot* I would rather die at once." "Monsieur," replied Harel, "follow me and summon up all your courage."

This must have aroused the darkest suspicions in the mind of the young Duke, but it was only as the little procession rounded the corner of the Tour de la Reine that these suspicions were confirmed. He found himself face to face with a firing squad.

The Adjutant, Pelé, advanced towards him and read the sentence. After a moment of silence the Duke asked for a pair of scissors. One of the soldiers had a pair, which was passed to him. He cut off a lock of his hair and asked Noirot to see that it was conveyed to the princesse de Rohan-Rochefort.

The Duke then asked for a confessor. He was told that all the clergy would be in bed. No priest worthy of the name would have refused such a call at such an hour, but no attempt was made to find one. A lantern was hung on the Duke's chest to offer a target to the firing squad.

In the gatehouse, which projected over the moat and whose windows on the eastern side, therefore, commanded the place of execution, Hullin was still feeling ruffled at not having been allowed to send his letter to Napoleon. He and his companions were waiting for their coaches, which had been refused entry into the courtyard of the château. "We were ourselves locked up so that no one could communicate with those outside," he wrote, "then suddenly a salvo of shots rang out, a terrible sound which penetrated to the bottom of our hearts and left us frozen with fear and dread." The deed had been done. The duc d'Enghien was dead.

It is perfectly clear that the whole process was controlled from Paris. If it was not Napoleon who commanded it, he must be subjected to the principle "le responsable c'est le chef". For the rest of his life the episode was clearly on

10 The Death of the Duc d'Enghien. An imaginative reconstruction by H. Piffard.

his mind and it came out sometimes in bold defence of its necessity and sometimes in a shabby implication that others were responsible.

In the *Mémorial de Saint Hélène* we find the latter. "I have learned since," he said to the Count of Las Casas, "that he [Enghien] was favourable towards me; I have been assured that he never spoke of me without a note of admiration . . . certainly if I had been informed in time of certain particularities concerning the opinions and the natural dispositions of the Prince; above all if I had seen the letter which he wrote to me and which was only passed to me, God knows from what motive, after he had ceased to be, I would most certainly have pardoned him."

But, in his last will and testament, Napoleon reverted to an attitude of defensive unrepentance. But at least he did accept responsibility. "I had the duc d'Enghien arrested and judged because it was necessary for the security, for the interest and for the honour of the French people, at a time when the comte d'Artois maintained, as he later admitted, sixty assassins in Paris. In similar circumstances I would act in the same way." Why the maintenance of hired assassins by one man could justify the assassination of another was not explained. But the matter was clearly on his conscience.

Under the Restoration a massive monument by Deseigne was erected in the middle of the sanctuary to the duc d'Enghien. Napoleon III, to whom it must have caused no little embarrassment, had it removed to the Queen's Chapel on the north side of the nave. It was the last time that a sovereign was to concern himself with Vincennes.

3

The Château de Fontainebleau:
The Valois

" DESIRE TO inhabit the Château de Fontainebleau," wrote Napoleon to Duroc, his Maréchal du Palais, in October 1807, "keeping each part for its original destination." "C'est la maison des siècles," he observed on another occasion, "the real home of our Kings."

Napoleon had seriously contemplated setting up his Court at Versailles, which would have identified his régime with that of the last three Bourbons. Here at Fontainebleau he could claim Henri IV and François I among his predecessors, and indeed Saint-Louis, for, true to the traditions of the French château, Fontainebleau retained, embedded in its Renaissance fabric, the medieval keep.

La Maison des Siècles – the real home of the Kings of France. The saying is even more true today. Almost every sovereign from François I to Napoleon III left his mark upon the palace. The last Court was held here in 1868.

Inevitably such a history meant the continual alteration of the buildings and the continual redecoration of the rooms. Nearly always the creation of something new entailed the destruction of something old; each gain involved a loss, but often the gains were great.

Fontainebleau is thus a medley of buildings in a patchwork of different styles. "It may not have been strictly speaking an architect's palace," Napoleon reflected at St. Helena, "but most certainly it was a residence that was well thought out and perfectly suited to its use. There was not in Europe a palace more commodious or more happily situated for the sovereign." Napoleon had more experience of the royal palaces of Europe than most men and he had strong opinions about how architecture should relate to imperial status. Yet, whatever their merits, the successive buildings of Fontainebleau proclaim that here is a house that has been loved and lived in, where the successive rulers of France have felt themselves more than anywhere else "at home". It was, of course, the immense Forêt de Bière which attracted them to this area by reason of the superb hunting which it offered. The pure waters of the Spring of Bléaud, the "Fontaine de Bleau" as it came to be spelt, determined the situation of the royal residence.

In 1519 François I, disappointed in his hopes of becoming Holy Roman Emperor, made straight for Fontainebleau to forget his sorrows, "pour mettre

11 The Cour de la Fontaine before rebuilding by Henri IV. Watercolour by Ian Dunlop.

en oublie mélancholie", in the indulgence of his favourite pastime. He found, on the edge of the forest, a deserted and almost ruinous castle, its buildings ranged round a courtyard that was roughly the shape of a magnet, its towers and *poivrières* reflected in the clear waters of a little lake. Of its appearance little is known.

A letter of Charles VII's, written in 1431, refers to "the rebuilding anew of the very beautiful and notable *hostel* seated in the Forêt de Bière". The word "hostel" usually signifies a dwelling as opposed to a fortification. The very thick walls of the keep were not continued in the adjacent buildings and the keep is best thought of as a sort of Peel Tower – a central stronghold to which one could resort in case of emergency rather than as part of any systematic scheme of defence. The house so much associated with Charles' mother, Isabeau de Bavière, was a house built "for comfort and delight" and it sounds the key-note of Fontainebleau.

To the west of this *hostel* was the convent of the Trinitarian or Mathurin monks. Albert Bray, Architecte en Chef in charge of Fontainebleau, conducted an archaeological excavation here in 1925. He has located the site of the conventual buildings as corresponding more or less with that of the great horseshoe staircase. The Galerie François I, according to the specification of 1528, was to end in a *corps d'hôtel* of the convent and a "little staircase" had to be made to descend from the gallery into the *corps d'hôtel*. This residential

32

block formed the east side of a quadrangle which included the cloister. To the north of this quadrangle the Church, which was correctly orientated towards the east, would have cut at right angles across the south end of the present Trinity Chapel, which is not orientated at all.

On 24 February, 1524, François I was defeated by the Emperor Charles V at Pavia and taken a prisoner to Madrid. He was not released until January 1526, and even then he had to leave his two sons as hostages. It was not until three years later that the "Ladies' Peace", negotiated by Louise de Savoie and Marguerite of Austria, enabled the return of the royal princes.

François had failed to win the glory which he coveted upon the field of battle. He now turned his attention once more to that other field upon which men may win the regard of posterity – the field of architecture.

On 28 April, 1528, François contracted with Gilles Le Breton for a programme of rebuilding at Fontainebleau. The Cour de l'Ovale, at first known as the Cour du Donjon, was to be rebuilt using the old foundations and retaining the Donjon or Grosse Vieille Tour as evidence of its antiquity. It was to be enriched with a magnificent entrance pavilion, the Porte Dorée, and with a dignified portico with a stone stairway leading to the Queen's Apartment. Le Breton was also to construct a gallery to link these buildings with the old convent. At first this was known as the Grande Galerie but later as the Galerie François I.

In 1530 Giovanni Baptista Rosso was summoned from Italy to undertake the decoration of Le Breton's buildings. Two years later he was joined by Francesco Primaticcio. Both were financed in a manner typical of the age – by preferment in the Church: Primaticcio became Abbot *in commendam* of Saint-Martin, and Rosso a Canon of the Sainte-Chapelle in Paris.

These two artists developed a style which is more or less unique to Fontainebleau. It was a complete reversal of François I's approach to the architecture of Blois and Chambord. Here his outward façades are richly decorated and the interiors, apart from a few monumental chimneypieces, left bare – presumably for tapestries. At Fontainebleau the façades were of an austere simplicity, while the interior received a rich and permanent decoration.

Le Breton used materials that were local and undistinguished; plaster walls with quoins and pilasters of a slatey coloured stone known as "grès". The pilasters were used to divide the wall space into panels into which the windows were inserted with little regard to symmetry. This sometimes produced problems which Le Breton only solved in a rather amateur manner. The three dormers immediately left of the keep are set so close to one another that there is not room for the projection of the pediments, which have had to be built at different heights.

For the main entrance Le Breton produced a more distinguished piece of architecture – the Pavillon de la Porte Dorée. The name probably derived from the French word "orée" meaning the verge of a forest, and should be spelt *d'orée*. It was from this side that François had access to his "délicieux déserts", the Forêt de Fontainebleau.

Here Le Breton has achieved the translation of a feudal gatehouse into a Renaissance entrance pavilion, but with a typical disregard for symmetry. The square tower to the right of the archway is broader than that to the left and the main roof is placed eccentrically. But, if he derived the inspiration for the superimposed loggias in the centre from the ducal palace of Urbino, Le Breton remained true to the French tradition in his vertical treatment of the flight of windows on either side. Ornament is restricted to the capitals, in some of which can be detected the F with which François so often placed his signature upon a building.

There is only one room in the palace today which really recalls the décor of François I and that is the Gallery which bears his name. Sixty-four metres long by six wide, it was originally designed as a passage to connect the royal apartments with the convent. Built in 1528 to the designs of Le Breton, it received in 1531 the decoration for which it is famous. But like so much at Fontainebleau it has suffered from frequent readjustments and restorations. It needs some patient unravelling to get back to the original appearance.

To begin with it had windows on both sides. It was Louis XVI who blocked in those on the north side when he created his Petits Appartements. This, of course, destroys the balance of luminosity in the gallery. The rhythm has also been altered significantly, for according to the Comptes des Bâtiments it was punctuated in the centre by two projections large enough each to form a little cabinet. One of these disappeared when Henri IV reconstructed the terraced arcade towards the Cour de la Fontaine; the other survived until Louis XVI's alterations.

The removal of the convent and the development of the main entrance from the Cour du Cheval Blanc led to the redesigning of the two end façades of the gallery. Apart from these, the decoration is entire but very much restored. The restoration has been of two sorts: an attempt by Louis-Philippe to rejuvenate a faded and mutilated décor, and a recent attempt to get back to that décor behind his restoration.

It is still a very pleasing and sumptuous ensemble. Each of the interstices between the windows – there are seven on either side – is treated as a decorative unit, the lower part in walnut panelling, carved by Francisque Scibec and lightly gilded; the upper part devoted to a large fresco set in an elaborate context – for "frame" is too inadequate a word – of stucco figures, strapwork ornament, and architectural compositions and further frescoes.

The first coup d'oeil of the gallery creates an overwhelming impression of richness and exuberance. The variety of the stucco figures is seemingly endless. Fat-buttocked *putti*, hirsute satyrs and austerely robed priests, young and elegant nudes, some of them converted into angels by the simple addition of wings, standing, posturing and running at full speed, convey an extraordinary movement and animation to the scene. Never before had this combination of painting and high relief been taken to such an extreme.

Within these complicated contexts, the fresco paintings add a further movement and animation to the scene. In detail the figures are often grotesque – not in the technical, stylistic sense of the word but in the sense of distorted and exaggerated; the anatomy is often unpleasant and the contortions fantastic.

It is impossible to inspect these juxtapositions of paintings and stucco-work for long and not to enquire their purpose. Why this particular choice of subjects?

Anyone versed in the mythology which was popular at the time could have identified many of the scenes – "Cleobis and Biton", "The Death of Adonis", "The Education of Achilles". Others, such as "Ignorance driven out", might have been inferred from a mere inspection of the painting.

But there was more in them than this. A hundred years after the decoration of the Gallery, the first author to write a book on Fontainebleau, the Père Dan, stated that Rosso "meant, by the various histories and subjects of his paintings, to represent the principal actions of the great King François". His patronage of the arts and sciences, his piety, his courage, his work, his skill, his loves and his victories are all cited, but not all related to any particular painting. Only the battle of Cerisoles is suggested as the true subject of the fight between the Centaurs and the Lapithae. The reverses suffered by François, he suggested, were likewise represented by such scenes as the Shipwreck. He further stated that they were "of different subjects which have no connections with each other". It is possible, however, that there was a sequence.

Themes which receive a major treatment in one panel recur as minor themes in another. The first fresco on the north wall nearest the entrance from the Chapel represents "Priestly Sacrifice". The same sacerdotal figures appear in the stucco groups diagonally opposite to either side of The Fight of the Centaurs and Lapithae. Moreover the altar in the "Priestly Sacrifice" bears the inital of François. The allusion could well be to the priestly nature of the King of France which was symbolised in the Coronation rite.

In the same way Venus is the main theme of the first fresco on the north side on entering from the royal apartments; the birth of Venus is also represented in the stucco cartouche beneath the fresco of "Ignorance driven out" at the far end on the opposite side. There could, therefore, be a diagonal relationship between the panels at the four extremities of the gallery. The whole subject has been studied by a team of scholars under André Chastel, but the exact significance of many of the elements of the décor remains a matter for learned speculation.

If, as has been suggested, the building of the Gallery was part of an attempt to reinstate the prestige of the King after the humiliations of Pavia and his captivity in Madrid, it is difficult to see how this could have been achieved by a cryptogram which only the most tortuous and erudite of minds could have deciphered. It must be concluded that what is opaque to us today, and has been opaque to writers since the Père Dan, was more easily translucid in the intellectual climate of the mid-sixteenth century.

A thorough restoration of the Galerie François I, undertaken during the 1960s, shed light upon the methods of fresco painting. As the paint had to be applied while the plaster was still moist, the area of plaster put on each day could not exceed the area which the painter was able to cover. These areas were known as *journées*, and often as many as twenty *journées* were required for one of the compositions. Their outlines are revealed on photographs taken with a raking light.

Once the plaster was applied, the cartoon was then traced onto it, usually by pricking through the paper. Sometimes the perforation is so regular as to imply the use of a roulette.

The original colouring, now once more revealed, shows a palette signifi-

12 Galerie François I, detail of stucco frame to "Combat des Centaurs et des Lapithes", showing priestly figure.

cantly different from that of the nineteenth-century restorers. The dominant colours are green and mauve, with here and there a salmon pink, a pallid yellow or a slatey blue. The figures have come out as almost two-dimensional, with very little depth of light and shade, and very little modelling of the mostly naked bodies.

A good deal of bowdlerisation, also, had taken place with the nineteenth-century overpainting. In the group entitled "Filial Piety", the rather inelegant nudity of the elderly mother being rescued from the flames had been shrouded in a large sheet, while a convenient wisp of drapery did duty for a fig-leaf on the figure of her husband. In "The Combat of the Centaurs and the Lapithae", the overtly sexual behaviour of two of the *putti* had been "pudiquement dissimulé" by a garland of fruit.

A considerable number of artists, some French, some Italian, some Flemish, collaborated under the direction of Rosso and Primaticcio and thus was formed what is known as the First School of Fontainebleau. The Galerie François I is not only a masterpiece in itself, but it formed the training ground for artists who firmly established the Renaissance in France.

This was to exercise an influence on other countries including England. In 1540, when Henry VIII was building Nonesuch, he had in his employment a certain Nicolas Bellin of Modena, known as Modon. Architecture was often the subject of Henry's correspondence with his Ambassador to France, Sir John Wallop. Of Fontainebleau Sir John writes: "I went into his [the King's] bedchamber, which I do assure your Majesty is very singular as well with antical borders as costly ceilings and a chimney right well made." On the proportions of the Gallery "no man can better show your Majesty than Modon who wrought there in the beginning of the same".

François I also took an interest in Henry's buildings. "He heard say," wrote Wallop on 17 November, 1540, "that your Majesty did use much gilding in your said houses and especially in the roofs, and that in his buildings he used little or none, but made the roofs of timber finely wrought with divers colours of wood natural."

In 1834 there was a rare oportunity of inspecting the ceiling of the Galerie François I, for it had been taken down in sections and laid upon the floor. The comtesse de Boigne describes it: "we were in a position to take note of the perfection of this work of the cabinet-maker – almost, I might say, of the goldsmith – executed with the precision which one would exercise in the making of a snuffbox".

Primaticcio's decoration of the King's Bedroom – now known as the Salle du Donjon or Salle Saint-Louis – to which Sir John Wallop refers has disappeared completely. That of the Queen's Bedroom has been likewise replaced with the exception of the fireplace. Here, in an elaborate stucco frame, Primaticcio has reproduced one of the works of his master, Giulio Romano, "The Love of Venus and Adonis".

We can form some idea of what these rooms might have looked like from the upper landing of the Escalier du Roi. This conserves on its south and west walls the decorations of the bedroom of Anne de Pisseleu, duchesse d'Etampes. The room originally had a coffered ceiling like that of the Galerie François I, but in 1836 this was replaced by the present pastiche of the style of

Primaticcio. The east wall also dates from the nineteenth century.

The duchesse d'Etampes held the position of first among the King's mistresses. Even at the height of her favour he was unfaithful to her and she to him. "Unfaithfulness," wrote Brantôme, "is not surprising in women who have made a career out of love and who have enjoyed its fruits, but she was a worthy and straightforward lady and did not abuse her position."

She was not really able to do so. Her chief hatred was for Benvenuto Cellini, but try as she would, she could not undermine the King's appreciation of his work. A famous occasion when the artist and the mistress clashed in public was in the Galerie François I at Fontainebleau. An Italian named Bologna was due to exhibit a number of bronzes cast from the antique. Cellini was to exhibit a silver statue of Jupiter.

The duchesse d'Etampes, in order that Cellini's figure should appear at a disadvantage, managed to delay the King until it was almost dark. But Cellini had cunningly concealed a taper among Jupiter's thunder-bolts. This was lit at the King's entry and the statue gently pushed forward by Cellini's assistant, Ascanio. François was deeply impressed. "This is much more beautiful," he exclaimed," than anything that has ever been seen before." The Duchess quickly intervened. "Have you lost your eyes?" she asked; "do you not see how many beautiful bronze figures there are, placed further back? The true genius of sculpture resides in them, not in this modern rubbish." The king, however, stuck to his opinion. "We must rate Benvenuto very high," he insisted, "his work not only rivals, it surpasses the antiques."

The Duchess, waxing angry, observed that Cellini had placed a light veil over his statue. She suggested that it was there to conceal its imperfections. Cellini now proceeded to withdraw the veil, "lifting it from below to reveal the statue's fine genitals ... she thought I had unveiled those parts to mock her".

The situation was becoming really ugly. The Duchess was thwarted and outraged. Cellini was beside himself with anger. François intervened. "Benvenuto, I forbid you to say a word: keep quiet and you will be rewarded with a thousand times more treasure than you desire."

The duchesse d'Etampes' bedroom occupied the full width of the building, with one window overlooking the lake and two looking across to the north of the Cour de l'Ovale which contained the Queen's Apartment.

In 1531 this façade was dignified by the addition of a double flight of steps leading up to a portico which gave access to the Queen's Apartments. It was sometimes known as the Escalier de la Reine. The authorship of this portico has been much disputed. Anthony Blunt, following Albert Bray, was satisfied that the portico was built in 1531 and was the design of Le Breton and not, as some have argued, Serlio.

The portico, with its rich composition of arcades and attached columns, must have afforded a striking contrast with the austerity of Le Breton's façade, of which the ground floor was devoid of ornament. Perhaps this contrast suggested the addition of the colonnade which runs round two sides of the court. It is not a very accomplished piece of architecture. Each column stands on a pedestal so tall that its height is reduced to that of the pilasters of the dormer windows. They just look like a row of posts.

The contract with Le Breton specified that a space should be left on the south side of the Cour du Donjon for the building of a chapel "quand sera le bon plaisir du Roi". Even while making his first enlargements, François was envisaging further additions. It is difficult to know to what extent the Fontainebleau which we see today was already conceived in the mind of François I, even if it had not been executed by the time of his death.

Certainly he planned the Grande-Basse-Cour (Cour du Cheval Blanc) though we have no evidence as to what his projects were for the central pavilion. He built the west wing, with the small gatehouse called the Porte aux Champs, all of which was demolished by Napoleon and replaced by the grille which we see today. He built the north wing, probably in the late 1530s, which retains its general appearance. He also built the two high pavilions which mark the extremities of the entrance front – the Pavillon des Armes (de l'Horloge) to the north and the Pavillons des Poëles (because of the German stoves inserted by way of central heating) to the south – and the latter was ready to house the Emperor Charles V on his visit in 1539. In 1541 the accounts record a payment to Antoine Jacquet de Grenoble for making a model for a doorway to the chapel "which will be built in the Grande-Basse-Cour". There is no reason to doubt that this refers to the chapel ultimately realised by Philibert de l'Orme for Henri II.

The year 1541 seems to have been a crucial one in the development of Fontainebleau. Most important of all was the decision to raise the south wing of the Grande-Basse-Cour and to make here a Long Gallery later known as the Grande Galerie or Galerie d'Ulysse.

It was to be a gallery the like of which had not been seen in France. Four hundred and fifty-six feet long by eighteen across, it was nearly two and a half times the length of the Galerie François I. Its façade was divided into thirty bays. There were fifteen windows overlooking the Jardin des Pins to the south, but thirty overlooking the court. This was probably because the Grande-Basse-Cour was intended for joustings, tiltings and tournaments and the windows of the gallery would have provided a convenient viewpoint for spectators.

The principal ornament of the Gallery was a series of fifty-eight paintings representing the history of Ulysses. These were placed in the panels between the windows. The Gallery was ceiled with a barrel vault, lit by the little round dormers, which received a decoration of grotesques and frescoes of the utmost complexity.

The decorative scheme was worked out by Primaticcio. Under him the accounts mention "Anthonie Fantozi" (Fantuzzi) who furnished the *patrons* – the patterns for the grotesques and other paintings – to twenty-eight other artists, nearly all of whom had French names.

The painting of the Gallery, which progressed from east to west, was only half completed at the death of François I in 1547. Five years later a new impulse was given to the work by the arrival of "Nicolas de l'Abbey" (dell'Abbate). He brought with him, according to Anthony Blunt, "a wide experience of north Italian illusionist painting" which created a noticeable change of style between one end of the Gallery and the other. The painting of the vault was not completed until 1563.

The Abbé Guilbert, whose book the *Description Historique des Château, Bourg et Forest de Fontainebleau* was written in 1731, not long before the demolition of the Gallery, was enthusiastic in his praise. The barrel vault was divided into fifteen compartments by fourteen frames of gilded stucco. Within these was a rich and colourful profusion of frescoes and cameos set in a complex network of grotesques and arabesques, "enriched with divers ornaments in gold and in colours, of birds, wild animals ... figures of men, women, satyrs, termes, swags of fruit and armorial trophies in so great a number and of such perfect beauty that the eye hardly suffices to admire the treasures and at which the most perfect eulogy could scarcely more than hint".

It is difficult to say how well the frescoes lasted. The Père Dan, writing in 1634, says that Henri IV had undertaken considerable repairs "having found this incomparable work in a state which threatened ruin ... its rare paintings are more to be admired for their art and their design than in the appearance of their colours which the ravages of time have greatly faded".

Strictly speaking, one cannot restore a fresco. The paint has to be applied to wet plaster and once this has hardened the process cannot be repeated. Any retouching must be a matter of surface paint. The "reparations" under Henri IV deceived the eye of the last person to describe the Gallery, an Italian named Algarotti who visited Fontainebleau on the very day that the demolition began.

It was on 19 November, 1738. The duc de Luynes had noted that there was a project for pulling down the Gallery, "qui est mauvaise et inutile", and for replacing it with new lodgings for the Court. Algarotti arrived just in time. "I saw once again at Fontainebleau the admirable paintings of our Nicolino; they still retained the freshness, the modelling and the strength of colour which they possessed when Vasari described them ... I cannot express the pleasure which I felt in admiring this painted poetry. But if I had delayed even a few hours it would have been too late ... the masons were already on the roof of the gallery which they were to demolish. The rubbish of the vault of this monument was falling on our heads and we had to beg the workmen to suspend for a moment their work of destruction to give us time to contemplate that faithful hound [Argus] who recognised and caressed his master; to see Ulysses, having bent his mighty bow, challenging with it these effeminate suitors to the hand of Penelope."

The following October, when the annual *Voyage* brought the Court once more to Fontainebleau, the duc de Luynes noted, "The Gallery of Ulysses is completely demolished."

All that has survived of François I's wing on this side of the court is the Grotto which overlooked the Jardin des Pins at its western extremity. It almost certainly dates from 1543. This was some two years after the arrival of Sebastiano Serlio to be in charge of the buildings at Fontainebleau. The figures of Atlantes which form part of the rustication of the masonry are typically Italian. It is reasonable to suppose that Serlio was the author of the design.

Serlio also began what is now called the Salle de Bal or Galerie Henri II on the south side of the Cour de l'Ovale. The original plan had been for an open loggia with a high vault painted in fresco. His design for it, published in the seventh book of his treatise on building, is strongly reminiscent of his façades at Ancy-le-Franc. The building was carried up to the spring of the vaulting arches, Serlio informs us, not without sarcasm, "and then along came a man in authority, with greater judgement than the mason who had made these provisions, and ordered a ceiling of wood".

The "man in authority" was probably Philibert de l'Orme who became Superintendent of Buildings upon the accession of Henri II and ousted Serlio, for the ceiling was contracted for on 13 July, 1548, fifteen months after the death of François. It was certainly he who completed the building, turning it into a Grande Salle with glazed windows. Serlio complains bitterly that, although he was living at Fontainebleau at the time, "my advice was never sought on the slightest matter".

Once again Primaticcio and Nicolo dell'Abbate created the decoration. It was highly praised by Vasari as a work of collaboration. "No one did him [Primaticcio] greater honour than Nicolo of Modena, who surpassed all the others in the painting of the Salle de Bal."

By the nineteenth century, however, the frescoes were found to be "in the most deplorable condition . . . here and there a few remains could be found". The painter Alaux was commissioned by Louis-Philippe to undertake a restoration. He had the original designs to inform him and by means of a layer of heated wax he was able to bring to the surface colours which had almost disappeared. He thus had the double guide of Primaticcio's line and Nicolo dell'Abbate's colours. His restoration was no mean achievement; like the

13 Salle de Bal. The Three Graces.

Galerie François I, the Salle de Bal creates today an immediate impression of noble harmony. But, like the gallery, it does not stand up to close inspection.

Louis Dimier, one of the great historians of Fontainebleau, is stern in his judgement: "the figures are lacking both in balance and in life; heads which are too small alternate with bodies which are too long." One instance will demonstrate the justice of his criticism. In the spandrel between the third and fourth windows on the courtyard side are the Three Graces. Never have three figures deserved that title less; their tiny heads serve only to accentuate their lumpy and misshapen anatomy. It would have been bad enough to leave such uncomely coarseness naked; Primaticcio – or was it Alaux? – has gone one worse and given them a ring of bells half way up the calf. It is the one point at which it is most inelegant to divide the human leg.

The building of the Salle de Bal obscured the windows on the west side of the Chapel of Saint-Saturnin. This was a two-storey building, after the fashion of the Sainte-Chapelle in Paris, with the Chapelle Haute on the same level as the State Apartments serving for the Court, and the Chapelle Basse on the ground floor serving for the members of the household. The chapels had been built by Le Breton in 1541 on the site of an older chapel which had been consecrated in 1169 by Thomas-à-Becket.

When Henri IV straightened out the Cour de l'Ovale, he built the Pavillon du Tibre up against the chapels, thus obscuring the windows on the other side. They were replaced by paintings by Jean de Hoey with the aid of the Ambroise Dubois.

In 1882 the architect Boitte rebuilt the lantern over the chapels. In doing so he gave way to a petty republicanism and inverted the initials to R.F. (République Française) which should have read F.R. (Franciscus Rex).

In 1547, a few months before his death, François I was taken seriously ill during a visit to Fontainebleau. "The likelihood of death," wrote the Père Dan, "seemed greater than the hope of recovery. At the same time nearly all the courtiers were seen to abandon the sun which was setting in order to run after the sun which was rising; I mean after the Dauphin Henri."

The King, however, recovered sufficiently to play a trick on the deserters. On the Fête Dieu he felt sufficiently strong to help carry the canopy over the Blessed Sacrament in the procession. He had himself carefully made up so that "he looked more like a young courtier than a man of his age and in the condition in which he was".

The news of his recovery reached the ears of those who had abandoned him and they began to come back one by one to the King "all very ashamed and embarrassed". This caused the King to laugh with all his heart. With customary magnanimity he did not hold it against anyone.

On 31 March, 1547 François I died at Rambouillet. The Oraison Funèbre preached at his funeral caused a theological crisis. Pierre Châtelain, Bishop of Macon, claimed that the late King had gone straight to Heaven, "without passing through the flames of Purgatory". This brought an immediate inquisition from the Sorbonne. The deputation was received at Saint-Germain by Jean Mendose, Premier Maître d'Hôtel, who fed them and wined them well and bundled them out of the palace explaining that François I was incapable of stopping anywhere, and if he had made a tour of Purgatory, no one could have persuaded him to remain for long. Whatever the value of its theology, the Bishop's oration was a fitting epitaph to a persistently peripatetic monarch.

At the death of François I, Fontainebleau was well on its way to becoming the palace which we know today. The buildings of the Cour de l'Ovale, the Grande-Basse-Cour and the Galerie François I, which formed the junction between the two, were all of them begun and many of them completed. But one area in the vast, irregular layout which had not received its present form was the Cour de la Fontaine. Bounded on the north side by the gallery and to the west by a range of kitchen buildings terminating in the Pavillon des Poëles, it was still open to the east except for a short wing which ran obliquely from the end of the gallery to the Pavillon de la Porte Dorée. This wing, which followed the lines of the medieval fortress, turned at an obtuse angle at which there projected a round tower with a conical roof. This part of the château was portrayed by Rosso at the foot of his large fresco of "Venus and Cupid" in the gallery.

The idea of enclosing another court here by the erection of a further block on the east side is first mentioned in a letter from Catherine de Medici to Primaticcio dated 24 April, 1565. She speaks of a "galerietta" that would give access to the gardens. It was not until 1568 that the wing was actually built and it was not in the form of a gallery but of a Grande Salle which later became known as the Salle de la Belle Cheminée. Between 1565 and 1568 the opposite wing, later to be the Appartement des Reines Mères, had been rebuilt by Primaticcio. Philibert de l'Orme had had more elaborate intentions for the architecture of this wing, but he was dismissed by Catherine de Medici immediately after the death of Henri II in 1559.

It was this wing that set the style for the Cour de la Fontaine. Its main features – rusticated ground floor, doric pilasters articulating the first floor and a high roof pierced by tall dormer windows – are simple enough. It demonstrates the versatility of Primaticcio. Here he is much more severe than in, for instance, the grotto at Meudon. On the Aisle de la Belle Cheminée he has produced an architectural composition which provides the most distinguished individual façade at Fontainebleau.

The two façades of Primaticcio almost demanded the refacing to match of Le Breton's façade to the Galerie François I, but the arcading in front of it only received its final form under Henri IV. This has seven apertures corresponding with the seven blank wall spaces between the windows. There had been here, since 1534, a simple arcade with a single column between each archway. Rosso's painting shows twelve arches, one of Du Cerceau's drawings shows eleven and the other nine. But Du Cerceau has "concertina-ed" this façade, making it far too short; the number of eleven is to be preferred.

The end pavilion on the west side of the court, the Pavillon des Poëles, had been built by François I and it was here that he lodged the Emperor Charles V on his way through France in 1539. In its architecture it reflected the Pavillon des Armes (now de l'Horloge) at the opposite end of the entrance front, but it had the further addition of a ground-floor gallery built out towards the lake. This offered a flat roof or terrace level with the windows of the first floor. From the terrace there was direct access to the Galerie d'Ulysse.

The *Chronique de François I* is superlative in its praise of the Emperor's apartment: "the rooms, chambers and galleries were so lavishly hung with tapestries and rich paintings and statues that it is beyond the power of mortal man to describe or recite, so that it seemed more like a paradise, or something of divine rather than of human workmanship, and all were astounded to see the place so nobly enriched and adorned and prepared in so short a time."

The existence of so sumptuous an apartment in so attractive a corner of the palace caused Henri II to abandon the King's Rooms and to make this his habitation. In 1556 he built a cabinet on the terrace which must have been a delightful little room.

Nearly a hundred years later, in June 1654, Louis XIV had another building erected on the terrace – a domed pavilion which formed an ante-room to the Galerie d'Ulysse.

In the same year in which Henri II had his cabinet built, he invited Philibert de l'Orme to construct an outer staircase in the centre of the terrace which ran the whole length of the main front of the château towards the Cour du Cheval Blanc. It was in the shape of two arcs which curled in upon themselves to meet at a landing from which a single flight completed the descent. Philibert de l'Orme did not hesitate to qualify his creation as "one of the most beautiful works that it would be possible to see". It was however, in need of considerable repairs in 1580 and was finally replaced in 1634 by the much more splendid staircase which we see today.

Three more additions to the Fontainebleau scene under the Valois dynasty require a mention: the doubling, under Charles IX, of the royal apartments on the north side of the Cour de l'Ovale so as to provide a new suite of rooms overlooking the Jardin de Diane; the placing, in 1563, of a plaster cast of the equestrian statue of Marcus Aurelius in the centre of the Grande-Basse-Cour, which from then on has been known as the Cour du Cheval Blanc; and the surrounding of the château by a moat in 1565 at the command of Catherine de Medici who felt in those troubled times a need for greater security. In the Cour du Cheval Blanc a triumphal arch was constructed by Primaticcio to house a drawbridge over the moat. This was dismantled in 1580 by Henri III and later re-used by Henri IV for his Porte du Baptistère at the entrance to the Cour du Donjon.

Henri IV was a great builder. He was to leave Fontainebleau nearly twice the size of the palace which he inherited.

14 The west front as it was in 1579 with Philibert de l'Orme's horseshoe staircase. Watercolour by Ian Dunlop.

Henry IV and Louis XIII

ENRI IV was in many ways the most remarkable man to have sat upon the throne of France. He had fought his way to it, but no victor ever saw more clearly the fatuity of reprisal. There were no executions; no persecutions. Mayenne, the last leader of the Catholic league against him, was invited to Montceaux where he was subjected to no greater punishment than a rather fast walk on a rather hot terrace, after which the King sent him two bottles of wine. The duchesse de Montpensier was invited to dinner at the Louvre.

It was this magnanimity which lay behind Henri's capacity for religious tolerance, in which he was far in advance of his age. Tolerance may proceed from indifference, or it may proceed from a higher view of religion than that which engenders schism. Both Henri and Sully were of the latter sort. Sully rejected the mutual damning of Catholic and Protestant. "If they die in the observance of the Ten Commandments, believing in the Apostle's Creed, loving God with all their heart and having charity towards their neighbour; if they put their hope in the mercy of God to obtain salvation through the death, the merits and the justice of Christ, they cannot fail to be saved." That is not the language of indifference.

The real cause of religious disunity was as much concerned with the power politics of the Church as with the articles of religion. The heart of the Gospel was far removed from the causes of controversy. One forgotten element of that Gospel was reinstated by Henri IV. It was the saying "Blessed are the peacemakers".

Under such a ruler the Arts of Peace could flourish once more and Henri showed himself a prodigious builder. It was not long before he turned his attention to Fontainebleau.

Although Fontainebleau already possessed two of the finest galleries in Europe, the first extension of the Château under Henri IV was to provide it with three more.

The enlargement was achieved by enclosing the Jardin de Diane on all sides. First, in 1599, an aviary – the Volière – was built on the north side of the garden facing the Galerie François I. In the following year this was joined to the Royal Apartments by a double gallery, the Galerie des Cerfs on the ground floor and the Galerie de la Reine or de Diane above it. On the west side the garden was enclosed by a short gallery, the Galerie des Chevreuils, which linked the Volière with the Pavillon des Armes at the north end of the present entrance front.

Henri IV made his own main entrance on the opposite side of the palace. Between 1601 and 1603 he straightened out the two wings of the Cour de l'Ovale so that they were parallel to one another and ended in two symmetrical pavilions. Midway between these he made a triumphal arch, the Porte du Baptistère, re-using Primaticcio's archway from the Cour du Cheval

Blanc and crowning it with a square dome, held like a canopy over its central arch. Finally he built beyond this the vast Cour des Offices, with three wings ranged symmetrically round three sides of a quadrangle, fronting the château. In the centre of the north range is a large pavilion which formed the first gateway to anyone arriving from the town. From here a paved drive led obliquely across the courtyard to a gateway directly opposite the Porte du Baptistère. It was not a well contrived approach and his successors showed an increasing preference for arriving by way of the Cour du Cheval Blanc.

The Volière, "made of a metal trellis, extremely fine, so that it receives light and air on all sides without allowing the captives to escape", was the first of the buildings which ultimately enclosed the Jardin de la Reine. It was thirty yards long, the Père Dan informs us, with a large dome in the middle. This provided room for an artificial rock with little cascades and fountains which fed a number of rivulets that ran in stone conduits across the ground. "It is a most pleasant place," he concluded, "in which are kept all sorts of birds which, by their melodious song, give apparent tokens that they are contented with their rich and royal home."

A visit to the Aviary was one of the favourite pastimes of the little Dauphin, the future Louis XIII. On 11 September, 1604, Héroard notes: "taken to the Volière, where he squirted water on the King; the King squirted water on him too. He was asked: 'Monsieur, which do you prefer, Saint-Germain or Fontainebleau?' He replied: 'Fontainebleau,' as he always did."

His preference for Fontainebleau may have been because he saw more of his father here. Héroard often depicts a delightful relationship between father and son. At no time was Fontainebleau more truly "the real home" of the royal family. A day or two before the occasion just described Héroard wrote: "at five o'clock the King returned from hunting and was in the Grande Galerie. He ran with outstretched arms to meet the King, who was overcome with joy and contentment, he kissed and embraced him for a long time and then walked with him hand in hand, changing hands when they turned about, without saying a word and listening to Monsieur de Villeroy who was making a report to the King. He could not leave the King, nor the King leave him." Louis XIII did not grow up to resemble his father; a passion for hunting was almost the only taste they shared.

It was only fitting that a château belonging to a race of mighty hunters should have a gallery consecrated to the chase and on 26 January, 1600, Henri IV signed a contract with Rémy Collin, maître-maçon, for a new gallery "to link the Donjon with the Volière". This was to be the Galerie des Cerfs, with the Galerie de Diane on the first floor above it.

The interior, perhaps inspired by the Gallery of Maps in the Vatican, was devoted to a series of aerial views of the forests belonging to the King and the châteaux attached to them, painted, according to Guilbert, by Toussaint Dubreuil. It would have been a priceless document to the architectural historian but, here again, the originals have been almost totally lost. Whether Dubreuil, who died in 1602, was alive when the gallery received its mural decorations, or whether so eminent an artist did really paint so pedestrian a series of scenes is open to doubt.

Under Louis XV the gallery was partitioned off to provide more lodgings

15 Henri IV. Bust by Jacquet de Grenoble.

for the Court. This arrangement was maintained under the Empire, for Pauline Borghese was lodged here. It was not until 1863 that a restoration to its primitive condition was decided upon by Napoleon III. The murals had so deteriorated as to be largely unrecognisable. Two artists, Guiaud and Lassone, using such prints and drawings as were available, repainted the scenes. It must be said that Guiaud's portrayals of Monceaux and Madrid are extremely good – but they do not represent contemporary documents on the appearance of these important châteaux.

The Galerie des Cerfs is always remembered as the scene of a semi-judicial murder. In 1648 Christina of Sweden was lodging at Fontainebleau. She had abdicated her throne and embraced the religion of Rome without becoming thereby any less dictatorial or any more Christian. She had among her suite a certain marquis Monaldeschi whom she accused of having betrayed her, though whether his offence was of a political or a gallant nature is not known. He was arraigned before her in the Galerie des Cerfs, condemned and forced to make his confession before being stabbed to death in the presence of the ex-Queen. Barbaric executions did not normally shock Frenchmen of the seventeenth century, but this action caused widespread indignation. Christina wrote to Mazarin to justify her action: "I have no cause to repent of it," she assured him, "but a hundred thousand reasons for rejoicing at it."

Above the Galerie des Cerfs is the Galerie de Diane, or Galerie de la Reine, which was the great work of the painter Ambroise Dubois. Over the mantelpieces were portraits of the King and Queen, the one as Mars and the other as Diana. Ten huge canvasses – they were sixteen feet long by seven feet high – represented the victories of the King. The Père Dan was enthusiastic in his praise, especially of the ceiling, in which his observant eye detected "amid the lustre of the gold and the beautiful pictures and paintings which represent certain fictions of the Ancients, the plan and prospect of certain towns and landscapes". These included two views of Fontainebleau. It is significant that these found their place in an artist's record of the great achievements of the regin, for the whole gallery was an apotheosis of Henri IV.

It is therefore tragic that it has not survived. The Galerie de Diane has been entirely redecorated, first by Louis XVIII and later by Napoleon III. In that process was lost the most important example of the new décor of Henri IV. In contrast to the scenes of domestic life so frequently portrayed by Héroard, it would have reminded us that the purpose of a palace was to present the Sovereign to the world in all the impressive majesty that only a noble building can provide.

In pursuance of this aim, Henri IV adorned the Grande Salle of Primaticcio in the Cour de la Fontaine with the monumental fireplace which gave that building its historic name of Aile de la Belle Cheminée. The fireplace was dismantled in 1725, but the central figure of Henri IV was re-erected by Louis-Philippe in the Salon du Donjon.

It was a colossal architectural ensemble – a reredos of stone and marble twenty-three feet high by twenty broad – which occupied the entire wall-space between the two doors at the north end of the Grande Salle. Supported on a plinth and framed between coupled Corinthian columns "of a very beautiful marble", the great equestrian statue of the King stood out in brilliant

16 The "Belle Cheminée". Detail of drawing by François d'Orbay.

relief against the black of the marble slab behind it.

It is the very image of Victory. The proud stance of the charger – inspired by those mounted figures above the doorways of Blois, Le Verger and the Town Hall at Compiègne – is complemented by the easy poise of its rider. With a crown of laurels upon his brow and his white scarf flowing in the wind, Henri IV is every inch a King. At his feet his helmet, ornate with finely chased designs, displays his celebrated panache, recalling his words at Ivry: "If you lose your standard bearers, rally to my white plume: you will find it on the road to victory and honour." Those were words to stir a Frenchman's heart. The battle of Ivry and the consequent surrender of Mantes and Vernon were depicted above the centre of the fireplace in a bas–relief of the most exquisite workmanship.

To either side of the central statue the figures of Clemency and Peace completed the composition. The themes were appropriate, for it was only by means of the former that it was possible to achieve the latter.

Clemency and Peace: the Abbé Guilbert states that these figures "ornaient le milieu des colonnes de chaque côté" – "ornamented the central space between the pillars on either side". François d'Orbay, however, whose beautiful drawing of the Cour de la Fontaine provides the only pictorial record of the Belle Cheminée, has placed the figures immediately to either side of the equestrian statue. It looks an improbable position, but for that very reason it was unlikely that d'Orbay, a careful and accurate draughtsman, would have been wrong about it.

In 1900 the architect Boitte made a reconstruction of the Belle Cheminée, using many of its dismantled members as evidence and placing the two statues according to Guilbert's description. But he has inserted right at the top a pair of inverted cornucopias which have recently been identified as coming from the doorway to the Galerie de Diane and he makes use throughout of the combined monogram of Henri IV and Marie de Medici. d'Orbay is to be preferred in putting the royal H on its own. The architectural part of the reredos was contracted in August 1598, more than two years before the royal wedding which took place in December 1600. The commissioning of the equestrian statue in March of that year suggests that the architectural surround was nearly completed.

"Henri IV," writes the Père Dan, "had this beautiful mantelpiece constructed with a quite particular care. It is the work of the Sieur Jacquet known as Grenoble, a very excellent sculptor who bestowed five years of labour on this rare piece." Thomas Coryat, who visited Fontainebleau in 1611, made a note of its price: "This chimney cost the king fourscore and twenty thousand French crowns, which amount to four and twenty thousand pounds sterling."

The Salle de la Belle Cheminée is associated with one of the most poignant moments of the King's life. In 1599 he obtained from the Pope an annulment of his marriage with Marguerite de Valois and hoped to marry his favourite mistress, Gabrielle d'Estrées. She openly boasted that she could only be robbed of the crown by the death of the King. She forgot to reckon with her own. On Good Friday she was struck down by some terrible and then unknown disease. The King, who had set out from Fontainebleau to be with her at the last, was met on the road by the Marshals d'Ornano and Bassompierre with the news of her death. Alone in the great Salle de la Belle Cheminée Henri wept for his worthless mistress while France rejoiced.

Before the year was out, however, Gabrielle had been replaced in the King's affections by Henriette d'Entragues whom he created marquise de Verneuil and foolishly promised to marry if she conceived a son within six months. She did conceive a son, but he was stillborn. The next year he made a diplomatic marriage with Marie de Medici. James I's Ambassador, Sir George Carew, reported that the new Queen's chief rival was Madame de Verneuil who "maintaineth still a strong hold in the King's affections; and the Queen by her eagerness doth work herself some disadvantage".

The Queen, however, acquitted herself in the eyes of the Court and country by the prompt production of a Dauphin, the future Louis XIII.

It was on 27 September, 1601. It had been decided that the birth should take place in the Salon Oval (Cabinet de Théagène), perhaps because of its ample

dimensions. The King had requested the presence of his cousins the Prince de Conti, the comte de Soissons and the duc de Montpensier; the duchesse de Bar, the duchesse de Nemours and the marquise de Guercheville were also in attendance. A special chair had been made, Héroard informs us, "judging that she could be more easily delivered on it".

Next door, in the oldest part of the château, the Salle Saint Louis, the courtiers waited. Everything depended upon the sex of the child. Outside, in the Cour de l'Ovale, couriers, ready booted for their journey, awaited the signal to gallop off with their despatches.

Henri was so confident that it would be a boy that he had appointed Héroard, a week previously, to serve as doctor "to my son, the Dauphin" and he had promised the Queen the magnificent Château de Montceaux if the child should be male.

The Queen was therefore tormented by the fear, not uncommon in the circumstances, that it would be a girl. The King had made a private arrangement with the midwife – la dame Boursier – that if it was a boy her first words would be "chauffe moi un linge", but when the moment came there was something about her expression which caused him to doubt the message. The poor Queen cried out "e maschio?" – "Is it a male?" At this the midwife, who had given the child the kiss of life, uncovered the appropriate portion of his anatomy. The King rushed to the Queen's side. "Mamie!" he cried; "réjouissez-vous. Dieu nous a donné ce que nous désirons; nous avons un beau fils.'"

Some years later the room was completely redecorated and, in memory of

17 Aile de la Belle Cheminée (above) and façade of Galerie François I as re-ordered by Henri IV. Drawing by François d'Orbay.

49

the birth of Louis XIII, dolphins figure among its ornaments. Louis XV disrupted the decorative scheme by the insertion of four large doorways, but otherwise it remains unaltered and offers the best example in the palace of the style associated with Henri IV and his son.

The walls are divided into two sections of almost equal height by a dado supported by fluted pilasters. Between these the panelling frames a number of small paintings, landscapes alternating with flower pieces of an exceptional delicacy. Above the dado the walls and ceiling were devoted to a series of large canvasses by Ambroise Dubois. There were originally fifteen of them; they do not mean much to anyone unfamiliar with "The Loves of Theagenes and Charicles" to which they form a series of illustrations. The Greek of Heliodorus had been translated into French by Amyot in 1547. A new translation by Vital d'Audiguier appeared in 1609 followed by three more during the reign of Louis XIII. It seems likely that the popularity of the book owed something to the prominent part which it played in the decoration of Fontainebleau.

The paintings were presumably finished by July 1609 when the richly ornamental frames were commanded from F. de la Vacquerie.

At the time of his birth, Louis XIII had received a form of provisional baptism denoted by the verb "ondoyer". This was a security in case he should die in infancy. The baptism proper was deferred until September 1606.

The Cathedral of Notre-Dame de Paris was chosen for the ceremony. The Duchess of Mantua, the Queen's sister, and the Pope agreed to stand sponsors. France was to see another demonstration of the Catholic loyalties of their King. He tried, however, to make a simultaneous gesture in the opposite direction. He had by now two daughters who were to be baptised at the same time. It occurred to him to invite the Protestant King of England, James I, to

18 Cabinet de Théagène as altered by Louis XV. Watercolour by F. Fournier.

be godfather to Elizabeth. James, however, intimated that he could not accept to be godfather in second place.

During the summer there was an outbreak of the plague in Paris and it seemed imprudent to make use of Notre-Dame. It was decided that the ceremony should take place at Fontainebleau. But the Chapelle de la Trinité was quite inadequate for such a purpose. Henri IV had not yet begun his redecoration and it was probably in no condition to serve. But the work on the Cour de l'Ovale had been completed and it was decided to fit the courtyard up as a gigantic chapel.

A great platform was built up level with the first floor, so that the windows and the leaded walk above the colonnade could be used by the spectators. The Salle Saint-Louis was made the chief means of communication between the château and the platform. In the centre of the courtyard an altar was raised upon a dais and hung about with the richest tapestries. All the treasures of the Order of the Saint-Esprit were on show and the copper basin encrusted with silver ornaments which was said to have served for the baptism of Saint-Louis was placed in readiness. Overhead was stretched a vast canvas ceiling, painted blue with figures of dolphins, royal ciphers and fleurs de lys cut out "which appeared to be made of gold, for the sky was very clear that day".

The ceremony was the occasion for a number of disputes about precedence which were all too typical of the Court of France. The duc de Bouillon, descended from the ruling house of Sedan, claimed the right to pass in front of the other dukes. It was not allowed and he left the palace in high dudgeon. The duc de Nemours objected that he should have carried the candle which had been allocated to the Prince de Vaudémont. He pretended to have had a fall when out riding and had himself excused. The duc de Nevers resented the fact that the duc de Guise had been asked to bear the ermine train of the Dauphin and likewise absented himself. The Dauphin was dressed in white satin with an ermine mantle. He was carried from his apartment in the Pavillon des Pöeles by his tutor, the marquis de Souvré. The procession crossed the Cour de la Fontaine on top of the terrace in front of the Galerie François I, entered the Salle Saint-Louis and passed out onto the platform.

The Cour de l'Ovale presented a magnificent spectacle. Tiers of seats had been erected round three sides of the courtyard for the spectators to sit on. Both men and women scintillated with jewellery. It was said that the diamonds covering the hilt of the duc d'Epernon's sword alone cost three thousand écus.

The Cardinal de Gondi, Bishop of Paris, performed the ceremony which was punctuated by childish interjections from the Dauphin. "That's cold," he protested when anointed with the oil. "I've swallowed it," he said of the salt; "it tastes nice." But, when he had to recite the Paternoster, the Ave Maria and the Credo, he did it "with such a grace that there was not one of the spectators who was not moved to tears".

In memory of this occasion the new gateway of the Cour de l'Ovale has ever since been called the Porte du Baptistère. Under Henri IV this became the main entrance to the château, but it had to be approached by the way of the Cour des Offices. This consisted of three wings ranged symmetrically round three sides of a quadrangle open towards the château. The agreement with

Rémy Collin, the architect and builder, was signed on 18 July, 1606, and three years later the building was complete. By means of an alternation of doors and windows on the ground floor, Collin had introduced a pleasing rhythm which is repeated in the dormer windows above. In the centre of the north and south ranges he constructed a complex pavilion whose high roofs and lofty chimney stacks lent great distinction to the whole.

The north pavilion opens towards the town with a colossal niche containing the archway through which the palace was reached. From here a paved drive led obliquely to another gateway opposite the Porte du Baptistère. Within the niche of the north pavilion was an inscription in Latin which is worthy of note. "Henri IV, the most Christian King of France and Navarre, the mightiest of warriors, the most clement of conquerors ... restored this palace at a propitious moment, enormously increased it and ornamented it more magnificently in the year 1609."

The most important of his interior decorations to survive is that of the Chapelle de la Trinité. The façade of this chapel is probably a rebuilding of that of Philibert de l'Orme by Primaticcio. His wing on the other side of the central pavilion is identical in style. It is somewhat unusual for a chapel to be thus dissimulated behind a secular façade; there is nothing from the outside to suggest that this part of the château contains a religious edifice.

The present decoration dates from Henri IV but was only completed under Louis XIII. The inscription, which was placed over the entrance on the ground floor "Adorate Deum deinde Regem" – "Adore God and thereafter the King" – sets the general theme. The paintings of the ceiling are of exclusively religious subjects, the Mystery of the Redemption, but the huge escutcheons at either end of the chapel, upheld by the most elegant angels, are those of France and of Medici.

The whole design was due to Martin Fréminet, under whose directions the sculptors and stuccators worked. Except for the replacement, during the eighteenth century, of the oval paintings between the windows, the décor has suffered less in the way of degradation and restoration than the earlier portions of the palace. Fréminet painted in oils on dry plaster and not in fresco.

It is related that the redecoration owed its origin to the visit of the Spanish Ambassador, Don Pedro, in 1608. On 20 July the King showed him all over the palace and finally asked his opinion. "The only thing lacking," came the answer, "is that God should be as well housed as your Majesty."

It cannot be true. In a letter of 25 March, 1608, Henri IV reveals that Mass was being said in the Salle de la Belle Cheminée because of works in the chapel. The invaluable Héroard also tells us how, on 20 August of that year, exactly a month after Don Pedro's visit, the Dauphin came across Fréminet, "painter to the king, he who did the designs and paintings for the chapel". He went with Fréminet up a wooden staircase to the scaffold beneath the vault on which were paintings which he inspected for some time then exclaimed "voilà qui est bien fait". The programme for these paintings could hardly have been initiated only four weeks earlier.

The long vault of the chapel, with Fréminet's paintings set in stucco frames ornately moulded and heavily gilded, lends great magnificence to the perspective and naturally focuses attention upwards – a position spiritually conducive to worship. It needed, however, to be supported by an architecture rich enough to avoid top-heaviness. This balance has been achieved in a most satisfying degree. The lower storey is in the form of an arcade, proportioned by a Corinthian order with coupled columns separating the arches, each of which opens into a side chapel. The arches are filled with openwork screens above each of which a little gallery or lodge could be contrived. On big occasions, such as a royal marriage, these lodges could be filled with courtiers. Galleries running along either side of the chapel in front of the windows provided further accommodation.

The focal point of a Catholic church should always be the altar. It was left to Louis XIII to provide the chapel with a suitably magnificent reredos. It was the work of the Florentine Bordoni, who also carved the statues for the niches framed between pillars to either side. They represent Charlemagne and Saint-Louis, but their features are those of Henri IV and Louis XIII. A great King and a pious King – it was not wholly inappropriate.

There is, however, something disappointing – a certain lack of climax about the east end of the chapel. Its chief defect is that it is badly lit and this is the direct result of the fact, already noted, that the chapel was not in any way designed as a chapel but merely inserted between the walls of a secular building. When Louis XIV finally built the chapel of Versailles, his architect, Robert de Cotte, could provide dramatic lighting to the altar from the windows of his apse.

Brantôme, who described the Fontainebleau of François I as "the most beautiful and pleasant house in all Christendom", went on to claim that Henri IV left it "a hundred times better in its decoration and embellishment, to such an extent that it is not recognisable today as what it was before". Not only was the palace greatly beautified and extended, but the town – now numbering some 2,500 parishioners – could boast at least thirty houses which might well be called palaces erected by "the Princes, Cardinals and great lords of France ... so noble, so beautiful, so properly compact and built that there are many great Cities which could not surpass it. Briefly, it is a little Paradise in France."

A "paradise" should mean, in John Aubrey's phrase, "a most parkly ground and romancy pleasant place"; and certainly the creation of the gardens at Fontainebleau was not the least of Henri IV's achievements. They were described by Coryat. He enumerates the new fountains and figures of Thomas Francini, but wrongly gives the name of Romulus to the figure which represents the Tiber. This was central to the great parterre which was later named after it, but usually at that time known as the "Grand Jardin".

The other gardens were laid out round the lake and provided a pleasant variety of walks. The journal of Héroard makes constant allusion to these gardens, where the little Dauphin had his own plot where he dug the ground and grew peas and beans. "The walks about the gardens are many," wrote Coryat, "whereof some are very long and of a convenient breadth, being fairly sanded and kept very clean." To the south of the lake was one "enclosed with two very lofty hedges, most exquisitely made of filbird [filbert] trees and fine fruits and many curious arbours are made therein." The "fine fruit trees" were mostly mulberry whose leaves are the favourite food of the silk worm.

But the great attraction of the gardens were the little streams which

19 Aerial view across Parterre du Tibre, before destruction of the Galerie d'Ulysse (left). Martin le Jeune.

accompanied these sandy paths. "By most of these walks run very pleasant rivers full of sundry delicate fishes." Upstream of all these was "the principal spring of all, which is called Fountaine Beleau which feedeth all the other springs and rivers and whence the King's Palace hath his denomination". In the middle of this water garden was the lake, described by Coryat as "a pond full of goodly great carps, whereof there is wonderful plenty".

It has sometimes been claimed that the oldest fish at Fontainebleau dated back to the Ancien Régime. This cannot be true, for during the Revolution the lake was drained dry and the subsequent sale of fish lasted for eight days. Henri IV was very keen on fish and most of the canals and streams were stocked with trout.

These fish were sometimes the quarry for a form of aquatic falconry developed under Louis XIII. In September 1631 there is the first mention of a "Gouverneur des Cormorants". "In order to get the best enjoyment from this sport," wrote Nicolas Defer, "it is necessary to have the fish in a canal which is neither too deep nor too broad, in order to be able to see from above the way in which the bird dives and pursues its prey. He becomes so perfectly streamlined and moves with a speed so fast that he seems to cleave the water like an arrow and when he has caught a fish he comes to the surface and throws it in the air to catch it in his beak in order to swallow it head first. This he does with an astonishing speed and dexterity." The birds were prevented from swallowing the fish by a copper collar round the neck. The fish had to be extracted head first and this was achieved without putting the fingers into the bird's throat, but by manipulation from outside.

The enthusiasm of Henri IV for fish may have been one of his motives for the creation of the Canal. There was already a long canal at the nearby Château de Fleury-en-Bière, which may have provided the inspiration, but the King wanted something much more magnificent and he took an almost childish delight in its construction. Malherbe records how he would sit sometimes from five or six in the morning until midday watching the workmen. When finally completed, it took eight days to fill with water.

There is little documentary evidence to suggest that Henri IV took a creative interest in his works of architecture. He was certainly proud of the finished product and was always ready to show visitors of distinction round in person. "Having put his hand on my arm as he does to many," wrote the Florentine Ambassador Camillo Guidi, "he began to show me his house, room by room, starting with his own apartments and galleries and continuing through all the others, pointing out to me anything which was worthy of note ... being very careful to distinguish what was the legacy of his predecessors from what His Majesty had added or restored." It took two hours and they went everywhere. They mounted the scaffolding to watch the painters at work. The King climbed and jumped with "such agility and freedom that I cannot get over my astonishment". Although Henri was fifty-six at the time of his death, the doctors agreed that he could well have lived for another twenty years.

Louis XIII continued the tradition of showing Fontainebleau and, according to the Père Dan, caused a gold medal to be struck "embossed with the royal arms, to offer to the Ambassadors, foreign Princes, lords and ladies whom his Majesty sends daily to see his house".

Louis XIII was not a great builder. Thanks to the great activity of his father's masons, he hardly had need to be, but he left his mark on Fontainebleau. In 1639 the accounts reveal an expenditure of 193,882 livres here, which compares significantly with the 37,740 expended on the Louvre that year. In particular he embellished his own bedroom and that of his Queen with the richly-carved and gilded ceilings which we see today.

But his most important addition was the magnificent fer-à-cheval staircase. It must be remembered that Philibert de l'Orme's stairway was simply a means of reaching the terrace from the court. It did not provide direct access to the apartments. It was only under Henri IV that a door had been opened in the pavilion to which this staircase leads. Although he never intended the Cour du Cheval Blanc to be the main entrance to the palace, he made the first important step in that direction.

His son made the next. Philibert de l'Orme's stairs could never have been a main entrance. They began with a single narrow flight rising to a landing from which two semicircular arms gave access to the terrace at two widely divergent points. Jehan du Cerceau's fer-à-cheval begins at the doorway and offers two broad and sumptuous means of access. If imitation is the sincerest flattery, the greatest compliment paid to du Cerceau's staircase was the building of a replica in the forecourt of the nearby Château de Courances.

This was built by the architect Destailleurs in 1775 for the baron de Haber, an ancestor of the present owner, the marquis de Ganay. It is interesting that at so late a date the Louis XIII staircase at Fontainebleau should have still been sufficiently admired to merit imitation.

It is possible also that the gardens at Courances, which are among the most beautiful and peaceful gardens in France, owe something to the former Jardin des Pins at Fontainebleau. In contrast to the great elaboration of fountains and statues at Vaux-le-Vicomte and Versailles, the gardens at Courances form a green and pleasant landscape to which man has given a symmetrical and ordered shape. The water, which comes from a number of local sources, finds its level in the moat by a series of small cascades and gentle overflows, providing a sweet and constant music to the ear. Such were the gardens of Fontainebleau before they were reshaped on more English lines by Hurtault for Napoleon.

Louis XIV, Louis XV and Louis XVI

WHEN LOUIS XIV came to the throne, Fontainebleau was by far the finest of his palaces. Saint-Germain was not in the same class. The Louvre, the Tuileries and Vincennes did not answer to his requirements and were all subjected to extensive additions and renovations. Versailles was still an insignificant *maison de chasse*. But Fontainebleau Louis accepted more or less as it was. Only in the gardens was he to leave his mark upon the exterior; the great Parterre du Tibre was laid out from designs of Le Vau in 1664. But within the palace, apart from the renewal and enrichment of much of the furniture and the hangings, he made no important alterations until right at the end of his reign, when his bedroom was enlarged and reorientated.

His old bedroom, then, was the one which formed the centre of the ceremonial of the Court for most of his reign.

Fortunately it is depicted for us by a tapestry from the Gobelins Manufactory which is one of the series known as *l'Histoire du Roi*. The one which survives is from the duplicate series woven from 1671-1676 by Jean Jans and represents a historic scene: "The Audience given by the King Louis XIV at Fontainebleau to the Cardinal Chigi, nephew and *Legatus a Latere* of Pope Alexander VII, on 29 July, 1664, for the satisfaction of the insult made to his Ambassador in Rome."

The Ambassador, the duc de Créqui, had claimed that the whole area round his Embassy, the Palazzo Farnese, was outside the jurisdiction of the Vatican; he had also omitted to pay a visit to another of the Pope's nephews, don Mario Chigi, who sent a detachment of the Corsican Guard to molest Créqui's servants. On 20 August, 1662, the house was in a state of siege.

Louis XIV demanded an apology which the Pope refused to give. Louis retaliated by seizing Avignon which was still in papal possession. This provoked the apology which Cardinal Chigi was deputed to deliver, to which Louis added the humiliation of erecting an obelisk to commemorate the event in the Corsican quarter in Rome.

The atmosphere, then, of the scene represented in the tapestry was highly charged. Le Brun has slightly emphasised the obsequious attitudes of the accompanying clergy and the triumphant looks of those surrounding Louis.

But for the student of Fontainebleau the real interest of this tapestry is the picture which it gives of the most important apartment in the palace.

The room is that still designated as the Salle du Trône since the days of Napoleon and still furnished as such. In other words, it was one of the suite of apartments with which Charles IX doubled those of François I on the north side of the Cour de l'Ovale, from which it opened out of the Cabinet de Théagène. The King's bedroom was smaller than it is today. The bed, surrounded on two sides by its balustrade, was set against the wall opposite the windows. The fireplace was in the partition wall to the right when one was facing the windows.

The accuracy of the depiction in the tapestry has been studied and confirmed by Yves Bottineau. The hangings on the bed can be identified in the Inventaire Général and it is recorded that these were taken back to Paris after the departure of the King, while the framework, the *bois du lit*, remained at Fontainebleau. "Taken from Fontainebleau, one furnishing of white *gros de Naples* embroidered with figures of birds and flowers from China, picked out in gold thread with fringes and tassels of gold." The walls were hung with "gilded leather on a white background with large *rinceaux* and festoons and figures of children in gold and many colours".

Other pieces of furniture can likewise be identified. It has been demonstrated by Pierre Verlet that the cabinet against the wall behind the King corresponds to no. 5 in the Inventory – "the door ornamented on either side by two pilasters of fluted ebony, with bases and capitals of ormolu". Even the carpet within the balustrade, with the monogram of interlaced Ls in the corner, can be traced in the Inventory.

To the left is a tall guéridon which can be identified as one of four "made by de Bonnaire, of which the body is formed by three figures supporting a vase above which is the stand; the said figures carried upon a base of three consoles ending in lions' paws".

Only the chimney piece leaves us in doubt. The tapestry shows a retangular landscape in the overmantel which cannot be identified. Le Brun's preliminary sketch, however, shows an oval picture framed by a much more ornate surrounding. It is difficult not to prefer the original drawing. The mantelpiece, however, was destroyed in 1714 when Louis enlarged his bedroom on this side, suppressing his father's oratory among other little rooms, to create the alcove here for his bed. The fireplace, which is the one we see today, was transferred to the partition wall where the bed had previously been.

Over this new mantelpiece Louis placed a portrait of his father by Philippe de Champaigne. One of the destructions of the Revolution was the burning of this picture, together with forty-eight other royal portraits, before the newly-erected statue of Marat. Napoleon filled the empty space with his own portrait which was removed by Louis-Philippe and replaced by another painting of Louis XIII by Champaigne.

Louis also made certain alterations to the Galerie François I. In 1688 he inserted a staircase at the western end, which meant piercing the panelling with a new doorway. But his chief activity was in the bowdlerisation of the paintings. In 1701 he gave orders "during the visit to Fontainebleau to deface two of the pictures in the Galerie des Reformés [as it was sometimes called] in which the postures were somewhat irregular and had them replaced by others by Boulogne le Jeune of decent subjects taken from the metamorphoses". These were the two paintings at each extremity of the Gallery.

There was another painting – "Les Amours de Jupiter et Semélé" by Primaticcio – over the chimney of the little projecting cabinet which marked the centre of the Gallery on the north side. This painting, "jugée impudique", was also removed by Louis and replaced by a more proper allegory of Minerva and the Arts by Bon Boulogne. Semélé, it will be remembered, was the mother of Bacchus.

This expression of puritanism throws an interesting light upon the outlook of the age. Henri Sauval, in his *Amours des Rois de France* launched a tirade against the indecency of the paintings at Fontainebleau which were "not only lascivious but incestuous and execrable". He claims that in 1643 the Queen Mother, Anne d'Autriche, burnt 100,000 écus worth of paintings and added that "if she had wished to burn all that was most abominable and dissolute, she would have had to have reduced almost the whole of Fontainebleau to cinders". Although Sauval's book was not published until 1724, he died in 1670 before the rather minor purges of Louis XIV had been effected.

No doubt in Louis' case the puritanical influence derived from Madame de Maintenon, but if Louis destroyed certain works of art to please her, he also created at Fontainebleau the most exquisite apartment for her to inhabit.

It was situated on the first floor over the entrance in the Pavillon de la Porte Dorée. In 1661 the open arcade had been glazed in; the glass was supplied by Claude Tisserand, the leadwork by Jean Girard and the fastenings by the locksmith Etienne Pompier. The apartment consisted of an anteroom, salon, cabinet de travail, bedroom and cabinet de toilette. In 1685 it was completely redecorated.

It has recently been the subject of a very careful restoration and is today one of the greater glories of Fontainebleau. Here we see the Grand Siècle in a very different mood from that of the State Apartments of Versailles. Here the artists have been asked to create something intimate and homely. There is a pleasing appropriateness that this should survive in the palace that was the "true home" of the Kings of France. Insofar as Louis XIV found any room for domesticity in his life, it was in the presence of his morganatic wife. It is clear from the chronicles that he managed to spend more time with her at Fontainebleau than elsewhere.

For this domesticity the artists produced a faultless blend of finery and cosiness. It would be a revelation to see these rooms with the fires and candles lit, for it was in the long autumn evenings that Louis mostly came here to relax.

The panelling was carved and gilded by Lalande, who received 1,500 livres for his work, new paintings by Jean Dubois replaced those of the sixteenth century, and nine mirrors were supplied by Guimard. More important for the general appearance of the room was the *meuble*, the silk hanging and upholstery of the bed and chairs. It is here that the miniature and the exquisite have been used to great effect in the delicacy of the braiding and fringing and in the fine floral pattern of the silk.

The *meuble* – no. 567 in the Inventory – is described as "a furnishing of blue satin lined with taffeta trimmed with lace in *point de France* in gold and silver and coloured silk with tinsel, consisting of a bed, two armchairs and six folding seats".

The two armchairs evoke the equality in private of the married couple and Louis' ever-increasing habit of coming here. Madame, writing to the Duchess of Hanover on 27 October, 1696, says: "The King is once again in private with his lady, so full of gravity; Monseigneur is with the princesse de Conti and her good friends, and I am alone, for there is neither man nor woman whose presence is indispensable for me." She was, in fact, more happy in the company of dogs.

But the presence of the King in the apartments of his wife was not always of a merely domestic nature. On 9 November, 1700, the King of Spain died. The Court went into mourning and the Jours d'Appartement, the comedies and other entertainments were cancelled. At three o'clock Louis summoned his Ministers to meet him in Madame de Maintenon's rooms. The council ended just after seven, but Louis continued his discussions with Torcy and Barbézieux until ten. Madame de Maintenon was present all the time. Next day, on his return from hunting, the Council was again summoned to the same place and Madame de Maintenon was again present. "Accustomed as the Court was," wrote Saint-Simon, "to the favour of Madame de Maintenon, it was not accustomed to see her public entry into affairs of State, and the surprise was very great to see these two Councils assembled in her rooms."

It was a momentous occasion. The decision had been taken to accept the throne of Spain for the duc d'Anjou. The public announcement was made at Versailles on 16 November, but the letter accepting the offer was dated from Fontainebleau on the 12th.

In the early days of his reign, Louis XIV's visits to Fontainebleau followed no sort of pattern. From 1678 – the year in which he embarked upon the final enlargement of Versailles – until the end of his life the Voyage de Fontainebleau became, with one or two exceptions, an annual event which took place in the autumn and was frequently linked with a visit to Chambord.

From 1688 the presence of the exiled James II of England – never referred to as anything but "Le Roi d'Angleterre" – and his Queen obliged Louis to a high standard of luxury and entertainment.

The English exiles were lodged in the Appartement des Reines Mères on the west side of the Cour de la Fontaine. "When they are at Fontainebleau," the *Mercure Galant* informs us, "they come to the King's Rooms at 7.30 in the evening and the King goes to receive them at the door of his ante room, where the music commences as soon as they are seated. The concert lasts for some three quarters of an hour, after which the King conducts their Majesties into his Cabinet where the Queen plays cards until supper is served, which is at ten o'clock. The King of England watches the gaming and the King goes and works with one of his ministers ... nothing could equal the care, the regard and the politeness of the King towards them, nor the air of majesty and gallantry which was observed on every occasion."

The Cabinet de Théagène or Cabinet Oval was the main reception room. Whereas at Versailles a suite of apartments permitted the dispersion of the company, at Fontainebleau all were accommodated in this room; the King and Madame (Saint-Simon is writing after the death of Monsieur) in armchairs, the princesses on tabourets, the duchesses on cushions and the rest on the floor.

The room was still as Louis XIII had left it. Louis XIV's only importation was a double dog kennel "made of oak, painted white with pilasters and mouldings in gilt, the whole painted in light sprigs of flowers and ornaments in colour". The royal dogs each had three mattresses upholstered in a red velvet known as *tripe écarlate*. It is somehow typical of Fontainebleau that this extremely domestic item of furniture should have been placed in the main reception room.

The members of the Court enjoyed a greater measure of freedom here than at Versailles. Saint-Simon noted that "we offer one another enormous dinners here more than anywhere". Louis did not feed his guests, but he did offer them the frequent entertainment of the Comedy. In 1698 Louis allowed his grandsons to attend for the first time. It was a performance of *Le Bourgeois Gentilhomme*. Madame recorded that "the duc de Bourgogne lost all sense of decorum; he laughed until tears ran down his cheeks; the duc d'Anjou was so entranced that he remained open mouthed as if in ecstasy, never taking his eyes off the scene; the duc de Berry laughed so much that he nearly fell off his seat".

The provision of theatricals for a Voyage de Fontainebleau was one of the major expenses – in 1697 it amounted to 10,729 livres. The courtiers did not always bother to attend it. In 1704 Saint-Simon records how angry Louis was to learn that some of the ladies neglected to change into *grand habit* for the Spectacle and that others did not attend the theatre in order to avoid having to change. "Four words from him and the check that he made to see that his orders were carried out brought all the ladies along assiduously dressed in *grand habit*."

During the absence of the Court, Fontainebleau was the responsibility of the Direction des Bâtiments and of the Garde Meuble. Colbert, in his capacity of Surintendant et Ordonnateur Général, received 3,800 livres for this in 1672 and the marquis de Saint-Hérem, Capitaine et Concierge du Château, received the same.

Particular care was taken of the pictures. The accounts mention Jean Dubois "painter, having the care and responsibility for cleaning the pictures, both in fresco and in oils, both ancient and modern, in the halls, galleries, rooms and cabinets of the said château: the sum of 600 livres for his appointment for the present year, and is charged to restore those that are damaged and to clean the picture frames and to furnish the wood, coal and faggots to burn in the said rooms where the said pictures are for the better conservation of the same".

The maintenance of the gardens was clearly an important item too. The widow Bray and Nicolas Poiret each received 800 livres for the upkeep of half the Grand Parterre; Jean Desbouts 600 for the Petit Jardin de l'Etang, and the Jardin des Pins. A man named Voltigeant was paid 200 livres for the upkeep of the boats on the lake and Jacques Dorchemer de la Tour 100 for winding and care of clocks.

It is clear from the repeated legislation to prevent them that the inhabitants of Fontainebleau threw their rubbish over the walls, put their cows in to graze in the gardens and allowed their children to bathe in the *pièces d'eau*. The arrival of the Court meant a hurried removal of the rubbish, the driving out of the cows and the donning by personnel of their official clothing. The *jardiniers* and *fontainiers* for example, were provided with a jerkin or *justaucorps* with a large braid stripe which cost 46 livres a time.

Up till 1700 Louis used to pay for any alterations which the courtiers wanted for the apartments, but that year, Saint-Simon records, "started with a reform: the King declared that he would no longer bear the expense for alterations which the courtiers made".

The history of Fontainebleau is to some extent the history of successive attempts to create an entrance worthy of the palace. François I had used the Cour de l'Ovale which he entered by means of the Porte Dorée. Henri IV used the same court but entered it from the other side by his new Porte du Baptistère. But the Cour du Cheval Blanc was by far the largest in its extent and the most imposing in its architecture. The great fer-à-cheval staircase seemed to have been designed to provide sumptuous access to the apartments. Yet the courtyard itself could only be approached either through an insignificant archway in the middle of the Aisle des Ministres or through the equally insignificant Porte des Champs directly opposite the great staircase.

It is clear from a number of accounts, such as that of the arrival of Cardinal Chigi, that Louis XIV made the main entrance by one or other of these routes. The *Mercure Galant* describes the reception of Marie-Adelaïde de Savoie on 5 November, 1696. "She arrived at about five o'clock at Fontainebleau by the Cour du Cheval Blanc. The King gave his hand to the princess; the duc d'Anjou and the duc de Berry, who were waiting for her at the top of the Escalier du fer-à-cheval, saluted her without kissing her." Saint-Simon also describes the scene. "It was a truly magnificent spectacle. The King led the princess, so small that she appeared to be sticking out of his pocket, and after walking very slowly the whole length of the terrace, they entered the Chapel for a short prayer."

The Cour du Cheval Blanc provided a capacious theatre for scenes of this sort and the horseshoe staircase with its terrace offered an impressive stage for the principal actors.

Right at the end of his reign, Louis XIV finally saw the necessity of creating a worthier entrance to the courtyard. A memoir written by Oudin de Massingi in 1716 claims the Porte des Champs as one of the principal "avenues" to the château – "since it is opposite the great horseshoe staircase; the late King Louis le Grand, of triumphant memory, determined to have the entrance pavilion demolished and in its place to construct another and very magnificent gateway". He did not live to realise the project. Louis XV, also in the last year of his reign, entertained the idea of a sumptuous entrance here, but also died before he could implement the plan.

By the mid-eighteenth century the old buildings were beginning to look hopelessly out of date and the ever-increasing number of courtiers required a corresponding increase in the number of apartments available. Under Louis XV, Fontainebleau came dangerously near to losing its domestic character as the "real home of the King", and to becoming a second, and second-rate, Versailles.

The present-day enthusiasm for conservation – bred of a lack of confidence in modern art and architecture – has put such a premium on the preservation of the past that it is difficult for us to sympathise with the readiness of our forebears to destroy their "architectural heritage" in order to replace it with their own modernity. The confidence of the eighteenth century in its own good taste was one of the most destructive forces. It seriously imperilled the great cathedrals of the Gothic Age and it deprived posterity of many of the finest décors of the Renaissance and the Grand Siècle, particularly among the royal palaces.

The presiding genius of this programme of destruction was Louis XV. He was a man dominated by two passions: one for the chase and the other for architecture. In the first he was the acknowledged master of the art; in the second, he had the status of a gifted amateur. He was never so happy as when he was seated with Madame de Pompadour and Gabriel and the table before them was spread with architectural designs. D'Argenson credits him with both taste and talent, especially in the contrivance of "les petites commodités de son apartement".

At Versailles he can often be forgiven his destructions in view of the many beautiful décors with which he replaced them. At Fontainebleau the balance is against him. His reconstructions here entailed the loss of the Belle Cheminée, the Pavillon des Poëles, the Galerie d'Ulysse and several of François I's finest interiors. The Galerie des Cerfs also, though later restored to its original appearance, has lost the authenticity of its topographical murals. In exchange for these losses, posterity has gained the delightful decorations of the Cabinet du Conseil, the palatial grandeur of the Gros Pavillon, a number of finely panelled interiors in the Appartement des Chasses and the dull and overpowering façades of the long wing which replaced the Galerie d'Ulysse and which took the name of Aisle Louis XV.

If he had realised all his projects, he would have left Fontainebleau altered almost beyond recognition. Robert de Cotte drew up plans for screening off the Cour de la Fontaine with a massive block surmounted by a dome, which would have deprived the château of its most charming and most typical perspective.

Louis XV was the only King to have been married at Fontainebleau. The ceremony took place in September 1725, and was the occasion for the dismantling of the Belle Cheminée for the better accommodation of a Court theatre in the space afforded. Marie-Leczinska had come from Wissembourg and on the night of 3 September she slept at Provins. The Court was already at Fontainebleau and Louis fixed on Moret-sur-Loing for their first meeting. It was raining as it had never rained before as he set out with his brilliant cortège. The muddy roads were almost impassable and at one point in Marie's journey no fewer than thirty horses had to be harnessed to her great berline. A dais had been prepared and bales of straw laid down to insulate the carpet from the all-pervading mud. Louis greeted his fiancée with a boyish enthusiasm which won all hearts. As he did so, the weather changed dramatically and the sun, piercing through the rain, crowned the scene with a rainbow. The young pair got into the King's coach and drove back over the bridge into Moret, where Marie spent the last night before the wedding in the old château.

A nine o'clock on 5 September, the coach was seen approaching along the road from Moret. In spite of the rain, which had started again, the avenues and forecourts of the place were filled with a populace delirious with joy. Within the more privileged precincts "the apartments, the galleries, the terraces were teeming like an ant-hill with princes and lords, both French and foreign".

The carriage made its way down the Chaussée de Maintenon to the Porte Dorée and, entering the Cour de l'Ovale, which formed a magnificent amphitheatre for spectators, drew up before Le Breton's portico at the foot of the Queen's staircase. On the first landing Louis was there to meet his bride and to conduct her to her apartment where she was to be robed as a bride and as a Queen.

It was an unforgettable moment. The daughter of a dethroned King of Poland, she had been brought up in the poverty and obscurity of exile in the modest Hôtel de Weber at Wissembourg. Here her father lived on an irregularly paid pension from the King of France and an ever-decreasing hope of regaining his throne. One morning, however, a few months previously, he had burst into Marie's room. "Oh my daughter," he had exclaimed, "let us fall on our knees and thank God."

"What, father," asked the astonished princess; "are you to be recalled to the throne?"

"Heaven has granted us more than that," came the reply; "you are to be Queen of France!"

It was unbelievable, but it was true. Party political intrigue between the House of Orléans and the House of Condé had ruled out any more obviously eligible candidate as unacceptable to one side or the other. Only a political nonentity could command their joint approval. As Marie was robed in her purple and ermine mantle and loaded with the Crown Jewels of France, a destiny that must have seemed beyond her fondest dreams was realised.

Meanwhile, in the Chapelle de la Trinité, the marquis de Dreux, Grand Master of the Ceremonies, was already placing the privileged guests. Tiers of seats had been erected in the side chapels and the windows taken out to make more room in the balconies.

On every side the architecture had been enriched with gorgeous hangings and gold embroidery. The canopy that had been raised over the King's throne at Reims for the Coronation now hung over the dais where the bridal couple were to kneel.

The magnificence of the decorations was further enhanced by the sumptuous apparel of the spectators. "To give some idea of the richness of the costumes," wrote Narbonne, "I will merely say that the greater part of the Lords were in stockings of spun gold which cost 300 livres a pair – and the rest in proportion."

At a quarter past one the Queen's procession moved off through the royal apartments, along the Galerie François I, down Louis XIV's staircase and into the Chapel. She was met by the King, dressed entirely in cloth of gold with every button on his coat a single diamond. The Cardinal de Rohan was waiting in the Chapel to perform the ceremony.

Two hours later Marie was back in her apartment and being relieved of the heaviest of her fineries when the duc de Mortemart was announced. He was the bearer of the *corbeil* presented by the King in accordance with tradition. It was a coffer lined with crimson velvet embroidered with gold and filled with the most exquisite pieces of jewellery. Marie was delighted. "This is the first time in my life," she said, "that I have been able to give presents," and she distributed them to her ladies.

The only immediate alteration to the Queen's apartment was the contrivance, in 1726, of a little oratory. Marie-Leczinska was sincerely devout and this provision met an obvious need. It was not until 1747 that her bedroom received the attention which it deserved.

The chronicler *par excellence* of the new reign was the duc de Luynes. If he lacked the literary ability of the duc de Saint-Simon, he made up for it by the scrupulous accuracy of his observation. Nothing seems to have escaped his watchful eye. He and his wife were among those closest to Marie-Leczinska and he was well placed to record the details of any changes in her apartments.

During the Voyage de Fontainebleau of 1745 he mentions that the Queen had been complaining of the smallness of her bedroom. "Her bed was in the corner by the fireplace, raised on a little dais which is very beautiful, and enclosed by a balustrade." In the course of this visit plans were agreed for the enlarging of this room, but the King had stipulated that the old ceiling, made for Anne d'Autriche, should be preserved intact. It is interesting to see Louis XV playing the part of conservationist.

Two years later the duc de Luynes was able to admire the new décor. The room had been extended by the addition of an alcove, made at the expense of an adjoining cabinet, and the ceiling of the alcove, with the monogram of Marie-Leczinska, was achieved in a style which carefully accorded with the old one.

"These additional ornaments," wrote the Duke, "are in the antique taste, since it was necessary that it matched the rest, but this antique has been executed so agreeably as to leave almost nothing to be desired."

The room was also enlarged by the advancing of the façade some eight feet into the Jardin de Diane. The window recesses were therefore decorated at this time and still carry the monogram of the Queen.

The advancing of the façade affected all the rooms on this side of the royal apartments, but the only one to receive a thorough redecoration was the Cabinet du Conseil. Louis XIV had also redecorated this room, but only his ceiling survives. Its many compartments dictated the rhythm of the panelling. Great care was taken over the new décor, "since the King's cabinets should be a masterpiece of its sort," wrote Monsieur de Vandières, the Directeur des Bâtiments. "I ask for the greatest possible attention." The result was a most attractive ensemble, though perhaps more suited to a drawing-room than a council chamber. Boucher, Van Loo and Jean-Baptiste Pierre have the major share of the credit, but the delightful floral decorations are by Pierre-Joseph Peyrotte. It is a splendid example of artistic collaboration. It needs the evidence of the Comptes des Bâtiments to reveal that the pink panels are by Pierre and the blue-grey by Van Loo. The paintings on the ceiling were done by Boucher. In October 1753, Luynes recorded that the work had been completed: "It is very beautiful and blends together the ancient and the modern ornaments."

The Cabinet du Conseil was one of Louis XV's great successes at Fontainebleau. The same cannot be said of the long wing which forms the south range of the Cour du Cheval Blanc. The King wanted fifty more apartments to offer his courtiers, Luynes informs us, twenty-two of which were to have their own kitchens. His first idea was to partition off the Galerie d'Ulysse, as he did partition off the Galerie des Cerfs. But the Galerie d'Ulysse was only two storeys high. A new block could be twice the height and offer far more accommodation. In 1738 Gabriel was invited to design a new wing containing seventy-two apartments.

He produced a façade thirty-nine windows long with no other architectural contrivance than a small central break ornamented with a pediment. Admittedly there was here no place for a flourish of architecture. Too grand a façade would have detracted too much from the entrance front and its horseshoe staircase. But Gabriel has not even introduced the gentle rhythm which can be created by the alternation of triangular and segmental pediments over the dormers or by a slight but regular grouping of the window bays. Only the drainpipes break the monotony of his composition.

There is today a striking imbalance caused by the lack of chimneys on the western half of the wing. This is the result of the creation within these walls of a Court theatre by Napoleon III. The great regiment of chimneys on the eastern half reflects the barrack-like provision of apartments within doors. The multiplicity of the fireplaces was the occasion for the exercise of economy. It was specified in the contracts that the marble should be of an inferior quality, "commun" or "non du beau".

At the opposite extremity of the château the Pavillon des Chasses contains some of the most beautiful panelling of the reign of Louis XV; it also preserves some of its saddest memories. For these were the apartments of the Dauphin Louis, son of Louis XV and father of Louis XVI. He never reigned but he would in all probability have made a better King than his father or his son. "There is no doubt about it," wrote Diderot to Sophie Vollant, "the Dauphin had read much and reflected much and that there were few important matters on which he was not very well informed." It was recorded that he and his first wife, the Infanta of Spain, would read together the *Mémoires* of Sully in order to learn how best to restore the country which they were to rule to peace and prosperity. Once on the terrace at Bellevue the young Prince had contemplated the City of Paris in pensive silence. "I was thinking," he said afterwards, "of the pleasure that a sovereign must experience in creating the happiness of so many."

The tragic early loss of his first wife was in course of time repaired by his affection for the second, Marie-Josèphe de Saxe. She was a person in many ways out of tune with the Court, but happy in the "délicieux deserts de Fontainebleau". She describes her feelings for the palace in terms which show, between the lines, the prevailing attitude of the times. "I love this wild place," she admitted; "they say I have bad taste; perhaps I have and I do not deny it – but it pleases me. I prefer this forest with its great rocks and its dense woods to Compiègne, which is more like a park than a forest. I know that the château here is ugly – it is quite true, but I love old things. When I think that Saint-Louis, François I and my beloved Henri IV lived here, I seem to see them, and I am delighted in my entresol. I am in a little palace alone in the middle of everything. In fact I find it charming." In those words she expresses one of the most penetrating appreciations of Fontainebleau that has been recorded.

Her happiness was not to last. In 1765 she lost her husband through a long and painful illness.

The Dauphin Louis possessed the two traditional virtues of a French King; he was a great soldier, and greatly loved by his soldiers, and he was a sincere Christian. As an admirer of Henri IV and Sully, he was the opponent of all persecution. Like a soldier and like a Christian, he knew how to die. "His death," wrote the duc de Croÿ, "was an edification to all through his courage and true piety, without bigotry and without weakness. Those who were furthest from religion gave him credit for it." Diderot records that, shortly before his death, the duc de Nivernais found the Dauphin reading the works of the atheist philosopher David Hume. They did not deprive him of his faith. After he had received the Viaticum the Dauphine entered his room expecting to find him exhausted. "I shall never forget," she said, "the look of contentment, of joy, of beatitude which shone in his eyes and permeated his countenance." His three sons were all to mount the throne of France as Louis XVI, Louis XVIII and Charles X.

One of the most recherché décors of this period was an octagonal salon built in the Jardin de Diane for Madame du Barry. It was placed, with what seems an astonishing lack of good taste, immediately in front of the windows of the Queen's apartment, occupied by Marie-Antoinette. One of Louis XVI's first actions was to have it destroyed.

On her first arrival as Dauphine at Fontainebleau, Marie-Antoinette had spent three hours being shown all over the palace and its gardens by the marquis de Marigny and the architect in charge. It was here that she first captivated the Court and, although only just fifteen, scored a number of triumphs against Madame du Barry and yet endeared herself to the King. "She is my duchesse de Bourgogne," was his significant remark. In the Court theatre, which occupied the Aisle de la Belle Cheminée, etiquette forbade applause, but when the duc d'Aumont inserted into a piece some verses complimentary to the Dauphine, she received a spontaneous ovation.

At the beginning of the new reign the Voyage de Fontainebleau continued to be a regular feature in the routine of the Court. "It is well known," wrote the comtesse de Boigne, "that the Court of France was never seen in greater magnificence than at Fontainebleau." The King was at his most affable; the Court theatre was at its most brilliant; first nights of the latest plays were produced here with a great wealth of costumes and scenic effects.

It was, of course, exceedingly expensive. A troop of comedians would be paid 650 livres for the performance and 10 livres a day for each member of the cast. Then there was all the "petit monde obligatorie à cette occurrence" – the tailors, embroiderers, sempstresses, perruquiers, laundresses, the designers, painters, makers and movers of scenery, and of course the enormous cost of transporting all these together with their baggage from Paris. In 1783 the figure for theatrical entertainment had amounted to 468,204 livres. In 1785 it reached 600,000.

The transport of furniture and tapestry was another heavy item of expense. In 1786 Thierry de la Ville d'Avray, in charge of the Garde Meuble du Roi, claimed that the Voyage de Fontainebleau provided "one vast theatre of corrupt dealings". The tapestries were all brought down before the arrival of the Court and, after its departure, rolled up and taken back to Paris. In an average year there were 101 "tapisseries à or", including a set done from Mignard's gallery at Saint-Cloud; there were 198 "tapisseries en soie", twenty-three of which formed a series of Julius Caesar, and 112 "Verdures" to be transported.

Finally there was the cost of the actual transport of the King and his Court. The English Ambassador, the Duke of Dorset, reported: "Their Majesties, the Dauphin and the rest of the royal family, are removed from Fontainebleau to Versailles. The expense attending these journeys of the Court is incredible. The duc de Polignac told me that he had given orders for 2,115 horses for this service. Besides this, an adequate proportion of horses are ordered for the removal of the heavy baggage." Calonne, he mentions, was obliged to borrow to meet this heavy expense. Mercy, Ambassador from Vienna, said the endless cavalcade "resembled that of an army on the march".

The ever-rising cost of the Voyage de Fontainebleau perplexed contemporaries because the courtiers were lodged there at their own expense. The invaluable comtesse de Boigne provides the details in a passage which deserves to be quoted in full.

"Those who were invited were only accorded the four walls of an apartment; one had to procure one's own furniture and one's own linen and live as best one could. In point of fact, since all the ministers and all who had "charges" at Court kept tables for those who attended them, one had no difficulty in obtaining invitations to dinner and supper. But no one concerned themselves about you except for providing the lodging. When the château was full – and a very large part was in such poor repair that it was uninhabitable – the guests, or rather those who were admitted, for one only had to enter one's name, were distributed about the town. Their names were written in chalk on the doors as in a posting house."

To this must be added an official document, dated 1786, "observations placed before the eyes of His Majesty by the Grand Maréchal du Logis on the increase which is occurring in the expense of hiring lodgings for the service of the Court at Fontainebleau".

There were, he states, 176 lodgings in the château itself. There followed a list of those entitled to such lodging – not to be confused with those "logés à la craye", in other words with those whose names were chalked on the doors of apartments in the town in the way which the comtesse de Boigne described. The list of those who required lodging in the château amounted to 245. 73 people who were entitled to lodgings in the château therefore had to put up in the town. To compensate them it was necessary to obtain larger and grander apartments. In 1783 the cost of these lodgings had been 35,280 livres; in 1785 it was 41,610; now in 1786 it had risen to 55,970. "The Grand Maréchal views the rapid progress of these expenses with regret for the present and alarm for the future."

There was no future. The year 1786 saw the last Voyage de Fontainebleau.

Faced with the figures, Louis XVI decided to discontinue the visits. It must have been a painful decision for him, for he loved the place and had just, in 1785 and 1786, created his own Petits Appartements. It must have been even more painful for Marie-Antoinette, for she had just had two of her rooms beautifully redecorated.

In 1785 Louis XVI determined on the building of a new block which was to double the Galerie François I towards the Jardin de Diane. All the windows on the north side of the gallery therefore lost their light. The new building was to contain the Petits Appartements and to provide a more intimate suite of rooms for the royal family, for by now the Queen had given birth to three children. The rooms themselves were certainly decorated and furnished; the report on the contents of the château by the Commissioners of the Convention leaves no doubt about that. But it is more than probable that they were not ready for use in 1786 when the last Voyage de Fontainebleau took place.

The two rooms redecorated for Marie-Antoinette, however, were almost certainly finished before the Court arrived – certainly the Boudoir was, for an actress named Mlle Contat persuaded the Maréchal de Duras to admit her to this much-talked-of inner sanctuary, and they were surprised by the Queen in the act.

The Salon du Jeu was in the very latest style known as "Pompeian", which was chiefly the work of the brothers Rousseau who painted the doors and panels. The overdoors, by that great master of trompe l'oeil P. J. Sauvage, and the ceiling by Barthélemy representing "Minerva crowning the Muses" complete the décor. Some of the original furniture has been recovered, notably the two magnificent commodes by Benneman, and the screen which retains its original covering of painted silk. This has enabled an accurate reconstruction of the general upholstery and hangings.

When the list of the furniture was drawn up during the Revolution, the Salon du Jeu was found to contain thirteen different gaming tables – each game in those days necessitating a special sort of table. In the early days of her reign, Marie-Antoinette had gambled for very high stakes, but her belated maternity had brought a great change in her way of life. In its new form the room was used more for concerts and is sometimes known as the Salon de Musique.

The Boudoir de Marie-Antoinette is usually acclaimed as the most perfect piece of interior decoration in the whole palace. It also served for one season only.

The word "bijou", as applied to architecture, is irretrievably debased. This is unfortunate, because the exquisite refinement of this little room belongs to the art of the jeweller. The overall colour scheme is of silver and gold. Almost all the surfaces are covered with decoration, but with so light and delicate a touch that it is never ornate. As so often at Fontainebleau, it is a work of collaboration.

Designed by Mique, it was executed by members of the same team that created the Salon du Jeu – Barthélemy for the ceiling, the brothers Rousseau for the paintings. But here the overdoors are not in trompe l'oeil but achieved in three dimensions by the sculptor P.L. Roland.

20 *Above:* Salon de Jeux de Marie-Antoinette.

21 *Below:* Boudoir de Marie-Antoinette.

In 1962 the Boudoir recovered some of its most important furniture, the bureau à cylindre, the work table and the fire screen. The bureau and the work table, which were made by Riesener, do not bear the customary marks, the MA surmounted by a crown and the words "Garde Meuble de la Reine", but Verlet has shown beyond reasonable doubt how their details are identical with those of the marble fireplace and how perfectly they match the colour scheme of the room.

If harmonious surroundings ever brought peace to a human soul, perhaps this marvellous little room afforded a few weeks of solace to that unhappy Queen.

The Nineteenth Century

IT WAS NOT until he was about to become Emperor that Napoleon took any personal interest in Fontainebleau. In June 1804, the architect Percier noted: "The Emperor seems to want to make this ancient royal house into a second country residence for himself for the autumn season." Percier told Napoleon that he could never form an accurate idea of Fontainebleau without spending twenty-four hours there on his own. On 27 June he made his inspection.

The palace was at the time occupied by a Military Academy and the first plan was to leave them in the Cour du Cheval Blanc and to restore the Cour de la Fontaine and the Cour de l'Ovale as an imperial residence. The work began at once, but in September a note of greatly increased urgency was added by the announcement that Pope Pius VII was to be lodged there at the end of November. The Appartement des Reines Mères had been designated for his reception. Work had to be done on the masonry, the roofs, the chimneys, the floors, the panelling, the windows and locks – and a multitude of rats had to be cleared out. It was a prodigious task to be accomplished in a matter of weeks, but it was done.

"The apartments," wrote Percier, "have been furnished as it were by magic. Those of the Emperor, the Empress and the Pope are decorated with a profusion of very beautiful mirrors. Most of the rooms are provided with carpets – Aubusson, Savonnerie or Tournai." Paintings of suitably religious subjects were hung on the walls; everything was thought of, even to the delicate allusion to another French sovereign who turned Catholic – a little statuette of Henri IV upon the mantelpiece. "It is due in particular to the care and foresight of the Maréchal Duroc that we owe our success in furnishing, in nineteen days, the whole of the Château de Fontainebleau. He personally selected and sent down from Paris the objects which were to be transported. Transport vehicles ran short: he provided artillery carriages. In the end the inhabitants of Fontainebleau could not but admit that never, in the days of the Monarchy, had they seen the château more brilliant or better furnished."

Meanwhile, on 2 November, the Pope had set out on his journey. It took him twenty-three days. He came not without misgiving. Napoleon's letter had been skilfully worded: "The happy effect on the morals and character of my people caused by the re-establishment of the Christian religion leads me to invite your Holiness to give me yet another proof of the interest which he takes in my destiny and in that of this great nation, in one of the most important occasions offered by the annals of the world. I invite him to come and give the highest possible religious character to the ceremony of the Anointing and Coronation of the first Emperor of the French." He had signed it "Your devout son, Napoleon".

But, in spite of this protestation of filial devotion, Napoleon was determined not to yield the precedence to his Holy Father. A formal reception at the palace would have necessitated a decision on this issue. To evade such a decision Napoleon arranged to meet the Pope "accidentally" as he traversed the forest. He therefore pretended to be out hunting and awaited his guest at the Croix Saint-Hérem. An informal greeting was all that such an occasion required.

In 1812 the same Pope Pius VII was to return to Fontainebleau in very different circumstances – as a prisoner upon whom the Emperor was determined to force a humiliating Concordat.

The preparation of the papal visit had been a hastily improvised affair, but the occasion had given impetus to Napoleon's desire to add Fontainebleau to his list of residences.

In 1806 a general refurnishing of the palace took place. As usual it was the work of the indefatigable Duroc, Grand Maréchal du Palais. He established a regular hierarchy in the rooms and graded the furniture accordingly. As under the Ancien Régime, both the Emperor and the Empress had a Grand Appartement and a Petit Appartement. The former were to be furnished "with the majesty and dignity appropriate"; the latter "with nobility, elegance and commodity, according to the demands of the interior decorations". Those of the Princes were to be treated "in a manner corresponding to their rank, but with a noble simplicity".

The Grand Appartement de l'Empereur began with the three rooms overlooking the Cour de l'Ovale – the Salle du Buffet (known then as Salon des Pages), the Salon Saint-Louis (Salon des Officiers de la Maison) and the Cabinet de Théagène (Salon des Grands Dignitaires). The suite was a deliberate contrivance of what the rhetoricians call "incrementum", a crescendo of importance culminating in the gilded splendour of the Salle du Trône.

This was the former bedroom of Louis XIV. In 1714, the last year of his reign, Louis had extended this room towards the north, thus creating the alcove in which his bed was to stand. Louis XV had the outer wall of the façade pulled down and rebuilt several feet further out into the garden. The duc de Luynes, who recorded nearly every change in the décor, found this room much to his taste: "The more one examines this room, the more magnificent one finds it."

It was therefore the most appropriate room for the Salle du Trône. All that Napoleon had to do was to replace the bed by a throne. Designed by Percier and executed by Jacob in the course of 1805, it closely resembled the throne in the Tuileries. It survived the Restoration with no more drastic alteration than the removal from the hangings of the imperial bees.

Having turned the bedroom into a throne room, Napoleon created his own Chambre de l'Empereur in the first of Louis XVI's cabinets which backed the Galerie François I. The architecture of the room, including the overdoors by Sauvage, he retained unaltered, but the panelling was painted by Moench in a style in keeping with the new furniture.

Joséphine took over the apartment of Marie-Antoinette, and it was not until 1806 that the magnificent silk hangings, woven at Lyons but never used under the Ancien Régime, were finally hung.

In 1807 the imperial court spent the whole autumn, from 21 September to 16 November at Fontainebleau. The duchesse d'Abrantès, like a skilful painter in watercolour, has caught the atmosphere and picked out the significant details. Fontainebleau is never so beautiful as in the autumn and that year, during October and November, the weather was superb. The ladies were often invited to follow the hunt. They wore a special uniform – a waistcoat of chamois leather, an *amazone* or riding habit with collar and facings of green cloth embroidered with silver, a hat of black velvet with a large *aigrette* of white feathers. "Nothing could have been more graceful than to see seven or eight calèches filled with these ladies, their heads covered with nodding plumes, their figures tightly laced into elegant riding coats, dashing through the magnificent Forêt de Fontainebleau." Every now and then the Emperor, at the head of a large field, would flash past "swift as an arrow", or the antlers of a great stag would appear for an instant at the summit of some rocky outcrop.

In the evenings they were still celebrating the marriage of the King of Westphalia: "Fontainebleau saw the Court, more brilliant than it had ever been in the days of Louis XIV, offer some new fête every day, and each more magnificent than the last." It seemed that this year was particularly remarkable for the number of beautiful women – the Princess Pauline, the Grand Duchess of Berg and, in true Louis XIV style, Napoleon's latest infatuation "la belle Génoise".

This galaxy of beauty, together with the diamonds, the jewels and the flowers; the pleasures, the love affairs and the spice of more than a little courtly intrigue, "faisait de Fontainebleau un séjour fantastique et enivrant".

But not for Joséphine. The death of the young Prince Louis (son of Jérôme Bonaparte and Queen Hortense), who had been treated by Napoleon as his son and heir, had brought back into prominence her own childlessness. Rumours of divorce were in the air and began, during this autumn, to take on a certain consistency. "We talked much at Fontainebleau," wrote the duchesse d'Abrantès, "but we talked in hushed voices." Napoleon was silent and pensive. It was noticed that he often rode out into the forest, regardless of the usually tight security, accompanied only by his faithful piqueur Jardin. "Joséphine was profoundly unhappy in spite of her efforts to appear contented and gay." On one occasion the Duchess observed her entrance to the Salle du Trône "looking with a melancholy and desolate eye which seemed to rest on every object as if to bid it farewell".

It was during this visit that Napoleon decided to evict the Military Academy with which he had hitherto shared the palace and to take full possession of Fontainebleau. On 4 October he wrote to Duroc: "The young men are subject to too much dissipation, living so close to the Court; it is necessary to set them apart from it. The recovery of this wing [the Aisle Louis XV] will give me extra lodgings of which I may have need."

The experience of a long period of residence led ·to a considerable rearrangement of the château which was really a return to the affectation of the rooms under the Bourbons. But in the course of this visit Napoleon made his first important contribution to Fontainebleau.

The west façade of the Cour du Cheval Blanc had never been distinguished. François I had not intended any major entrance from this side. A meagre pavilion, the Porte des Champs, offered a narrow archway to those who used it. By 1807 this outward façade had been considerably degraded and its symmetry upset by lean-to additions which half obscured it. Instead of replacing the Porte des Champs with something more magnificent, Napoleon abolished the offending wing, replacing it only by an iron grille which opened up the whole, huge perspective of the courtyard. The imposing architecture of the west front with its great horseshoe staircase was now revealed.

The astonishing fact, however, is that Napoleon, with all his appreciation of the "maison des siècles", actually contemplated the destruction of this façade. There exists in the Archives Nationales an elevation, attributed to Hurtault, of the projected new front – as dull and monotonous a piece of neo-classicism as was ever designed. In pursuance of the same intention the Aisle des Ministres was to be replaced by a copy of the dull Aisle Louis XV.

The *Moniteur* of 24 September, 1810, contained an article on the new project. "Lovers of art," it claimed, "all hope that the fine horseshoe staircase will be allowed to remain – a piece of architecture that is unique, both for the beauty of its outline and for the grace and elegance of its contours."

As Napoleon added victory to victory until he had the whole of Europe, with the exception of England, at his feet, so he became progressively obsessed by a *folie de grandeur* which affected his ideas about the formation of his Court and the furnishing of his palaces.

In the State Rooms at Fontainebleau it was clear from the enumeration of the articles of furniture that the new Court was to follow the pattern of the Ancien Régime. Only the sovereigns were allowed armchairs, two of which were provided for all the rooms used for State receptions. The folding stool, known as the "ployant d'étiquette", was reserved for the most distinguished courtiers and twenty or thirty of them were also provided. In the Chambre de l'Imperatrice, the balustrade, designed by Jacob-Desmalter, re-established the old disposition which emphasised the distinction between the wife of the Emperor and ordinary mortals.

It was, however, in the Petits Appartements that Napoleon was to make his second but most distinctive and permanent contribution to the interior of Fontainebleau.

It was largely a question of refurnishing. Built by Louis XV or Louis XVI, the rooms have retained most of their original fireplaces, panelling and other architectural ornaments. Into this framework were inserted the silk hangings and draperies, the chairs, tables, sofas, consoles and gueridons of Marcion, Bellangé and Jacob-Desmalter.

An excellent example is the Salon Jaune of Joséphine's suite. The cornice, decorated with swags and garlands of flowers, is identical with that of the Salon d'Etude which can be dated 1772. The marble fireplace is plainly Louis XVI. In contrast, the panels of gold silk, hung here for Joséphine, are plain rectangles. The furniture by Jacob-Desmalter is plain and rectilinear also. It stands on a magnificent Aubusson carpet specially designed for this room.

All was done to the precise instructions of Napoleon. He had, on his own admission, "le goût passionné du détail". In Joséphine's Cabinet de Toilette he ordained every fitting. "It is desirable," he wrote, "that the bath should be sunk so that there are not more than eight or nine inches above floor level in order to accommodate the sofa which is to cover it." The sofa, in fact, concealed the bath when not in use and opened out to form a screen round it when needed.

Joséphine did not have long to enjoy these new luxuries. In October 1809 Napoleon arrived at Fontainebleau straight from Schönbrunn and the victory of Wagram. The whole Court was summoned and Joséphine hastened here from Saint-Cloud. She found that the door between her and her husband had been walled up. Two months later her dismissal was announced and preparations made for Marie-Louise of Austria to succeed her.

Beyond Joséphine's rooms were those of Madame Mère, who kept herself rather apart from the Court saying: "In public I call you *Sire* and *Majesté*, but in my own rooms I am your mother and you are my son." These rooms were within the former Galerie des Cerfs which had been partitioned off under Louis XV.

Marie-Louise showed much consideration to her mother-in-law. The duchesse d'Abrantès, whose attachment to Joséphine made her critical of her successor, records an occasion when Napoleon was away. Marie-Louise went to call on Madame Mère and invited her to dinner, adding, "Je ne viens pas comme l'Impératrice, je viens tout simplement chez vous." Her mother-in-law immediately embraced her and reversed the invitation, saying, "I will receive you as my daughter, and the wife of the Emperor will dine with the mother of the Emperor."

Napoleon's marriage with the Archduchess of Austria, the niece of Marie-Antoinette, and the birth of their son, gave him a new and overweening confidence. "The yoke of Bonaparte was becoming intolerable," wrote the comtesse de Boigne. "His alliance with the House of Austria had turned his head completely." The son was to be known as King of Rome, a title previously reserved for the heir to the Holy Roman Empire. Sooner or later the old, old question as to who had the primacy, the Emperor or the pope, was bound to arise. There was no question in Napoleon's mind. He did not wish to abolish the Papacy but to transfer its seat to Paris and to subject it to his own control. His first step was to annexe the papal States; his second to make the Pope himself a prisoner; his third to transfer his prisoner to safe keeping in the middle of France. Fontainebleau, where Pius VII had stayed eight years previously when he came to crown the Emperor, was fixed upon for his residence. On 19 June, 1812, he arrived in the last stages of exhaustion.

It was not until the following February that Napoleon succeeded in forcing upon his captive the signature of a Concordat which deprived the Pope of the right to appoint any Bishop not nominated by the Emperor. The great Salon des Reines Mères, with its magnificent black and gold ceiling was the scene of this public humiliation. The signatures on the document tell all that needs to be told – the Pope's pathetic scrawl and the Emperor's triumphant flourish. Pius was so overcome with shame afterwards that for days he would not even say the Mass.

But time was on the Pope's side. The star of Napoleon was setting fast and the Allies were advancing on Paris. It was soon to be the Emperor's turn to taste at Fontainebleau the bitterest humiliation and defeat. He struggled hard to obtain a treaty which only involved abdication in favour of his son. It was of no use. On 6 April, 1814, he signed the act of total abdication.

His agony during the next few days is better imagined than described. The defection of most of his Marshals must have been the bitterest blow of all. But in the end he mastered himself and on 20 April, the day fixed for his departure to Elba, he rose magnificently to the occasion. With the soldiers of the Old Guard sobbing in the courtyard, he descended the great horseshoe staircase, embraced General Petit and then kissed the flag on which were recorded so many of his victories. "Que ce baiser passe dans vos coeurs!" he cried and then, promising to write of all their great achievements together, he bade them farewell – "Adieu mes enfants" – and threw himself into the carriage that awaited him. From that moment the Cour du Cheval Blanc has been known as the Cour des Adieux.

Fontainebleau was to see him again for a few hours during his meteoric trajectory from Elba to Waterloo. He issued a few orders, greeted a few friends and was off saying, "This evening I shall be at the Tuileries."

A touching sequel to the whole painful episode was added three years later when the Pope, whom he had so ill used, learned of his approaching death at St. Helena and with truly Christian generosity pleaded his cause. "He can no longer be a danger to anyone; we would wish that he might not be a subject for remorse to anyone either."

For the next seventeen years Fontainebleau was almost abandoned. Louis XVIII came once; Charles X only with a small following for a few days' hunting. It was Louis-Philippe who started the great work of restoration which was continued by Napoleon III. With it came a renewal of the Voyages de Fontainebleau, but with a great difference. Under Louis-Philippe and Marie-Amélie a visit to Fontainebleau was more like a visit to some great country house. The first of these took place in 1834. Among the guests was the comtesse de Boigne.

"It was the beginning of October," she wrote; "the weather was magnificent throughout the whole of our stay. I was conducted to a very handsome apartment, arranged with minute attention to detail both with regard to beauty and to comfort. An enormous fire warmed the bedroom and the Salon which preceded it. Five minutes after my arrival a valet de chambre entered bringing a tray heaped with fruits and cakes with carafes of wine and iced water."

Her observant eye soon detected the influence which Fontainebleau began to exert upon the "bourgeois King". "There was during this voyage a certain *parfum de trône*, at least there was evidence of a slight inclination to mount one

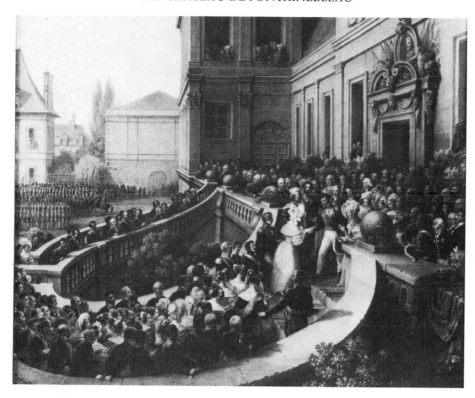

22 Salon François I. Fireplace by Primaticcio as restored by Louis-Philippe.

23 Arrival of Princess Helen of Mecklenburg-Schwerin, bride of the duc d'Orléans. Sèvres plaque by Develly.

step of the ladder of royalty. The foreign Ambassadors noticed it and rejoiced. I acknowledge in good faith that I shared their contentment."

Louis-Philippe, it must be remembered, was the son of the duc d'Orléans who had played an active part in the Revolution and signed the death warrant of his cousin Louis XVI. He had taken the name of Philippe Egalité. It did not save him from the guillotine. The comtesse de Boigne now watched his son with interest.

"It was the first time since the Revolution that I saw the King dare to remember that he was the descendant of Henri IV. This very aristocratic residence of Fontainebleau recalled the blood of the Bourbons to his veins and he developed a taste for it."

In the Salon de Famille a table was spread with prints and drawings illustrating the history of the palace and on the first evening the King took his guests on a conducted tour. "It would be impossible to imagine a guide more instructive, more amusing, and amused, than King Louis-Philippe. His wonderful memory provided him at every moment with some anecdote of history or art which was really piquant and which brought to life all the places through which he passed, so that although he kept us for two and a half hours on our feet, no one was conscious of any fatigue."

The most important event to take place at Fontainebleau during the reign of Louis-Philippe was the marriage of his eldest son, the duc d'Orléans, to Princess Helen of Mecklenburg-Schwerin on 30 May, 1837. The couple were lodged in Gabriel's Gros Pavillon and the Chambre de la duchesse d'Orléans

24 Civil marriage in the
Salle de Bal.

25 Catholic marriage in
the Trinity Chapel.

still retains its sumptuous furniture. The bed, with two armchairs to match, was that made in 1787 for Louis XVI at Saint-Cloud. The magnificent commode by Benneman came from Compiègne. But of greatest interest in its context is the jewel cabinet made for the Princess herself and inset with large plaques of Sèvres porcelain painted by Develly with scenes representing the arrival of the bride at Fontainebleau, the civil marriage in the Salle de Bal and the Catholic marriage in the Chapelle de la Trinité and the Protestant wedding in the Galerie des Colonnes.

The comtesse de Boigne, who was invited to Fontainebleau again for the royal wedding, provides the commentary for Develly's pictures.

Her arrival at Fontainebleau shows the impressive setting which the horseshoe staircase and terrace afforded for such receptions. The Princess mounted the steps with an eagerness and a speed which her fiancé could scarcely follow, and was greeted at the top by the King with the words: "My daughter! my dear daughter!" upon which he and the Queen embraced her tenderly. "From that moment," writes the Countess, "she belonged to them and became an integral part of that very united family."

The next day the three nuptial ceremonies were performed. First, in the Salle de Bal, was the civil ceremony, presided over by the baron Pasquier. "Everyone agreed that the civil ceremony was the most worthy, the most solemn and even, if I dare express myself thus, the most *religious*."

Madame de Boigne was full of admiration for the decoration of the Salle de Bal. This huge room had not been restored by Louis XVI or by Napoleon. It seems mostly to have been used as a Salle de Gardes, and by 1834, when she first saw it, the frescoes were in a pitiful condition. "One could best describe the degradations that had occurred," wrote Poirson, "by saying that they presented the appearance of immense holes in an old tapestry." The restoration by Alaux, which was completed in time for the wedding ceremonies, was highly praised – "as remarkably elegant as it was magnificent".

From the Salle de Bal, they descended to the Galerie des Colonnes on the ground floor. Here the Protestant ceremony took place. The Galerie des Colonnes was Louis-Philippe's own contribution to Fontainebleau. Madame de Boigne did not care for it: "These heavy massive columns, which support nothing and which take away that spaciousness and light with which Monsieur Fontaine had been so lavish in the palaces."

They then proceeded to the Chapelle de la Trinité. Develly shows it sumptuously lit with chandeliers in the window recesses and side chapels, all of which were packed with spectators. But he also portrays the rather detached and uninterested attitude of the clergy, for the Catholic marriage was celebrated "with very little ecclesiastical pomp and few prayers, no more being permitted for mixed marriages".

The duc d'Orléans – still always known as "Chartres" to his family – was the strongest hope of the new dynasty. "Witty and talented and deeply versed in a wide variety of subjects, he was of a charming appearance – liberal, generous, magnificent . . . he was loved by all for his good grace and desire to give pleasure. But where he was absolutely adored was by the army . . . joining with all in the camaraderie of the bivouac as in the face of the enemy, only claiming first place where the danger was greatest, he had established his influence over the troops to such a degree as to become their idol."

To this brilliant and hopeful heir to the throne, Princess Helen of Mecklenburg-Schwerin was a worthy partner. "Her figure was supple, her neck long and gracefully curved," observed the comtesse de Boigne, "and she moved like a swan on the water." She had a majesty that was natural and which could therefore be worn lightly. "The duchesse d'Orléans in a most attractive négligée seemed to me more charming than in her diamond tiara, and every bit as much the *grande dame*." She had the same outgoing charm as her husband and the same desire to please.

If anybody could have rescued the throne of France at this critical moment in its history, it was these two. But it was not to be. On 13 July, 1842, the duc d'Orléans was killed by a fall from his carriage. The keystone of the arch had been wrenched from its position; it was only a matter of time before the arch itself collapsed. In 1848 Louis-Philippe was forced to abdicate.

It was left to Napoleon III to complete the restoration of Fontainebleau. In 1856 there was a disastrous fire in which the Court theatre of the Aisle de la Belle Cheminée was burnt out. Louis-Napoleon decided to have a much more professional theatre built and decided on the west end of the Aisle Louis XV for its emplacement. Hector Lefuel was chosen as architect. He has clearly taken his inspiration from Marie-Antoinette's theatre at the Petit Trianon. In May 1857, the new Court theatre was inaugurated in the presence of the Grand Duke Constantine of Russia.

In 1859, Louis-Napoleon transferred the library from the Chapelle Saint-Saturnin to the Galerie de Diane. The redecoration, which had been begun by Napoleon and completed by Louis XVIII, was largely lost by the introduction of bookshelves.

In 1868 the Emperor appointed Octave Feuillet librarian, and it is through his letters that we get our last picture of Fontainebleau as a royal palace. Feuillet was deeply impressed with the old château – "very far removed from what we have seen at the Tuileries, at Saint-Cloud and at Compiègne. All the glory of the Valois dynasty stands out in full relief in these galleries with their wall paintings, their woodwork and their ceilings, all elegant and superb. The uniformed officials and the ladies in Court dress were dwarfed by this overwhelming décor."

On 16 June, Feuillet dined for the first time with the Court. The dinner was in the Salle de Bal, known usually as the Galerie Henri II. To Octave Feuillet this room was "the most beautiful Banqueting Hall in any Palace in the world".

After dinner they went down to the Salon Chinois. This was in Gabriel's Gros Pavillon. Eugénie sat on a large sofa with her back to the huge windows which opened onto the lake. Fontainebleau, with all its historical associations, seems to have dictated the conversation of its new inhabitants: "We talked till midnight on every subject – the palace and the memories that it recalled of Marie-Antoinette, of Monaldeschi and of Madame de Motteville. We were gay – the Emperor more than usual."

The moment of calm is often precursor to the storm. It was during this visit to Fontainebleau that the first results of the election came in. In the Jura the imperial candidate had lost to the republican by eleven thousand votes to twenty-two thousand.

The fête continued with the typical mixture of magnificence and informality cultivated by the imperial couple. Eugénie loved to lead walking parties into the forest; she walked fast, "son pas élégant et intrépide, la tête haute", talking with animation on her favourite topic, history. To Feuillet she seemed like "some fantastic memory of Diane, of La Vallière, of Marie-Antoinette".

Marie-Antoinette: Eugénie was always haunted by that figure of tragedy, in whose steps she so often trod, and was subject to premonitions that she might share her fate. She sometimes talked about these to Feuillet, who duly reported to his wife. "A heroic impulse in the face of danger," he wrote, "would come easily to her, but to be resolutely calm and collected every day and every hour does not come to her without effort."

One day in July, Madame Miramon came to Fontainebleau and had a private audience with Eugénie. Her husband had been shot at the side of Maximilian of Mexico. The details of the execution were particularly harrowing.

A little later, Louis-Napoleon and the Prince Imperial went to Paris for a distribution of prizes. They returned late and in sombre mood. All that evening Eugénie was seen applying smelling salts to her nose and murmuring "mon petit garçon, mon petit garçon". The Prince Imperial had had a hostile reception from the crowd. Feuillet began to be apprehensive. "I do not know if my imagination is deceiving me," he wrote, "but I see difficult times advancing with great strides towards us." The visit to Fontainebleau was due to end on 5 September. Already Eugénie had noticed a fall in the temperature. "Autumn has come," she said; "I feel sad."

On the last day there was a display of fireworks and all the inhabitants of Fontainebleau were invited to attend. The courts, the terraces, the parterres were all invaded by an immense crowd. Only the Jardin Anglais was reserved for members of the Court. Eugénie was at the balustrade talking happily to members of the populace, who were enchanted.

When darkness fell the Emperor appeared, bearing a flaming torch with which he lit the first rocket as a signal for the display to begin. Suddenly the whole scene was illuminated. Red, blue and silver flares lit up the walks and alleys and threw the bosquets into dramatic relief of brilliant highlight and cavernous darkness. Fountains of coloured fire rose and fell in cascades of gold and silver rain. Rockets streaked into the air and burst into great petals of fire with a roar that made the ground tremble. Suddenly, as the fires died down, there was a fanfare of trumpets and the Avenue de Maintenon was seen to be filled with ghostly figures on horseback. The regiment of Imperial Dragoons was conducting a torchlight retreat. Everyone followed them into the Cour du Cheval Blanc where they executed a carrousel.

Octave Feuillet was in ecstasies: "It was like one of the magnificent fêtes of the Valois." It was the last ever to be held. The next day the Court left for Biarritz. They never returned. Fontainebleau was never again to serve as a royal palace.

4

The Château de
Saint-Germain

ONE OF THE most distinctive features of the Second Empire was the
prodigious expenditure on building. It took two forms: the creation
of the new and the restoration of the old. Paris as we know it today is
largely the achievement of the baron Haussmann, and his architecture is not
without dignity. But France was already overcrowded with ancient monuments, many of which had suffered badly from the Revolution and even more
from subsequent neglect.

The restoration of the great Gothic cathedrals, entrusted by Napoleon III to
Viollet-le-Duc, Boeswillwald, Lassus and others, and the setting up of the
Commission des Monuments Historiques under Prosper Mérimée was to
preserve for France a great architectural heritage which was in grave danger.

Viollet-le-Duc also undertook the exacting task of restoring the feudal
fortress of Pierrefonds; Félix Duban salvaged the Renaissance façades of Blois;
in 1862 Eugène Millet was charged with the restoration of the former royal
palace of Saint-Germain-en-Laye. Thirty years earlier it had been turned into
a Pénitencier Militaire. It was a fate worse than death.

In August 1855, Queen Victoria, who was staying with the Emperor
Napoleon III at Saint-Cloud, was taken to visit Saint-Germain where she
particularly wished to see the rooms inhabited by James II in his exile. "Her
Majesty," according to Lytton Strachey, "always maintained that she was an
ardent Jacobite." She did not, however, say much about the visit in her
journal. "The Emperor," she noted, "has recently recovered the property,
and intends to try and do something with it; but he was much disgusted when
he saw the state of ruin and filth in which it was." It was not until 1862 that he
decided to adapt the building for use as the Musée Gallo-Romain, which has
since become the Musée des Antiquités Nationales.

The restoration of Saint-Germain from the state of degradation in which
Victoria saw it posed a problem. The Renaissance château of François I had
been enlarged under Louis XIV in order to give more accommodation to the
Court and more symmetry to the façades. The additions of Mansart were by
no means an improvement. The question therefore arose as to whether the
task committed to Millet should not be that of restoring the building to the
form in which François I had left it. In the end it was decided to take this
course. Mansart's additions were demolished and the Renaissance château was
thoroughly restored.

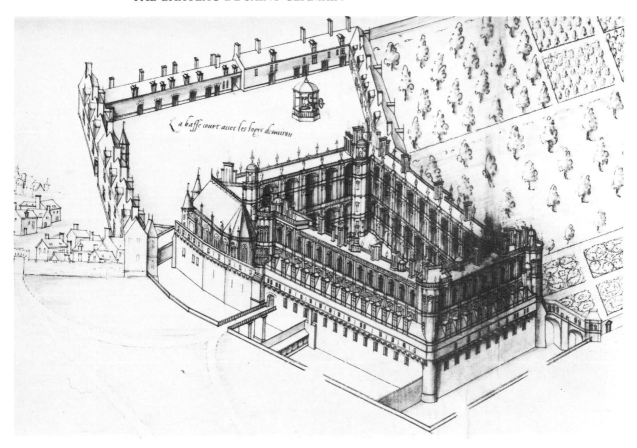

La basse court auec les loges de murin

26 Aerial view from the south-east. Drawing by J. A. du Cerceau.

Like so many restorers, however, Millet succumbed to the temptation to "improve" on his original, but in spite of these flights of imagination, the château that we see today is recognisably that built by François I.

It is an amazing structure – neither one thing nor the other; dignified in the grandeur of its conception, crude in the pettiness of its ornament; a palace of the Renaissance in the size and regularity of its windows, a château of the late Middle Ages in the vaulting of its ceilings and its many corkscrew stairways. It is both, and yet it is neither. It lacks the Italian refinement of Lescot at the Louvre without retaining the flamboyant magnificence of, for instance, Maintenon.

The more one looks upon the façades, the more the question imposes itself – who was the author of so curious a design? The earliest answer comes from Du Cerceau: "The King took such an interest in the building that one might almost say he was the architect." It is a plausible claim and one which the history of the building supports to a certain extent.

When, in March 1539, François I decided to erect a palace on this site, it already boasted what Fleurange could call "a very beautiful castle with a good park and good hunting". That was at the time of the royal marriage between François, then comte d'Angoulême, and Claude de France, daughter and heiress to Louis XII and Anne de Bretagne. It took place on 18 May, 1514 – "the most beautiful wedding that was ever seen," continues Fleurange, "for there were ten thousand men dressed as richly as the King and Monsieur d'Angoulême who was the bridegroom."

However beautiful the castle may have been, it did not, in the eyes of Fançois I, merit conservation. Once again Du Cerceau provides information: "He had the old buildings pulled down, without, however, altering the foundations, as can be seen from the courtyard, which is a rectangle gone mad." This "rectangle" was in fact a five-sided figure devoid of right angles, of which the shortest side was that occupied by the Sainte-Chapelle, built by Louis IX and correctly orientated, the apse towards the east.

The relationship between this chapel and the Sainte-Chapelle of Paris has already been discussed. Saint-Denis and Saint-Germain are clearly by the same hand. If one were to draw the perimeter of the south rose at Saint-Denis just inside the outer ring of trefoils, one would have a tracery identical to that of the west rose at Saint-Germain. If one were to take the clerestory of the choir and apse at Saint-Denis and place it immediately on top of the arcading at ground-floor level, one would have a building indistinguishable from Saint-Germain, except in one respect. At Saint-Denis the clerestory windows are set within a pointed arch. At Saint-Germain the pointed arch is set within a rectangle, the whole of which is glazed. It is not a change in style, but a logical progression for an architect in search of a maximum area of glass to illuminate his building.

The chapel at Saint-Germain has lost its glass, a tragedy which throws into relief a simplicity of style which is almost austerity. Branner has pointed out that just as Blanche de Castille, Saint-Louis' mother, made it a rule "to dress well enough to maintain the respect of people, but not so ostentatiously as to excite their envy", so in the architecture of her son there is a great dignity of style combined with an extreme economy of detail.

Little else is known about the building to which Saint-Louis appended this

27 Interior of court with section of Salle des Fêtes (right).

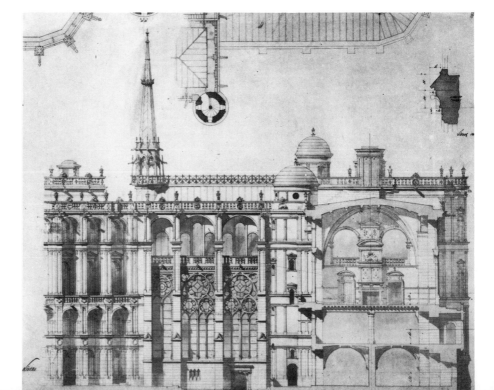

chapel, but its size must tell us something of the importance of the château. Here, as at Vincennes, Charles V made important alterations. But at Vincennes he demolished Saint-Louis' chapel to build a larger one, whereas at Saint-Germain the chapel was retained.

Charles V bequeathed to his successors a castle with a curious rhomboid plan which had to be the basis of any further structure on the site. Not only did François I accept these limitations imposed by the foundations, he further restricted his designs by the retention of the Keep. This was in line with the general attitude of the French aristocracy towards the preservation of ancient towers.

Besides the Keep, it is possible that the rather unusual *chemin de ronde*, which runs right round the base of the building, is also a survival of the château of Charles V. It resembles the one which he built at Vincennes and the numerous irregularities in the size of the bays would be difficult to explain if the building had been begun anew by François I. The first letters patent issued in connection with the project are dated 12 March, 1539, and were issued to Nicolas Picart. The preamble begins: "As we have decided to have pulled down certain blocks of apartments [*corps d'hôtel*] and to make several repairs in our château of Saint-Germain-en-Laye..." All that we know, then, is that some buildings were pulled down and some were repaired. It is at least possible that the *chemin de ronde* came into the second category. On the exterior façades this gave the architect a base or "podium" upon which to raise the dignified façades of the north, east and south fronts. But on the inward façades of the courtyard he was obliged to create his own podium and the result was less successful. It led to the superimposition of one two-storeyed structure upon another.

Although the courtyard is not devoid of grandeur, and even of a certain beauty, its façades are too tall for its size and there is still an uncomfortable feeling of prison about it. In spite of its numerous irregularities, it does not possess the charm of a frankly irregular building; nor, for the same reason, can it offer the aesthetic satisfaction of a beautifully-ordered façade.

The same hybrid architecture typifies the interior. The biggest rooms were vaulted, the others ceiled with enormous beams and rafters. Its main staircase follows the Renaissance in its straight flights and coffered ceilings, but the landings are covered with ribbed vaulting. The building does not give the impression of being the work of someone fully conversant with Renaissance architecture, and yet 1539 was comparatively late in the reign. Already at Blois, Chambord, Madrid, Fontainebleau and Villers-Cotterets, François I had been involved as patron of much more "advanced" buildings. Alongside these, Saint-Germain looks crudely provincial and archaically Gothic.

It must be remembered that the Gothic tradition survived well into the sixteenth century. Marius Vachon, who has made a particular study of the Chambiges family, draws our attention to "a period of renewal of Gothic architecture which, at the hour of its declining seems, like the sun, to emit the same radiance and to shine with the same brilliance as at its rising". It was Pierre Chambiges who was in charge of the building of Saint-Germain.

Pierre Chambiges was trained in the Gothic tradition. He had succeeded his father as Clerk of the Works during the final stages of the building of Beauvais

Cathedral. But Chambiges only appears upon the scene at Saint-Germain on 22 September, 1539 – that is to say six months after the letters patent addressed to Nicolas Picart. The position of Chambiges appears to have been that of an entrepreneur who was brought in to oversee the works, rather than that of an architect whose designs must have been in existence long before the issue of the first letters patent.

The question of the authorship of the design of Saint-Germain may well remain unsolved, but in the process revealed by what we do know it is quite possible to admit the guiding mind of François I according to Du Cerceau's assertion.

In one respect Saint-Germain was well in advance of its time. It was provided with a flat roof which offered the most delightful walk to the inmates of the palace. "This terrace," claims Du Cerceau, "is, I think, the first of its sort in Europe and a thing worthy to be seen and considered." François I, however, did not live to see it accomplished; it was not until January 1549 that these "terraces" were built "in pierres de liais de Notre-Dame-des-Champs in Paris, the whole estimated at 6,000 livres Tournois".

The great Salle des Fêtes, on the west side of the courtyard, was also far from finished and this, too, was brought to completion under Henri II. It extended right across the western end of the Sainte-Chapelle. François I has been reproached for blocking in the great rose window in the western wall, and it is true that his Salle des Fêtes was designed to extend across this façade, but there exists an account for September–November 1548 for putting plain glass windows in the new extension "to give more light and clarity in the said chapel". The rose window was, therefore, not at this time blocked in. It was not until Mansart made his extensions in 1683 that the rose finally disappeared. It was only rediscovered by Millet.

The work on the Salle des Fêtes was carried out by Philibert de l'Orme, "commissaire des dits bâtiments". As the official Court architect for Henri II, Philibert de l'Orme completed the château of François I. He was also commissioned by Henri II to design and build a sort of annexe which became known as the "Château Neuf". Once again Du Cerceau provides an introduction. "After the death of King François, Henri II, his second son, came to the throne, who had the same love for this place. Also this King, in order to increase the beauty and convenience, began a building in the form of a theatre, between the river and château."

This was in 1553. Two years later, on the death of Henri II, Philibert de l'Orme was dismissed from all his posts and replaced by Primaticcio. He wrote in affronted self-justification: "If they had had the patience for me to have completed the new building which I had begun . . . I am convinced that there would be nothing like it to be seen today, and nothing more worthy of admiration, as much for the porticos, vestibules, theatres, steam baths, bathing rooms, as for lodgings." He promised to make his designs known in a further volume which never appeared.

The picture is that of a sort of "royal lodge" where the King and the Queen could be housed in greater comfort and in greater privacy and apparently greater hygiene than in what was already within fifteen years beginning to be called the "Vieux Château". In the "old" château one had to mount to the

28 The Château Neuf with its terraced gardens. Engraving by A. Francine.

roof in order to enjoy the magnificent view. The Château Neuf was perched on the very edge of the high ground and commanded the view directly from its windows and terraces.

Both Du Cerceau and Philibert de l'Orme used the term "theatre" to describe the courtyard. It was built in the form of a square of which each side bellied out into a semi-circle. One of these semi-circles formed the concave entrance front of the château; answering it across the court were two quadrant arcades springing from either side of the triumphal arch which formed the gateway. It is possible that this court was used as a theatre in the ordinary sense of the word.

André Chastel, in his interesting and original book *Fables, Forms, Figures*, has traced a connection between the architecture of the Renaissance courtyard and the frequent use of that courtyard for theatrical performances – in particular the concave front, or concave colonnade masking the square corners of the court, and the flights of steps so often associated with these features. "The inner courtyard," he writes, "appearing as a place of privilege and a setting for theatricals, a significant contrast can come into existence between the simplicity of the exterior architecture and the sumptuosity of the interior."

The main entrance gave access directly to the largest room, the Salle des Audiences. To the left, or north, of this was the King's Apartment and to the right, the Queen's. Each apartment was extended north and south by a gallery. The extremities of these galleries were joined by open arcades to the end pavilions which formed the King's Chapel and the Queen's Oratory. The King's Chapel is the one surviving portion of the Château Neuf today.

It shows the colour scheme – brick dressed with stone – the opposite, in fact, of the Vieux Château – but in the more stately parts the columns were of marble *rouge de Languedoc*, which was to be the marble of Versailles.

The death of Henri II brought an end to the works, but before his death an event took place for which Saint-Germain will be for ever famous, the judicial duel between Jarnac and La Châtaigneraie: the last to be fought in France.

Words had passed "touchant l'honneur de la Dame de Jarnac". François I had refused to countenance a duel, but the moment that Henri II succeeded to the throne, he gave permission, by letters patent dated at Saint-Germain 11 June, 1547 – "the causes of this difference being beyond proof, as the result of which the truth can only be known and the one who is innocent justified, by means of combat". That was the medieval formula. All that was spectacular and all that was misconceived about chivalry was set forth on this, the last occasion.

The duc d'Aumâle, later duc de Guise, stood sponsor for La Châtaigneraie and the Grand Ecuyer de Boisy for Jarnac. The Connétable de Montmorency was appointed arbiter and the King, the Queen and Diane de Poitiers and most of the Court were present. La Châtaigneraie was the undoubted favourite. He was the better fencer and he enjoyed the support of Diane de Poitiers. He made his entrance with three hundred supporters dressed in his colours, scarlet and white, and he had prepared a magnificent banquet ready to celebrate his victory.

Jarnac, more prudent and less ostentatious, had been to a fencing master called Caize who had taught him a new stroke.

On 10 July the two adversaries appeared upon the "esplanade" between the old and new buildings. A herald announced, on behalf of the King, that while the two assailants were engaged in combat, "everyone present was to keep silence, not to talk, or cough, or spit, to make no sign with foot or hand or finger which might help or hinder either one or the other of the adversaries on pain of death".

The signal was given – "upon which each rushed furiously upon the other", and for a little while the issue was in doubt. And then it came – *le coup de Jarnac*. Suddenly placing his shield above him, he ducked low and cut the calf of his adversary. A second cut brought La Châtaigneraie to the ground. Jarnac then called to him, "Rendez-moi mon honneur". It was received in silence. A second time Jarnac addressed his opponent: "Châtaigneraie, mon ancien compagnon, soyons amis." The appeal met with no further success. Finally Anne de Montmorency persuaded the King to intervene. He ordered Châtaigneraie to be carried off and greeted the victor coldly with the words, no doubt intended for his adversary: "You have fought like Caesar and you have spoken like Aristotle." Châtaigneraie refused medical help and died of his wounds three days later. But Henri II had learned his lesson; never again was a point of justice to be decided by combat.

One of the first acts of Henri IV was to pursue with vigour the construction of the Château Neuf at Saint-Germain. He found it half built. On one of Du Cerceau's drawings in the British Museum the artist has noted: "The Theatre, of which the half on the side towards the river is more or less complete." Of the gardens he records: "The terrace with the gallery is not yet made and the foundations only in part."

On 29 November, 1599, Thomas Platter, Gentleman of Geneva – a traveller whose observant eye has left many valuable details on the palaces of Elizabeth I – made a visit to Saint-Germain. He passed over the Vieux Château "which the King no longer inhabits", noticing only the flat roofs and terraces. But his main interest was to see the Château Neuf and he leaves some interesting details.

"In the Grande Salle [Salle d'Audience] there are many beautiful paintings; particularly remarkable is a small frame attached to the wall and painted both sides. Seen from below, this little picture represents a hunt. But if one looks into a mirror which is attached to the ceiling, one sees two lovers in an embrace. It is a picture painted with much skill."

Coming out of the château towards the river, Platter found himself at the balustrade of the double fer-à-cheval staircase which formed the first of a series of descents which led to a riverside parterre. "Beneath the balcony of these stairs," he continued, "is an underground room constructed with much skill, in the centre of which is raised a fountain with corals and sea-shells. The water is spewed by a griffon, and nightingales, activated also by water, sing most agreeably."

On 26 June in that very year there had arrived from Rouen "twelve cases and twelve large barrels in which are shells, periwinkles, mother of pearl, lumps of coral, tufa stones and other marine rocks ... all to be employed on the grottoes and fountains which His Majesty is having made at Saint-Germain". What Thomas Platter saw must have been the Grotto of Mercury.

They were also at work, he was told, on another in which there was to be an organ. "The King has brought over an Italian," he noted, "specially for this work, who has made these grottoes and fountains and one must say that he has made some fine things."

This Italian was Thomas Francini. He had been working for the Grand Duke of Tuscany, but at the age of twenty-seven he received an invitation from Henri IV to come and practise his art at Saint-Germain. It was his son François who was to create the waterworks at Versailles. The Francinis formed a dynasty, the last of whom died, Intendant Général des Eaux et Fontaines de France, in 1784.

On 27 February, 1623, Louis XIII appointed Thomas Francini "Intendant of our waterworks, fountains, grottoes, movements, aquaducts, artifices and water pipes in our houses, châteaux and gardens of Paris, Saint-Germain, Fontainebleau and others". The preamble to the deed begins: "Waterworks and fountains being one of the principal ornaments of houses and châteaux..." It was not only as ornaments that they appealed to the mind of the sixteenth and seventeenth centuries, but as opportunities for practical joking. There were facilities for soaking one's guests at Kenilworth Castle at the time of Queen Elizabeth's visit in 1575. Perhaps the most complete ensemble to survive is that of Schloss Hellbrunn near Salzburg.

The Grotte de la Demoiselle qui joue aux Orgues was typical of Francini's creations. Her fingers were activated by water pressure so that she played her organ, producing a music, it was claimed, "hardly inferior to the best of concerts". But the most intricate and dramatic of these productions was the Grotte des Flambeaux, illuminated, as its name implies, entirely by torchlight.

This revealed a vast theatre in which the scene was constantly changing. First the sun rose in all its glory upon a calm sea, clear as a mirror, dotted with islands and peopled with marine monsters in playful mood. Then the clear sky was overstretched by ominous clouds, the winds blew and the sea was lashed to a fury to the accompaniment of thunder and lightning; ships were wrecked and sailors swam for the shore. Then after the storm came peace once more. The scene changed to a lordly mansion set in a noble park. "In the background rose the Château de Saint-Germain with its magnificent terraces. The King could be seen walking in the midst of an eager crowd of courtiers, while the Dauphin, the future Louis XIII, came down out of the sky on a luminous chariot supported by two angels who held a royal crown."

One of the favourite pastimes of the little Dauphin was to visit Francini. The journal of Jean Héroard, his doctor, refers to them frequently – "taken to the lodgings of the Sieur Francino, who made him a little fountain". Louis even dreamed of them. Héroard's entry for 16 April, 1605, reads: "Woken at seven o'clock, he tossed about in his bed saying he was going to see the fountains and turn the taps on: he went *fss, fss*, then said to me 'Dites grand merci à mucheu [Monsieur] Francino'."

The picture of the infant Prince drawn by Héroard brings the life of the royal family momentarily into sharp focus. The Dauphin's apartment was in the Vieux Château, but on most days he was taken across to the Château Neuf, where the galleries, terraces and grottoes were his normal playground. He only appears to have slept at the Château Neuf when there was danger of smallpox.

The young Dauphin showed many signs of precocity. When he was still not yet four years old (5 April, 1605) Héroard could say of him: "He sees and hears everything, without appearing to; retains everything and remembers it, and relates past events to whatever he sees or hears tell of." It is clear that, at this early age, building, gardening and above all music appealed to him. On Sunday, 14 August, 1605, Héroard records that he asked for the choir to come and sing in his room. They sang a Laudate; "he listened in transports, so much did he love music." Otherwise military interests came first. "His play and his talk are all soldiers and wars."

His language was often that of the barrack room. Different ages draw different lines between the frank and the indecent. In the days of Henri IV it was drawn a lot lower than today. Before his fourth birthday Louis was conversant with the facts of life and demonstrated his knowledge both in words and gestures; but when the conversation turned to his own sexuality he spoke with lowered head and downcast eyes *"honteusement"*.

When the Dauphin was about six his father wrote to his governess, the marquise de Montglat: "I desire and order you to whip him every time he shows stubbornness or does anything wrong, knowing as I do that nothing in the world can be of greater profit to him than that; I know this from experience having profited by it myself, for at his age I was frequently whipped." He was usually beaten first thing in the morning, while still in bed, for the offences of the previous day and this, says Héroard, even when Madame de Montglat had promised not to the night before. " 'Mamanga,' he said one night, 'dont't beat me tomorrow." She replied: 'Monsieur, I have promised not to.' 'Ho! I know that you will,' came the answer; 'you will hear my quatrains and then you will say 'now bare your arse.' "

The severity of his upbringing in no way affected his high spirits, nor indeed his stubbornness, but the bawdiness of the Court may have affected him deeply. His adult life was marked by a chastity unusual among Kings and which seems to have largely included his relations with his wife, Anne d'Autriche. It was not until twenty-three years after their marriage that their first child, the future Louis XIV, was born.

On Sunday, 5 September, 1638, at about eleven in the morning, the Queen gave birth to a Dauphin. The King immediately ordered the singing of a Te Deum in the Chapel and messengers were dispatched to Paris with the joyful news. They would have crossed the Seine by the Pont de Neuilly, but the bridge was down and the message had to be conveyed by signals. Arms crossed on the chest were to indicate the birth of a daughter; the throwing of hats in the air the birth of a son. The news that it was a boy was transmitted with an appropriately impressive salvo of headgear.

The character of Louis XIII was marked by a love of sobriety both in the adornment of his person and in the satisfaction of his appetites; he ate little and drank less; he was devout and gave most of the money reserved for his personal expenditure to the poor. But he compensated for this lack of outward show by a majesty that was natural to him, for he was a man of magnificent physique and robust constitution and a horseman without equal. "The King on foot is King of his subjects," wrote Pluvinel; "the King mounted is King of Kings."

He was, like most of his race, a passionate hunter and he found in the forests of Saint-Germain and Marly ample opportunity to indulge his taste. It was while hunting on 15 January, 1621, that he came upon a little hamlet on the edge of the forest called Versailles. There was something about the place which appealed to him and here he determined to build a small hunting lodge for his own use. In due course he developed a deep affection for the place, which can be best appreciated from his words to the Père Dinet, his Confessor, shortly before he died. "If God gives me back my health, as soon as I see my Dauphin attain his majority, I will set him in my place and retire to Versailles with four of your fathers to converse with them of things divine, and have no thoughts but of the concerns of my soul and my salvation."

The Château de Saint-Germain was to be the scene of the baptism both of Louis XIV and of his eldest son, the Grand Dauphin. Like his father, Louis XIV had been provisionally baptised – *ondoyé* – at the time of his birth. This was performed in the little oratory of the King's Apartment in the Château Neuf – the only part of that building to survive today. The real ceremony of baptism was deferred until the boy was five and a half.

It took place on 21 September, 1643, in the Sainte-Chapelle of the Vieux Château. Robed in a mantle of silver taffeta he was described as being "beautiful as an angel and exhibited on this occasion an extraordinary modesty and restraint". Mazarin was godfather and the princesse de Condé godmother. At his entry into the Chapel, the Choir "sang a motet most harmoniously" and the Bishop of Meaux, as Grand Aumônier of France, administered the Sacrament.

The King was not present. He was already on his deathbed and died on 14 May. The seventy-two years of Louis XIV's reign had begun.

It was a difficult point in the history of Europe. Revolution was in the air. Richelieu had died a little before the King, and France was now ruled by a Spanish Queen and an Italian Minister. Both the Parlement de Paris and some of the upper aristocracy made a bid to increase their power. In England a much more serious rebellion had broken out which was to attack the Monarchy itself.

On 25 July, 1644, Queen Henrietta Maria of England sought in France an exile from the horrors of the Civil War. She was given an apartment at the Louvre and, as a summer residence, the Château Neuf at Saint-Germain. Thus began the connection between Saint-Germain and the English royal family which was to last until the death of James II.

Having fled to France to escape from one revolution, Henrietta Maria had to endure the discomforts imposed by the Fronde. It reduced her to such penury that she was, according to the Cardinal de Retz, unable even to afford a fire in her rooms in January.

On the night of 5 January, 1649, the Court decided to escape from Paris. The occasion is vividly described in the memoirs of Madame de Motteville and Mademoiselle de Montpensier. On arriving at Saint-Germain, wrote the former, they found the palace "with no beds, no officers, no furniture, no linen and with absolutely nothing which was necessary for the service of the royal family and those who had followed them ... Madame la duchesse d'Orléans slept the first night on straw, and Mademoiselle also. All those who followed the Court shared the same lot, and, in a few hours, straw became so dear at Saint-Germain that money would not buy it."

Mademoiselle de Montpensier records her own experience. "I lay in a very beautiful room in the attics, with beautiful painting and beautiful gilding, large but with very little fire and no glass in the windows, which is not agreeable in January."

The Abbey of Saint-Denis was the centre of the royalist troops and enjoyed intervisibility with Saint-Germain. A beacon was lit on one of the towers of the Abbey to mark any notable event or victory and was answered by another from the terrace of the Château Neuf.

Towards the end of 1652 the Parisians were getting tired of the fighting and invited the King to re-enter his capital, which he did on 21 October. The Fronde was over.

With the advent of Louise de la Vallière in 1662, Louis XIV began to reside more frequently in the two châteaux de Saint-Germain. He came to enjoy the free air and the fine prospect and the opportunities which a country residence afforded for indulging in his amours. The proximity of Versailles proved an added attraction.

Louis also had at his disposal by now the team who had created Vaux-le-Vicomte. On 11 April, 1663, Le Vau wrote to Colbert: "Monsieur Le Nôtre is here with a number of workmen to make the parterre opposite the end of the Grande Galerie of the King's Apartment . . . the earth is levelled and they will begin planting the box hedges tomorrow."

This parterre was designed to be seen from the King's windows. Le Nôtre himself described it as "a place made for nurses and nursery maids; it is not for walking in but it forms an agreeable outlook from a second storey". Beyond the parterre the long perspective of the Allée des Loges introduces what was to be a typical feature in most of Le Nôtre's gardens.

In 1665 Le Nôtre planted five and a half million trees to bring the line of the forest out to his great terrace. This vast undertaking offered a walk, or a ride, of some 2,400 metres on the edge of the high ground as it slopes down from the Château Neuf towards the river. The terrace commanded one of those incomparable prospects which the Hauts de Seine so liberally afford. It overlooked an immense sweep of countryside. To the south and east it enjoyed the view painted by Bonington and Corot, extending from the wooded slopes of Louveciennes – to whose skyline Louis XIV added the gigantic balustrade of the Aqueduc de Marly – to Paris, set between the hills of Mont Valérien and Montmartre, and across the wide meander of the Seine to the single spire of Saint-Denis – "ce doigt silencieux levé vers le ciel" – the last resting place of the Kings of France.

Between 1664 and 1680 nearly four million livres were spent on the improvement of Saint-Germain. In particular this concerned the King's apartment. In 1669 the sloping roof of the *chemin de ronde* was replaced by a leaded walk enclosed by an iron balustrade, finely-wrought and richly-gilded, which provided the perfect vantage point from which to admire the parterres.

At the same time the King's Chambre d'Apparat was squared up and the space left to the east of it used by Mansart for the creation of a miniature apartment of five tiny cabinets. This was the state of the King's rooms that was

93

29 The Château Neuf from across the Seine in about 1665. Van der Meulen.

described by Le Laboureur, the bailli de Montmorency, who made a tour of the château in company with Le Brun. He tells of a richness and a brilliance of décor which has long since vanished from Saint-Germain. Owing to the irregular ground plan, the rooms were often oddly-shaped; they were also badly-lit. This defect was overcome by the use of mirrors. "All the walls and ceilings," wrote Le Laboureur, "are covered with mirrors with frames and ornaments of which the gilding was not the richest part."

The furniture equalled, if it did not surpass, the magnificence of the decorations. "In every corner, and in a hundred other places, there are great vases of silver, loaded with flowers, and columns and *terms* of the same material carrying filigree work in gold." In the King's bedroom, high up in the vaulted ceiling, within the cupola, three little *amorini*, "painted in the most inimitable manner", joined hands "with a marvellous eagerness" to uphold a chandelier. On the sides of the cupola were painted "les maisons de plaisance du Roi . . . Saint-Germain, Versailles et Fontainebleau".

In the corner tower of the King's apartment Le Laboureur saw a "great silver vase which makes a hundred little fountains which can be made to play at will and that can serve as required to give an agreeable refreshment to the place in summer".

Francini's fountains were by no means confined to the gardens. The King had in his little cabinets a tiny grotto with a large *jet d'eau* reaching almost to the ceiling, and in 1673, when an apartment was being created for Madame de Montespan, she demanded a fountain on the flat roof outside her windows. On 6 December, Petit, Colbert's agent, reported; "I have made them work all these last days and even stay up until after midnight on all the works which His Majesty has commanded for the rooms of Madame de Montespan; the said works were completed last night. The King and the aforesaid lady were content with my labours. The said lady is also very satisfied with the *jet d'eau* in the middle of the garden on one of the balconies of her room; she takes great pleasure in making it play."

On 21 March, 1668, Louis' eldest son, always known as the Grand Dauphin, was baptised at Saint-Germain. As at Fontainebleau for the baptism of Louis XIII, the whole courtyard of the Vieux Château had been specially decorated and furnished for the occasion. The scene is accurately portrayed in an engraving by Brissart.

Tapestries lined the walls and an amphitheatre had been built up to the level of the first-floor windows. At the entrance to the Court two great buffets had been erected for the display of ceremonial silver. In the centre was a platform raised upon four steps on top of which stood the silver basin which served as a font and over the font was suspended a great dais of silver brocade, thirty feet high, ornamented with dolphins and the interlaced Ls that formed Louis' monogram.

Against the windows of the Queen's apartment, opposite the entrance, was built a magnificent reredos. It took the form of a triumphal arch in the Corinthian order, twenty metres in width and some eight metres high. In front of the central arch was placed the altar on which there was a further display of silver. Galleries for the musicians were contrived to either side.

The Dauphin had spent the night in the Château Neuf, which had been "adorned with a wonderful magnificence". He was dressed, in accordance with tradition, in silver brocade and silver lace with a long train lined with

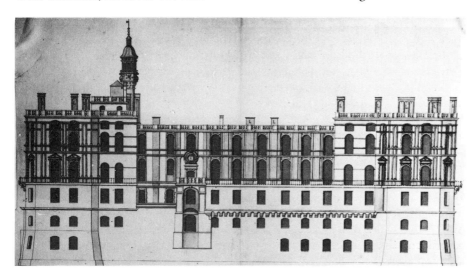

30 The entrance front as enlarged by Louis XIV.

95

ermine, and he advanced between two Dukes, the duc de Créquy and the duc de Mercoeur. The cortège came in procession from the Château Neuf, round into the Basse Cour, and entered the Vieux Château by what is still the main entrance. The Pope, Clement IX, was godfather and Henrietta Maria, Dowager Queen of England, godmother.

In the same year the first important enlargement, known as the "Enveloppe", was made to Versailles. Although Saint-Germain was still officially the seat of the Court, it was in no way a palace worthy of Louis' conception of Monarchy. In spite of its remarkable situation "unique for its combination of the marvellous view, the immense expanse of the forest immediately adjoining it . . . the beauty of the trees, the advantage of fresh springs at such an altitude, the charm and the commodity of the Seine", Saint-Simon complained that those courtiers who were accommodated in the palace found themselves lodged "étrangement à l'étroite".

In 1680, when the final enlargements of Versailles were already in hand, Louis commissioned Mansart to add large blocks of apartments to the corners of François I's building. The result was aesthetically disastrous. Two years later the Court left for Versailles never to return.

Saint-Germain might have remained unoccupied had it not been for the "Glorious Revolution" in England. In 1689 James II and his Queen came to spend their exile in France. They were offered the Vieux Château. Mary arrived first on 4 January and was met by Louis with great marks of respect together with a few false promises. Two days later, James arrived safely and Louis personally conducted him to his wife's apartment, saying, "Je vous amène un homme que vous serez bien aise de voir."

On 16 September, 1701, James II died at Saint-Germain. The Herald at Arms immediately proclaimed his son, James Edward Stuart, King of England and Ireland as James III and James VIII of Scotland. Seventeen years later, Mary of Modena followed her husband to the grave. The duc de Saint-Simon wrote her epitaph: "Her life, since she came to France, has been one long succession of misfortunes, which she bore heroically right until the end, in offering herself to God, in detachment, in penitence, in prayer and in continual good works. The life and death of this Queen of England is to be compared, at the least, to that of the greatest saints."

When the Stuarts were no longer considered a danger to the House of Hanover, George IV had a mausoleum constructed in the Parish Church of Saint-Germain. In 1855, Queen Victoria made a pilgrimage to the last home of her unfortunate ancestor.

5

The Château du Louvre

"I HAVE OFTEN been tempted," wrote Henri Sauval, the seventeenth-century historian of Paris, "to say nothing about the Louvre, and I have great difficulty in overcoming this temptation, because, after all, its origins are so obscure, the progress of the building so uncertain, all the plans so often changed, that there is no great honour in undertaking a history that is subject to so much controversy and is so totally and generally ignored." Sauval was writing at about the time when Louis XIV's many projects for the Louvre had resolved themselves into a design for the Cour Carré much as we see it today. The honour of unravelling this tangled skein fell to the twentieth-century historian of art, Louis Hautecoeur.

There is certainly nothing obscure about the origins of the Louvre. It began as quite a small castle which formed part of the general scheme for the re-fortification of Paris under Philippe-Auguste, who placed it as an outwork of his defensive system. Charles V somewhat diminished the military significance of the Louvre by building an outer line of fortification beyond it and by turning the building into something more like a palatial residence than a *château fort*. Subsequent kings allowed the expansion of Paris to envelop the Louvre and the process of in-filling came right to its walls. When the idea of building something really large here began to take shape, the site was already heavily encumbered.

François I took the decisive step of pulling down the Keep, the famous Tour du Louvre, and starting to build a purely palatial structure. But the word "palatial" can only be applied to its style and not to its dimensions. François I's Louvre was to have been no larger than that of Charles V. By proportioning his façades to so small a building, he created a problem for those who were later to enlarge it.

The next difficulty arose from the decision of Catherine de Medici to build herself a palace outside Charles V's line of fortification, but near enough to the Louvre for it to seem obvious to her and her son Henri III to link the two together. The connection between the Louvre and the Tuileries was not the least of the problems which were to confront their successors.

These difficulties, however, might have been overcome had there been any persistent determination to do so. But the Kings of France showed a recurrent reluctance to live in Paris. Vincennes and Saint-Germain were in many ways more attractive to them. As a result, the many projects for transforming the Louvre from fortress to palace were pursued in a less than wholehearted fashion. Progress at the Tuileries was steadier and it was often possible for the King to lodge here while the louvre was under scaffolding.

Therefore, although the Louvre was for centuries regarded as the seat of the Monarchy – rather like St. James's in England – it was not often inhabited for any considerable length of time. Louis XIV abandoned it definitively for Versailles. Its connection with the creation and exhibition of works of art was already established by then and in due course was to determine the future of the building.

The original fortress of Philippe-Auguste was probably started at the same time as the curtain wall, in other words in 1190. Certainly by 1202 – for which year there survive various accounts for the fixture of the windows – it was well advanced. The building stood four-square with towers at each corner. In the centre of the south and east façades were twin towers guarding narrow entrances. A single tower marked the centre of the other two façades, providing covering fire to the whole wall. The south and west ranges contained apartments but on the north and east the courtyard was bounded by a curtain wall. Outer defences, with a barbican before the eastern gatehouse, culminated in the Tour du Coin where the original city wall reached the river and which answered the Tour de Nesle across the Seine.

Inside the courtyard, and placed eccentrically in the north-east corner, was the Grosse Tour – a huge cylinder of stone some eighteen and a half metres in diameter and standing in its own moat.

This appears to have become the current formula of defence, for a number of châteaux, of which Coucy, built in 1230, was the most important, were based on this design. In one case the desire to emulate the Louvre was explicit. At Dun-le-Roi in the Cher it was stipulated that it should be "made to the measure of the Tower of Paris" – "faciendo ad mensuram Turris Parisius".

The next phase in the development of the Louvre was undertaken by that great builder, Charles V. He used the architect Raymond du Temple to carry out the work. In 1360 we have the first order for stone – not from a quarry, but from the demolition of the Hôtel de Valence at Saint-Germain-des-Prés.

The first work which Charles undertook was to enlarge the encircling wall of Paris. Starting from the Tour du Coin, he carried the line of fortification along the Seine to a point about half way along what is today the Quai des Tuileries. Here he built the Tour du Bois. From this tower the line of the wall turned at right angles from the Seine cutting across the present Cour du Carrousel and continuing in the direction of the Porte St. Denis. The wall curved round until it finally came back to the riverside at a point upstream of Paris near which the Bastille was built.

The building of the Bastille relieved the Louvre of one of its functions – that of providing a prison for persons of distinction. The defensive rôle of the Louvre was already diminished by its being placed within the new line of fortification. Whereas the Bastille remained a grim fortress until it was destroyed by the Revolution, the Louvre began to develop into a *maison de plaisance*.

Most of Raymond du Temple's reconstructions were aimed at making the

31 View from across the
Seine. Miniature by Pol
de Limbourg.

old fortress more habitable. New lodgings were created on the north and east sides of the courtyard; new staircases in the corners of the quadrangle facilitated communications. In 1365 a much more important Grand Escalier was built onto the new north range. Its form was spiral, as is implied by its name "la grande *viz* neuve du Louvre". It appears to have been built out as a projection from the façade in the manner of François I's staircase at Blois. The inside of the cage was ornamented with statues in niches representing the King and Queen, the duc d'Anjou and the duc d'Orléans, the duc de Berry and the duc de Bourgogne. There is enough reference to sculpture in the accounts to confirm that the staircase was an affair of the greatest elaboration and elegance.

Besides the creation of improved communications, Raymond du Temple was concerned with the provision of better lighting. Eight windows to each storey brought a new flood of daylight into the rooms of the Grosse Tour. Two rectangular projections on the east front were probably also intended as a means of increasing the illumination of the apartments. Out of doors a leaded walk behind the battlements afforded a delightful view over the city on the one side and the country on the other. By 1370 the château of the *Très Riches Heures* had been created.

Owing to its origins in a fortress not unlike the Bastille, the Louvre of Charles V had a compactness and a symmetry which were its most distinctive features. Pol de Limbourg shows the south and east façades, each of which centred upon a gatehouse with twin towers surmounted by a tall pavilion roof. The corner towers gave birth, above their battlements, to small towers capped by *poivrières* with delicately swept profiles. Two of these upper towers are backed by staircase turrets which repeat their silhouette in miniature. Towers, turrets and pavilions are crested with gilded weather vanes and banners painted with the royal fleurs de lys. The accounts for 1365 mention "Maistre Jehan Coste, peintre et sergeant d'armes du Roy" as having painted these banners. Tall, white chimney stacks climbed up the towers or sprouted from the roofs, adding an important contribution to the already exciting if not overcrowded skyline. The whole complex of pavilions, towers, turrets and chimneys soars to its climax in the great conical roof of the Grosse Tour, rising to a height of thirty-one metres above the level of the court. There was something of the spectacular roofscape of the central block of Chambord in the total silhouette created.

On 28 February, 1527, an event took place which was not only a decisive point in the development of the Louvre but an enormous advance in the introduction of the architectural ideas of the Renaissance. François I ordered the demolition of the Grosse Tour du Louvre and a certain Jean aux Boeufs contracted for 2,500 livres to execute the command. The disappearance of the tower was deplored in the *Journal d'un Bourgeois de Paris*. "In the said year of 1527 in February they began to pull down the Grosse Tour du Louvre, by order of the King, in order to convert the Louvre into a 'logis de plaisance' and for him to live in. And the King maintained that the said tower was an encumbrance to the said château and its courtyard. But all the same it was a great shame to take it down, for it was very beautiful, tall and strong and was appropriate for keeping prisoners of great distinction."

It is probable that the "Bourgeois de Paris" was speaking for most of his

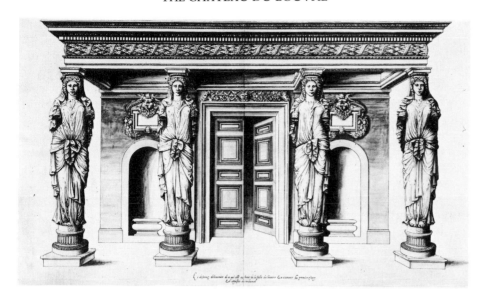

contemporaries. For centuries the Grosse Tour had been the architectural
symbol of the Monarchy in Paris. Royal rights were said to appertain to the
Tour du Louvre. It was the central stronghold of the régime.

Traditionally in France the rebuilding of a château respected the *Tour*. At
Chenonceaux, at Brissac and at Villandry in the Loire valley and more
significantly at Fontainebleau and at Saint-Germain among the royal houses,
the medieval towers were incorporated in the new building, often rather at
the expense of symmetry and convenience.

Germain Brice, whose *Nouvelle Description de la Ville de Paris* was written in
1684, records that François I had summoned Serlio, "one of the most
renowned architects from Italy", to submit designs for the new building. The
designs, "although very beautiful", were not accepted; those of Pierre Lescot,
Seigneur de Clagny, of a notable family of Parisian lawyers, "having been
judged infinitely more regular and more magnificent", were preferred.

Lescot was trained as a painter and as an architect. His approach to the
design of a façade was essentially decorative. It is significant that he worked in
close collaboration with the greatest French sculptor of the time, Jean Goujon.
Together they produced a style classical in its use of orders, but distinctly un-
Italian in the richness of its decoration; a style that is fully Renaissance and at
the same time unmistakably French.

François died some six months after he had commissioned Lescot, but Henri
II at once confirmed him in his contract while asking for significant
alterations. On 10 July, 1549, an agreement was drawn up "to make certain
demolitions . . . in accordance with the new plans that you have drawn up at
our command".

The "new plan" removed the staircase from the centre to the right-hand
pavilion. It was a staircase in the Italian manner, consisting of two straight
ramps beneath a barrel vault on which Goujon did some of his most
distinctive carving. "The roof over these stairs," wrote Coryat, "is exceeding
beautiful, being vaulted with very sumptuous frettings or chamferings,

wherein the forms of clusters of grapes and many other things are most excellently contrived.''

The moving of the staircase to the end of the building made room for two Grandes Salles, one above the other, occupying the whole of the first two storeys. Of the upper one we only know that it had "a gilt roof richly embossed". The lower, the famous Salle des Cariatides, still gives some idea of its original appearance.

The caryatids took the place of pillars in what was really an elaborate and purely ornamental porch to the doorway. Facing the caryatids at the opposite end was a remarkable and original feature known as the "Tribunal". It was a kind of triumphal arch upheld by groups of pillars of an almost Grecian simplicity, which formed the architectural context and canopy for the King's throne. In other respects the room has largely lost its original appearance. The great beams which upheld the ceiling were replaced in the days of Louis XIV by the present vault. The decoration was renewed again by Percier and Fontaine for Napoleon.

Adjoining this wing, Lescot built a corner pavilion which housed the King's apartment and consequently took the name of Pavillon du Roi. The external architecture was very much plainer than that of the courtyard. This was no doubt deliberate. A palace often reserves its fairest for its most intimate friends. But it was also top-heavy. In order to obtain the extra height which he needed, Lescot merely superimposed another main floor on top of the attic storey.

But, if the outward architecture was austere, the rooms which it contained were of a richness that was something new in France. Walls and ceilings were clothed with a wooden panelling of the most ornate workmanship and so lavishly gilded that some spectators took them for solid gold. Thomas Coryat describes what he calls the Presence Chamber – more usually the Grande Antichambre or Salle Henri II – as "very fair, being adorned with a wonderous sumptuous roof, which though it be made but of timber work, yet it is exceeding richly gilt, and with that exquisite art, that a stranger upon the first view thereof, would imagine it were beaten gold''.

On 12 February, 1556, Lescot produced the designs for the ceiling and contracted Francisque Scibec for its execution.

A very rich cornice, underscored by a continuous festooning on the frieze, upholds a ceiling of deeply-recessed and heavily-carved compartments. According to Sauval it was made in sections so that it could be taken down and cleaned more easily. In the centre a huge circular frame in full relief surrounds the Arms of France, all of which was thickly gilded. Here is the evident prototype of the later ceilings in the royal apartments of Fontainebleau.

Matching the rich elaboration of the ceiling, the doors and window embrasures were the subject of an equal care. The doors originally were surmounted by rounded pediments, each with a helmet in full relief against the tympanum. Louis XIV replaced these pediments with the gilded trophies which can be seen today. The room no longer occupies its original position in the Pavillon du Roi. In the nineteenth century the ceiling and panelling were re-erected in a new position behind the Colonnade.

In 1556 the Spanish Ambassador, Gaspar de Vega, described a visit to the

Louvre. He provides some of the all-too-rare information about the accommodation of those who were not members of the royal family. In particular he noted "a gallery for the ladies in the manner of a Convent dormitory, with cubicles on either side of the central corridor". It is probable that the ladies did not often make use of these cubicles for in those days the Louvre does not appear to have been used so much as a residence, but more as the setting for certain important receptions and entertainments. The King resided for the most part in the Hôtel des Tournelles.

It was here, on 30 June, 1559, that Henri II was killed while jousting by the splintering of a lance. His widow, Catherine de Medici, abandoned the Tournelles which she then had demolished and transferred her residence to the Louvre.

The Louvre thus became the central theatre of the most tragic and horrific period in the history of France. It was caused by fanaticism which was in the first place religious but which was, as so often, used as a pretext by unscrupulous seekers after power. There were three main parties. The House of Lorraine, headed by the duc de Guise and the Cardinal of Lorraine, represented extreme Catholicism and did not scruple to betray their country by the calling in of Spanish troops. The house of Bourbon, headed by Henri de Navarre and his brother the prince de Condé, neither of them fanatics, but anxious to protect the Huguenot cause since their supporters were drawn largely from this source, represented the other extreme and was likewise ready to welcome such help as Elizabeth of England was prepared to offer. They were ably seconded by the Admiral de Coligny. The "Politiques", headed by the noblest of the characters upon that stage, the Chancellor Michel de l'Hôpital and the Maréchal de Saint-André, were Catholic but not extremist and were rejected by both the others as men "who prefer the salvation of their country to the salvation of their souls". Between these parties the Court, under the leadership of Catherine de Medici and the three Kings who were her sons, tried vainly to mediate. But their mediation only too often took the form of veering first to one side and then to the other.

In 1572 an alliance was formed between Charles IX and Henri de Navarre, who became engaged to the King's sister, Marguerite de Valois. But no sooner was the alliance formed than Catherine began to resent the ascendancy of Coligny over her son. It was only through him that she could maintain her own authority. On 23 August, during the celebrations for her daughter's wedding, she ordered the assassination of Coligny. The attempt failed. In the panic which ensued she managed to persuade Charles to make a sudden change in his alliance and to order the massacre of all the Huguenots who were in Paris for the wedding – Henri and Condé always excepted. On Saint Bartholomew's Day, the massacre began in the very courtyard of the Louvre. It was the most disgusting act of perfidy and brutality and it availed nothing, except to give the Huguenots an increased sense of justification for their reprisals. Two years later, Charles IX died at the age of twenty-four, haunted by the memories of that night of carnage.

Such times were hardly propitious for the building of palaces and work on the Louvre was virtually suspended. Catherine de Medici was more interested in building a palace for herself on a site just outside the walls of Paris beyond

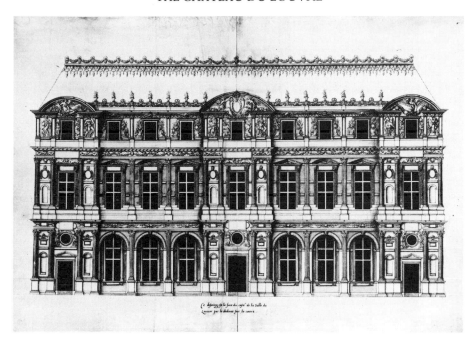

34 *Left:* Façade of Pierre Lescot. Drawing by du Cerceau.

35 *Below:* Façade of Pierre Lescot. Detail of doorway by du Cerceau.

the Louvre which was called the Tuileries. It was her intention to join the Tuileries to the Louvre by means of a very long gallery. But since she intended to make use for this of the foundations of the curtain wall of Charles V, she had to make provision for another building to link her gallery with the Louvre, for the line of Charles' fortification was well in advance of the south façade of the palace. The building which was to link the two was called the Petite Galerie. It has since become more famous as the Galerie d'Apollon.

To Charles IX succeeded Henri III, the last of the Valois. His was a character full of contradictions. Happily married to the demure and devout Louise de Lorraine, he surrounded himself with elegant and overdressed young men who were known as his "mignons' and who scandalised Paris. Sincerely Catholic and convinced of the necessity of a single religion within the State, he was ready to join the Protestant Henri de Navarre against the Catholic League. "Passionately addicted to beauty, good manners and fine clothes," according to the Venetian Ambassador Priuli, he was also morosely penitent and joined himself to the Flagellants.

This had begun at Avignon in December 1574. The Chronicler l'Estoile describes how he dressed himself with the regulation sack which covered his head, leaving two apertures for the eyes like the cowl of an Inquisitor, and joined the "procession des Battus". It was the first of many such occasions and it brought him into ridicule in his own palace. On 29 March, 1583, L'Estoile records: "On this day the King had a hundred and twenty pages and lackeys whipped in the Salle Basse [Salle des Cariatides] at the Louvre for having performed a mock Procession of Penitents with handkerchiefs over their faces with holes for the eyes."

This public flogging was not the worst scene that was to be enacted in the Salle des Cariatides. On 12 May, 1588, Henri III had to flee from Paris. On 1 August the following year he was stabbed to death at Saint-Cloud by a Dominican monk named Jacques Clément. Paris was in the hands of the League, dominated by a Council known as the Sixteen. By their orders the President Brisson and certain other Magistrates were put to death. The duc de Mayenne had the four members of the Sixteen responsible for this outrage tried before him in the Louvre and hanged them then and there from the beams of the Salle des Cariatides.

It was in the Louvre also that Mayenne convoked the States General with the avowed purpose of electing a Catholic King.

If there had been one consistent note in the character of Henri III it was his belief in the absolute necessity of the legitimate succession. On the death of his brother, the duc d'Alençon, on 10 June, 1584, he had no alternative but to accept as his heir presumptive the King of Navarre, a distant cousin but a direct descendant through the male line of Saint-Louis.

On his death-bed, he reaffirmed this acceptance and ordered his followers to accept Henry as their rightful King. But Henry was a Huguenot. To become King he would have to be anointed and crowned according to the ancient rite. The ancient rite included the oath "to exterminate heresy and to protect and advance the Catholic religion without tolerating any other".

Henri IV had one great asset: he was the sort of person who appeals to the French. When he made his manifesto – "We are all Frenchmen and fellow citizens of the same fatherland" – men listened. When he added, "We must be brought to agreement by reason and kindness and not by severity and cruelty which serve only to arouse men," they responded. But not Paris; their new leader, Mayenne, declared the Cardinal de Bourbon King.

Henri IV saw that to be master of France and not master of Paris was to be unable to rule. He had on several occasions refused to abjure his religion in order to gain the throne. But now that he had won his throne he was prepared to reconsider the matter. On 25 July, 1593, he was solemnly received into the Catholic Church at Saint-Denis.

The conversion of the King, however, did not have the desired effect on Paris, but the League was in fact already broken. Mayenne fled, leaving the City in the hands of its Governor, Charles de Cossé, comte de Brissac. Brissac, though a devout Catholic, was statesman enough to realise that further resistance was useless if not actually undesirable. In the early hours of 22 March, 1594, he opened the gates of Paris to the royalist troops.

Henri IV and his great Minister Sully had the gigantic task of rebuilding a France in ruins. In this they were remarkably successful. But they were builders also in the literal sense of the word. "If you do not return to Paris in two years' time," wrote Malherbe to a friend, "you will no longer be able to recognise it." Before the end of 1594 Henri had announced his intention of continuing the work on the Louvre.

Henri IV took far more interest in Saint-Germain and Fontainebleau than in the Louvre, which he used more for occasional receptions than as a regular residence. His influence on architecture was more on the administrative than on the artistic side. Since the days of Lescot and de l'Orme the King had always been in direct touch with his architect and the architect was his own contractor. Within five weeks of his entry into Paris, Henri IV had put a stop to this by creating Jean de Fourcy Intendant des Bâtiments. From now on the King only dealt with the architect via his Intendant. The architect in charge at the Louvre was at that time Jacques Androuet du Cerceau. In October of the same year, Fourcy appointed Louis Métezeau to the same post as du Cerceau, "also our architect". To have two architects on the job is to place oneself in the position of arbiter, which is a position of power. In this Fourcy foreshadowed the role of Colbert in the royal buildings.

Louis Battifol has studied the transactions of Jean de Fourcy issued by his notary Rossignol. These documents leave no doubt that the building of the long Galerie du Bord de l'Eau which linked the Louvre with the Tuileries was Fourcy's creation. It is specified that the old curtain walls of Charles V and its towers were to be pulled down. On their foundations were to be built the outer wall, towards the Seine, and new foundations were to be dug for the inner wall.

The entire work was therefore Fourcy's, but the plan was considerably older. The idea of joining the two palaces dates back to Catherine de Medici. It presupposes the retention of the city wall, cutting across the present Place du Carrousel. The architecture made a break in style at the point at which it crossed the city wall at the Porte Neuve. The part of the gallery inside the city was richer and more ornate; that which was outside was simpler.

On 9 January, 1595, at the Hôtel de Fourcy, the adjudication was made and contractors appointed to carry out the work according to their estimates – some of the work "dans la ville", some "hors la ville". The prices "dans la ville" were lower because the foundations of Charles V's wall were to be retained and the stones of the wall itself re-utilised.

By 1607 the work was well advanced. On 3 May, Henri IV wrote to the Cardinal de Joyeuse: "In Paris you will find my great gallery which goes to the Tuileries, finished." This can only have referred to the outer shell of masonry and roofing. When Thomas Coryat made his visit in 1608 he wrote that the gallery was "imperfect, for there was but half the walk boarded and the roof very rude".

At one extremity of the gallery, where it joined the Tuileries, was the Pavillon de Flore. It was built on piles which had to be driven into the sandy sub-soil, but this precaution was not enough: Napoleon III had to rebuild the whole block. At the other extremity was the Petite Galerie, a building started by Catherine de Medici which formed the junction between the Grande Galerie and the Louvre. It is now the Galerie d'Apollon, but was known then as the Galerie des Rois from the decoration which it was accorded.

Thomas Coryat was extreme in his enthusiasm for this room, which "excelleth in my opinion not only all those that are now in the world, but all whatsoever that ever were since the creation thereof ... having in it many goodly pictures of the Kings and Queens of France, made most exactly in wainscot, and drawn out very lively in oil works upon the same. The roof of most glittering and admirable beauty, wherein is much antique work, with the picture of God and the Angels, the Sun, the Moon, the Stars, the Planets and other celestial signes."

It was from the Louvre on 14 May, 1610, that Henri went to visit Sully, who was ill at the time. He went without guards, informally with three or four friends. At the corner of the rue de la Ferronerie there was a blockage caused by a pig, and the coach had to stop. François Ravaillac happened to be standing at the corner. He was a fanatic who had sworn to kill the King. He seized his opportunity, thrust himself into the coach and stabbed him twice in the heart. By the time the coach had returned to the Louvre, Henri IV was dead.

Ravaillac died a hideous death, but he had himself to blame. He had killed the only man in France who was likely to have shown mercy on him.

When the surgeons performed their post mortem on the King, they found "all his members healthy and in good state ... the doctors said that in the course of nature he could have lived another twenty years". It is a matter for wistful speculation what might have been the future of France had Henri IV been spared these twenty years. It is more than probable, among other things, that the Louvre would have been completed.

In the Galerie des Cerfs at Fontainebleau, Henri IV had ordered mural paintings of all the palaces and hunting lodges of the King. The Louvre was depicted not as it was in 1600, when this gallery was begun, but as it was intended to be. The painting became badly defaced and was heavily restored in the nineteenth century. It is not reliable evidence for the details of the design, but it shows the magnificent perspective of the lay-out – an enormous complex of courtyards occupying most of the area which it occupies today.

In the foreground the Cour Carré sets the scale and imposes the proportions of the whole design. The west side of the courtyard is made up of Lescot's original façade, a large central pavilion and a repetition of Lescot's façade to complete the symmetry. The other buildings form a square upon this side.

It was left to Richelieu and his architect Lemercier to put this plan into execution. He pulled down the remaining north range of the old Louvre, with the Tour de la Librairie, the Tour du Milieu and the famous spiral staircase. By the end of June 1624, all was ready for the King to lay the first stone "du bâtiment neuf".

On 14 May, 1643, Louis XIII died and his widow, Anne d'Autriche, left the Louvre and went to live in the Palais Cardinal – now the Palais Royal – which Richelieu had bequeathed to her. It was not until 1652, when the Fronde was over, that the royal family came back. On 21 October the *Gazette de France* bore the headline: "The return of the King, so deeply desired by his good city of Paris;" and on the same day he made his entry. He did not, however, go to the Palais Cardinal. As Madame de Motteville wrote, "he had learnt by humiliating experience that these private houses without moats were not for him". He returned to the Louvre.

It was at that time a complete architectural mess, in process of transition from a fortress to a palace, and it was still surrounded at close quarters by a jumble of other buildings.

To the east was the Petit Bourbon – the remains of a private hôtel which had been confiscated on the occasion of the defection of the Connétable de Bourbon in 1527; there were still traces about its doors of the yellow paint with which it had been daubed by the public executioner as a sign of infamy.

But its Grande Salle, a vast room running parallel with the river, was used as an extension of the Louvre and its Chapel was the Chapel Royal.

The Petit Bourbon was separated from the château by a moat crossed by a drawbridge. The archway which formed the main entrance was set between two ancient towers and was only six feet wide. Its passageway was so dark that someone had once bumped into Henri IV when entering. To the left and right of the entrance front were two more towers with tall conical roofs, built in the days of Philippe-Auguste.

From the left hand of these towers the south front of the palace, which contained the royal apartments, presented a façade of ten windows towards the Seine. It was an architecture of the greatest austerity, relieved only by the row of triangular pediments over the first-floor windows. It merely continued the style of Lescot's Pavillon du Roi which marked its western extremity. Beyond this the façade was extended for the space of three windows to join at right angles the building which contained the Galerie des Rois, running south towards the river as far as the line of the old wall of fortification. Here it turned west again into the long range of the Grande Galerie. Halfway along this, the old Tour du Bois and Porte Neuve, dating from Charles V, were still standing.

Within the quadrangle the new buildings had not progressed very far. From the Pavillon du Roi Lescot's original wing, prolonged by Lemercier, formed the west side of the courtyard, but the corner pavilion was only up to the level of the ground-floor windows. The north side of the court was as yet unbuilt and the private houses in the rue de Beauvais were still standing. The east front, set between its corner towers, still preserved the proportions of the old quadrangle.

At first the concerns of the royal family were more with redecoration than with reconstruction. In March 1655, the Queen Mother had the ground-floor rooms beneath the Galerie des Rois turned into her *appartement d'été*. It was a suite of six rooms. Louis le Vau had just been nominated Premier Architecte du Roi and was working on the new buildings at Vincennes. He provided the design for the architecture. The scheme for the decorations was furnished in the same year by Romanelli, a painter whom the King had summoned specially from Italy. Romanelli did the painting of four of the ceilings himself. With him worked Michel Anguier who did most of the stucco ornament and figures. Anguier had been working for Nicolas Fouquet at Saint-Mandé. These ceilings still survive and already show a family likeness with that of the King's Bedroom at Vaux-le-Vicomte. The style known as Louis XIV began here at the Louvre and in the new wings of Vincennes, was developed at Vaux-le-Vicomte and found its fullest expression at Versailles.

On 31 October, 1660, the King "being resolved, on the advice of M. le Cardinal de Mazarin, his first Minister, to complete forthwith both the building of his Château du Louvre and that of the Palais des Tuileries, to be joined together according to the ancient and magnificent design which has been made by the Kings who preceded him", ordered the demolition of the remaining parts of the medieval Louvre and the continuation of the building of the great courtyard, the Cour Carré.

The architect was still Le Vau. He completed the south front, following the

36 Lescot's façade with Lemercier's pavilion.

procedure of Lemercier, by building an ornate central pavilion and repeating Lescot's façade beyond it, terminating in a repetition of the Pavillon du Roi. In all it made a façade of twenty-nine windows.

But before the work had progressed far, on 6 February, 1661, the Galerie des Rois was destroyed by a disastrous fire. The first reaction to this outbreak was of a purely spiritual nature. The Blessed Sacrament was sent for from the Parish Church of Saint-Germain-l'Auxerrois and was solemnly processed towards the location of the fire. Buckets of water, however, just in case, were being passed by means of a human chain which was rapidly formed. The gallery was destroyed, but the Queen Mother's apartments on the floor beneath it were miraculously spared. The Blessed Sacrament was processed back to the church, attended by the King and Queen "and all the Court with the most exemplary devotion".

The rebuilding of the gallery, now to be known as the Galerie d'Apollon, introduces a new name. On 3 May, 1663, approval was given that work be done here 'to the design and model and under the direction of M. Le Brun, Premier Peintre du Roi''. In the following year the stucco work was executed by the brothers Marsy, Girardon and Régnaudin. Already some of the great names that were to be connected with the creation of Versailles were found associated in this impressive work of artistic collaboration. Already the great theme of Apollo had been attached to the mythology of Louis XIV. He had probably first assumed it when dancing the famous ballet as the Sun.

Louis Hautecoeur, one of the chief authorities on the Louvre, has drawn attention to the possible connection between the theatre of the mid-seventeenth century and the style of decoration which is known as Louis XIV. If we could only witness the masques and operas as they were performed at that time, we would see with the eye of recognition these painted ceilings and stucco figures, in which Gods appeared in gilded chariots and floated on solid cumuli of cloud: "le décor des appartements répétait celui de la scène."

The performance of ballets by the members of the royal family was an important part of the entertainment of the Court. It taught them also to move, on ceremonial occasions, with the gracefulness of a trained dancer. Israel Silvestre, one of the most prolific depictors of the period, has captured just such an occasion in a pen and ink drawing. It represents a ball given on 29 January, 1662, in the Grande Antichambre at the Louvre, now known as the Salle Henri II. The occasion is described in the *Gazette de France*. "The magnificence of the Court of France was there set forth in such a degree as to astonish Don Cristobal de Garivia, Emissary of His Catholic Majesty, who was present with all the Ambassadors and other ministers of foreign Princes. All were charmed by the grace with which His Majesty and the Queen danced the overture to this *divertissement*; after the dance a collation was served in the most royal manner."

The young days of Louis XIV were the great days of the Louvre as a royal palace; they were also to be the last. 1661 was in many ways an *annus mirabilis*. Everything indicated that France stood upon the threshold of a golden age. Although the young King had announced, on the death of Mazarin, that he intended thenceforward to be his own first minister, he found in Colbert a man whose genius for administration was to dominate the scene for twenty years. Even in his relations with his family and with his mistresses, Louis depended on the devoted discretion of his minister. "Colbert," writes Inez Murat, "was one of the rare men of whom Louis was absolutely sure."

Inez Murat, in her deep and sympathetic study of Colbert, gives a brilliant thumbnail sketch of the great minister. "The eyes dark black, the countenance pallid, the look severe and with a glacial coldness of manner, the whole character of the minister created a sombre severity which terrified those who approached him but which was reassuring to the King. Each is in his proper place: Louis XIV in that of King, Colbert in that of Minister; to the one, the effulgent display of the divine nature of the Monarchy; to the other the conscientious rigour of the servant of the State. The incredible capacity for work of Colbert is pleasing to a King whose respect for work is beyond doubt. Colbert's methods harmonise with the character of Louis XIV. Unlike Mazarin, both men share a love of detail. "Le détail de tout" is what the King demands of his Minister."

And yet there were certain fundamental differences of outlook between the two. To Louis, the Monarchy was the all-important symbol of unity in a country that was still an incoherent mass of local customs. To Colbert it was the State. True, at that time the identity of both coincided so nearly that the distinction was seldom perceptible. Whether Louis actually pronounced the words or not, "l'Etat c'est moi" was an aphorism which held true. But the difference of outlook was there. In religion, for instance, the principle of toleration was more acceptable to Colbert than to this master. The revocation of the Edict of Nantes had to wait until after Colbert's death. But nowhere was this difference more marked than in their respective attitudes towards the capital. "Paris," wrote Colbert to his eldest son, "being the capital of the kingdom and the seat of the King, it is certain that it sets the pace for all the rest of the country, that all internal affairs begin with it."

But Paris, in terms of the seating of the King, meant the Louvre. Colbert's great ambition was to see the King housed in splendour in the centre of his great metropolis. He saw the Louvre, as he told Bernini, as the "séjour principal des Rois dans la plus grande et la plus peuplée ville du monde". The whole building in all its parts was there "to impress respect on the minds of the people".

On 1 January, 1664, Colbert became Surintendant des Bâtiments. For reasons which remain obscure, he did not like Le Vau, whose plans for the Louvre were regarded as accepted. "Colbert," wrote Perrault, "was not satisfied with this design; it became a matter of honour with him to provide this palace with a façade worthy of the Prince who was having it built, so he began by causing the design of Le Vau to be examined by all the architects in Paris ... Nearly all the architects found fault with Le Vau's project." They were, of course, all hoping to get their own designs accepted.

Antoine-Léonor Houdin and François Mansart were among the first. They were followed by François Le Vau, a little embarrassed to enter into competition with his brother; then came Jean Marot, François Dubois and Pierre Cottart. It is not worth discussing their designs in detail; they none of them succeeded in solving the basic problem. There is a limit beyond which a classical façade cannot be extended without monotony. The proportions of Lescot's buildings and the scale of Lemercier's additions imposed a problem which may have been insuperable. Of the French candidates, only François Mansart appeared to appreciate the problem. By varying the height of his roofs and by the insertion of a very large central pavilion which looked more like a church than the gateway to a palace, he at least avoided monotony. But he refused to tie himself to any design. Always ready to pull down what he had just built if he did not quite like it, he was, from the point of view of the client, an expensive and exasperating architect.

Colbert now turned to Italy. "It is a question," he wrote to Poussin, "of bringing to perfection the most beautiful building in the world and of making it worthy, if that were possible, of the greatness and magnificence of the Prince who is to inhabit it." Poussin was being charged to contact the most eminent architects in Rome – Rainaldi, Cortona and, of course, Bernini.

It was only in the imagination of Colbert that the Louvre could ever have been considered the most beautiful building in the world. It was nothing of the sort. Colbert himself had no use for the royal apartments – "rats' holes", he called them, unworthy of the Majesty of the King or the grandeur and beauty of the design of the Louvre. The real fault was that they were badly lit. "The King's bedroom," wrote Sauval in about 1660, "has not been put right, where at high noon one has to feel one's way about. This darkness is all the more unfortunate in that it obscures the most beautiful room in the world belonging to the greatest King on earth." Badly lit rooms are the sign of a badly designed house. There were two courses open to Colbert. One was to accept the architecture and the scale imposed by Lescot and Lemercier and to try to get the best design available for the east front. The other was to pull it all down and start again.

The Italians were more likely to adopt the latter course. But Rainaldi's design was dismissed by Perrault as "extremely bizarre and without any taste of beautiful and simple architecture".

The only project taken seriously was that of Bernini. Arrogant as an artist, temperamental as a prima donna and radically incapable of appreciating anything French, he flew into a temper at the least criticism of his designs and personally insulted most of the people whom he met. It had become clear that the matter could not be settled by means of correspondence and Bernini had been invited to France. He arrived on 29 April, 1665.

The duel between Bernini and Colbert which ensued makes good reading. "It would be difficult to find two spirits more opposite," declared Perrault. Bernini was concerned simply and solely with creating theatrical effects of architecture. Colbert, with his usual eye for detail and for practicality, insisted on asking "where and how the King was to be lodged, how the service could be effected most commodiously"; he wanted to know everything about the distribution of the rooms, "even to the smallest which are no less necessary than the most important". Bernini "did not understand and did not wish to understand any of these details, fancying that it was beneath the dignity of a great architect like himself to condescend to such minutiae".

Louis had originally expressed a desire to preserve the work of his predecessors, but finally agreed, or pretended to agree, with Bernini's advice "de tout jeter par terre". Indeed, the Italian's project for a huge plaza before the east front would have meant pulling down everything between the Louvre and the Pont Neuf. He would have created a huge palace in a wholly Italian style. He made no concession to the difference of climate, let alone to the difference of architectural tradition; it would, as Fréart de Chambray pointed out, have overwhelmed the Tuileries.

Somewhat surprisingly, however, the design was accepted and the foundations were even begun. But the moment Bernini left the country the work was abandoned.

Colbert turned once more to the French architects. "Considering that none of the architects, either of France or of Italy, had wholly succeeded in their designs for the Louvre and having come to the conclusion that this work demanded the genius, the knowledge and the application of several persons who could contribute their different talents, helping and assisting each other mutually, and for this purpose having in mind M. Le Vau, Le Brun and Perrault", he summoned them to his presence. In April 1667, the Petit Conseil des Bâtiments came into existence. From this group originated the design, often attributed to Perrault alone, of the Colonnade, much as we see it today.

It is impossible to say exactly to whom the credit is due, but in a batch of designs, marked in Perrault's handwriting "Divers plans and elevations of the Louvre – useless", is an exquisite drawing by François d'Orbay, showing the right-hand pavilion and part of the façade adjoining. It contains most of the features of the actual building but avoids the only two which might expose it to adverse criticism – the disproportionately large central windows to the end

37 Project for the
colonnade of the Louvre
by François d'Orbay,
1667.

37 Project for the colonnade of the Louvre by François d'Orbay, 1667.

pavilions and the monotony of the skyline. D'Orbay has filled the semi-circles above the windows with bas-reliefs, thus reducing their height, and has crowned his balustrade with an impressive row of trophies.

Henri Sauval makes the interesting statement that "these great works were begun in 1667 and continued to the state in which they are seen at present in 1670, under the oversight and from the designs of Louis Le Vau.... François d'Orbay his pupil made no mean contribution to the perfection of this beautiful work and it is to these two excellent artists that should be given the glory for the design and execution of this superb edifice." It looks as if someone was trying to rob them of their credit.

In 1678 Louis decided on the final enlargement of Versailles. Work still continued on the Louvre until 1680, but the annual sums show a steady decrease. The history of the Louvre as a royal palace comes to an end. That of the Louvre as a museum of art had already begun.

It is not clear why Louis abandoned the Louvre. Some authors have linked it with a supposed dislike of Paris caused by the humiliations of the Fronde. But Louis's long period of residence both at the Louvre and the Tuileries does not support this theory. Two other considerations suggest themselves. One is that the isolation of Versailles had a symbolic value in representing the unique position of the Monarch. However magnificent the architecture of the Louvre, it could not avoid the suspicion of being *primus inter pares* among the other great buildings of the city. The other is simpler still. Versailles was not only a palace: it was a palace with a garden. The latter was, if anything, the more important of the two in the eyes of Louis.

6
The Château de Versailles:
Louis XIV

W HEN YOU ARRIVE at Versailles," wrote Voltaire, "from the courtyard side you see a wretched, top-heavy building, with a façade seven windows long, surrounded with everything which the imagination could conceive in the way of bad taste. When you see it from the garden side, you see an immense palace whose defects are more than compensated by its beauties."

Voltaire writes with all the self-confidence of eighteenth-century "good taste" but he does identify the essential duality of Versailles. Nobody seeing for the first time a picture of the entrance court alongside one of the garden front could ever infer that they were two sides of the same building.

Only an accurate understanding of its history can enable us to make sense of Versailles. It is a theme which it took a century and a half to develop. The topography of the building is no less complex than its history. "One might compare the palace of Versailles," wrote the comte d'Hézècques, "to a vast labyrinth. One needed a long familiarity to find one's way about." The visitor today requires the same. Here, more than anywhere else, a previous study of the history of the château and a leisurely approach to its seemingly endless rooms, pictures, statues, fountains and outbuildings will repay the trouble. Today we do not without adjustment see eye to eye with the France of the Grand Siècle. "Their small, bright world," wrote Lytton Strachey, "is apt to seem uninteresting and out of date unless we spend some patient sympathy in the discovery of the real charm and the real beauty that it contains."

Not only must we bestow this patient sympathy upon our study of Versailles, we must never let the glittering wealth of detail obscure the central meaning of the whole. More than any other royal house of France, Versailles was built as the expression of a theory of monarchy of which Louis XIV was himself the truest impersonation.

His formative years had seen the humiliations of the Fronde, when the natural indiscipline of the French, freed from the iron hand of Richelieu, had risen up in an almost frivolous revolt. The object of their hostility, however, had been the Queen Mother and her minister Mazarin. During a tour of the provinces the young King had been received with acclamations, but the cry had been "Vive le Roi tout seul".

By 1661 all that was over. On 9 March, Mazarin died at Vincennes "in an atmosphere of piety and abundance". It was the moment of Louis' true coming of age. "Only then," he wrote in his memoirs, "did it seem to me that I was King: born to be King." He expressed his intention to do the job – "de faire son métier de Roi". In this endeavour he was more than commonly favoured. He was himself endowed with a natural majesty. Everything that he did he did with elegance. "If fortune had not made him a great King," wrote a Venetian Ambassador, "it is certain that Nature gave him the appearance thereof." He was also a hard worker and he regulated his life with the minutest punctuality. "With a calendar and a watch," claimed Saint-Simon, "one could say what he was doing three hundred leagues away."

It was his good fortune to be served on all sides by men of the first quality. Some of the greatest names of French history, those distinguished in war, in politics, in art and literature and science were associated in the creation of Versailles and in the enrichment of the life of the Court. "It is with this august cortège of immortal genius," wrote Cardinal Maury, "that Louis XIV faces the judgement of posterity, backed by all the great men who had reached and retained their positions through his direction."

Versailles was the architectural expression of the Grand Siècle, but it was no lifeless monument, no "laboured quarry above ground". It was a theatre in which a drama was enacted, almost a cathedral in which a liturgy was performed, but the object of its worship was the person of the King. The *dramatis personae*, the priests and acolytes of the liturgy, bring the walls of the palace to life, filling the rooms with memories and decking the gardens with all the colourful paraphernalia of the Court of France. To those who know its history Versailles can never present the mournful aspect of an empty house.

For the life of the Court, those who experienced it must be allowed to speak for themselves. It is interesting how the key-note changes with each successive phase. They begin with a flourish and a fanfare; they settle down to the sheer grinding boredom that ensued. "Court life," wrote La Bruyère, "is a serious and melancholy game which requires application." Supreme among the memorialists of the reign is the duc de Saint-Simon. "Throughout the endless succession of his pages," writes Lytton Strachey, "the enormous panorama unrolls itself, magnificent, palpitating, alive." That is the impression that we must somehow recapture at Versailles.

Under Louis XIV Versailles was to grow from a little hunting lodge into the greatest palace in Europe. When completed it covered nearly twenty-five acres of ground; it contained 2,143 windows and 1,252 fireplaces. Towards the garden front it displays its vast length of 670 metres, the square block of the State Apartments projecting proudly against the elongated architecture of the Aisle du Nord and the Aisle des Princes. Towards the town it deploys its ever-widening series of forecourts – the Cour de Marbre, the Cour Royale, the Cour des Ministres. But when all had been built, the original hunting lodge – the "façade of seven windows" which Voltaire derided – remained embedded in the fabric forming the inner sanctuary known as the Cour de Marbre. It was in this part of the building that Louis finally placed the room which was the ceremonial centre of the palace – the Chambre du Roi.

In the course of its growth from Hunting Lodge to Palace, Versailles passed through two intermediate phases. The first was a *maison de plaisance* – a pretty

country house of brick and stone conveniently near Saint-Germain. It was a place to which Louis could invite a few favoured guests for a few delectable days of brilliant entertainment. It came to be known as the "Petit Château." The second phase was the enclosing of this *maison de plaisance* on three sides by a great stone palace known as the "Enveloppe". In the final enlargement this was to form the projection of the State Apartments on the garden side. The architect of both the earlier phases was Louis Le Vau, ably assisted by François d'Orbay. The final enlargement was the work of Jules-Hardouin Mansart.

The Petit Château is known to us by many drawings and engravings but above all by the superb oil painting by Pierre Patel in the Musée de Versailles. Patel has filled his canvas with perfect precision and faultless perspective, and by the skilful use of a shadow cast by a cloud has brought a vivid sense of realism to the scene. In the centre is the château, a bright array of brick and stone and slate and gilded lead "which makes it look," observed Sir Christopher Wren, "like a rich livery". All the leaden ornament on the roof was picked out in gold leaf which glittered in the sun.

The château proper is built round three sides of a quadrangle. At each of the four corners, where on an earlier building one would expect a tower, a square pavilion stands almost free of the main block. Corner touches corner just sufficiently to allow the rooms to connect, but imposing the aesthetic drawback of doorways in the angles of the rooms.

The open end of the courtyard is crossed by an arcade which forms a bridge, a passageway from wing to wing between two wrought iron balustrades, richly-gilded. The outer balustrade is continued in the form of a balcony right round the château, like a girdle of golden lace, and providing an exterior corridor to the rooms. For, as was usual in the seventeenth century, the building was one room thick, each room giving access to its neighbour. Le Vau further improved communications by adding four little staircases in the angles between the main block and the pavilions.

The most significant of Le Vau's improvements is shown in the new Cour des Offices. Two symmetrical blocks answer each other across the courtyard, standing back, as it were respecfully, so as to leave clear the vista of the château proper. Their architecture is dignified but simple, reflecting that of the main building but without its grandeur, as befitted their more humble status. The forecourt is nearly three times the width of the inner quadrangle of the château. In creating this disposition Le Vau foreshadowed the triple widening of the courtyards of the finished palace.

The block to the left of the Cour des Offices was devoted to stables; the one opposite contained the kitchens. To the right of this Patel shows a square building with a reservoir on its roof. This was the famous Grotte de Thétis. It was begun in 1665 and not finished until 1677. The King complained that he had never known anyone work so slowly as Denis Jolly.

The Grotto presented towards the Parterre du Nord a simple, one-storeyed façade pierced by three arches and decorated with rustic panels. The arches were closed by wrought iron gates of a most original design. The head of Apollo, Louis' personal device, was placed in the centre of the middle arch. The gilded bars of all three gates radiated from this centre and became as it were the shafts of light from the setting sun.

The gates opened into a vast, vaulted chamber on the opposite wall of which three enormous niches corresponded with the three arches of the façade. These were destined to receive the sculptures from which the Grotto took its name. The walls and ceilings were encrusted with shells. It took Jean de Launay, "rocailleur", two years to achieve this work, for which he was paid 20,619 livres. In August 1666 a water organ was purchased from the Sieur Desnots at Montmorency. It took Denis Jolly three years to transport and re-erect this in the Grotto.

As at Saint-Germain, the organ was activated by water pressure controlled with the most delicate skill; as at Saint-Germain the water also activated the voices of a whole chorus of little birds. "To the sound of the water," wrote Félibien, "the playing of the organ harmonises with the singing of the little birds ... and, by an artifice even more surprising, one hears an echo which repeats the gentle music so that the ears are no less charmed than the eyes."

In 1666 the first piece of sculpture was positioned and Girardon and Regnaudin paid a total of 18,000 livres for the central group. Apollo is shown having run his daily course across the sky and descended to the submarine abode of Thetis, where a group of nymphs refresh him after his labours. Marsy and Guérin received 14,318 and 7,750 livres respectively for the flanking groups of Apollo's horses being rubbed down by tritons. "When the Sun is tired and has accomplished his task," wrote La Fontaine, "he goes down to Thetis and enjoys a little relaxation. In the same way Louis goes off to take his ease." As the palace of Thetis was to Apollo, so was Versailles to Louis XIV – a place of pleasant recreation and amorous respite.

Louise de la Vallière, "the violet which hid itself in grass and blushed alike to be a mistress, a mother and a duchess", was at this time the focal point of Louis' life. The Abbé de Choisy, who has been a childhood friend of hers, leaves us a glowing description: "Mademoiselle de la Vallière was not one of those exquisite beauties whom one admires without loving. She was extraordinarily lovable and La Fontaine's verse: 'Her charm was more beautiful than her beauty' might have been written for her. She had a lovely

complexion, blonde hair, an agreeable smile, blue eyes and so tender and yet so modest a gaze that it won the beholder's heart and esteem equally." To this she added a character "gentle, generous and shy; she was always conscious of her failings and strove ceaselessly to overcome them".

On 5 May, 1665, Louis gave the first and most famous of the great fêtes at Versailles, the Plaisirs de l'Ile Enchantée. Officially it was offered to the Queen and the Queen Mother, but in fact it was all done to impress Louise de la Vallière.

Some six hundred guests had been invited. The duc de Saint-Aignan, as Premier Gentilhomme de la Chambre, was in charge of the operation. He chose from Ariosto's *Orlando Furioso* the theme of Roger and the magician Alcine.

An enchanted island had mysteriously appeared off the coast of France and from its fairy shores came Roger and his Knights to entertain the ladies with a tournament. It was a good pretext for the men to show off their brave demeanour and accomplished horsemanship in an impressive costume. The King, as Roger, took good care that no one should outshine him.

The second night the troop of Molière gave a performance of the *Princesse d'Elide*. The perspective of the Tapis Vert, framed in a proscenium of verdure by Carlo Vigarani, provided the setting. On the last evening Roger was delivered from the spell of Alcine and the Palace of the Magician disappeared in a tremendous display of pyrotechnics.

Thousands of candles and flambeaux lent their flattering light to the occasion and the woods and alleys resounded to the music of Lully.

In this, as in all things, it was Louis' destiny to be served by men of genius. Comedies specially written by Molière, set to music specially composed by Lully, created a standard of entertainment which can hardly ever have been surpassed.

Already the gardens were beginning to take the shape with which we are familiar today. Their use for these nocturnal receptions of the Court was to influence their design, for Louis needed a variety of large but enclosed spaces in which to set his theatricals, his concerts and his *al fresco* supper parties.

One of the pleasures of the "Plaisirs de l'Ile Enchantée" was a visit to the newly-built Ménagerie. There was as yet no Canal, but the Ménagerie is best located on a modern map as answering Trianon at the end of the south arm of the canal.

The building was in the form of a large octagonal pavilion crowned with a dome and cupola. It was two storeys high with a wrought iron balcony running right round beneath the first-floor windows. Each window overlooked a segment of the surrounding court, for the runs were disposed fanwise around the central pavilion. A small forecourt to the east, or entrance side, provided two apartments with bedroom, ante-room and garde-robe.

It was all extremely expensive. As early as 28 September, 1663, Colbert was becoming anxious about the money spent on Versailles. "This house is more a matter for the pleasure and diversion of Your Majesty than for his glory. . . . While he has been spending such large sums on this house, he has neglected the Louvre, which is assuredly the most superb palace that is in the world and more worthy of the greatness of Your Majesty . . . Oh! what a pity that the greatest and most virtuous of Kings should be measured by the yardstick of Versailles."

During the next few years the projects for the Louvre finally resulted in the acceptance of Claude Perrault's design for the Colonnade, but Versailles was gaining ground in the heart of the King. In 1668 Louis chose it as the scene for the Grand Divertissement Royal. There could be no question of such an entertainment being given indoors. The château was not large enough, but the gardens were, and a series of outdoor salons was specially contrived to provide the setting for this unforgettable occasion.

The success of the entertainment, the facilities which were offered by the gardens and the insufficiency of the house itself – all must have been present in the King's mind when the fateful decision was made. Versailles was to be considerably enlarged.

This was the turning point in its history. The Petit Château as depicted by Patel offered a really beautiful example of a French country house of the mid-seventeenth century. It occupied its knoll in a satisfying manner, making use of the sloping ground on all sides to provide an Orangery to the south, a long perspective to the west and gently-inclined parterre to the north. It was delightful, but it was too small. Any extension of its architecture would have merely ruined its appearance. The problem of enlargement was extremely difficult.

In the end it was solved by the creation of the building which we see today – Voltaire's "immense palace whose defects are more than compensated by its beauties". The palatial façades of Europe usually err either in the direction of the monotonous or of the over-ornate. The garden front of Versailles avoids both of these defects and fully merits Voltaire's praise. But it was only achieved by a costly process of trial and error.

As early as 1665 Louis was contemplating plans for pulling down the Petit Château and replacing it with a far grander building. Le Vau's designs for this project, which were discovered in Stockholm by Alfred Marie, included vast octagonal rotundas at the corners of the west front. Colbert, who disliked Le Vau, was scathing in his criticism. "The round figures which he affects for his Vestibules and Salons are in very bad architectural taste, especially from the outside." In a series of memoirs he underlines the errors in Le Vau's project, sets forth the arguments for retaining and for abolishing the Petit Château and demonstrates the inadequacy of the site. "It is impossible to create a great house in this space. The steep declivity of the parterres and avenues does not permit of any extension or further occupation of the site without turning everything upside down and incurring a prodigious expense."

Nevertheless the building of Le Vau's project was put in hand. In 1665 and 1666 some 175,000 livres were paid for "masonry at Versailles". But then the payments cease. Charles Perrault mentions this abortive attempt. "A beginning was made with certain buildings which, when half built, were not satisfactory and were pulled down forthwith. Later, the three blocks were erected which surrounded the Petit Château and which fronted the gardens on three sides."

That was not until 1668. There seems to have been a period during which Louis XIV rather lost interest in Versailles. It was just at this time that Le Vau and d'Orbay were commissioned to complete the Tuileries. In 1665 Bernini was invited to submit designs for the Louvre. Colbert must have hoped to see his dearest dreams fulfilled. He was to be disappointed. In 1668 the new project of Le Vau's was put in hand which was to result in the second phase of Versailles, the Enveloppe.

We can easily form an idea of the Enveloppe by making certain adjustments in the imagination to the present garden fronts. Walking through from the Cour Royale to the Parterre du Nord we have, stretching away to the left, the great façade of the Appartement du Roi. The first section of the front, as far as the fourth window, is of Mansart's building. The twin pilasters, crowned with a corresponding trophy on the skyline, mark the beginning of Le Vau's Enveloppe.

The façade is punctuated by three porticoes; between each pair of porticoes there is a niche, with a rectangular bas-relief in the panel above. The architrave above the niche marks the original height of Le Vau's windows, which were not round arched but surmounted by similar bas-reliefs. Le Vau's windows came down to floor level, but there was no balustrade. This lower positioning of the windows created a top-heavy appearance. Mansart raised the height of the windows by half their width in the form of a semi-circular arch. He also raised the apparent base of the window by the insertion of a balustrade. He thus gave a sort of face-lift to the façade which was a great improvement.

On the west front the same adjustment must be made mentally to the windows, but here there was a dramatic difference of form. The façade today divides into three sections, each of which centres upon a portico. These divisions are marked off by twin pilasters on the first floor and by half trophies on the skyline. These half trophies were clearly meant to mark a corner. And so they did. In Le Vau's building, the central section of the façade only existed at ground-floor level. The façade of the first and second storeys was recessed back behind the terrace so formed, leaving clear a front of three windows on either side. This gave a bold relief to the west front which Mansart had to sacrifice in order to build the Galerie des Glaces.

The year 1678, with the annexation of Franche Comté, marked the flood tide of Louis' military glory. It was no longer endurable that his magnificence should be inadequately housed. It was decided that Versailles should become the permanent seat of both the Court and the Government.

We have already seen the way in which Mansart tackled the final enlargement. Two great wings, thrown out to north and south, left the stately block of the Enveloppe a mere projection on the garden front, while on the entrance side a more satisfactory solution was found to the fusion of the two styles different in scale, colour and materials.

Beyond the Cour Royale another courtyard, wider still – the Cour des Ministres – afforded accommodation to the Ministers of the Crown, while across the Place d'Armes, in the angles formed by the convergence of the three avenues, the Grande Ecurie and the Petite Ecurie were built for the reception of 2,400 horses and 200 coaches. These beautiful buildings have a corresponding symmetry which helps to unite them with the palace and to perfect the whole. Within the concave sweep of each façade there stretches a network of great vaulted galleries and spacious courtyards which drew from the Elector of Hanover the confession that he was not so well housed as the horses of the King of France.

Besides the royal horses, the Grande Ecurie housed the royal pages. To become a page of the Bedchamber one had to show proof of nobility dating back for two hundred years. In return, the boys received a good, if spartan, education.

South of the Cour des Ministres was the building known as the Grand Commun. It contained six hundred rooms and offered sixty apartments to the high functionaries of the Court. Some fifteen hundred people, including such distinguished artists as Le Nôtre, lived here in the Grand Commun, which had a life of its own and even its own chapel.

The Great Kitchen was also in the Grand Commun and here was prepared and served the food for those whose position entitled them to "bouche à la Cour" – the right to eat and drink at the King's expense. The Bouche du Roi, where the food for the King's table was prepared, was required by etiquette to be within the palace. The King's Kitchen was in the main building between the Grand Commun and the Aisle des Princes. The food, the "Viande du Roi", was taken in solemn procession through the château to the room in which the King ate.

What was left after the King had eaten went to the table of the Gentilshommes Servants, known collectively as the "serdeau". What *they* left was sold to the townspeople at a special market known as the "baraques du serdeau".

The years 1684 and 1685 were those of the greatest activity. In 1684 4,598,190 livres were spent on Versailles. In 1685 the figure rose to just over six million; the highest figure recorded. On 24 August, 1684, Dangeau noted "during the last week there was an expenditure of 250,000 livres on Versailles. Each day there were 22,000 men and 6,000 horses at work."

40 The Enveloppe from the entrance side. Engraving by I. Silvestre.

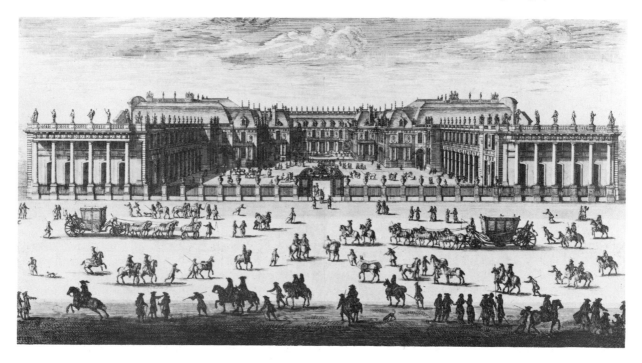

The remarkable painting by Van der Meulen at Buckingham Palace showing the forecourts of Versailles during the final enlargements, portrays the conditions in which the Court often had to live. A procession of royal coaches is seen arriving in the middle of the crowds of workmen and the clutter of their materials and machinery. The Court was often obliged to occupy a palace, much of which was under scaffolding, and to endure the proximity of thousands of workmen who laboured both day and night. In May 1682, the Dauphine, about to give birth to the duc de Bourgogne, had to move from her room, the hammering of the carpenters being so loud as to prevent her sleeping.

In 1684 Louis spent the autumn at Chambord and Fontainebleau. He fixed 15 November for the return to Versailles and Louvois went on ahead to hasten the works. Every evening a courier arrived from Fontainebleau to collect his report which Louis received at his *lever* the next morning. His comments, written in the margin, reached Louvois the same day. The weather had been very bad and Louvois had to break the news that the work was nowhere near finished. Louis accepted the inevitable, merely adding: "Pay more attention to my bedroom than to the rest ... the smell of gilding is most unpleasant." Louvois replied: "Bontemps [Premier Valet de Chambre] has been instructed to keep a large fire going and to open the windows from time to time."

In most of the rooms an open fire was the only form of heating, but among the many installations of this period there is reference made to a "machine pour donner la chaleur". Unfortunately it is not related what the machine was nor how it provided heat.

On 15 November, 1684, the Court returned from Fontainebleau to find the Galerie des Glaces complete in all its glory and lit with a thousand candles. It met with immediate acclaim. "Nothing could equal the beauty of this gallery at Versailles," wrote Madame de Sévigné; "this sort of royal beauty is unique in the world."

It is difficult today, standing in this noble apartment, empty and unfurnished, to recapture the astonishment and admiration with which it was seen for the first time. It was the apotheosis of Louis XIV. Two hundred and thirty eight feet by thirty-five, it did not have the disproportionate length of the Galerie d'Ulysse at Fontainebleau, which was nearly twice as long and only half as wide. To do honour to the greatness of France, even the classical orders were set aside; in place of the Doric, the Ionian or the Corinthian, Le Brun had been charged to design an *ordre français* which incorporated the Sun, the *fleurs de lys* and two cocks set against the palms of Victory.

But it was in its furnishings that the greatest glory of the gallery was to be seen. Against the background of the marble pilasters and the tall windows, each reflected in its corresponding mirror, and Le Brun's ceiling with its crowd of allegorical figures, each reflecting some corresponding victory of Louis', we must set two enormous Savonnerie carpets covering the full length of the floor; curtains of "thick, white damask brocaded in gold with His Majesty's monogram" lined the windows; between each window stood a solid silver table of the most exquisite workmanship and in each window recess a massive silver tub containing an orange tree; seventeen great silver chandeliers and twenty-six smaller ones of crystal and countless smaller

candelabra on gilded gueridons lent an indescribable lustre to the scene.

It is probably easiest to evoke the effect of the Grande Galerie by visiting the copy made of it at Herrenchiemsee by Ludwig II of Bavaria in 1873. His artists were among the first real scholars of Versailles since the Ancien Régime and their replicas are accurate in most respects. It is lit on certain occasions by 1,848 candles.

It must be remembered, when looking at Versailles, that much of the life of the Court was night life and the rooms are seen at their best by candlelight. The gilding and the marble, which can look so oppressive by day, spring magically to life when highlighted at a thousand points by the flames of the candles. The imagination must also supply the additional decoration of the gorgeous costumes and scintillating jewellery of the courtiers. "Add to that," wrote the author of the *Mercure Galant*, "the brilliance of the Court in full dress and the sparkle of the precious stones with which most of the ladies' dresses are adorned."

By daylight the Gallery must not be considered in isolation from its view. Its seventeen windows, Blondel noted, provided it with "the most beautiful outlook that it would be possible to imagine". Blondel, writing two generations later, was not uncritical of the style Louis XIV, yet he could describe this gallery as "le plus beau lieu du monde". As for Le Brun's ceiling, the painting there "ensures the immortal glory of the French school".

School was the right word. As Anthony Blunt has pointed out, "Le Brun produced no single work which one is tempted to linger over ... but in creating such an ensemble as the decoration of Versailles he was a master".

The Grande Galerie formed the connecting link between the three main

41 The final forms of the entrance front before the building of the Chapel. I. Silvestre.

apartments of the palace. At the south end, in the corner of the block, was the Salon de la Paix. From here ran the Appartement de la Reine occupying the first floor of the whole of the south façade. At the north extremity of the gallery was the Salon de la Guerre from which ran the Grand Appartement occupying the whole of the north façade. Behind the gallery, in the original west range of the Petit Château, began the Appartement du Roi, which continued all along the north side of the Cour de Marbre. At the end of this, and giving access both to the King's rooms and to the Grand Appartement, was the magnificent staircase, the Escalier des Ambassadeurs.

Three times a week, on Mondays, Wednesdays and Thursdays, the King gave a reception for the Court in the Grand Appartement. A fascinating account has been left of one of these "jours d'Appartement" by the Abbé Bourdelot in 1683.

Full of eager anticipation, and not a little trepidation, he waited in the thronged Vestibule. Here Bontemps, the Premier Valet de Chambre, scrutinised all comers "with the eyes of Argus". Then Monsieur de Joyeux entered and called his name; the Abbé dived after him towards the Cabinets du Roi, "the door closed and I found myself in the middle of the royal household". The Queen was there, and the Dauphine, the duchesse d'Orléans, the duchesse de Bourbon and the princesse de Conti. The duc de Vermandois, son of the King by Mlle de la Vallière, came and spoke to him.

From here he passed into the Grand Appartement. "Nothing in the world could be more beautiful, more magnificent nor more astonishing. Just imagine the brilliance of a hundred thousand candles in this great suite of apartments; I thought it was all ablaze, for the sun in July is no brighter. The furnishings of gold and silver had their own particular lustre, as did the gilding and the marble."

The magnificence of the decorations was only equalled by the splendour of the company. "In the Grand Appartement the flower of the Court was gathered, all the Princes and Princesses, Lords and Ladies, Officers of the Crown, Generals of the Army, besides an infinite number of Persons of Quality, superbly dressed. I found myself in the middle of all this pomp, the only man from the University and accustomed to a life of retirement."

In the Salon de Mars the tables were set for gaming; "the crowd was immense, but without noise or tumult; there is something august about the place which imposes respect." Next door, in the Salle de Diane, the King was playing billiards – "he is the master in this as in everything else".

Doubling back through the Salon de Mars, Bourdelot now crossed the Salle de Mercure; "from there I passed into a room [the Salon d'Apollon] which enchants with every object which meets the eye. The King's throne stands there. The hangings of crimson velvet embroidered with gold impose respect. The pilasters are in high relief; their bases and capitals seemed to be the work of goldsmiths: nothing could be more august or majestic."

The paintings left the Abbé in raptures: "Ought one not to go down on one's knees before that Paul Veronese of Our Lord at Cana?" The dancing also delighted him: "There were many ladies, both young and beautiful and scintillating with jewellery; they were marvellously graceful. The princesse de Conti, 'la Belle', carried off the prize for dancing; all eyes were fixed on the young princess." But the central attraction was always the King himself. "He did not sit on his throne; there were four cushions on the edge of the dais; I was astonished to see him sitting there quite informally."

It is easy to imagine the feelings of this quiet, academic man as he drove away from the brilliant Court of which he had been the privileged spectator. The vividness of the impression which it made upon him is clear from the liveliness of the account which he wrote. In strong relief against the marble and crimson velvet and gold embroidery, and in brilliant contrast to the more than ordinary splendour of the guests, stands out the figure of the King, magnificently informal against the formal setting which he had created, "faisant les honneurs de chez lui en galant homme". "The supreme pleasure", wrote Madame de Sévigné in the same year, "was to spend four whole hours with the Sovereign, to partake in his pleasures and he in ours."

Certain additions need to be made to Bourdelot's account from the description of Nicodémus Tessin, an architect sent by the King of Sweden to report on the decorations of Versailles in 1687.

In the first place Tessin came in summer and Bourdelot in winter. There were two sets of hangings for all the rooms, a *meuble d'été* and a *meuble d'hiver*. They were changed during the Voyage de Fontainebleau which always took place during the autumn. Bourdelot describes the *meuble d'hiver* which was of a rich velvet designed to show off the pictures to their best advantage in candlelight. The *meuble d'été*, which was meant to be seen in broad daylight, was of an almost unbelievable richness.

In the Salle de Mercure there was a State Bed. It was known as a *lit de parade* and was not meant to be used. Louis did sleep in it for a few weeks in 1701 when his new bedroom was being redecorated and here, for nine days after his death, he lay in state. We must refurnish this room in our imagination with a great four-poster, surmounted by an impressive canopy, fringed and tasselled in gold and proudly plumed with ostrich feathers. The hook from which this canopy was suspended can be seen on the ceiling. We must isolate the bed behind a solid silver balustrade and provide a silver table, silver chandelier and eight silver candelabra to match.

"The magnificence of this room," wrote Tessin, "is quite astonishing; the hangings are separated by pilasters of gold embroidery, standing out some three inches in relief; the figures are all nearly life sized and are picked out in solid silver to represent the naked flesh. The rest is embroidered in gold, standing out, in some places, up to five inches, particularly in the trophies in the lower parts."

The *meuble d'été* had been made under the direction of Madame de Montespan at the convent of St. Joseph. It was a technique known as "in the Persian manner" which could deceive the most practised eye, "mistaking for the work of the chisel that which was pure embroidery". When Louis XV had these hangings melted down in 1743 they realised 52,000 livres.

This was the fate also of all the silver furniture, but as early as 1689. Dangeau recorded in December of that year: "The King desires that throughout the kingdom all the silver which is used in the rooms should be melted down and taken to the Mint . . . and to set an example himself he had melted down all the beautiful silver furniture, regardless of the richness of the workmanship."

Some 2,500 pieces were removed and realised 2,500,000 livres.

One cannot help being conscious, when reading the accounts of life at Versailles, of a great change which came over the Court as the seventeenth century neared its close. Gone were the gay crowds who had swarmed after Louis on his *promenade des jardins*, applauded the fêtes, complained about the lack of accommodation and rolled wearily back in their great coaches to Paris or Saint-Germain at the break of day. They may not have come from purely disinterested motives – "jeunesse du Prince, source de belles fortunes" – but there had been a spirit of freshness and of unfeigned enthusiasm for the delights which they were offered. Now the courtiers settled down to the regular routine of interest and intrigue, of flattery and back-biting. At the beginning of the century, Saint-François de Sales had written: "It is a great loss of time to be at Court, and for many it will mean losing Eternity also." Now, at the end of the century, even Mlle de Lafayette, formerly so enthusiastic about Versailles, commented on the sameness of everything and every day: "Always the same pleasures, always at the same hours, and always with the same people."

Above all La Bruyère exposed the degrading influence of the life of the Court upon the character of the courtiers. "The Court does not make one contented; it prevents one from being contented anywhere else." "The Court is like a building made of marble: I mean that it is composed of men who are very hard but highly polished."

Towards the turn of the century, considerable alterations and redecorations were carried out in the interior of Versailles. They chiefly concerned the suite of rooms lit by the first-floor windows of the Cour de Marbre which formed the King's personal apartment – "private" would be the wrong word in talking of Louis XIV.

In the centre of the east façade was the Salon Carré; originally intended as a sort of withdrawing room from the Grande Galerie, it was built two storeys high and accorded a solid architectural décor, with white pilasters fluted in gold and a rich cornice and frieze. It was the most important and imposing room in the suite and doubtless it was this consideration which led Louis to make it his bedroom, for the ceremonial functions of the Chambre du Roi made it necessarily the centre of the life of the Court.

The two ceremonies of the *lever* and the *coucher* were of the deepest significance. To Louis etiquette was no mockery, no hollow façade behind which a King might hide his human frailty, but the liturgical expression of Absolute Monarchy. Voltaire, in his *Siècle de Louis XIV*, observed that the Frenchman regarded his King "as a sort of Divinity", an opinion which is reflected in Louis' memoirs where he defined God as "a superior Power of which our royal power is a part". In this spirit he exacted, and was accorded, a deference not far removed from worship, and the routine acquired thereby a ceremonial significance. It also achieved the final atrophy of the nobility. Men who found it beneath them to do work of the least utility craved for admittance to the most ordinary details of Louis' life; the height of honour was to hold the candle for him at his *coucher*.

Framed in a shallow alcove and cordoned off behind a gilded balustrade, the bed occupied the focal point in the apartment. It was a stately four-poster crowned with ostrich feathers at the corners. It had two sets of hangings, one of crimson velvet laced with gold for use in winter, and one of gold and silver flowered damask for summer. Courtiers made their low obeisance to this bed even in the absence of the King. So greatly was the holy of holies revered that the customary precedence in going out of a room was reversed, it being the greater honour to remain a moment longer in the royal presence. Thus do priests reverse their precedence for leaving the sanctuary.

For many who were not distinguished enough to have the *entrée* for the more exclusive functions, much of the day might be spent waiting in the Anteroom outside Louis' bedroom. In 1701 this was also redecorated and it was decided to make use of the space above the cornice for a decorative frieze. Louis himself determined what the subject matter was to be: "jeux d'enfants". The playing boys form as it were a garland round the ceiling, and their dancing figures and flowing lines of their scant vesture give an almost Grecian elegance to the room.

Although it was the *oeil de boeuf* window which gave the room its name, the playing-boy frieze is of greater significance, for it marks the birth of a new style at Versailles. Unconsciously, the duchesse de Bourgogne was its mother.

In 1697 she had come from Savoy as a girl of twelve to all the stale solemnity and settled routine of Versailles; as Saint-Simon so aptly put it, "she brought the whole place to life". Without interesting herself particularly in architecture, she was the source of a great rejuvenation in the heart of the King which found its expression in the redecorations of 1701. For her the Ménagerie was enlarged to provide a little private residence. Mansart was instructed to draw up the plans and as usual Louis noted his comments in the margin. They are most revealing. "It seems to me that there is something to be changed," he observed; "that the decorations are too serious and that there must be youth mingled with whatever is done." On another occasion he struck the same note. "Il faut de l'enfance répandue partout."

Marie-Adélaïde de Savoie was the granddaughter of Henriette d'Angleterre, the first wife of Louis' brother the duc d'Orléans. Not pretty, but of an inexhaustible vivacity, she had made an immediate impression upon Louis and upon Madame de Maintenon, and it was in her company more than anywhere else that they may be said to have enjoyed a family life together. She brought a breath of fresh air to the *après soupers* of the royal family, perching on the arms of chairs, throwing herself onto Louis' lap, rummaging among his papers and offering her opinions where they were not asked for. Louis was delighted. The one thing that he had lacked most, the easy charm of a private home, was now brought to him by his little granddaughter-in-law. It made him young again and brought the vital spark once more into the palace in which he had immured his Court.

The rejuvenating effect of the duchesse de Bourgogne must be set against the austere influence of Madame de Maintenon, to whom Louis was secretly married. While the younger set were becoming carefree and irresponsible, their elders were inclining towards a life of strict religious observance.

The religion of the courtier was not necessarily insincere; the letters of Fénelon are sufficient witness to that, but there were, as ever, hypocrites as well and, as always, they were the more conspicuous party. Saint-Simon has

42 The Enveloppe from
the north with the Etang
de Clagny in foreground.
I. Silvestre.

an anecdote about the ladies who attended Vespers punctiliously – provided
that the King was there. One day Brissac, major of the Guards, played a
practical joke upon them: as soon as the ladies were assembled he ordered the
guards to retire, saying that the King would not be coming. The guards were
turned back by their officers, who were in the secret, but not before most of
the ladies had withdrawn. Presently the King arrived and was astonished by
the smallness of the congregation. "At the conclusion of the prayers, Brissac
related what he had done, not without dwelling upon the piety of the Court
ladies. The King and all who accompanied him laughed heartily. The story
soon spread, and these ladies would have strangled Brissac if they had been
able."

Madame de Maintenon – "votre solidité" as Louis once called her – ended
by acquiring a real disgust for the Court. She had attained the highest position
that she could have dreamed of attaining and it merely left her unsatisfied; "je
meurs de tristesse dans une fortune qu'on aurait peine à imaginer."

Born a Huguenot and converted in later life to Catholicism, she has often
been reproached for the bigoted and puritanical nature of her religion. But
this could have been the inevitable reaction against the vices of the Court.
Among these the sin of Sodom was assuming alarming proportions. François
Hébert, curé de Versailles, mentions in his memoirs the representations which
he made to Madame de Maintenon on the subject. She assured him that she
had pressed Louis to take action but had received the answer: "Am I then to
begin with my own brother?"

Madame de Maintenon was also reproached, especially by the duchesse
d'Orléans, with responsibility for the ferocious persecution of Huguenots
connected with the revocation of the Edict of Nantes. The marquis de la Fare,

however, put the blame elsewhere. "It is said that Le Tellier and Louvois did not desire the revocation for which the sanctimonious hypocrites were campaigning so enthusiastically. Yet when Le Tellier signed the declaration in his capacity as Chancellor, he exclaimed in the words of Simeon: 'Lord, now lettest thou thy servant depart in peace.'"

Whatever the true nature of Madame de Maintenon's religion, her secretary Jeanne d'Aumâle leaves us in no doubt as to the extent of her charity towards the poor. "I have made up her accounts on more than one occasion," she claims; "she donated between fifty-four and sixty thousand livres a year from her own income." Charity and devotion, bigotry and hypocrisy — all had their place in the religion of Versailles.

It would be wrong, however, to connect the building of the new chapel with the influence of Madame de Maintenon. She opposed the idea on the grounds of extravagance and because she thought the King would be unable to continue living at Versailles.

The chapel was Louis' last important contribution to the palace. The original project of Mansart had been for a building very much in the style of the Grand Appartement, particularly in the use of the same brawn-like marble for the walls. But the project was delayed by the War of the League of Augsburg. In 1699, when it was taken up again, Louis had changed his mind in one important respect. Instead of the marble he decided to use the beautiful white stone known as *banc royal* which gives the chapel its particular charm.

Mansart, now Surintendant des Bâtiments as well as Premier Architecte, was ably seconded by his son-in-law Robert de Cotte. It was he who was responsible for the lighter treatment of the decorations which announced the beginning of the eighteenth century.

True to the traditions of lay and ecclesiastical architecture, the chapel of Versailles provides the only important vertical accent in this vast lay-out of horizontal lines. Although it is made up of purely classical elements, the conception is recognizably medieval in form, but with the relative importance of nave and triforium inverted, for the royal tribune is on the level with the first floor of the palace. The last twelve piers of the nave — reflecting in their number the twelve Apostles — support the twelve columns of the tribune, which in turn uphold the barrel vault, pierced by clerestory windows, which illuminate the painted ceiling.

The decoration of the twelve piers, done in a low relief that gives an almost brocade-like texture to the stone, represents the Stations of the Cross, but it is a most unusual treatment of that theme in which the artist has taken the line of discreet allusion to avoid offending the eyes of a fastidious Court or disturbing, by any too stirring scenes, the architectural *ordonnance*. Thus a cherub holding the purse of Judas suffices to evoke the Agony in the Garden and a crowing cock to convey the bitter remorse of St. Peter.

One is tempted to compare the chapel at Versailles with that of Timon's Villa:

> *On painted ceilings you devoutly stare*
> *Where sprawl the Saints of Verrio or Laguerre,*
> *On gilded clouds in fair expansion lie*

And bring all Paradise before your eye.
To rest the Cushion and soft Dean invite,
Who never mentions Hell to ears polite.

In 1710 the chapel was finished. On 25 April Louis had a motet sung to try the effect of music in it; on 22 May he went again, inspected the whole minutely and had another motet sung. The acoustics of the chapel are magnificent and the music written for it answers admirably to the stately pomp of the architecture and the colourful animation of the painted ceiling. A performance here of Lully's *Plaude Laetare Gallia*, intended for use at the baptism of a Dauphin, or of Lalande's *Te Deum* is an experience never to be forgotten.

At either end of the royal tribune the balcony curves into a small quarter circle to round off the corners. These projections were used for the accommodation of two little glazed kiosks, each "une lanterne dorée et fermée de glaces", where princesses who were indisposed could hear the Mass. One of them was always occupied by Madame de Maintenon.

To appreciate the chapel we ought to reverse the order of the regulation visit and to follow the *chemin du Roi*. Every day Louis went from his Bedroom into the adjoining Cabinet du Conseil, entered the Grande Galerie and passed right down the imposing enfilade of the Grand Appartement to attend Mass in the Chapel. Every room was a profusion of coloured marbles, silver furniture and gilded decorations. The doors of the Salon d'Hercule were thrown open and the King passed into the Vestibule of the chapel ...

The contrast is astonishing. In place of the heavy marble, the pure, pale-cream stone and delicate play of light upon the carvings create an entirely different atmosphere, cool and refreshing; it is as if one had cast off the colourful paraphernalia of royalty. But if colour is the attribute of royalty, that of divinity is light. The tall windows, the open colonnade and the pale stone of the chapel make the fullest use of this element.

The side windows of the ground floor offer a restricted illumination to the nave, but those of the apse, where the arcade curves into a graceful ambulatory, provide dramatic lighting to the altar. Gilding – conspicuously absent from the rest of the chapel – is used to focus attention on the sanctuary and to conduct the eye thence, by way of the organ case, to the brilliant profusion of the painted ceiling by Antoine Coypel in close collaboration with Charles La Fosse, who was responsible for the scene of the Resurrection in the quarter dome or *cul de four* above the apse.

It would be a fitting note on which to end a tour, for the building of the chapel marked the completion of the palace.

The landscape painters of the seventeenth century acquired an astonishing skill in imagining from the air what they could only see from the ground. One of the greatest of these painters, Jean-Baptiste Martin, has left us a bird's eye view which is the perfect portrait of Versailles.

The artist has set himself to tell us all the truth. His accuracy is scrupulous but his detail never obtrusive. He shows to its full advantage the long, regular procession of the forecourts, the complex, many-faceted construction of the roof. He has drawn his axis slightly oblique, thus counterbalancing the

asymmetry of the chapel, which stands like a miniature cathedral, its golden belfry riding high above the rooftops of the palace.

From an increased altitude, such as the viewpoint taken by Patel, the whole lay-out of the gardens would have appeared behind   to the left the Orangerie, swelled to a gargantuan size, and beyond it the Pièce d'Eau des Suisses, lying like a silver mirror beneath the sombre woodlands of the Heights of Satory; to the right the smaller but more ornate ensemble of the Bassin de Neptune. Behind the château an elaboration of parterres gives place to the regimented plantations of the lower gardens with their marble colonnades and kiosks, their statues and urns standing, like outposts of Art, against the walls of foliage, with here and there a stately fountain raising its crystal column among the treetops. Below lies the great cruciform Canal with a gay flotilla riding its waters – the huge brigantine, flying the royal standard and decked with an awning of blue and silver; four chaloupes in red, blue, green and yellow, and the violet of the Neapolitan felucca presenting a very colourful spectacle to the eye.

But the imagination is not answerable to the law of gravity: it must soar to greater heights if it is to comprehend the whole of the Grand Design. At a more considerable elevation, when the features of the park appear as a plan reduced to a scale that would include not only the Ménagerie and Trianon, but the town of Versailles, the Château de Clagny and more distant Marly, a new feature of the countryside would become apparent: the great chain of

43 From the Pièce d'Eau des Suisses, before the building of the Chapel.

reservoirs linking Marly to Versailles, Versailles to Rambouillet and Rambouillet to the Valley of the Eure to provide water for the embellishment of the royal garden.

The interior of the palace offered a scene no less majestic, revealing a noble unity of design and an astonishing richness of furniture. Everywhere it seemed as if Midas had run his fingers over the decorations, leaving them sparkling gold.

And yet there was something lacking.

The whole character of the place had been one of growth – a character which gives the study of Versailles in the interest of a biography. But, like so many things on this earth, it proved more enjoyable in the getting than in the possessing. It had been Louis' ambition to own the greatest palace in Europe. He had achieved it, yet the happiest moments in his life were when that ambition was as yet unattained. It had been his ambition to surround himself with a brilliant Court, but the most brilliant moments had been those of the first fêtes. The finished product seemed only to testify to the truth of La Bruyère's words: "A healthy mind acquires at Court a taste for solitude and retreat." They testify to the truth of the paradox that nothing fails like success.

How different was the Versailles of those last days! And yet it was chiefly different in that it remained the same. Change and development had been the keynotes of its history; now they were silent. Only the seasons now brought their successive changes to the trees and hedges of the garden, clothing their naked branches with a light veil of foliage and making the avenues cool and shady for the ensuing summer; but to no purpose. In vain did autumn succeed summer, covering the plantations with its gold and umber mantle "comme une vieille tapisserie de château"; but spring held no promise and autumn no enchantment since the death of the duchesse de Bourgogne. That had been the bitterest blow to Louis, "la seule grande douleur de sa vie". But it was more than that; it was the end of the Grand Siècle at Versailles. "Tout est mort ici," sighed Madame de Maintenon; "la vie en est ôtée."

Pitifully reduced in numbers, the Royal Family continued to assemble, as it always had, in the Cabinet des Perruques after supper. Madame, delighted to be admitted to the inner sanctuary of a Court which she had always criticised with malevolence, now joined the circle, and the old Maréchal de Villeroi, veteran of Louis' campaigning days, came and sat with them in the gathering gloom of the evenings. Then the musicians in the next room would fill the air with the light strains of Lully, and almost imperceptibly the conversation drifted into reminiscence and they talked on into the night of the fêtes of the old days and the *Plaisirs de l'Ile Enchantée*.

The Gardens

"A BEAUTIFUL HOUSE," wrote the English philosopher John Locke, "but even more a beautiful garden." Unfortunately Locke did not have the gift of lucid description and his account of Versailles is disappointing, but he does give us an interesting sense of priorities. It would be absurd to consider the Versailles of Le Vau and Le Brun without the complementary landscaping of Le Brun and Le Nôtre.

Locke made his first visit on 23 June, 1677. The château was still in the state in which Le Vau had left it, but the gardens had already, in broad outline, assumed the form with which we are familiar today. Above all the Great Canal had been created, which set the scale for the whole gigantic lay-out.

Seldom can a hundred hectares (some 250 acres) of land have undergone such a metamorphis. The duc de Saint-Simon described the original site as "the most sad and barren of places, with no view, no water and no woods". Colbert, as we have seen, warned Louis of the difficulties which confronted him: "It would not be possible to create a great house in this space without a complete upheaval and without incurring a prodigious expense." But Louis was undeterred. "It is in the difficult matters," he wrote in his memoirs, "that we give proof of our ability." Since Nature had not provided the Val de Galie with any features of distinction, Le Nôtre set out to create a landscape worthy of its destiny, and he went about the task with that broadness of vision which was his title deed to greatness.

It was he who ordained the lay-out of the Grand Design, giving the land itself a new symmetry and a new shape – now making use of the natural declivity of the site (there is a drop of some thirty-two metres from the Palace to the Canal) to form a series of terraces; now hollowing out a vast amphitheatre for the Parterre de Latone; now clothing the slopes with woods and hedges within which were contrived bosquets of an astonishing variety.

It is impossible to appreciate the work of Le Nôtre without seeking to answer the question: "What was the purpose of his elaborate creation?"

We might begin by taking note of the nomenclature of Le Nôtre's garden. The words with which he describes its features are largely drawn from the vocabulary of the interior of a house – names like the *Galerie* des Antiques, the *Salle* du Conseil, the *Salle* des Festins, the *Cabinet* or even the *Appartement* de Verdure; words like the *Tapis* Vert, the *Buffet* d'Eau or the Parterre de *Broderie*, which are all suggestive of indoor architecture and furnishing. It is as if the gardens were conceived as a vast open-air extension of the palace, and in fact the uses to which these Cabinets de Verdure were put reflect, as often as not, those of the State Rooms. We find them serving for supper parties, for concerts, for theatricals, for dances: was not the most elaborate of the bosquets known as the *Salle de Bal*?

The principle of the *bosquet* is clearly illustrated by painters such as J.-B. Martin. His view of Versailles from the north, showing the huge Bassin de

Neptune in the foreground, accurately portrays two thickly wooded enclosures which lay to either side of the Allée d'Eau: to the left the Bosquet de l'Arc de Triomphe and to the right the Bosquet des Trois Fontaines. In the centre of each, and closely embowered by the surrounding trees, is an open space, exposed to the sun but sheltered from the wind, which forms the *salle* or *cabinet*, set off by an elaborate architectural feature and decorated with an alternation of fountains and statues, in the design of which Le Brun, Claude Denis and François de Francine had all collaborated. Part of the credit may also be shared with the King. A water-colour design of the Bosquet des Trois Fontaines, preserved in the Bibliothèque de l'Institut, bears the caption: "De la pensée du Roi, exécuté par M. Le Nôtre." In the mid-eighteenth century Blondel praised the manner in which the Trois Fontaines had been designed, adding that "this bosquet alone would have sufficed to establish the reputation of Le Nôtre".

As if to heighten the impression of being outdoor rooms, the statues were set against a united wall of foliage in the form of a *charmille,* or hornbeam hedge. In 1685 an order of 2,870,000 hornbeam plants was sent to Versailles from the Forêt de Lyons.

The bosquets provided a raison d'être for many of the features of the garden. But there was more to it than this. The whole layout was an attempt to impose upon the landscape a form conceived by the human intellect – a form in which every part was related to the whole in a manner which was readily grasped and easily understood.

Le Nôtre trained as a painter in the studio of Simon Vouet, whose style was described by Anthony Blunt as "Baroque, still qualified by classical tradition". The principles underlying such compositions arc laid down by Fréart de Chambray as built on "proportion, symmetry and agreement of the whole with its parts, taught above all by geometry, the source and guide of all the arts".

In the eighteenth century, the classical lay-out of Versailles was condemned for failing to conform with the already Romantic ideas that were gaining ground in England, where Alexander Pope ridiculed the formal garden for not being informal:

> *"No pleasing intricacies intervene:*
> *No artful wildness to perplex the scene;*
> *Grove nods at grove, each Alley has a brother,*
> *And half the platform just reflects the other."*

In France the most perceptive critic was Blondel, who was by no means unappreciative of the work of Le Nôtre. He saw the need for formality in the immediate surroundings of the house. The garden was to provide a delicate and graduated transition from the refinements of architecture to the beauties of Nature. "After having ornamented the parts nearest the building," wrote Blondel, "one should find in Nature enough to satisfy the view." He was therefore more ready to praise the gardens of Meudon, Marly and Saint-Cloud, where the natural contours of the ground and the delightful prospects afforded by the site provided the continual contrast between "the regularity of the forms and the beautiful disorder of valleys, hillsides and mountains, the one setting off the other to its best advantage".

At Versailles there was no such natural complement. Apart from the great perspective to the west, the gardens were enclosed on every side. The formality of Le Nôtre, having no counter-attraction offered by Nature, became oppressive.

Such was Blondel's argument. In talking of "beau désordre" and praising the irregular beauties of Nature he had already departed from the principles of Le Nôtre and was foreshadowing those of Jean-Jacques Rousseau. "The error of self-styled men of taste," wrote Rousseau in *La Nouvelle Héloïse*, "is to want Art on every side and never to be content for this Art to be concealed." For him, the contribution of the landscape gardener was like the putting of a barely perceptible touch of make-up on an already beautiful face.

To him the straight line was abhorrent: "is it not amusing," asks Julie of Saint-Preux, "how, as if already bored by their promenade at the outset, they prefer to make it in a straight line in order to come as quickly as possible to the end of it?"

Blondel would not have agreed. By recognising the need for "ornamenting the parts nearest the house", he remained true to the seventeenth century.

The parts of the garden nearest the house were governed by the principle that the eye is best satisfied by seeing the whole at once. Louis XIV's own advice – the *Manière de voir les Jardins* – was to walk out of the château and proceed straight to the edge of the Parterre de Latone, and there, having first admired the prospect before you, to turn and look at the façades of the palace. If this were really one's first view of Versailles, the impact would be overwhelming.

In order to give full power to this impact, Le Nôtre designed the Parterre d'Eau, where everything is kept flat in order not to intrude upon the great panorama of architecture. In pursuance of this end the figures representing the mighty rivers of France – the Seine, the Loire, the Rhône, the Garonne – are all treated as recumbent.

Thus Le Nôtre not only provided a surrounding area to the château which set off the building to its best advantage, but also celebrated the greatest of the triumphs of Louis, the creation of a water supply at Versailles. "Though a place naturally without water," wrote John Locke, "yet it hath more jets d'eau and waterworks than are to be seen anywhere, and looking out from the King's Apartment [in those days there was no Galerie de Glaces] one sees almost noe thing but water for a whole league forwards, this being made up of several basins ... and a very large and long canal."

Locke was fortunate in being able to see Louis XIV and Madame de Montespan surveying the gardens. "The King seemed to be mightily pleased with his waterworks, and several changes were made then to which he himself gave sign with his cane, and he may well be made merry with this water since it cost him dearer than so much wine, for they say it costs him three shillings every pint that runs here."

When Locke saw the gardens the water was still being circulated by a system of windmills and horse pumps which returned it from the Canal to the Etang de Clagny. The ten windmills – "the best sort of windmills I have seen anywhere" – worked a chain of copper buckets. A hundred and twenty horses, working in relays of forty, laboured night and day.

Of the three deficiencies listed by Saint-Simon – "no view, no water and no woods" – the lack of water was by far the most formidable obstacle to overcome. Le Nôtre's design ultimately comprehended 1,400 fountains which required a continual and very copious supply.

As the townspeople of Versailles deposited most of their garbage in the Etang de Clagny, the water, which circulated endlessly between this and the Great Canal, became progressively polluted. In 1681 Primi Visconti, commenting on the foulness of the air occasioned by the excavations, added: "and the waters, which are putrid, infect the atmosphere, so that during the month of August everyone was taken ill, except the King and myself only." Clearly the system described by Locke was far from adequate. Charles Perrault records that Louis even contemplated abandoning Versailles "to go and build on a happier site".

But Louis was not easily deterred. "In a great state," he wrote in his memoirs, "there are always men suited to any sort of activity. The only thing is to know them and to put them in place." This was the real greatness of Louis: his ability to make use of the talents of others. As Chateaubriand was to write: "It is the voice of genius of all sorts which sounds from the tomb of Louis: from the tomb of Napoleon only the voice of Napoleon is heard."

Louis was right: the man for the task was a priest, the Abbé Picard. Essentially he was an astronomer, but it had occurred to him to apply telescopic lenses to the instruments of surveying, thereby greatly increasing their efficiency and accuracy. With him was a Dane, Olaüs Romer, the first scientist to determine the speed of light. The creation of Versailles stimulated technological progress in much the same way that a war may.

In 1678, thanks to the precision of Picard's levelling, a new source of supply was obtained from the ridge beyond the Heights of Satory. Reservoirs were established at Trappes and Bois d'Arcy and a watercourse created, with canals, aqueducts and siphons which greatly augmented the supply. "What I urge you most," wrote Louis to Colbert from the camp at Gand, "is with regard to the reservoirs and channels which are to provide water. This is what you must make them work on without respite."

The work resulted in an extension of the watercourse for some thirty-four kilometres, two thirds of which were of solid masonry, right into the Forêt de Rambouillet. Although this provided a most welcome addition to the supply, Louis was still hoping for something more spectacular. His hopes were fulfilled by an offer from two engineers from Liège, baron Arnold de Ville and Rennequin Sualem. Their proposal was to raise the waters of the Seine at Bougival up the 162 metres of hillside and down some eight miles of aqueduct to Versailles, by means of a gigantic pump.

Fourteen enormous water wheels communicated their movement to 221 pumps, which worked in relays up the hill. On 13 June, 1684, the mechanism was completed and the operation proved successful. At its best it could produce as much as 25,000 cubic metres of water in twenty-four hours. This needs to be compared with Blondel's figure for the consumption of water at Versailles. For the fountains to play *à l'ordinaire* from 8 a.m. to 8 p.m. required 12,960 cubic metres. But many of the *jets d'eau* were only at half pressure. For the full glory of the Grandes Eaux, a spectacle only turned on for the visit of an

1 *Above:* A royal hunt at Vincennes. *Van der Meulen*

2 *Left:* Fontainebleau: the Galerie François I and Porte Dorée before Primaticcio's additions. Fresco by *Rosso* in the gallery

3 *Above:* Fontainebleau: Louis XIV's bedroom. The reception of Cardinal Chigi. (Tapestry from *Musée de Fontainebleau*)

4 *Below:* Fontainebleau: the Galerie François I, 'Combat of the Centaurs and Lapithae'. Tapestry revealing its original state. (*Kunsthistorisches Museum, Vienna*)

5 *Left:* Fontainebleau: aerial view from the south-east before the destruction of the Galerie d'Ulysse (*extreme left*). *P. D. Martin*

6 *Below:* The Louvre from the Pont Neuf. From right to left – Le Vau's façade, the Galerie d'Apollon and Grande Galerie. Across the river is Le Vau's college, now the Institut Français. (*Anonymous*)

7 *Right:* Saint-Germain: the Château Neuf and its terrace from the east, across the Seine. *Ecole française, eighteenth century*

8 *Below:* Versailles: the final enlargement under construction. Extreme right, the Grande Ecurie. *Van der Meulen*

9 *Left:* The completed Versailles from the Place d'Armes. *P. D. Martin*

10 *Below:* Versailles from the north, showing the Bassin de Neptune (*foreground*), the Bosquet de l'Arc de Triomphe (*left*) and the Bosquet des Trois Fontaines (*right*). *J.-B. Martin*

11 *Right:* Grand Trianon: the entrance court with Trianon-sous-bois on the far right. *P. D. Martin*

12 *Below:* Petit Trianon: the Hameau with the Tour de Marlborough. *J. C. Nattes*

13 *Above:* A hawking party at Marly, showing the whole lay-out from the north. *P. D. Martin*

14 *Left:* The Tuileries: the Salle de Spectacle by Percier and Fontaine used as a banqueting hall. *Emmanuel Viollet-le-Duc*

15 *Above:* Compiègne: Curée à flambeaux before the entrance screen. From Napoleon III's hunting album

16 *Below:* Saint-Cloud. Louis XVI's bedroom, later Salon de l'Impératrice under Eugénie, at the time of Queen Victoria's visit. *F. de Fournier*

ambassador or other very important person, the fountains consumed 9,458 cubic metres in two and a half hours.

It was not until the end of 1685 that this water reached Versailles. Louis was delighted and granted a gratification of 100,000 livres to Arnold de Ville. Exactly what his contribution was will never be known. On his tomb in the church at Bougival, Sualem is described as "the only inventor of the Machine at Marly".

If Blondel's figures are correct, 25,000 cubic metres a day should have sufficed. But by 1685 a new and important addition had been made to the Royal palaces of France – the Château de Marly, "pièce capitale de tout le décor du Grand Siècle". Painted in fresco and perched after the manner of Italian villas on the side of a richly-wooded hill, this delightful château was surrounded by gardens teeming with cascades and fountains. It was rather obvious that the Machine de Marly should supply the Château de Marly, and Louis again set out in search of a dramatic increase to the waters of Versailles.

In the same month that had seen the completion of the Machine de Marly – August 1684 – Louis announced at his *lever* at Fontainebleau a new undertaking: "les travaux de la rivière de l'Eure". It was nothing less than the diversion of the river Eure from Pontgouin, some forty kilometres upstream of Chartres.

The most spectacular portion of the works necessitated by this scheme, from Berchères to Maintenon, consisted of a great embankment, sixty feet high, leading to the aqueduct, where the river was to recross its own valley within sight of the Château de Maintenon. This aqueduct, much of which can still be seen today, was over five thousand metres long and nearly seventy metres high. It was to have had three tiers of arcading. We must imagine another row of arches of nearly the same height surmounting the present arcade and a further storey, half the height of the lower ones, on top of that.

Thirty thousand soldiers were placed at the disposal of Vauban for this Herculean task; nearly nine million livres were poured into it. In July 1686, Dangeau noted that the work was well advanced and that the success of the enterprise seemed assured. But the war of the League of Augsburg intervened and the troops had to be withdrawn. The main effort was thus abandoned and gradually the lesser works ground to a standstill. The granting of a pension to M. Pigoreau, "ci-devant directeur des travaux de l'aquéduc de la rivière de l'Eure", seemed to admit that the project was abandoned.

Saint-Simon hurled not unmerited abuse at Louis for his gross disregard for the price that had to be paid for "his cruel folly". "Who could count the cost, in money and in men, of this obstinate endeavour? . . . it was forbidden, under the severest penalties, to talk of those who were taken ill, and above all those who died, who were killed by the arduous labour and even more by the gasses given off by so much movement of earth."

Napoleon adopted an attitude of quiet superiority. Referring specifically to the *rivière de l'Eure* project, he wrote: "It would not have been abandoned if I had undertaken it, because, before I started, I would have seen everything, examined everything and I would have assured myself that it could all have been finished."

The ruins of the Aquéduc de Maintenon remain an impressive monument to a costly failure. Nevertheless, the 1,400 fountains did display daily and brought an animation to the gardens without which they would indeed be dull.

The waters, which thus arrived in more or less sufficient quantity into the reservoirs of Versailles, had to be conducted by a complex network of underground pipes to the basins and then translated into an infinite number of *jets d'eau* of an astonishing variety of form.

On 2 April, 1672, the author of the *Mercure Galant* reported: "I would never come to an end if I were to tell you all the marvels which the waters produce in this delectable spot. Le Sieur Denis conducts them by means of the most admirable pumps and aqueducts, and Monsieur de Francine makes them do things which are beyond our imagining."

This is the great loss of the Grandes Eaux today, which largely consist of jets spouting in various directions. The art of François de Francine, the second generation of his family to work as *fontainers* for the Kings of France, is seldom if ever practised today and not much of its original achievements have survived. Apart from the devising of a large number of rather puerile practical jokes, it required the construction of nozzles and other fittings which so directed the water as to form spheres, hemispheres, urns, bells and other such-like shapes.

One of the most ingenious of the waterworks at Versailles was made at the suggestion of Madame de Montespan. The bosquet was called the *Marais*; its central feature was a tree, cast in bronze with leaves of tin, but according to Félibien "so cleverly made that it seemed to be natural. From the extremities of all its branches come an infinite number of little jets ... there is also a large number of others which spring from the reeds (also made in tin) which border the pond." The bosquet was lined with three tiers of marble steps, "from which water played by means of special fittings which took the shapes of ewers, of goblets, of carafes and other sorts of vases, which looked as if they were made of rock crystal garnished with silver gilt".

It was this sort of skill that earned Francine the enormous salary of 10,000 livres a year; it was to procure this sort of decoration and animation to his gardens that made Louis so determined to achieve an adequate supply of water.

"No view, no water, no woods." If Nature had not endowed these gardens with a view, then Art must needs contrive a great variety of vistas. The green walls of trellis and hornbeam that lined the alleys were used as a background to one of the largest sculpture galleries in the world.

The ordering and designing of the whole array was entrusted to Le Brun. It was important that the decoration of the gardens should be by the same hand that had ordained the décor of the State Apartments. A noble unity of style was the result.

The palace and its gardens were to be the visible symbol of Louis' own conception of the rôle and status of the French Monarchy. He took the Sun as his emblem and it was to provide the iconography for almost the whole lay-out – "this vast poem of mythology", as Mauricheau-Beaupré called it, "in honour of Apollo, which dominates the whole conception of the gardens".

Apart from the actual history of Apollo, this theme could be made to embrace such topics as the hours of the day, the seasons of the year, the four quarters of the globe and the seven ages of man. Since Diana was Apollo's sister, scenes of hunting could be included which were highly appropriate to that mighty dynasty of Nimrods, the Bourbons.

The "Sculpture Gallery" of the gardens provides the most striking evidence of Colbert's policy of encouraging artists to develop the same style. This was achieved by means of the Academy of Painting and Sculpture. As in all other fields, the ideal of the mid-seventeenth century was an Art which was the product of Reason and which appealed therefore to the educated man. Rules of proportion, rules of perspective and rules of composition provided the foundation for the training of the painter. Colour, which was felt to be sensuous and ephemeral, was secondary to form, which was thought of as permanent and rational in its appeal.

The great works of classical Rome provided the prototype, and the most promising students of the Academy of Painting and Sculpture were sent to Rome, where a further Academy for French students had been founded in 1666. Here, under the tutelage of Charles Errard, they copied the greatest works of Antiquity. In 1685 a certain Benedictine monk, Dom Michel Germain, wrote from Rome to one of his brethren: "The Romans greatly envy the beautiful copies which the French Academicians are making for the King of all the ancient figures. . . . But they can find no ground for adverse criticism."

Not only was the Academy there to produce a uniformity of style; it was there to ensure that the style was French. There was a conscious effort to win for France that supremacy in the world of Art which had hitherto been enjoyed by Italy.

In due course France claimed superiority over Italy in all branches of the Arts. The Sieur Combes, who wrote an "Explication de ce qu'il y a de plus remarquable dans la Maison Royale de Versailles et en celle de Monsieur à Saint-Cloud", boldly asserted: "Italy must now yield to France the prize and the crown which she had won over all the countries of the world, until today, in all that regarded the excellence of architecture, the beauty of sculpture, the magnificence of painting, the art of gardening, the structure of fountains and the invention of aqueducts. Versailles alone suffices to ensure for ever for France the glory which is now hers, of surpassing all other countries in the science of building."

The result of Colbert's policies and the system of the Academies was that by the mid-1680s there were nearly a hundred sculptors all trained in the same principles and all working in the same style as Le Brun. The outcome was one of the most remarkable examples of artistic collaboration ever known. It would be difficult, if not impossible, to distinguish the hand of one from the hand of another among the countless statues and urns which people the gardens.

Great care was taken to ensure the highest standard possible. Le Brun, surely the most prolific of designers, usually produced the first sketch. Models were then made and offered for inspection to the King, who liked to see a design in three dimensions. The different figures were then farmed out to a

44 The Bassin d'Apollon and the Canal with its flotilla. Engraving by Perelle.

selection of sculptors, who first had to submit a plaster mock-up, so that the effect could be tried out on the spot. The success of the finished group of statues was almost a foregone conclusion.

Behind all this artistic creation was the solid administration of Colbert. In March 1678, Louis wrote to him: "You are doing wonders with money, and every day I am more pleased with you. It gives me pleasure to tell you so." It was Louis' good fortune to be served by men of first-rate ability in every department of the State.

"No view, no water, no woods." Perhaps the last was the easiest of the three problems to solve. In the passage already cited from the *Mercure Galant* of 2 April, 1672, the author mentions "the great number of orange trees planted in the ground, and also the large trees which have been transported for the widening of the Allée Royale – something that has never been seen before".

A letter from Charles Perrault to Bontemps, dated 8 March, 1673, marvels at this method of "instant forestry". "This same Prince wishes to make a long alley with trees whose tops surpass in height those of the surrounding woodland: at once the alley is made, and the labour of a single day equals the work of Nature during two or three centuries."

To achieve this, Le Nôtre made use of a special mechanism known as the *Machine pour transplanter les Arbres*. It was based on the pulley and the lever and was known among the workmen as the Devil on account of its enormous strength.

It was one of Louis' greatest pleasures to take his guests on a conducted tour of his gardens. On 17 April, 1671, Madame de Sévigné wrote: "Mme de Lafayette was at Versailles yesterday. She was very well received – very well indeed, which is to say that the King put her in his *calèche* with the ladies and took pleasure in showing her all the beauties of Versailles, just like a private

45 The Colonnade.
Anonymous drawing.

individual whom one was visiting at his country house."

Louis XIV has left, in his *Manière de voir les Jardins de Versailles*, his own instructions as to how such a tour was to begin. "On leaving the château by the Vestibule of the Cour de Marbre, you will go out onto the terrace; you must halt at the top of the steps to consider the situation of the parterres, the pièces d'eau and the fountains of the Cabinets; next you must proceed to the top of Latona."

From here one looks over the Bassin de Latone, down the Tapis Vert to the Bassin d'Apollon and out onto the long vista of the Canal behind. The statuary announces the main theme of the decorative ensemble. Latona was the mother of Apollo. She is shown appealing to Zeus for protection against the peasants of Lycias who were pelting her with clods of earth. Zeus retaliated by turning them into frogs.

The Bassin d'Apollon shows the moment of sunrise; the chariot of Apollo is labouring to get clear of the water before it breaks forth upon another day. The whole group, which was Tuby's masterpiece, gives the most magnificent impression of eruption as the tritons scatter to either side and announce on their raucous conches the advent of Le Roi Soleil.

On the south side of the Tapis Vert is the Salle de Bal or Bosquet de Rocailles – so called from the thousands of exotic shells, specially imported from Madagascar, with which it is encrusted. The sloping ground has been hollowed out into the form of a steep-cut arena, with cascades tumbling from tier to tier between gilded gueridons on which candelabra could be placed, bringing the magic of candlelight to the nocturnal festivities of the Court.

Further down on the same side is the Colonnade, the most elaborately architectural of all the bosquets. To Blondel, this was the supreme achievement of the whole lay-out: "its aspect alone would be enough to give an idea

of the splendour and the prospering of the arts during the reign of Louis le Grand." The design, executed in 1685, was by Mansart, but nearly all the great names associated with the sculpture of Versailles were involved in its production. In the centre stands a marble group representing the Rape of Proserpine, the last and greatest work of Girardon.

On the north side of the Tapis is another important ensemble, the Bains d'Apollon. The figures, representing Apollo and his horses being rubbed down after a hard day's ride, should be seen as complementary to the group in the Bassin d'Apollon. They represent respectively sunrise and sunset. The central group of the Sun God and his attendant nymphs is by Girardon and Regnaudin; the groups of horses attended by tritons by Marsy and Guerin.

Originally these were housed in the Grotte de Thétis which stood to the north of the old château. The grotto disappeared when the Aisle de Nord was built and the statues set up beneath gilded canopies in the Bosquet des Dômes. In 1776, when the trees were being replanted, Louis XVI invited the painter Hubert Robert to design a new setting for the groups more in keeping with an already Romantic age. The result was the enormous rock with its cavernous recesses representing the Palace of Thetis.

The Bains d'Apollon lie just beneath the Parterre du Nord at the far end of which is the Fontaine de la Pyramide. It is one of the earliest of the fountains to survive in its original position. It was the work of Girardon and was finally completed in 1672. Originally the figures of tritons, dolphins and crayfish were gilded and the other ornaments bronzed. It is composed of four marble saucers of diminishing size down which the water, overflowing from one to the other, formed, as Félibien puts it, "so many crystal bells".

Next to the Pyramide is the Bassin des Nymphes. The natural declivity of the ground dictates a high reredos and this has been used by Girardon for a delightful bas-relief of ladies bathing, executed in lead, which was, as always at Versailles, gilded and regilded every year. The design is attributed by Charles Perrault to his brother Claude, but it clearly reflects that of a painting by Dominichino. Perrault generously agreed that Girardon had improved upon his design, making it "one of the most beautiful bas-reliefs that have so far appeared".

At the bottom of this slope, known as the Allée d'Eau, is the huge ensemble of the Bassin de Neptune. It is preceded by the Bassin du Dragon in which the fountain was made to play at two different heights – twenty-seven metres if the King was in that part of the gardens: eleven if he was not.

The Bassin de Neptune was designed by Le Nôtre in 1679, but it was not completed until 1741. The first state is shown in a painting by J.B. Martin which must have been done before 1710 when the new chapel was built. With the construction of the Bassin de Neptune the whole vast lay-out of the Grand Design may be regarded as having been completed.

In all this huge display of terraces and colonnades, of statues, vases and urns, of canals, basins and fountains, of bosquets, alleys and hornbeam hedge, there is one element of which no mention had yet been made, but which, for most people, would be the first requirement of a garden: flowers. Louis had a passionate love of flowers and the first Versailles had been adorned, between the château and the Orangerie, with the Parterre des Fleurs. Enclosed by a

46 *On page 144 above:* The Bosquet des Domes. Drawing by I. Silvestre.

47 *Below:* The Bosquet de l'Eté, showing the "walls" of hornbeam. Anonymous drawing.

gilded balustrade and lined with vases painted to resemble procelain, it had been "filled with a thousand varieties of flowers". The parterres to north and south of the château accounted annually for 150,000 plants. But the real flower garden was to be at Trianon.

Trianon

TRIANON WAS FIRST conceived as a garden. André Félibien was among the earliest to record its charms: "One could with reason name it the Abode of Spring, for in whatever season one goes there, it is enriched with flowers of every kind and the air which one breathes is perfumed with the jasmines and orange trees beneath which one walks."

The orange trees lined the parterre; they did not stand in clumsy tubs waiting to be trundled back into some vast orangery for the winter, but were planted in the soil. At the coming of the first frosts, the gardener Le Bouteux erected a greenhouse over them which was removed in the following spring.

It was the only concession which he made to the elements, for the garden was kept supplied with flowers throughout the year by the expedient of placing them every day fresh from the hothouse into the beds which they were to occupy. Thus, even in mid-winter, Louis was able to take his guests for a stroll in a spring garden. The accounts for the period are full of references to the purchase of flowers on a gigantic scale. Colbert's letters and instructions underline the same concern. On 5 May, 1670, he wrote: "The garden is progressing well; Le Bouteux is being provided with all that he needs." Louis noted in the margin: "It will be well to urge Le Bouteux on and not to let him lose one minute." It is clear that he was a man who needed supervision. "Visit Trianon often," wrote Colbert to Petit. "See that Le Bouteux has flowers for the King for the whole winter and that he has enough workers ... You must render an account to me every week of the flowers that will be available."

To the Intendant de Galères at Marseilles Colbert wrote: "I beg you to buy me all the jonquils and tuberoses that you can possibly find." In order to sustain this continual transformation scene, Le Bouteux kept the almost unbelievable number of one million, nine hundred thousand flower pots.

The siting of Trianon was closely connected with the extension of the Grand Canal into the great cruciform lake which we see today. A graceful double stairway, the Fer-à-Cheval, forms the vista to anyone navigating the north arm of the Canal and the new gardens were laid out at the top of the stairway.

It was not a place endowed by Nature. There are frequent mentions in the accounts to the transporting of "good earth" to provide the gardens with a top soil and an immense quantity of manure was also imported.

From the top of the Fer-à-Cheval one had access to the lower parterre, a large square sheltered between two trellis pergolas. The centre of this square was in the main axis of the garden. To the left a woodland alley framed the distant prospect of a single fountain. To the right, elevated upon a terrace of eight steps, the château, which provided the architectural focus of the gardens, was now visible – a Doric pavilion with a high and highly-decorated roof which seemed to be made of blue and white porcelain.

Its lay-out is best appreciated from the other side, which formed the entrance. It was a château in miniature. The main block with its two attendant pavilions were set as tangents to an oval forecourt which was closed on the fourth side by an iron grille and gateway. To either side of the grille two quadrant walls embraced an open forecourt in the shape of a half oval, to the right and left of which were two smaller pavilions reflecting in simpler form the architecture of the other three.

It was the architecture of the Cour de Marbre at Versailles. The main block presented towards the courtyard a façade of five windows of which the three central ones were contained within an attached Ionic portico surmounted by a pediment. The windows to either side of the portico were flanked with busts supported on consoles. Above the cornice was a balustrade adorned with urns and leaden figures and above the balustrade there rose a mansard roof ornately crested at both levels with an alternation of vases and exotic birds. Also reminiscent of the Cour de Marbre were the two wrought iron aviaries at either extremity of the façade for the accommodation of singing birds.

Such was the architecture. The decoration was more exotic. The dominant theme was of blue and white porcelain, either real in the form of pottery tiles, or painted to resemble them. Even the glazing bars of the windows and the iron bars of the grilles and gateways were treated in this way from which the château derived its name of "Trianon de Porcelaine".

48 Trianon de Porcelaine from the garden side. In the background Clagny and the 'Enveloppe'. Engraving by Perelle.

49 The bed in the
Chambre des Amours.
Drawing by N. Tessin.

The affectation of the rooms betrayed the purpose of the building. To the right of the central Salon was a bedroom known as the Chambre des Amours.

During the siege of Lille in the summer of 1667, Athénaïs de Montespan had become the King's mistress. She did so by insinuating herself into the good graces of the Queen by her regular religious observance and at the same time by attaching herself to Louise de la Vallière. "By these means," wrote the marquis de la Fare, "she contrived to be permanently in the King's immediate entourage and she did all that she could to please him, in which she succeeded very well, being plentifully endowed with wit and charm, in contrast to La Vallière who was sadly defective in these qualities." In due course Louis fell passionately in love with her and her slightest wish was his command. The building of Trianon and Clagny were directly connected with this romance.

The Chambre des Amours was furnished with "un lit extraordinaire". It was in the form of a couch with a large mirror for a dossier and overhung with a canopy of great complexity with the curtains flounced up into festoons – "the whole of white taffeta with blue embroidery . . . the said bed trimmed with gold and silver lace and with tasselled fringes and braid also of gold and silver".

In the central Salon, according to Félibien, the walls were of stucco "very white and high polished with ornaments of azure". A curious fact revealed by the accounts is that this work was done by Carmelite monks "who sent two of their brothers to paint white the apartments of Trianon". An appreciable contribution was made to the creation of Versailles by monks and priests who possessed some expertise not apparently related to their religion.

Beyond the Chambre des Amours was a cabinet furnished with a "lit de repos". One window looked west onto the parterre, another – obviously a *porte–fenêtre* – gave access to the gardens by means of a flight of steps. It was answered symmetrically by an opening – presumably closed by a bird-proof mesh – into the aviary.

The symmetry of Trianon was exact and the rooms to the south of the central Salon reflected in every respect the Appartement des Amours. They were named after Diana and also boasted "un lit extraordinaire". It is not clear for whom this suite was intended.

The central Salon, the largest of the rooms, merits the shortest entry in the Inventory, but the furniture, consisting of two armchairs and eighteen *tabourets* suggests a room for formal use according to the etiquette of the Court. The *tabouret* was a folding cross-legged stool reserved for the use of duchesses.

The lack of mention of any wall hanging here raises the question of the many fragments of porcelain recovered from the site. In the Salle des Bains de Marie-Antoinette at Rambouillet are panels made up of porcelain tiles traditionally supposed to have come from Trianon. They were copied for the kitchen at Amalienburg, the "trianon" in the grounds of Nymphenburg near Munich. Similar rooms exist at Schloss Brühl near Bonn and at Rosenborg in Copenhagen. It is at least probable that the Salon at Trianon was decorated with these colourful tiles.

The title "Chambre des Amours" makes clear the primary purpose of the Trianon de Porcelaine. A secondary purpose is revealed by an annotated plan

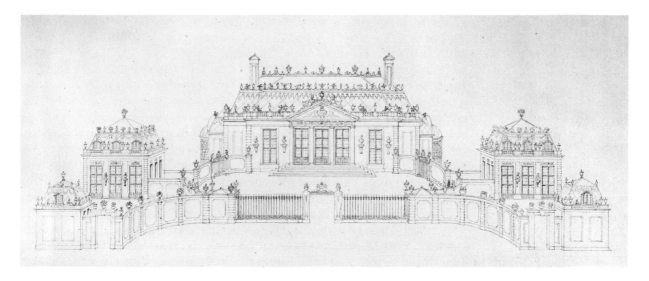

in the Cabinet des Estampes. The rooms in all four attendant pavilions were consecrated to the preparation of food. On the left or south side, the small corner pavilion is marked "pour les entremets" and the larger one, divided into two rooms, is "pour les potages" and "pour les entrées et hors d'oeuvres". Between them, in a lean-to against the wall, is marked "pour faire le rost". Across the court, the small pavilion is reserved "pour travailler aux confitures" and the large one, divided into five small rooms, serves "pour dresser les fruits", "pour la table des Princes et Seigneurs", "pour la table de la desserts" and two "pour le buffet". Louis was one who took his pleasures seriously.

"This palace," wrote Félibien, "was regarded from the first by everyone as being enchanted, for, having only been begun at the end of the Winter, it was found ready by Spring, as if it had grown out of the ground with the flowers which accompanied it." It was not quite as magical as that, but it was built in a matter of months. The first account for masonry is dated 1 March, 1670. Perhaps its completion was marked by the entry for 17 October of the same year: "gratification of the joiners, locksmiths, sculptors and others in consideration of the diligence with which they have worked at Trianon."

It is difficult to know whom to believe about Madame de Montespan. The duchesse d'Orléans wrote: "La Montespan had a whiter complexion than La Vallière; she had a beautiful mouth and fine teeth, but her expression was always insolent. One had only to look at her to see that she was scheming something. She had beautiful blonde hair and lovely hands and arms, which La Vallière did not have, but at least La Vallière was clean in her person, whereas La Montespan was filthy."

On 18 September, 1680, Madame de Sévigné wrote to her daughter: "I don't know which forked tongue among the courtiers first pronounced the new name, but they are calling Madame de Maintenon *Mme de Maintenant*."

Françoise d'Aubigny, marquise de Maintenon, was born in almost total penury in the conciergerie of the prison at Niort. She came of a well-known Huguenot family which was out of favour with Richelieu. At the age of fifteen she married the poet Scarron, already so crippled that he described himself as being shaped like a Z. It was a marriage *faute de mieux*: the only alternative was a convent.

Left a widow at twenty-three, she became a welcome guest at the house of the Maréchal d'Albret where she attracted first the attention and then the friendship of Madame de Montespan. In due course the mistress became a mother and the mother needed a person "sûre et discrète" to whom she could confide the care of the children with whom Louis so regularly provided her. Thus Françoise d'Aubigny came into contact with the King. It was to Madame de Montespan that she owed, in the words of Saint-Simon, "the decisive introduction which led to the unbelievable fortune that was to be hers".

In about 1683 she became the wife of Louis XIV and in all but title Queen of France. She disliked Versailles, she disapproved of the Court and she made little use of the advantages of her position. "Je meurs de tristesse," she confided to a friend, "dans une fortune qu'on aurait peine à imaginer."

Under the new régime established by Madame de Maintenon Louis became a reformed character. The Trianon de Porcelaine, so closely connected with his double adultery, may well have become embarrassing. Its fragile decoration also required incessant repair.

In July 1687, the marquis de Sourches records, the King pulled the little château down "to build a larger one, in order, he said, to be able to give a few *fêtes* and *divertissements*. That was the pretext, but they thought that he was having the building put up in order to withdraw himself more, and it was of this that the courtiers were mortally afraid." And they were right. Trianon became a place to which only the very privileged few were ever invited.

Perhaps no building at Versailles illustrates more clearly Louis' method of building. It was the way of the amateur, a succession of trials and errors, of building, pulling down and rebuilding, which may have produced the desired result but was certainly the most expensive procedure possible.

From the outset Louis exercised the closest supervision over the construction. "He even often went," wrote the marquis de Sourches, "to pass the *après-dîners* in a tent there where he worked with Monsieur de Louvois and cast an eye over the works from time to time to see that they were advancing."

As at Versailles, so at Trianon, Louis began with the intention of retaining the petit château and surrounding it with new buildings, but this time he was soon led to abandon the idea. The first plan that is known to us retained the shell of the main block of the Trianon de Porcelaine while greatly extending the side pavilions so as to form the wings to right and left of the present entrance court. These were joined to the central block by oval salons set obliquely. No doubt because of this retention of the old building the new wings were originally covered with the same mansard roofs. But their architecture was in the new style that gave its name to the building of the Trianon de Marbre.

It was at this stage that Nicodemus Tessin wrote his description. "The frieze and all the pilasters are of a brown and red and yellow marble; the Ionic capitals and bases are of white marble and the rest in ordinary stone which contrast with one another in the most disagreeable manner in the world."

It was not long before Louis changed his mind. On 18 September Louvois wrote to Mansart, who was taking the waters at Vichy: "The King, not being content with the effect produced by the building on the garden side" (in other words the petit château) "ordered that it should be demolished. His Majesty did not wish the continuation of work on the roofs either, which he found too heavy and to give to Trianon the appearance of a big house."

The roofs, it was now decided, were to be flat and concealed behind a balustrade. The chimneys also were to project no more than twelve inches above the roof, "His Majesty preferring the risk that they might smoke to their being visible from outside". At the same time Louis decided to fill the gap left by the demolition of the petit château by an open peristyle, which may have been inspired by Rousseau's celebrated Perspective painted in trompe l'oeil on one of the pavilions at Marly. "His Majesty desires that it should be something very light, upheld by columns in the form of a peristyle, and it is for this that he would like you to do a design at your earliest convenience – understanding as he does that while you are taking the waters it is difficult for you to apply yourself."

On 22 September, Louvois informs Mansart that Louis will not wait for his return from Vichy but is asking "Monsieur De Coste" (Robert de Cotte) to provide designs for the peristyle. It had already been determined to have an arcade on the side of the entrance court and the foundations had been laid. The area within the peristyle is described as "une pièce". Louis wanted to be able to enjoy from this *room* a view of the Canal and of the whole garden. There is strong evidence that the arcade was at first glazed towards the courtyard forming a loggia open towards the garden.

On 2 October the King left for Fontainebleau announcing his intention to return on 12 November; "in other words," observed the marquis de Sourches, "until the time when he hoped to have an apartment habitable at Trianon, which he desired with impatience, for he pressed the work on with an incredible diligence."

Letters from Louvois continued to pass on the King's instructions on the minutest of details, always accompanied with the insistence that the work must be done "the earliest that it is possible to do".

On 13 November Louis returned from Fontainebleau between two and three o'clock at Versailles "where he took coach immediately to go to Trianon". Fortunately for all concerned the work had progressed equal to his expectation. Dangeau records that he found it "very well advanced and very beautiful". He made six more visits before the end of the month, during which "he walked a great deal about the buildings which he is having put up and with which he is very pleased at present".

There can be little doubt that Louis' was the controlling mind throughout the creation of Trianon and that his architects were merely there in the rôle of interpreter. The result was a building which no architect was ever likely to have built. Its extraordinary plan can only be explained in relationship to the gardens as they had been laid out for the Trianon de Porcelaine.

The controlling factor was a garden room called the Cabinet des Parfums. This was situated at the north-west corner of the parterre immediately surrounding the château and it faced south towards the Canal. Running from the Cabinet des Parfums the whole length of the north end of this parterre was a trellis pergola. In the finished design of the Trianon de Marbre the pergola was replaced by the Galerie and the Cabinet des Parfums by the Salon des Jardins at its extremity. Finally, since there was nowhere else to put it, a further block of lodgings was appended at right angles to the gallery, which was known from its sylvan setting as the Trianon-sous-Bois. It was an architecture dictated by the lay-out of a garden.

By the end of 1688 the Trianon de Marbre was finished and furnished. Perhaps the fairest description of it comes from the duc de Croÿ, who was writing towards the end of Louis XV's reign when it was no longer fashionable to describe the buildings of the Grand Monarque in terms of uncritical adulation. "It is the most charming piece of architecture in the world," he wrote, but he added the qualification: "the view from the entrance to the court is admirable, but the rest does not answer to it." This is very true, for the façade towards the avenue, giving no hint of the full extent of the whole, suggests a building of a size proportionable to the single storey and Ionic Order. But seen from the parterre, the château deploys its monotonous length, interrupted only by the peristyle turns at right angles to present the fourteen windows of the Gallery and its attendant Salon and finally regains its original orientation in the further façade.

One could easily believe that Trianon-sous-Bois, with its two storeys, smaller windows and plain stone façades, was an afterthought; its beautifully-carved masks and consoles suggest a later date. But it was not so; Trianon was conceived and built as a whole.

The historical imagination must make one alteration to the façades, which would mitigate the monotony of the skyline. It must replace upon the balustrade that regiment of urns and statues which gave an animation of the façades which they lack today.

The King's guests were put up at Trianon-sous-Bois, and here the duchesse d'Orléans found a lodging to her heart's content. She looked out over a little garden known as "les Sources" which was unhappily destroyed in the general replantation of trees in 1775. It must have been a very attractive corner – "a little bosquet so closely planted that at high noon the sun did not penetrate". Beneath the trees fifty little springs gave birth to as many rivulets and the rivulets formed a diversity of islands, some of them large enough to set table and chairs for a game of tric-trac.

The King's private garden was contained in the angle between his lodgings and those of Madame de Maintenon and joined diagonally with the Jardin des Sources. For the rest, the gardens remained much as they had been in the days of the Trianon de Porcelaine, the formal parterres soon giving place to the woodland, pierced with long, green alleys punctuated at their intersections with little basins and fountains, their brightly-gilded figures shining among the trees like the last outposts of art in a landscape which was rapidly merging with its natural surroundings.

Within doors, Trianon contained a suite of interiors which still afford, in their carved friezes, panelling and overdoors, an important souvenir of the Grand Siècle, though most of the décor has been modified either by Napoleon or Louis-Philippe, both of whom made use of Trianon. To picture these rooms as they were in the days of Louis XIV we need the evidence of the Inventory. We must see the walls hung with tapestry or red damask, in much of which the Chinese taste still lingered. Fourteen rooms are marked as having furniture "upholstered with Chinese stuffs" and beds hung with satin "sprinkled with flowers and animals from China". Only the Gallery seems to have reflected the style of the parent palace. Its furniture was carved and gilded and covered in crimson damask, with curtains of red taffeta to match.

But its real décor came from the set of paintings which lined the walls, twenty-four of them, mostly by Cotelle, representing the chief beauties of the gardens and the park of Versailles. The Paintings of the Galerie des Glaces told of the civil and military accomplishments of the Grand Monarque; those at Trianon commemorated another achievement of which Louis could be as justly proud. As he walked down his gallery, he could compare with advantage the successive views of parterres, bosquets and fountains with the state of Versailles as he first remembered it – "the most sad and barren of places, with no view, no water and no woods". Cotelle's paintings showed the incredible alteration which had been witnessed by the last quarter of a century. But the last and loveliest of the views came not from a painting, but from the windows of the Salon des Jardins at the end of the gallery – over the parterre and across the Canal to the Ménagerie. No longer could it be said that Versailles was wanting in views, nor in woods nor in water.

On 11 July, 1691, Dangeau describes an idyllic evening at Trianon. "A great supper party was given under the peristyle to seventy-five ladies, who were joined by the King and Queen of England. They came by the Canal, where the whole orchestra remained. Arriving in gondolas and chaloupes, they landed at Trianon, which was brilliantly illuminated; they walked in the gardens; then supper was served at five tables."

The French word *féerie* is needed to describe the magic of these nocturnal occasions, these spectacles of *son et lumière*, in which the sound was that of Lully's orchestra, enhanced by the strange echoes of a woodland setting, and the light was the warm, smokeless glow of dry faggots which lit the façades from below, inverting the normal shadow projection so that they appeared as figures before the footlights.

Understandably, an invitation to Trianon was one of the most coveted privileges which could be conferred upon a courtier. Such invitations were given or withheld in order to keep the nobility assiduous in their efforts to remain in the royal favour. Saint-Simon reveals how the niceties of etiquette were used to his own discomfiture. When a lady was invited to Marly, her husband accompanied her without need for personal application, but this was not the case if the invitation was to Trianon. By consistently inviting the duchesse de Saint-Simon to Trianon and by equally consistently refusing her applications for Marly, Louis was able to convey in no uncertain manner his displeasure with the Duke.

The Château de Marly

THE ENVELOPPE, the Trianon de Porcelaine, the Château de Clagny, the gigantic lay-out of the gardens, the private houses of the courtiers which began to line the Avenue de Saint-Cloud and the Avenue de Sceaux – at some point during this evolution it must have become clear to Louis that Versailles must replace Saint-Germain as the true seat of the French Monarchy.

It is possible that the year 1677 was the decisive one, for it was on 7 November of that year that Louis signed the contract for the purchase of land at Marly. He had come upon the site, Jean-Antoine du Bois informs us, while out hunting: "finding himself by chance in a kind of marsh, where the situation seemed to lend itself to his plan . . . he found there a fine vista opening towards the river and the place surrounded by several magnificent woods, its whole aspect determined the King then and there to choose and to take this plot."

"I must needs say," wrote the English traveller Martin Lister, "it is one of the pleasantest places I ever saw, or I believe is in Europe: it is seated in the bosom or upper end of a valley in the midst of and surrounded by woody hills. The valley is closed at its upper end, and gently descends forward by degrees, and opens wider and wider, and gives you the prospect of a vast plain country and the river Seine running through it." What he called a valley is in fact a vast re-entrant of which the principal contour line takes the form of a capital U. The open end of the U, which commanded the prospect referred to, was to the north.

This, then, was the natural conformation which Louis identified as one which lent itself to "his design". The first drawings of Marly, made by Jacques Hulot in 1679, reveal the broad outlines of this design. At the focal point of the rounded end of the U was to be a house for the King, the Pavillon du Roi. On the same contour line which forms the two arms of the U were to be separate pavilions for his guests, set some distance apart and linked by a trellis pergola. Within the area thus circumscribed the land continued to slope downwards and inwards and was to be cast into terraces between which would be contrived a succession of ornamental lakes.

The intention is clear: to recreate the charming *maison de plaisance* that Versailles had been but could never be again; to have somewhere where privileged house parties could be offered brilliant entertainments and to which invitations would be greatly coveted. In due course the highest hopes of assiduous courtiers were to be summed up in the formula of application for invitation: "Sire, Marly?"

Although the château is no more; although none of its attendant buildings have survived; although the statues, the fountains, the cascades and most of the pièces d'eau have disappeared, it is still well worth a visit to Marly in order to form a just impression of the scale and contours of the land. None of the paintings or engravings gives an adequate idea of either.

154

There is something about the site itself, and it must have been this that first attracted Louis. The high, wooded hills give a pleasing sense of privacy, and with it intimacy and exclusiveness. But it is not completely shut off from the world. To the north the land falls away and the prospect opens across the wide meanders of the Seine towards Saint-Germain, Le Vésinet and Argenteuil. But, although the gardens are thus left open to the north, their insulation is secured by the skilful use of ground levels. In order to obtain sufficient space for the last of the lakes, the Pièce des Nappes, the lower gardens have been considerably banked up and end abruptly in a high terrace overlooking the Abreuvoir. The privacy, the intimacy and the exclusiveness are maintained.

"He who planted this garden," wrote Diderot to Mademoiselle Volland, "realised that it was necessary to keep it out of sight until the moment when one could see it in its entirety." It was only to those privileged to enter the precincts that the whole glorious lay-out of Marly was revealed.

Turning in at the gates, the carriages crossed a circular court flanked by quadrant arcades, behind which lay the stables, and began cautiously the long and steep descent of the Allée Royale. From this moment the château was plainly visible, framed between two neat outbuildings and nestling comfortably amid the luxuriant foliage of its surroundings. The impression created was one of extreme richness. The balustrade, with its figures and vases, was brilliantly gilded; so were the frames of the windows. The bas-reliefs which decorated the pediments and the panels above the windows were picked out in

51 General view from the entrance side. Reconstruction by A. Guillaumot.

155

gold against a royal blue. The tall pilasters were of marble, *rouge de Languedoc*, and the whole was underlined with a base in *vert antique* – or so it seemed at a distance; a closer inspection revealed that the entire architecture and decoration of the façades was painted on a flat wall in trompe l'oeil.

This external painting made Marly extremely colourful. The *Mercure Galant* gave the credit to Le Brun for the whole décor which was done "from his designs and under his directions". But the Comptes des Bâtiments leave no doubt as to who played the major part in the execution. The payment of 74,476 livres to Jacques Rousseau, compared with that of 49,495 divided among twelve others, leaves little to the imagination. Rousseau also painted the Salle de Vénus at Versailles and the Orangerie at Saint-Cloud.

Rousseau's most celebrated work at Marly was known as the "Perspective". In order to identify its position in the lay-out it is necessary to have a clear conception of the area to east and west of the Pavillon du Roi. To the east, the two "neat outbuildings" already mentioned were the Chapel and the Salle des Gardes. These stood to either side of the entrance grille at the foot of the Allée Royale. The Allée Royale was reflected by another avenue on the opposite slope; at the foot of this alley were two pavilions which answered the Chapel and the Salle des Gardes. At an early stage in the evolution of the design these two pavilions were joined by a building which presented a blank wall towards the Pavillon du Roi. It was on this wall that Rousseau painted his Perspective.

The effect was that of an open peristyle, similar to the one created three-

52 Section and elevation of the "Perspective".

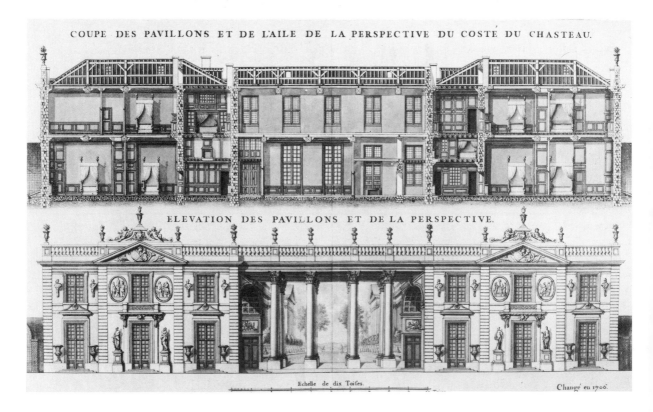

COUPE DES PAVILLONS ET DE L'AILE DE LA PERSPECTIVE DU COSTÉ DU CHASTEAU.

ELEVATION DES PAVILLONS ET DE LA PERSPECTIVE.

Echelle de dix Toises.

Changé en 1706.

156

dimensionally at Trianon. Between its stately rows of columns appeared two long, colonnaded wings and a distant prospect of classical landscape. In due course the painting gave its name to the whole block of office buildings.

In the centre of the area between the Perspective and the Chapel and Salle des Gardes, and raised upon a platform or terrace eight steps high, stood the Pavillon du Roi. The building was an exact square and each façade was identical – a rather smaller version of the west front at Chatsworth which in many ways resembles Marly. The front of Chatsworth is 175 feet long; that of Marly 144.

Within doors the square plan was based on an Irish cross formed by a central octagonal Salon and four radiating Vestibules. In each of the four corners of the square was an apartment – one for the King in the north-east angle, overlooking the main axis to the north and the Salle des Gardes to the east – these were upholstered in crimson damask; one for the Queen, overlooking the Chapel to the east and the south gardens on the other – these were upholstered in blue; one for Madame in the south-west angle, with hangings of a gold pink known as "aurore", and one for Monsieur upholstered in green.

The octagonal Salon was the centre of the building and the centre of the life of Marly. On four sides, glazed doors gave access to each of the Vestibules. On the other facets were four fireplaces surmounted by tall mirrors. The Salon occupied the full height of the building, a Corinthian order marked the ground floor and upheld an ornate entablature. At first-floor level the pilasters were replaced by caryatids, between which four more windows opened into an inward corridor. Before each of these windows was a balcony overlooking the Salon. The only direct daylight came from the roundel windows above opened from skylights onto the roof.

It made an imposing background to the entertainments offered by Louis to his guests. A stage could be erected in the space of half an hour in one of the vestibules, or musicians accommodated in the first-floor balconies and the Salon turned into a ballroom or concert hall; often there were lotteries – a means of distributing expensive presents to the ladies – and, in the absence of any particular entertainment, card tables were always in readiness. Its greatest drawback appears to have been its susceptibility to draughts. "One is beaten by a wind," complained Madame de Maintenon, "which reminds one of the hurricanes of America." Half a century later Marie-Leczinska made the same complaint: "I deserted the Salon yesterday, the wind was as strong there as in the garden."

The exact symmetry of the Salon made it easy for guests to lose their bearings. "Those who are not familiar with Marly," noted the duc de Luynes, "often mistake the way by which they should go out." The only means of orientation was the fact that there was a billiard table in the south Vestibule.

The main building was completed in 1683, when payments were made for the roofing, but the first recorded house party took place three years later. Racine was one of the first to record his impressions. "You could not believe how agreeable this house of Marly is," he wrote; "it seems to me that the Court is quite different here from what it is at Versailles."

There was nothing so flattering to the courtier as to be allowed to lay aside for a few days the etiquette of the Court. Those who had been to Marly

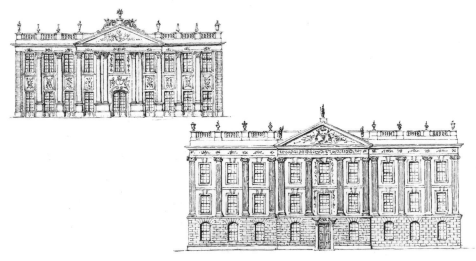

53 Façades of Marly (top left) and Chatsworth drawn to the same scale. Ian Dunlop.

formed an inner ring which placed them in a position of quiet superiority over those who had not. It was one of the privileges of Marly for men to remain covered in the presence of the King, but it still required the royal command. As Louis left the Pavillon du Roi to conduct his guests round the gardens, he would say: "Chapeaux, Messieurs."

The whole design of Marly was conceived to sustain this flattering sense of intimacy and exclusiveness which lent their savour to an invitation.

In the area immediately adjacent to the château, everything was closely-packed and heavily-overhung by high banks and steep woodlands. To east and west were four *cabinets de verdure*, two on either side and so placed as to leave clear a broad alley between them. Their very names – Cabinet Sombre, Cabinet de la Rêverie, Cabinet Secret and Cabinet de l'Ombre – suggest the atmosphere of cosiness and seclusion which was one of the delights of Marly.

To the south was the Petit Parterre, from which a noble flight of steps led to the level of the all-encircling *berceau de charmille*, a green tunnel of hornbeam hedge which followed the main contour line, linking the pavilions and providing a shady walk around the perimeter. Beyond this, and continuing the main axis of the gardens, the great cascade known as the Rivière brought its tumultuous waters down the steep avenue from the Reservoir du Trou d'Enfer. Under Louis XV the Rivière fell into disrepair and was replaced by a grass ride, leaving only the pond known as the Déversoir which had formerly received its waters. The basin remains today, but the panels of red and green marble and the gilt lead figures have long since disappeared.

It is to be presumed that Le Nôtre was responsible for the original lay-out of Marly, although the evidence is slight. In 1694 a letter from Cronström, the Swedish Ambassador, to Nicodenius Tessin mentions that "it is no longer Le Nôtre who is in charge of the gardens nor of Trianon: it is Monsieur Mansart".

In 1679 Le Nôtre had been sent to Italy. Colbert explained in a letter to the duc d'Estrées that he was there "to seek diligently if he might find anything sufficiently fine to be worthy of being imitated in the royal houses". It is not recorded whether he derived any inspiration from his visit.

To the north the apartments of the King and the duc d'Orléans overlooked the wider prospect of the lower gardens. On the same level as the château, but set well back to either side, were the twelve pavilions for the guests. Each pavilion contained two apartments, one on each floor, connected by a tiny oval staircase. Each apartment contained a comfortably-sized bedroom and a small anteroom. Behind the bed was a narrow garde-robe with a privy contrived within the thickness of the wall.

In 1687, when visits to Marly were becoming longer and more frequent, one of the pavilions was sacrificed to make a bathroom. It contained twin baths and there were two "lits de repos" in the adjoining room. In 1703 the King sacrificed two more for the housing of two enormous globes, made by Coronelli. On the celestial globe the stars were shown as they would have been on 5 September, 1638, which was Louis' birthday.

The amount of accommodation sacrificed was not serious, for in 1698 Louis had added a number of apartments to the office buildings behind the Perspective. "Another block of lodgings is being made here," sighed Madame de Maintenon; "Marly will soon be a second Versailles." Alfred Marie, one of the greatest authorities on Louis' buildings, has estimated that, at its peak, Marly could offer 1,339 beds. All but about sixty of these were for servants and staff.

The main apartment of the Perspective was occupied by the Grand Chambellan, the duc de Bouillon. Here also was a dining room for the guests and a room in which coffee, chocolate and liqueurs were served. The men usually dined at the table of one of the Grands Officiers – that of the duc d'Antin being especially reputed for its cuisine and its cellar.

The King ate in the Anteroom of the Queen's Apartment, which was occupied by Madame de Maintenon. There were three tables laid and all the ladies invited had the privilege of being seated with him. To watch Louis XIV at table was an experience not easily forgotten. "With the first two spoonfuls of soup," wrote Saint-Simon, "his appetite opened and he ate such prodigious quantities . . . that one could never become accustomed to the sight." Madame filled in the details: "I have seen the King consume four different plates of soups, a whole pheasant, a partridge, a great plateful of salad, some mutton in gravy and garlic, two brave slices of ham, a dish of pastries and then fruit and preserves." It was noted with amazement at his autopsy that his stomach was twice the usual size.

The self-control which typified Louis' deportment at Versailles was noticeably less rigid at Marly. Saint-Simon records his having risen from table and broken a cane across the back of a valet whom he had seen pocketing a biscuit. "These scenes," he added, "always occur at Marly." Louis was even known to drop his royal dignity altogether and throw bread pellets at the ladies, who had permission to return his fire. Madame could not contain her indignation: "It no longer bears the slightest resemblance to a Court."

The coming of the duchesse de Bourgogne made the same impact here as at Versailles. The Pavillon du Roi underwent a considerable redecoration which started, typically, in the Chambre du Roi, where the new ceiling announced the new style – plain white, centring upon a delicate rosette of stucco. The fireplaces, too, designed by Le Pautre, which carried their tall arched mirrors

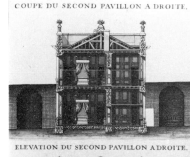

54 Section and elevation of a guest pavilion.

COUPE DU SECOND PAVILLON A DROITE.

ELEVATION DU SECOND PAVILLON ADROITE.

Echelle de cinq Toifes.

"right up under the cornice", revealed in their decoration a lightness of touch which fittingly ushered in the eighteenth century.

The years 1699, 1701 and 1703 were those of greatest activity, reflected by correspondingly heavy figures in the accounts. Work proceeded at the usual breathless pace. Madame, astonished to find a wood where she remembered a lake, hastened to describe the transformation: "You would have thought it was the fairies that were at work here." The men worked in relays through the night and the coming and going of so many points of light, together with the ghostly illumination of the façades, certainly had something of the aspect of fairyland. "More work has been done in one week at Marly," wrote Cronstöm to Tessin in October 1699, "than would formerly have been done in six months." Diligent labour did not go unrewarded. There occur in the accounts such entries as: "Memoir of a hundred louis d'or which His Majesty gave me on 10 November, 1703, to be distributed among the labourers who have worked at Marly with such precipitation."

In particular the transformation of the gardens concerned the two areas to east and west of the main axis behind the two rows of pavilions, the Bosquets de Louveciennes and the Bosquets de Marly. "What strikes me most," wrote Diderot, "is the contrast between refined art in the plantations and pergolas, and rude nature in the solid mass of luxuriant foliage of the great trees which dominate and form the background. This continual interplay between nature and art and between art and nature is truly enchanting."

The Bosquets de Louveciennes, where the contours were steeper, were richer in waterworks. Up nearest the château, behind the circular arena of the entrance court, was the Amphithéâtre, a flight of grassy steps leading from a statue of Hercules to a round pond with a tall fountain in the centre; alongside this was the Cascade Champêtre – a miniature version of the Rivière, lined with an alternation of marble statues and gilded vases.

It was devised by Père Sébastien Truchet, one of the odd, ecclesiastical figures of the seventeenth century who appear to have interested themselves in almost anything but theology and the affairs of the Church. A member of the Académie des Sciences and the friend and associate of the great engineer Vauban, Truchet was more or less attached to the Court and there is no doubt that he played an important role in the creation of Marly. For the building of the cascade he established a little railway on either side with a pulley wheel which enabled one truck to descend, acting as a counterweight to the other which was being pulled up. From the Amphithéâtre and the Cascade Champêtre, two parallel walks ran behind the line of the pavilions at increasingly divergent levels until they both opened out into the last feature of the bosquet, Parnassus or the Bassin des Muses.

Behind all these elaborate contrivances the Bois de la Princesse, named after Marie-Adélaïde, struck a new and lighter note which was to usher in a new style of gardening, for, in and out of the straight intersecting alleys, little tortuous paths wandered with the completest inconsequence, opening unpredictably into small *Cabinets de Verdure*. One of the most delightful, the Cabinet des Fleurs, contained a little temple – a blue dome upheld by marble pillars, its inner cavity painted like trellis-work and powdered with birds and flowers. It was the work of Belin de Fontenay, "peintre fleuriste", and Louis was so delighted with his achievement that he granted him a special bonus.

The number of garden games was also multiplied. There was already one course laid out for *mail* – an ancestor of golf – in the Bosquets de Marly. Another was now added up on the high ground near the top of the Rivière. Here also was the Roulette. A steep incline, starting near the Trou d'Enfer, was equipped with a sort of switchback railway on which ran a toboggan, carved and gilded, in which the young princess and her friends could descend at exhilarating speed into the valley below.

She also collected carp of the most varied colours to enliven the fishpools. They each had a name, to which she claimed that they answered. Madame observed that the poor fish seemed sad in the clear water and bewildered amid their sumptuous surroundings. Madame de Maintenon noticed also and said to Madame de Caylus: "They are like me; they are regretting their native mud."

In 1701 it seemed that the redecorations were complete. In July Dangeau noted in his journal: "The King spent all the morning and all the afternoon walking in the gardens. He told us that he could not imagine the possibility of any further embellishments to Marly." In spite of this statement he continued "creating artificial lakes and filling in natural ones", planting fully-grown trees in thick spinneys and changing the disposition of the statues and decoration of the fountains until the year before he died.

In 1714 the magnificent set of coloured drawings was compiled, which may still be seen in the Archives Nationales, showing every detail of the finished design. It was, as Louis Bertrand puts it, "the complete and perfect realisation of the thought of Louis XIV, and assuredly his masterpiece".

Louis XV made frequent use of Marly and adapted it to his own, more private way of life. His taste was for the small and the exquisite. The large rooms of the royal apartments were reduced by the insertion of an entresol and to give light to the new rooms thus created he had oval windows inserted between the two storeys. It made nonsense of the façades.

One of Louis' first moves after the arrival of Marie-Antoinette was to arrange a Voyage de Marly. The royal family lived at closer quarters here than at Versailles and the Dauphine would be brought into contact with Madame du Barry. It did not have the desired effect. "The King showed me a thousand kindnesses and I have the most tender affection for him," she wrote to her mother, "but his weakness for Madame du Barry is pitiable. She is the most stupid and impertinent creature that it would be possible to imagine. She joined us for cards every evening at Marly; twice she sat next to me, but she did not speak to me and in fact I have not entered into any conversation with her."

The refusal of Marie-Antoinette to address a single word to the King's mistress became a major issue at Court. The Austrian Ambassador Mercy, reporting on the character of the favourite, ended with the words: "Her whole desire is that Madame la Dauphine would speak to her just once." Letters passed from Versailles to Schönbrunn and from Schönbrunn to Versailles. Maria-Theresa expressed the hope that her daughter would comply with the wishes of the King. "If they were requiring you to stoop in any way, or to show any familiarity, neither I nor anyone would advise you to do so; but some unimportant word – not for the sake of the lady in question, but for your grandfather, your Master, your benefactor ..."

Marie-Antoinette's position was not as secure as she might have thought. Through no fault of her own she had not fulfilled her primary function as Dauphine – the production of an heir to the throne. Royal marriages had been declared null and void before now and princesses had been sent back to their countries of origin. The whole Franco-Austrian alliance hung in the balance. Europe waited with bated breath upon the outcome of the issue.

On 1 January, 1772, Marie-Antoinette made up her mind. New Year's Day was the occasion of one of the big receptions of the Court. The favourite, introduced by the duchesse d'Aiguillon and the Maréchale de Mirepoix, was as usual presented to the Dauphine. Having addressed a few words to the Duchess, Marie-Antoinette looked the Countess in the eyes and said: "Il y a du monde aujourd-hui à Versailles."

It was enough. The Palace Revolution was averted. But Marie-Antoinette had had her first great disillusionment. She had seen the Court of France at its fatuous worst and her opinion of it was never to recover.

On 10 May, 1774, Marie-Antoinette became Queen of France and a great change came over the life of Versailles and its dependencies. It was typical of the new Court that it did not like Marly. "Everything there," wrote Madame Campan, "seemed to have been created by the magic power of a fairy's wand;" the painted decorations made it look like a scene from an opera. After dinner the Queen and her ladies went out in their light carioles to drive in the park, where the trees had by now reached a prodigious height. Nevertheless, some of the fountains still raised their crystal columns above the treetops, and the sparkling cascades and silvery sheets of water formed a brilliant contrast to the sombre background of woodland. But only Madame Campan seems to have appreciated their beauty.

The Salon was still overcrowded and the stakes at pharaon were higher than ever. Any rich financier could come and play, but he was dubbed a "polisson" and of course he was not accorded an apartment.

During her first visit as Queen, Marie-Antoinette had the innocent desire to see the sun rise from the Belvédère which overlooked Saint-Germain. Unfortunately the King did not accompany her and the incident gave rise to the first of the calumnies against her name. The same voyage saw the arrival upon the scene of a character who was to cast an ominous shadow across the life of the Queen – the jeweller Boehmer, already occupied with the creation of his fabulous diamond necklace.

In June 1789, during the critical meetings of the newly-formed National Assembly, Louis XVI retired to Marly to deliberate his response to the situation and to mourn his eldest son, who had died earlier that month at Meudon. It was the last time that Marly was to serve as a royal palace. It was not destined to survive the Revolution.

On 21 January, 1793, Louis XVI went to the guillotine. The scaffold was erected in the Place de la Concorde just at the entrance to the Champs-Elysées. To either side of the avenue were two equestrian statues by Coysevox, "Renommée" and "Mercure sur Pégasse". They used to stand at either end of the terrace overlooking the Abreuvoir at Marly, but had been replaced in 1745 by Cousteau's more famous "Cheavaux de Marly". It seems probable that these statues were the last objects which Louis saw.

The Château de Meudon

IT IS SURPRISING how little damage the Revolution did to the royal palaces of France. No building could have more obviously symbolised the Ancien Régime than Versailles, but the only deliberate damage done by the revolutionaries was the removal of fleurs de lys, coats of arms and other attributes of royalty.

The palaces were exposed, however, to a new threat: they had lost their raison d'être. Neglect and misuse can be as fatal to a building as vandalism. Marly was the victim of both. Put up for sale by the Nation in 1793, it was bought by a manufacturer and converted into a cotton mill. The business did not flourish and the owner recovered what he could from the estate by selling the materials of the buildings. When Madame Vigée-Lebrun returned from exile in 1812, her first thought was to revisit the "hermitage" of Louis XIV. "I ran to see my happy, noble Marly." Nothing remained except a single stone which seemed to mark the centre of the Salon.

Another royal establishment to suffer a similar fate was the two châteaux of Meudon. The Old Château was turned into a munitions factory and badly damaged by an accidental explosion. Napoleon had the ruins cleared away in order to make the New Château into a residence for his son, the King of Rome. He even dreamed of establishing here a "School for Kings". In choosing Meudon for his son and heir, he followed royal precedent: Meudon was historically the home of the Dauphin. It had been here, on 4 June, 1789 – just when the storm clouds of the Revolution were accumulating – that the eldest son of Louis XVI and Marie-Antoinette had died at the age of seven and a half.

"The young prince," wrote Madame Campan, "had fallen, in a few months, from flourishing health to a rickety condition which caused a curvature of the spine and an attenuation of the features and which made his legs so feeble that he had to be supported like a decrepit old man to enable him to walk." "Everything that poor little boy says," wrote the marquise de Laage de Volude, "rends his mother's heart. His attitude towards her is one of extreme tenderness. The other day he begged her to dine in his room. Alas, she swallowed more tears than food."

He had been sent earlier that spring, with his Governor, the duc d'Harcourt, to live at Meudon, always reputed for the purity of the air. Occasionally his frail little form, dressed in a sailor suit crossed by the ribbon of the Saint Esprit, could be seen on the terrace before the château. By the beginning of June he was visibly failing. He faced his premature end with "a courage and a resignation beyond his age". In the small hours of 4 June he died. At his birth all France had been delirious with joy. Now the throne to which he had been born the heir was toppling to its fall.

Two days later, when the stricken parents were at prayer in the chapel before the mortal remains of their little boy, there arrived at Meudon a

55 Entrance court in the days of the duc de Guise.

deputation from the Tiers Etat, demanding to see the King. Three times they were told of his affliction; three times they persisted in their demand. Finally Louis acquiesced, but exclaiming in his outrage: "Is there not one among these men who is a father?"

Meudon had come into the possession of the royal family as a private residence for Louis XIV's son, the Grand Dauphin. It was a more convenient situation than that of Choisy-le-Roi, which he had inherited from Mademoiselle de Montpensier – la Grande Mademoiselle. Like Saint-Cloud, Meudon belonged almost naturally to Versailles, but each was assimilated into the royal domain in its own proper time. Meudon had been slowly brought, by a succession of owners, to a state of perfection which called for its annexation by royalty. On 5 June, 1695, just after the acquisition of the estate by the Grand Dauphin, the King was taken round the gardens by Le Nôtre. "For a long time, Sire, I have wanted you to have Meudon," said the great landscape artist; "I am delighted that it is yours now; but I would have been annoyed if it had come to you earlier, because it would have been less beautiful."

It had taken a hundred and seventy years to reach this point of maturity. The story begins with a churchman named Antoine Sanguin in the reign of François I.

Canon of the Sainte-Chapelle in 1522, Abbot of the important Monastery of Fleury-sur-Loire in 1523, Bishop of Orléans in 1534, Cardinal in 1539 and finally, in 1543, Grand Aumônier de France, Antoine Sanguin had risen steadily through the upper ranks of the ecclesiastical hierarchy. It is possible, however, and certainly not out of keeping with the age, that he owed his preferment not so much to his own intellectual and spiritual prowess as to the physical attractions of his niece, Anne de Pisseleu. Her advancement was no less impressive than her uncle's. From being one of the King's mistresses, she became the favourite; she was made a Countess in the same year as Sanguin became a Bishop, and was elevated to the rank of Duchess two years later. She is best known to history as the duchesse d'Etampes.

In 1527 Antoine Sanguin gave her the Château de Meudon. Solid facts about the dates of the building of Meudon are rare, but, in the course of a repointing of the stonework of the façades in the seventeenth century, the dates 1539 and 1540 were recorded on two of the staircase towers in the Cour d'Honneur. If, as this suggests, the building was nearly complete at that time, then Meudon is contemporary with François I's building at Madrid, Fontainebleau and the later parts of Chambord.

The house was built between four pavilions round three sides of a courtyard. A fifth pavilion marked the centre of the entrance front. These pavilions were elevated above the façades by half a storey and carried their lofty pyramids of roof high above the general silhouette. Together with their tall attendant chimney-stacks, they created that deeply indented skyline so dear to the French builder.

To either side of the courtyard, on the inward façades, a new and attractive feature was contrived – a loggia affording a covered passage between the pavilions and providing a leaded walkway above communicating with the first-floor windows. These "terraces" – as they are designated on the ground plans – were set between square staircase towers which nestled in the angles of the pavilions. These towers were crowned by little cupolas which made a further contribution to the skyline.

Another interesting feature of the style is the survival of vestigial towers. Four little turrets, built out on corbels at first-floor level, marked the corners of the pavilions at the entrance to the courtyard. They are shown on the plans as providing little circular retreats from the end rooms which may have served a very private purpose. As guardians to the entrance court they do not look out of place, but their reappearance on the garden front was something of an absurdity. These are shown on the plans as being solid; they were therefore purely ornamental and as ornaments they failed. The garden front would have looked better without them.

For here, on the south front of Meudon, there appeared, probably for the first time, what was to become the classical French façade for centuries. Exact in its symmetry, satisfying in its proportions, and built throughout with an impressive economy of ornament, the style combined the austerity of an Italian façade with the exuberance of a French roofscape. For the three pavilions and their two connecting *corps de logis* provided an alignment of five separate roofs of two different heights. Montceaux, Coulommiers, Richelieu, Vaux-le-Vicomte, Clagny and Choisy-le-Roi – to mention only some of the most important – were to follow this formula. On the eve of the Revolution, Barré's new wing at Le Lude still incorporated this articulation of roofs over the separate pavilions.

On 8 January, 1553, the duchesse d'Etampes sold Meudon to Charles, Cardinal de Lorraine. A younger brother of the duc de Guise, and therefore destined not only for the Church but for a plurality of lucrative preferments, he was Archbishop of Reims at the age of thirteen; he was also Abbot of Saint-Denis. He thus had the unusual privilege of officiating both at the coronation and at the funeral of the King. To this eminent position in both Church and State, Charles de Lorraine added the distinction of a first-class mind. He was a fine scholar and a considerable connoisseur of art. He was destined to live in troubled times and in the Wars of Religion the Lorraine family emerged undoubted champions of the ultra-Catholic cause. But during the periods of truce he found time to entertain Ronsard and the members of the Pléiade at Meudon and to endow the terrain with one of its most important features. This was the famous Grotto.

As at Fontainebleau, the Italian Primaticcio contrived here a building which was unmistakably French. It was a lofty, three-storey pavilion containing a *Salon Frais* encrusted with shells and cooled by many little fountains. The vaults, according to Vasari, were decorated with a combination of stucco relief and mural painting by Dominico Barbiere. More often referred to as "Dominique Florentin", this versatile artist is known to have worked at Fontainebleau just when the Galerie François I was under construction. It sounds as if the Grotto at Meudon was in a similar style.

To either side of the Grotto were two attendant pavilions, known as the Tour de Ronsard and the Tour de Mayenne, which appear from the engravings of Chastillon and Silvestre to have remained roofless and incomplete. It was not until the days of Abel Servien that they received the mansard roofs shown in Aveline's engraving.

Servien, who succeeded the Guise family as proprietor of Meudon, did more than complete the Grotto. He carried out a thorough renovation of the château and he undertook the prodigious earthworks of the terrace.

Israel Silvestre, in his engraving of the entrance front of Meudon "in the days of Messieurs de Guise", shows the château standing on a bleak and rocky escarpment more or less as Nature had made it. The building up of the terrace to form the gigantic platform that we see today was an enterprise that could only have been contemplated by a millionaire or an Intendant des Finances. This lucrative position fell to Abel Servien in 1653. He took the title of marquis de Sablé and in 1654 he purchased Meudon, an acquisition which marked the zenith of his career.

There is a long and interesting account written by "Two Young Dutchmen" who visited Meudon in September 1657. Their horses had been unable to mount the steep ascent and they were obliged to proceed on foot. "At last we arrived on the terrace, which is at least 500 or 600 yards square. It was not yet finished, but a great number of men are continually at work levelling the earth and removing the mound which made it impossible to have a large forecourt or a fine avenue." It is necessary to visit the site today to get the full impression of the colossal scale of this *terrassement* and to marvel, as the two

Dutchmen marvelled, at the great containing wall, so high that it seemed to them "like a precipice".

But above all they admired the view. "From this terrace there is a view which is without equal both for its beauty and for its diversity, which is the most happy blend that it would be possible to imagine, for one can see the river Seine meandering across a rich and charming plain, an incredible number of beautiful houses and large villages, some in the valleys and others upon little knolls, and the whole is so beautifully disposed that one seems to have before one's eyes the picture of an idealised landscape. But what is best about it is that one overlooks in its entirety the biggest, the richest and most magnificent city in the whole of Christendom."

Bernini, who visited Meudon in 1665, was characteristically derogatory in his observations. To his more sophisticated eye, Paris was just "a heap of chimneys" only to be compared to a carder's comb, whereas Rome, of which he proceeded to give an inventory of the monuments and palaces, presented from a distance a prospect "very magnificent and superb". Of the château itself, he was no more complimentary. In the Vestibule he declared that Servien's new staircase, singled out by the two Dutchmen as "a masterpiece of art", would be unacceptable even in an Italian inn.

In addition to the terrace, Servien provided Meudon with a park proportionate to its importance. The woods of Clamart and Trivaux were added to the domain, enabling Servien to prolong his avenues to the east and to the south. Lands were brought adjoining Chaville and Sèvres and the Valley of Fleury. Finally at the end of August 1657 he obtained permission "to extend his park and to surround it with a wall, although the properties acquired are *dans le voisinage des plaisirs de Sa Majesté*".

Servien died at Meudon on 5 February, 1659. His son, "extremely debauched", so ruined his fortune that he was reduced to living on the charity of the King. He somehow managed to retain Meudon for twenty years, but on 31 October, 1679, he sold it to François-Michel Le Tellier, marquis de Louvois, son of the Chancellor and one of Louis XIV's most valued Ministers.

The Le Telliers already owned Chaville, a modest but well-appointed country house, adjacent to Meudon. There could have been no more striking symbol for the rise to power of Louvois than his purchase of the great house by which his father's little château had always been overshadowed.

He could hardly have seated himself better. Meudon was renowned for its pure air, its beautiful gardens and its incomparable outlook. It was handy for Paris, it was handy for Saint-Germain, but above all it was handy for Versailles. In 1678 more than two million livres had been spent on the latter – well over twice the sum accounted for in the previous year. It was by now quite clear that Louis XIV intended to make this his definitive seat of the Court and the Government.

The duc de Saint-Simon has left a glowing account of the new Minister's abilities. "M. de Louvois was the greatest man of his kind that has been seen for several centuries. Nothing could be more comprehensive, nothing more fertile, nothing more just than his head for great undertakings. He was indefatigable at his work, and a work which was all day and every day, evaluating, discerning, directing with unimaginable ease all the details of which not even the smallest escaped him. Magnificent in everything, noble in everything, of an open-handed generosity, making to friends and relations presents that were truly princely. The best parent in the world and "Father of the Poor" to whom he never refused anything . . . living at home like a little King and yet with no insolence, talking without embarrassment of his humble origins and of the social difference between himself and his in-laws." He had married, in 1662, Anne de Souvré, a daughter of one of the most distinguished houses of France.

Such was the man who became, in 1679, the new châtelain of Meudon. It was he who was to put the final touch to the picture by extending the gardens – an undertaking for which he naturally employed Le Nôtre.

Louvois and Colbert, who had brought the domain of Sceaux in 1670, both had the example of Fouquet to warn them. Louis XIV did not tolerate being outshone by his ministers. "I have often understood," wrote Louvois to Le Peletier, "that the crowds of people who went to Sceaux displeased the Master." He was careful not to make the same mistake at Meudon. His correspondence also with La Tuilière, Director of the French Academy in Rome through whom he purchased works of art, reveals his moderation as a connoisseur. When Cardinal Nini's collection came up for sale, Louvois asked La Tuilière to purchase some "provided that you do not consider them worthy of a place at Versailles".

On 2 July, 1685, Louvois offered a fête at Meudon for the King and all the Court. He had provided sedan chairs to enable everyone to visit the lower gardens, of which the *Mercure Galant* recorded that "a great number of very beautiful fountains formed one of the principal ornaments". The marquis de Sourches remarked also on the magnificence of the collation offered to the distinguished company "during which all the violins and hautbois of the Opéra were playing airs from Lully. Afterwards the King went on foot in the gardens, which are the most beautiful in the world."

The gardens of Meudon derived their attraction from the happy use made by Le Nôtre of the natural contours of the land. The windows of the south front looked out onto a *parterre de broderie* beyond which the ground fell away sharply. It was cut back into two terraces, the lower of which contained the Orangerie, with its parterre before it, forming a natural sun-trap. Only from the top of the terrace was the whole perspective visible. The great avenue, the Allée de Trivaux, maintained a level contour between two *pièces d'eau*, the Grande Carré and the Etang de Chalais, and then began its upward sweep to a point at which it should have been crossed by the park wall. To avoid this intersection of the view, Le Nôtre had the charming inspiration of replacing the wall by a moat from which there rose a number of slender jets, each some twenty feet high and so closely set as to merit the name of La Grille d'Eau.

To the north of this axis the Grotto dominated another *parterre de broderie* which overlooked the steep descent to the Jardins Bas and the grand Parterre de Gazon, beyond which lay the meadows of Fleury backed by the wooded slopes of Issy and Clamart.

The Jardins Bas were too steeply set to be visited except on foot, but to the west of the Grotto were the Jardins Hauts where the gentler slopes permitted the use of a calèche. The most notable feature of the upper gardens was a vast

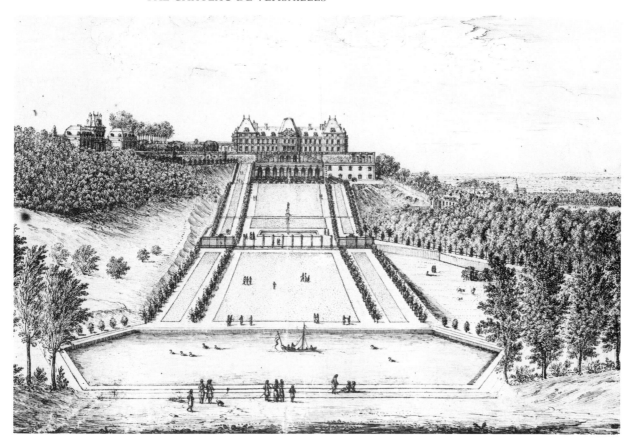

56 Garden front and Orangerie with Grotto left. Drawing by I. Silvestre

oblong enclosure formed by a double avenue of oaks, of which the upper branches, meeting overhead, suggested the ribs and tiercerons of a Gothic vault. This resemblance earned it the name of Le Cloître. The Abbé Boutard, writing in 1703, was so overcome by the numinous impact of this venerable plantation that he attributed its origin to the Druids.

The beauty of the gardens ministered to the attractions of the house. The view from the windows was not the least important element in the décor. The apartments in the east wing enjoyed the panorama of the Seine valley – "the most beautiful view in Europe," claimed the *Mercure Galant*, "because from here one overlooks the whole of Paris, and there is but one Paris in the world." At right angles to this suite, the rooms on the south front looked out over the Parterre de l'Orangerie and across the Etang de Chalais to the endless avenue of the Allée de Trivaux. From the room in the south-west angle – the Salon du Petit Pont – the windows commanded the lovely outlook onto the Grotto by means of a French window and a little bridge, this room gave direct access to the upper terraces.

From this Cabinet d'Angle, the Grande Galerie formed the west wing of the château. Louvois had always fancied the role of Ministre de la Guerre, and the main decoration of the gallery consisted in the alternation between paintings by van der Meulen of the victories of Louis XIV and military trophies sculptured in full relief that formed the drops between the paintings.

169

This great suite of apartments, numbering seventeen rooms in all, ranged round the three sides of the courtyard, was largely hung with tapesty. Those in the east wing had in common a background of trellis pergolas, from which the whole suite derived the name of "l'Appartement des Berceaux". As a delicate compliment to the King, the first room was hung with twenty paintings of the gardens of Versailles by Cotelle. These may have been his sketches for the larger series painted for Trianon in 1693.

Pictures, which were mostly copies from Italian originals, hung on the walls that were not devoted to tapestries. The unifying theme to all these rooms was the great series of overdoors painted by Jean-Baptiste Monnoyer. Monnoyer, often known as Baptiste for short, worked a great deal in England, especially for the Duke of Montagu, and many of his colourful flower paintings are to be seen today at Boughton. Monnoyer's flowers linked the beauties of the garden with the decoration of the château.

On 16 July, 1691, Louvois died, shortly after a shouting row with Louis XIV. That evening the young Saint-Simon noted narrowly the countenance of the King. "He appeared to me in his customary majesty, but with a certain air of light-heartedness and liberation which I found rather surprising."

Four years later, the King offered to Louvois' widow the Château de Choisy, together with the sum of 900,000 livres, in exchange for Meudon, which now became the official residence of the Grand Dauphin. Saint-Simon devotes one of his most devastating passages to the poor man. "As for his character, he had none. He was without enlightenment or knowledge of any kind and radically incapable of acquiring any; very idle, without imagination or productiveness, without taste, without discernment; neither seeing the weariness he caused others nor that he was a ball moving willy-nilly at the impulsion of others." This unfortunate victim of the Duke's merciless, penetrating perception was to live "absorbed in his fat and his ignorance" in Louvois' château where he was capable, so the duchesse d'Orléans said, of spending the whole day lying on a sofa tapping his feet with a cane.

Madame, however, has left posterity a more shrewd assessment of the character of this prince. Writing on 16 September, 1699, from Fontainebleau, she calls him "the most incomprehensible man in the world. He is not at all stupid, and yet he behaves as if he were. This is because of his dullness and indifference." It can have been no easy thing to have been born the son and heir of the Grand Monarque.

Saint-Simon was wrong in asserting that the Grand Dauphin had no taste. The history of Meudon makes it clear that he had a taste of his own, in important ways distinct from his father's, and the main apartments were redesigned to suit his own ideas.

By the summer of 1699 the new decorations were more or less complete and on 3 July the King dined at Meudon in order to inspect them. On the very eve of the eighteenth century the style which was to typify its earlier years had already been created. The genius of the new style was Bérain; his work is misleadingly described as "grotesque": it would be better named "*fantaisiste*". The word is better left in French, for the English "fantastic" has rather lost contact with the creative implications of "fantasy".

In the Chambre du Dauphin a very special fireplace was devised. It cost a total of 8,774 livres. Fourteen different specialists were involved in its creation, among whom the great name of Boulle is outstanding. The style involved an elaborate inlay of bronze and tortoise-shell similar to that in most of Boulle's furniture. Unfortunately no example of the application of this technique to interior decoration has survived, but there is at Versailles a portrait of the Grand Dauphin which shows in the background his Cabinet in that palace, which includes a monumental chimneypiece of the same sort as that which was achieved at Meudon. In all, 1,021,847 livres were spent on the redecoration of Louvois' château.

The new châtelain of Meudon was at pains to house the royal family in the greatest of comfort. To the King was allotted the apartment on the first floor of the south front, from the central Salon des Maures to the Salon du Petit Pont at the eastern extremity. Madame de Maintenon was treated as Queen and occupied the rest of the same floor. The furniture in her apartment mostly came from the late Queen's rooms at Vincennes. To this added a "fauteuil de commodité" – a sort of portable private latrine known as a "confessional", upholstered in gold and silver silk.

The Dauphin himself took over the Appartement des Berceaux, from the windows of which he could command the famous view of Paris, and he inserted an entresol for the accommodation of his mistress, Mademoiselle Choin. Another mistress of his, Françoise Raisin, was, according to Madame, obliged to observe the Dauphin's strict régime of fasting. When Madame asked him why he did so, he replied: "My intention was to commit one sin, but not two." By the time the apartments had been allotted to such members of the royal family as the duchesse de Bourbon and the princesse de Conti, and of course their servants, there was not much more in the way of accommodation left. Meudon was too small for a royal house.

A first extension was achieved by developing a little quadrangle to the right of the entrance court, known as the Aisle des Marronniers. This soon proved inadequate and in the autumn of 1705 the Dauphin decided to build a second château on the site of the Grotto.

The "Château Neuf", which was the last commission to be undertaken by Mansart, was quite simply an annexe and needs to be judged as such. Louis XIV found that it "resembled more the house of some financier, rather than that of a Prince". The façades were dignified without being in any way distinguished, but in the slight arching of the ground-floor windows, and in the way in which their pediments borrowed the same lines, the lighter touch of the eighteenth century may be discerned.

Inside, the plan was developed with barrack-like precision. A long corridor ran from end to end of each floor, dividing it into two equal halves. These were devoted each to six identical apartments consisting of a bedroom, a cabinet and a garde-robe. Seen as a ground plan it suggests a monotonous austerity, but in fact the Château Neuf at Meudon paved the way for the more commodious grouping of rooms which became typical of Mansart's successor and son-in-law, Robert de Cotte. Hitherto it had been usual for each room to open into the next, so that the last room in the suite could only be reached by passing through all the others. At Meudon every apartment had three separate means of access.

57 Entrance front with
Château Neuf to the
right. P. D. Martin.

The Grand Dauphin did not have long to enjoy his new creation. On 14
April, 1711, he died at Meudon of smallpox. Louis was beside himself with
anguish, but Saint-Simon records maliciously that Madame de Maintenon sat
on a sofa with him "and attempted to cry". Mademoiselle Choin – perhaps
the most disinterested of all royal mistresses – departed into oblivion and died
in 1732 after twenty-one years of modest and pious retirement.

The Château de Meudon, no longer the centre of interest to assiduous
courtiers, went into a gentle decline from which it was never to recover. But
in 1717 two foreign potentates were to pay it their highest compliments. On
19 May, the Tsar Peter the Great, who had not scrupled to express his
disappointment with Fontainebleau, visited Meudon accompanied by Prince
Rakoczy and the Maréchal de Tessé; he declared that "the situation of this
royal house and its view gave him more pleasure than all the rest". In October
of the same year, Joseph-Clement, Elector of Cologne, wrote to Robert de
Cotte for designs for his Buen Retiro, a *Lustschloss*, to which he wanted to be
able to retire from Bonn "to seek tranquillity and to rest his mind from public
affairs without being importuned by a crowd of courtiers." He specified that
he wanted the decorations to be "like the apartments were of the late Dauphin
at Meudon".

The château became the property, first of the duc de Bourgogne and then
of his sister-in-law the duchesse de Berry. On her death it reverted to the

Crown and was used to provide "grace and favour" lodgings for distinguished courtiers. The duc de Saint-Simon and his wife were lodged in the Château Neuf and found the gardens "a charming place for every manner of walk".

With the arrival of a new Dauphin, the eldest son of Louis XV, Meudon reverted to its former function of housing the heir apparent, and for a few years recovered its original splendour. On 14 May, 1733, the *Gazette de France* records that the Dauphin and his sisters were taken by their Governess to pass the summer months here "to strengthen his constitution by walking and by the sweet air that one breathes there". They returned to Versailles at the end of September "in perfect health".

Towards the end of Louis XV's reign, the situation had deteriorated badly. In June 1770 the Contrôleur Le Dreux sent an impassioned appeal to the King. "I see only tears and despair," he wrote; "the children of Boisselet, the Park gardener, the only workmen that remain to him, have left their father . . . The garden will become a wilderness." The few workmen who remained did not even receive their proper wages. "Rossignol, gardener of the Orangerie, waters the orange trees with bare feet, bare legs and bare head . . . he has neither eaten meat nor drunk wine for two years."

The gardeners had even been obliged to petition Madame du Barry for the payments which they had not received. Under-payment led to neglect and neglect to invasion. "The fences were in such disrepair that you might see all the people of Paris in the most beautiful gardens of Europe."

But Louis XV was not interested in the upkeep of an old-fashioned and obsolete domain. He was building at the gates of Meudon the Château de Bellevue for Madame de Pompadour and was doing his best to turn Versailles from a monument to the Grand Monarque into a building which reflected the lighter, more intimate taste of the mid-eighteenth century.

Louis XV

THE VERSAILLES of Louis XIV was the architectural expression of his own conception of Monarchy. It was the vast theatre of a continuous pageant of royalty. It was, practically, in no sense a "machine à habiter". When, in the mid-eighteenth century, Blondel gave his verdict on Versailles, he made a criticism which it would not have occurred to the seventeenth century to make; he complained of the lack of "essential commodities". This made the building out of date, "the distribution of rooms being one of the branches of Architecture in which we have made most discoveries since the building of this palace".

Blondel was also severe in his criticism of the façades. Even those towards the garden, which usually attracted the praise of the eighteenth century, offended against his rules of good taste. The repetition of round arched windows on two successive storeys shocked him; the use of the Ionic order for so large a building struck him as "intolerable"; as for the architecture of the entrance courts, he went so far as to call it "semi-Gothic". It was to his mind already *proved* "how contrary it was to propriety to place a visible roof over the residence of a crowned head".

Versailles in the eighteenth century, therefore, was in twofold danger. It was regarded as uncomfortable and it was condemned as being in bad taste. Gabriel's great project for rebuilding the whole palace "au goût du jour", however, resulted only in the reconstruction of half a wing in the Cour Royale. Louis XV was more interested in the comfort and decoration of the interior.

"Louis XV," wrote Dufort de Cheverny, "was, in his domestic life, the most lovable and the best of men; as a private individual, as the father of a family, he would have been held in affection, esteem and consideration."

In the person of Louis XIV the natures of private individual and King were hardly to be distinguished, so completely was the man identified with his rôle. With Louis XV the distinction was so marked as to amount almost to dual personality. "To separate Louis de Bourbon from the King of France," wrote Madame Campan, "was what this monarch found most piquant in his royal existence." This unresolved discord of his inner nature left him a deeply dissatisfied man.

There was only one person who seems to have understood his deepest needs and to have discovered the means of ministering to them, and that was Jeanne-Antoinette Poisson, Marquise de Pompadour. Once again Dufort de Cheverny observantly distils the essential truth: "She had the great art of being able to divert the most difficult man in the Kingdom to amuse, whose natural taste was a love of privacy, but who felt that his position demanded the opposite; with the result that as soon as he could extricate himself from public appearances, he would descend by a secret staircase to her rooms and lay aside his character of King."

This dualism at the heart of his existence expressed itself nowhere so clearly as in his attitude to architecture. Next to hunting, building was probably his favourite diversion. Madame de Pompadour admitted that he was only really happy when he had a batch of architectural designs spread before him. On 8 July, 1739, the marquis d'Argenson noted in his journal: "The King is continually making the young Gabriel do his designs in front of him in private." The style to which he gave his name was well on its way before Louis XV began to exercise his patronage. Robert de Cotte, who had brought a new lightness to the last buildings of the previous reign, was the first architect also of the new régime.

In place of the impressive majesty of the Grand Siècle, which matched the stiff discomfort of the courtly life, the *style Louis XV* offered a combination of luxury and superficiality. Alexander Pope might have been writing of the old style in "Timon's Villa":

> "So proud, so grand; of that stupendous air,
> *Soft* and *Agreable* [sic] come never there."

Soft and *Agreable* were to be keynotes of the new style. The angles are rounded off, the straight lines give place to gentle curves; the mouldings are gracefully turned, their arches breaking into delicate scrolls that curl in upon themselves and blossom out into a spray of tiny flowers or become lost in a lace-like rosette at the foot of the panel. The furniture, too, the chairs, the sofas, tables, consoles and commodes, borrow the same undulating lines and obey the rhythm of the whole décor.

But the change came gradually and, to begin with, the great tradition in architecture was maintained. The finishing of the immense Salon d'Hercule, already planned by Robert de Cotte, in no way suggested the destiny which the next forty years was to reveal in the interiors of Versailles.

The Salon d'Hercule, the link between the Vestibule of the Chapel and the Grand Appartement, not only continued the style of Louis XIV; it surpassed much of it in excellence. It was the ceiling which gave this room its special lustre. It is a heroic conception, the Apotheosis of Hercules, and it was the work of a humble postillion's boy, Antoine le Moyne. "There is hardly in Europe," wrote Voltaire, "a painting more vast than the ceiling of le Moyne, and I do not know of any more beautiful." It took three years to paint and on 26 September, 1736, it was finally unveiled. "That day," wrote the painter Donat Nonnotte, "the King, going to Mass as usual, looked at the work of le Moyne with an expression which announced the good fortune of the painter." on his way back the King stopped again to look at the ceiling and created its author then and there Premier Peintre du Roi.

The Salon d'Hercule was the last variation upon a noble theme. It was not in the Grands Appartements that the new style, *le style Louis XV*, was to be created, but in what were known as the Petits Appartements du Roi. These were the rooms on the first floor of the north side of the Cour de Marbre. Under Louis XIV these had consisted of a number of small rooms and the Petite Galerie painted by Mignard. Such names as "Cabinet de Tableaux" and "Cabinet des Curiosités" proclaimed their purpose. These rooms housed most of Louis' art treasures, and he was very agreeable to the admission of those who were genuinely interested.

The Abbé Bourdelot obtained admission through his acquaintance with Bontemps, the Premier Valet de Chambre and a person of considerable influence at Court. "He had me conducted into the Petit Appartement du Roi," writes the Abbé, "which is none the less large, magnificent and sumptuous." The pictures, which were arranged according to the artists' names, were provided with little curtains which were drawn for his benefit. He was in his usual transports of admiration.

This easy access to the King's private apartment was typical of Louis XIV. Publicity was an art which he had studied; the magnificent spectacles to which all were admitted; the elaborate firework displays which all could enjoy; even some of the most domestic occasions in the King's life were accessible to the humblest bourgeois who could dress decently and hire a sword to gain admittance to the palace. It was as if Versailles was a royal museum and the person of the King was the chief exhibit.

It is essential to bear this publicity in mind when approaching the Versailles of Louis XV, for he came to dislike it and his dislike is clearly reflected in his alterations to the palace.

In the Petits Appartements on the first floor of the Cour de Marbre and in

58 Section of the Petits Cabinets showing the reduction in the height of the rooms by the insertion of an entresol.

the Petits Cabinets on the second floor above, and encroaching progressively upon the inner courtyard known as the Cour des Cerfs, Louis created the interiors which concerned his private existence. He began at the top. High up under the roof he started, as early as 1727, to construct a network of cabinets linked by narrow galleries and little winding stairs. Here were tiny libraries of the neatest invention and the most elegant design; a bathroom with a bedroom attached in which he could relax after his ablutions; above was a workshop fitted with a lathe where he could work ivory under the direction of Mademoiselle Maubois; there were still-rooms and a bakery where he made chocolate and sweetmeats with the expert assistance of the pâtissier Lazur; there was a roof garden with trellis screens and a little aviary.

Here, with a small circle of intimate friends, Louis could shut himself off from the heavy formality of the Court.

The rooms were decorated with delicately-carved panels painted in a distemper known as *chipolin* and finished with a polish known as *vernis Martin* which gave them the gloss and freshness of porcelain. This was the most typical feature of the new style; gilding was either banished or confined to the frames of pictures and mirrors and its place was taken by soft colours. "Les peintures couleur d'eau, petit vert, jonquille, lilas, gris de perle, blue de Prusse font la gaieté des appartements."

First to be built were the libraries; they were ranged round the north side of the Cour des Cerfs and formed a little suite of four rooms, of which one, the Galerie de la Géographie, was little more than a corridor equipped with "very beautiful maps" mounted on spring rollers. The carved decorations were almost confined to the window recesses, but of course the books themselves – "well chosen and very beautifully bound" – formed an important part of the decorative scheme, and, where space did not permit of the genuine article, the walls were lined with the backs of books specially ordered from the Sieur Collombat, the Court bookbinder. Ten large folios bore the title "Descriptions de Pays inconnus"; another set was devoted to "the Pleasures of Celibacy".

On the opposite side of the Cour de Cerfs from the libraries, and overlooking the Cour de Marbre, was the Petite Galerie. The five dormer windows provided a feature of which Gabriel made the happiest use, creating thereby a series of delightful panelled recesses which are still to be seen, but the gilding dates from the redecoration of this suite for Madame du Barry. The wall opposite the windows was hung with six paintings representing scenes of big-game hunting which formed the most important decoration of the gallery.

There were two dining-rooms, both dating from 1735. The Salle-à-Manger d'Eté was right up on the third floor and must have commanded a most interesting roofscape. The Salle-à-Manger d'Hiver was moved from place to place, ending up on the east side of the Cour des Cerfs next to the Petite Galerie.

These were the scenes of the intimate supper parties for which the Petits Cabinets were above all famous. One of the most interesting accounts of these parties comes from the duc de Croÿ. İt seems that he was half-expecting to be involved in some orgy which did not in fact take place. He was torn between the desire to be admitted among the élite and the fear that by doing so he might be obliged to compromise his moral integrity. He took elaborate precautions to have the King reminded of his presence. Invitation at that time could virtually only be obtained through Madame de Pompadour. Those who hoped to be asked presented themselves at the door of the Cabinet du Conseil after the King's return from the hunt. Louis then marked off the names of those to be invited which were then read aloud. "An usher," wrote the comte d'Hézècques, "announced the names of the elect, who slipped proudly into the apartment, while the rejected ones returned to their own rooms to hide their vexation and sat down sadly to their own repasts."

"We entered one by one," wrote the Duke, "and we mounted into the Petits Cabinets." One can imagine the thrill of climbing the little oval staircase and penetrating this inner sanctuary of the Court. "The Dining Room was delightful, the supper enjoyable, without restraint. We were only served by two or three Valets of the Wardrobe, who retired after placing all that was necessary before each of us. The King was easy and gay, but always with a certain grandeur which one could not overlook; he did not appear in the least shy, but very much at home and talking very well. We were there for about two hours with great freedom and no excess."

The Salle-à-Manger d'Eté opened directly onto the leaded roofs of the palace and on summer evenings the King and his guests would sometimes walk round behind the balustrade. "For some time," recounts the duc de Luynes, "he has been going up onto the roof of the château and walking with those who have the honour of dining with him right to the end of the new wing, and from there right to the end of the Aisle des Princes." It is the most fascinating walk in the whole of Versailles. Over the courtyards they could look down into the illuminated windows of the palace and sometimes Louis would make surprise visits to his courtiers. "He has been several times to converse with Madame de Chalais," continues Luynes, "by a window which opens onto the roof, and with Madame de Tallard by the chimney."

More often the evening after a supper party was spent at the tables of the Salon du Jeu. Here Louis made and served the coffee himself to avoid the constraint imposed by the presence of servants. Everyone was permitted to sit and the evening passed without formality until the King, with a gay "allons, allons nous coucher", gave the signal to retire. The ladies made their reverences and departed and the men descended to present themselves in the ordinary way for the *coucher*.

For sixteen years Louis continued to sleep in the bedroom of his great-grandfather in spite of the impossibility of heating so lofty an apartment. The cold at Versailles could be severe and Louis sometimes found it necessary to pass into the Cabinet du Conseil to warm himself before going through the ceremony of the *lever*. But he did not like to do this too often because it entailed waking his personal servants before the usual time. "If I get up before the *entrées*," he told Luynes, "I light my fire myself . . . if I go through into my Cabinet I would have to call them. These poor people must be allowed to sleep, I prevent them often enough." There was a certain endearing simplicity and modesty about Louis.

When he was ill it was his custom to have his bed made up in the Cabinet du

Conseil for the warmth and convenience which it afforded, and this may have given him the idea of making a smaller bedroom for his personal use.

During the voyage of the Court to Compiègne in the summer of 1738, the first of the old Cabinets of Louis XIV on the north side of the Cour de Marbre was enlarged and redecorated by the sculptor Verberckt and furnished as the royal bedroom. The panelling survives today intact, but the character of the room has been somewhat lost by the disappearance of the balustrade and pillars from the alcove. The latter were in the form of palm trees whose undulating branches enclosed the upper half of the recess.

Here it was Louis' practice to sleep, but first he held the *coucher* in the official bedroom and laid himself solemnly in the ancestral bed; when the company had withdrawn he got up and went into his new bedroom where he slept until it was time to get up, go back and get into the official bed and receive the *entrées* for the *lever*.

From the alcove in the new bedroom a little door led into a Garde–robe where Louis installed, in 1738, a "chaise à l'anglaise" or water closet. It was made of marquetry by Jean-Philippe Boulle and it cost 600 livres. Verlet has also brought to light some of the details of the other furnishings. Two little "fumoirs chinoises" made of white porcelain, with a pot pourri to match, together with a "fontaine à parfums" maintained the freshness of the room. Louis was known to shut himself up here for total privacy when he was sulking or in tears.

If Etienne Martin, the inventor of the *vernis Martin*, was the name chiefly to be remembered in connection with the Petits Cabinets, the two sculptors Jacques Verberckt and Antoine Rousseau established their reputations in the creation of the Petits Appartements on the first floor. Verberckt in particular was not only to cover acres of wall-space with his exquisite carving; he was to become the first exponent of the *style Louis XV*. These rooms, larger in scale and accessible to a wider public, were accorded a more princely decoration in white and gold according to the fashion of the age.

Next to the bedroom is the Cabinet de la Pendule, which only received its present form in 1760. It is important to note, however, that much of the decoration dates from its earlier form, when it was known as the Cabinet Oval, which was constructed in 1738 at the same time as the bedroom. Verberckt, in making the extra panels for the new rectangular room, copied his former style exactly. This was the result, often perplexing to art historians, of the economy observed by the new Contrôleur des Bâtiments, the marquis de Marigny, who was the brother of Madame de Pompadour. Whenever possible he ordered the re-use of old material. The plan of the Cabinet de la Pendule had Marigny's note in the margin: "How much will it cost if we use all the old, and what is there in the workshop?" In spite of this economy there is no more perfect example of the *style Louis XV* in the whole of Versailles.

The most notable piece of furniture in this room is the astronomic clock from which it takes its name. Designed by Passement, constructed by Dauthiau and ornamented by Caffieri, the clock showed not only the hour, but the day, the month, the year and the phase of the moon. It is surmounted by a crystal globe in which the planets perform their revolutions according to the system of Copernicus. Louis XVI, also a lover of things mechanical, used to sit up in this room until midnight on New Year's Eve to observe the complete change recorded on this clock.

Beyond the Cabinet de la Pendule is the Cabinet Intime, occupying the corner overlooking the Cour de Marbre and the Cour Royale. It was Louis' favourite room; in 1741 the duc de Luynes described him as being "almost always in the cabinet which is beyond the Cabinet Ovale". It is another perfect example of the style and it is again the result of successive stages of redecoration employing "all the old" in its final re-shaping in 1760. It is again the product of collaboration between Verberckt and Rousseau.

In this room stands the elaborate bureau à cylindre of which there is a copy in the Wallace Collection in London. Designed and begun by Oeben, it was completed after his death by Riesener and finally delivered in 1769. It has an ingenious locking device whereby a single turn of the key closes the roll-top and locks the drawers.

The room has been known by many names – the Cabinet d'Angle, Cabinet Intérieur or Cabinet Intime. Perhaps the last is the most appropriate, for the room is associated with the most moving scene recorded in Louis' private life, the funeral of Madame de Pompadour.

It was fixed that the cortège should leave Versailles at six in the evening; etiquette forbad the presence of the King. Outside was raging a fearful tempest and the rain lashed incessantly on the windows of the palace. Alone with his valet de chambre Champlost, Louis had locked himself into the Cabinet Intime and was standing on the balcony which overlooks the Place d'Armes and the Avenue de Paris. The picture is painted by Dufort de Cheverny. "He maintained a religious silence, watched the convoy threading its way down the avenue, and despite the foul weather and the exposure to the air, to which he seemed insensitive, following it with his eyes until the whole procession was lost to sight." He turned and re-entered the room. Two large tears stood on his eyelids and ran down his cheeks. "Voilà les seuls devoirs que j'ai pu lui rendre" was all that he could say.

There is strangely little at Versailles today to recall the passage of Madame de Pompadour, although she was the inspiration of the age. Her rooms on the ground floor, beneath the Grands Appartements, must have been among the most exquisite in the palace. The Inventory, published by Jean Cordey, evokes a level of luxury at which every little domestic item becomes an objet d'art. Everything was done regardless of expense and regardless also of the exigencies of time. The Voyage de Compiègne and the Voyage de Fontainebleau provided the indispensable breathing space which afforded the opportunity but also fixed the limits for any campaign of redecoration. In 1751 this new apartment had to be begun after the departure for Compiègne and ended with the end of Fontainebleau.

The administration was in the hands of Madame de Pompadour's uncle, Le Normant de Tournehem. It was made more difficult by the lack of money. "I cannot conceal from you," wrote Lécuyer to Le Normant, "that they are absolutely without funds." Verberckt was having to pay out wages at the rate of 300 livres a day while 37,812 livres were still owing to him. Guesnon, charged with supplying the panelling to the rooms, was little better off. Of fifty thousand livres owing to him only four had been paid and he was obliged to borrow at interest to keep his workshop open. On top of everything Madame de Pompadour announced her intention of returning a week earlier than expected from Fontainebleau. "Il faut faire l'impossible pour que cela soit prêt" was all that her uncle could order.

It had been the same under Louis XIV, but this time there was no Colbert to provide for the King's extravagance. Versailles had, under proper control, contributed to the greatness of the Grand Siècle. The colossal expenditure had at least created an incomparable collection incomparably housed and had established the supremacy of France in the world of art. "Who could have told," asked Montesquieu, "that the late King had established the greatness of France by building Versailles and Marly?"

Louis XV maintained this supremacy, but he could no longer afford to. In the fullness of time Versailles was to play a not unimportant part in the downfall of the Monarchy.

Curiously enough the coming of Madame de Pompadour improved the relationship between Louis XV and his wife. "The King has carried his attentiveness to the Queen," observed Luynes in December 1746, "to the point of noticing an old inkstand which the Queen has been using for some time and he sent her another, very beautiful one." It was not inkstands, nor even little attentions, which Marie longed for, but the thought was a kindly one and in all probability it came from Madame de Pompadour; she had a sharp eye for such details and a genuine desire to please the Queen.

The life of Marie-Leczinska at Versailles was not destined to be a joyful existence. Too ready to find pleasure in what she knew to be her duty, she had fallen passionately in love with her handsome young husband. But she was not made to inspire similar affections for very long in Louis' heart. Their relationship soon degenerated into timidity on her part and indifference on his. Too nervous to say anything of importance to him, she took to communicating by letter.

Madame du Deffand, who was a niece of the duchesse de Luynes and knew the Queen well, described her in a letter to Horace Walpole. "Her integrity and irreproachable conduct were combined with a rare discernment and great modesty, and her desire always to give pleasure made her company delightful." But she was more than a virtuous woman: she was a Queen. "This same princess," wrote Président Hénault, "so good, so simple, so sweet and so affable, carried herself on state occasions with a dignity which commands respect. She keeps up in the Court that concept of grandeur such as that of Louis XIV is always represented to us." It was only in her part of the palace that the true traditions of the French Monarchy were maintained.

Among Marie's friends the most notable were the duc and duchesse de Luynes. Described by Hénault as "the most estimable man in the world", the Duke was one of the few at Versailles who was above those considerations of interest which undermined the morals of so many. His second wife became the Queen's dearest friend, and as often as the King supped in his Petits Cabinets, Marie went down and supped with the Luynes in their apartment.

The Duke's brother, the Cardinal de Luynes, was a man of genuine, if simple piety and of an endearing absence of mind. His sermons were directed with unerring aim at the vices peculiar to the Court – no other vices being known to him. The standard of behaviour in the Chapel left much to be desired. The marquise de la Tour du Pin tells how the ladies who followed the Queen to Mass were met at the door of the Salon d'Hercule by their lackeys armed with huge red velvet sacks fringed with gold. As soon as the royal family had entered, the ladies dived into the galleries to left and right of the royal closet and scrambled for the seats nearest to the King. Their lackeys then arranged the velvet sacks about their knees and feet and tucked their trains in beneath the seats.

It was this sort of conduct which moved the Cardinal to eloquence. "How is it that luxury follows you to the very steps of the altar? How is it that these cushions and sacks of velvet covered with fringes and tassels precede your arrival at the Temple of the Lord?" Unfortunately, having composed this tirade for the benefit of the Court, he read it, in a moment of complete abstraction, to an entirely bucolic congregation. "Quittez, quittez ces habitudes somptueuses!" he urged the bewildered peasants, who were as innocent of the irreverence imputed to them as they were ignorant of the articles described. The story got round, Madame Campan informs us, and so amused the Court that titled ladies used to get up early to go and witness for themselves these strange miscarriages of zeal.

In the Queen's apartment at Versailles the memory of Marie-Leczinska is somewhat eclipsed by that of her successor, Marie-Antoinette. Nevertheless, the decoration of the Queen's Bedroom dates for the most part from 1737. It was the first of the State Rooms to be altered and its alteration raised the inevitable protest from the diehards. "What could be more august," asked Saint-Yves, "than the King's State Room at Versailles? Seeing it one could almost fancy oneself in the midst of Ancient Rome. Those who are charged with the decoration of the Queen's would have done better to have copied exactly what they have just destroyed. Our moderns, prodigal in ornament, are but indifferent decorators." It is possible to disagree with his opinion.

Although the main decoration dates from 1737, it has been discovered by Pierre Francastel that the panel between the windows was renewed "à la moderne" by Robert de Cotte in 1730. It was he, therefore, and not Gabriel who set the style.

Tall mirrors, placed between narrow panels which take to some extent the place of pilasters in the decorative scheme, answer each other from opposite sides of the room between the doors and the alcove. The uprights of these mirror frames are in the form of palm trees, whose foliage curls in at the top to hold an oval picture. Above the mirrors were portraits of the King and Queen, and between the windows was one of the Queen's father, Stanislas Leczinski.

Here Marie lived most of her life as Queen, wife and mother. Here more than anywhere else in the palace, the old etiquette of the Court was punctiliously observed. A single example will show how careful Marie was to accord everyone their little distinctions. Duchesses had what was called the "droit du tabouret", that is to say the right to sit, on certain occasions, on a stool known as a "tabouret", in the royal presence. In 1736 M. de Châtillon, Governor of the Dauphin, was made a Duke and his wife was presented to the Queen. Marie was at this moment on her feet and about to go to the comedy, but she tactfully sat down for a few moments to allow the new Duchess to enjoy her privilege.

The great rooms of the State Apartments were the scene of these exacting public appearances. Behind these rooms, round the inner courtyard known as the Cour de la Reine, Marie-Leczinska had her own Petits Cabinets, which were by all accounts equal to those of the King for charm and delicacy of ornament.

Here it was her custom to retire for some two hours every day. Her time was given up to music, painting and reading poetry. Only the duchesse de Luynes dared to disturb her in this private retreat. Marie-Leczinska was a talented artist and musician. She took painting lessons from Oudry and some of the pictures on the walls of her cabinets were her own.

Her patronage of music was more important. "The concerts given in the Queen's Apartment twice a week were the centre of the musical life at Court," writes Barbara Scott; "the performers included all the greatest instrumentalists of the day, such as the violinist Mondonville and the cellist Giovanni Battista Bononcini."

Marie was a pupil of Couperin and no mean performer herself. She also played a form of bagpipes known as a *musette de cour*.

Her love of music was passed on to her daughters and especially to Madame Adélaïde, who was in some way the most colourful personality in the family. She was an accomplished violinist, but perhaps it was more in keeping with her tomboy character that she could sing bass nearly as loud as her brother.

Happily the Salon de Musique in her beautiful suite of rooms adjoining the Petits Appartements du Roi remains intact. Designed by Gabriel and executed by Verberckt, the decorations date from 1752, but in 1767 the alcove with the lovely drops of musical instruments was added. One is tempted to believe that the style of these trophies requires an earlier date, but Verberckt was perfectly capable of reproducing his earlier style and the payment to him in this year of 2,000 livres "for the Cabinet of Madame Adélaïde" does not suggest the use of older material.

The room recalls the visit of the young Mozart in the winter of 1763–64. He was only seven at the time. His father Leopold Mozart describes the occasion. They were invited to attend the Grand Couvert. "Not only were we placed near the royal table," he wrote, "but Wolfgang stayed the whole time at the Queen's side, chattering almost continually, kissing her hands and eating from the dishes she offered him. The Queen speaks German as well as we do and since the King does not understand a word, the Queen translated for him everything that Wolfgang said."

Adélaïde's apartment was made at the expense of Louis XIV's Petite Galerie. This had been used for some time by Madame de Pompadour for the private theatricals in which she took such a delight. But it was too small and it offered no facilities for scenic effects.

In 1748 she persuaded Louis to allow the Escalier des Ambassadeurs to be used. La Vallière was charged with the construction of a theatre which could be erected in twenty-four hours and dismantled in fourteen. "It will be finished during Fontainebleau," wrote the duc de Luynes; "it has been put up in the cage of the Grand Escalier de Marbre or des Ambassadeurs without doing damage to the marbles or to the paintings. This theatre will be dismantled for all the ceremonial occasions when it will be necessary, as for example, the ceremonies of the Order."

The staircase had been much admired in the previous reign by reason of the magnificence of its marbles, the excellence of its paintings and the heroic scale of its proportions. But above all it was admired for its overhead lighting. For Le Vau had made a virtue out of necessity and provided the staircase with a skylight. "The impossibility of obtaining light from any other source than the centre of the vault," wrote one contemporary, "produces the most wonderful effect. It results in a greater harmony in the paintings and the light from it is majestic."

Now, in 1752, it was falling, like so many other monuments of the Grand Siècle, into disfavour and disrepair. It was virtually only used for the ceremonial procession of the Knights of the Saint-Esprit on New Year's Day.

It was for such spectacles that Versailles had been designed; first came the Petits Officiers, then the Grands Officiers, then the Chancellor of the Order in rochet and violet cape, immediately followed by the "novices" in their short cloaks. Those who had already been admitted to the Order were gorgeously arrayed in silk trunk hose and stockings, their tunics crossed with the blue ribbon of the Order, and wearing the long robe of blue velvet embroidered with tongues of fire and doubled with ermine upon which lay the golden collar with the Cross and the Dove which were the special insignia of the Order.

The duc de Croÿ described the stiff discomfort of these robes. "One was suffocated, strangled, overwhelmed by these immense mantles and it was impossible to turn round. Mine cost some 8,000 livres not counting the rest of the outfit and it weighed horribly on me causing great pain to my collar bone."

Le Brun's decoration provided a worthy theatre for such pageantry, but it was no longer in keeping with the spirit of the reign. The demolition of the staircase was part of Gabriel's great project for rebuilding the whole of the entrance court. The short wing known as the "Aisle Gabriel" was all that was ever realised.

Although the taste for little apartments and private theatricals was as typical of the eighteenth century as grandeur and pageantry had been typical of the seventeenth, the large-scale receptions and public spectacles were common to both. It is possible that the fête given by Louis XV for the marriage of the Dauphin and the Archduchess of Austria, Marie-Antoinette, was the most magnificent ever seen at Versailles.

It was the occasion also of the last important addition to the palace, the Salle de Spectacle or Opéra.

As early as 1748 Gabriel had brought out his designs comprising the elegant new façade, whose simple, rectilinear proportions and stately attached portico are reflected in the reservoirs at the extremity of the Aisle du Nord. But it had to wait many years before the project was realised.

The custom had been, when any really large-scale entertainment was given, to rig up a ballroom for temporary use. This was often done in the *manège* of the Grande Ecurie. But now, in 1767, the marriages of the Dauphin's children

59 The Opéra used as a banqueting hall. Moreau le Jeune.

were looming up on the horizon and disquieting the royal exchequer. To improvise four temporary, but costly, entertainment rooms and to have nothing to show for it at the end was extremely wasteful. Papillon de la Ferté, Intendant des Menus Plaisirs, addressed a memorandum to the King urging the completion of the theatre of the Reservoirs. Costly though it would be, it might be regarded as an economy since it would put an end to the constant expense of temporary structures.

It was not, however, an extravagantly-conceived design. In the interests of economy no less than of acoustics, most of the structure of the auditorium was of wood painted to resemble marble. The colour scheme is one of the most successful at Versailles. The marbling is achieved in a warm salmon pink against a background of dull grey-green known as *verd-de-mer*, both of an infinitely subtle variety of tones and lavishly enriched with gilding. Contrasting with this is the cold, bright cobalt of the silk hangings and the more sombre blue of the patterned velvet upholstery.

The auditorium, in the shape of a truncated ellipse, is encircled by a colonnade which breaks into a graceful apse above the royal box. Each bay of the colonnade is backed by a mirror and each mirror reflects and thus completes a half chandelier which hangs against its surface. The rest of the house was lit by fourteen great chandeliers, each of them one and a half metres high and each containing ninety-six crystal pendants. In the apse was an even larger one, two and a half metres high and containing more than three hundred pendants. It took eight men to hoist it. A total of three thousand candles was required for the lighting of the whole. The duc de Croÿ noted that the chandeliers were left illuminated throughout the performance, "thus lighting up from below a superb ceiling, they produced the most admirable effect".

The Salle de Spectacle was also a potential Salle de Bal. It was equipped with a floor which could be laid down over the entire pit, thus joining the auditorium to the stage, the scene set to reflect the amphitheatre, and the whole opera house turned into one enormous ballroom or banqueting hall.

On 17 May, 1770, the Dauphin and Marie-Antoinette were married in the Chapel at Versailles and at 9.30 that night the *Festin Royal* inaugurated the ceremonies. In the Salle de Spectacle the floor had been laid down and a table with covers for twenty-two was set in the middle and surrounded by a balustrade. A hundred and eighty musicians were accommodated on the stage and the Court, in all the scintillating glory of full dress, occupied the boxes round about. The duc de Croÿ went into raptures. "For a whole hour I did not tire of admiring it from all sides; seeing it one was tempted not to regret the two and a half million which it cost."

In the evening the Galerie des Glaces formed the setting for the gaming. "Everything had been lit up," continues Croÿ, "and the dresses showed up with a greater lustre by their light. It is astonishing how it shows them up and brings out the gold and silver just as daylight tones them down."

The three days of celebrations ended with a firework display and illumination of the park which were perhaps the most magnificent ever seen at Versailles. A wonderful impression is given in Moreau's sketch. There were some two hundred thousand admitted that night to see this never-to-be-forgotten spectacle. Years after the Revolution, when the English traveller Nattes visited Versailles, his guide still remembered the fantastic pyrotechnics of that evening. "This immense park, illuminated through all its extent, was far more brilliant than when lighted by the sun in all its splendour. The waters in their varied falls reflected in a thousand ways the effects of the illuminations; some, falling from a great height, seemed to shed torrents of light, while others, elevating their streams in the air, appeared to descend in a shower of fire." It was impossible for him to do justice to the scene, there were so many things which "at the time dazzled the eye and astonished the mind"; in vain did he string together the details that he remembered – "all that you read of Fairyland would give but an imperfect idea of the whole".

The fireworks had surpassed anything of the kind that had ever been seen. The Court watched the display from the windows of the Grand Galerie. The curtains were drawn back and the magnificent spectacle of the illuminated parterre was revealed. The King gave the signal for the fireworks to start by hurling a flaming lance from the central window. "It was concluded," wrote Nattes, "by a Giranda of twenty thousand rockets, which, by its prodigious detonation and the immense blaze of light, produced the effect of the terrific eruption of a volcano."

It would be pleasant to be able to end on that note, but that would be to tell only half the truth. In 1769, when work was in hand on the Opéra and the Dauphin's apartment, Marigny wrote to the King: "All the contractors for these parts are in the deepest discouragement." Two hundred out of some two

60 Galerie des Glaces in
the days of Louis XV.
Cochin.

hundred and fifty workmen had been withdrawn from the Opéra; the agent
supplying the panelling for the Dauphin's rooms refused even to begin until
he had been paid. To the comtesse de Noailles Marigny wrote: "For the last
eighteen months I have hardly had the disposition of a single penny for the
relief of a throng of wretches who are dying of hunger, and to whom, at the
moment, wages are due for a year and a quarter."

The marquis d'Argenson was not far wrong when he predicted that
"buildings are bringing desolation to the country and will be the ruin of it".

Louis XVI

ON 10 MAY, 1774, the young couple who were the centre of all these
rejoicings became King and Queen of France. "The Dauphin and I,"
wrote Marie-Antoinette to her mother, "are appalled at the prospect
of reigning so young." Their succession, however, was the joy of all France
and in particular of the younger generation at Court. "As for us, the gilded
youth of France," wrote the comte de Ségur, "we walked upon a carpet of
flowers which covered an abyss."

Most of the memoirs of this reign were written long after the events.
Looking back across of bloodshed and exile on the last days of the Ancien
Régime, it seemed to many that it had been a golden age; their writings have
evidently acquired some of the gilt of nostalgic reminiscence, but they are far
more interesting to read than the chronicles of disputed precedence of the
previous reigns. Thanks to their more human approach, the picture comes

into sharper focus for the final scene. A landscape is never so vivid as in the last hour before the sunset fades.

Outstanding among these memorialists are two ladies, the marquise de la Tour du Pin and the comtesse de Boigne. They are each in their own way severe in their criticisms of this so-called golden age.

"The licentious reign of Louis XV," wrote Madame de la Tour du Pin, "had corrupted high society. The nobility of the Court set the example of all the vices. Gaming, debauchery, immorality and irreligion were flaunted openly." Writing many years after the events, she came to the conclusion that the Revolution "was no more than the inevitable result, and I would even say the just punishment, of the vices of the upper classes".

Brought up in the household of her great-uncle the Archbishop of Narbonne "in which all the rules of religion were daily violated", her formative years had exposed her to "everything that could have corrupted my mind, perverted my heart, depraved and destroyed all idea of morality and religion".

His château of Hautefontaine, between Compiègne and Soissons, was common to both memorialists, for Madame de Boigne was also related to the Archbishop. Her mother, the marquise d'Osmond, found the tone of the household most distasteful. One day an old Vicar General, seeing her obvious embarrassment, tried to comfort her. "If you wish to be happy here," he advised, "try and conceal your affection for your husband; conjugal love is the only one which is not tolerated."

It was a fairly general attitude. The duc de Guisnes said to his daughters when he presented them at Court: "Remember that in this country vices are of no consequence, but one ridiculous action is fatal."

Such a generation had little respect for the great tradition which was its heritage. The works of Lully were "brought up to date", those of Molière dismissed as "in exceedingly bad taste"; the gardens of Le Nôtre were found insupportable and the palace of Le Vau and Mansart ripe for reconstruction. "Anything that was long-established," wrote Ségur, "seemed to us tiresome and ridiculous." To this, however, there was one fatal exception: the long-established privilege of birth.

Despite the new atmosphere, life at Versailles seems to have continued very much the same. Chateaubriand, after his presentation in 1787, made the significant remark: "Louis XIV was still there." In the State Bedroom, now hung with purple and gold brocade and lit by porcelain candelabra, the ceremony of the *coucher* continued in all its splendour. "At eleven o'clock," wrote the comte d'Hézècques, "the service and the Court arrived. Everything was prepared; a magnificent gown of gold brocade and lace; on a red morocco armchair, the nightdress of white silk embroidered at Lyons; the shirt, wrapped in a piece of taffeta; on the balustrade, a folded cushion on which were laid the nightcap and the handkerchiefs. By their side the slippers, of the same stuff as the grown, were placed near the Pages of the Bedroom, who leant against the balustrade."

The comte Hilarion de Beaufort, who was page to the comte de Provence, the elder of Louis' two brothers, had described the function of the pages at the *lever*: they stood by a marble-topped commode. "I knew every vein in it," he wrote, "for I had much idle leisure in which to study it." They waited while the Usher threw open the doors to the Grande Service, with a courteous "Pray enter, Gentlemen", they waited while the marquis d'Avaray helped His Royal Highness on with his shirt – sometimes affording the pages a glimpse of His Royal Highness's posterior, "plump and white", while he tucked in the shirt tails; they waited while His Royal Highness donned his Court coat of embroidered satin; they waited while the barber enveloped His Royal Highness in a huge wrapper of muslin and lace to protect his clothing while his hair was powdered and curled; they waited while his face was gently wiped with a soft cloth in case any specks of powder had trespassed upon it. "Now came the great task for which the two pages had been waiting. Just imagine: it was no less than to step forward and each remove one slipper from the Prince's feet. We carried them back with as much respect and solemnity possible, to the commode by which we had been standing."

Young Hilarion had joined Monsieur's household in January 1776. He describes how his headmaster, the Gouverneur des Pages, conducted him to the palace for his presentation; "proud as a young peacock in my embroidered coats, I was convinced that I was already a personage at Court." His disillusionment was immediate: Monsieur received him in silence – "scarcely deigning an indifferent glance at my small person, he gave me only the courtesy of a barely perceptible nod".

In contrast to his brother, Louis XVI took a delight in his pages and not infrequently joined in their youthful escapades. Between the Queen's Apartment and the King's was a passage which the King often used. It was lined with upholstered benches on which a number of the palace servants slept, providing an irresistible temptation to bored but spirited young gentlemen – their open mouths inviting a syringe full of water or their closed lips the delicate application of a moustache by means of a burnt cork. In this they received encouragement from their sovereign, and when the victim awoke, blinking and spluttering, "the King, laughing heartily, would flee from the scene of battle with as much speed as his young army". Naturally this sort of behaviour endeared him to the young. "These childish pranks I have just described have, for me at least, the consoling merit of adding yet another tribute to the memory of the finest man the world has ever seen."

Not everyone would have so described Louis XVI, but on his virtues the verdict of those who knew him is unanimous. But, owing to the deficiencies of his education, he suffered from a shyness which expressed itself in a *gaucherie* which could be most unfortunate in a King. "In private," wrote Madame de Boigne, "the King used to complain bitterly of the manner in which he had been brought up. He said that the only man for whom he had ever felt hatred was the duc de la Vauguyon [his Governor]."

Madame de Boigne gives an example. "With the best intention of being obliging to someone, he would advance towards him to the point of making him retreat until his back was against the wall; if nothing to say occurred to him – and this was often the case – he made a great guffaw, turned on his heel and walked away. The victim of this public exhibition was always the sufferer and, if he were not an habitué of the Court, departed in high dudgeon, convinced that the King had wished to offer him an insult of some sort."

"Louis XVI was a good King," wrote his page, the comte d'Hézècques; "but unfortunately he lived at a time when his very virtues led inevitably to his ruin ... To a shy character, the fruit of a neglected education, this Prince joined such a kind-heartedness that, in an age of egoism, one never saw him in any circumstances, not even at the moment of danger, put his personal interest in the balance against that of his subjects." But with this goodness, this kind-heartedness, this readiness for self-sacrifice there was a pathological inability to make decisions – and he was called to reign at a time when decision-making was all important.

Louis himself valued the stately ceremonial and dignified traditions of Versailles, and he was right. "The French," wrote the comte de Ségur, "in spite of the light-heartedness with which they are reproached, or perhaps even because of it, soon cease to respect the authority of those who govern them once they see them without the garb of gravity." "Strip the Prince of the glory with which he is surrounded," observed Hézècques, "and he will be no more in the eyes of the populace than an ordinary man."

"Louis XVI," wrote the prince de Montbarrey, "would have liked to have retained the ancient forms; but he did have the strength to command their continuance, and his complaisant weakness allowed the change to take place against his will." The public could still watch him eat "with a good humour which it did one good to see" – and they were still admitted to the gaming, but the former occasions became more rare and the latter more short. "The Queen's private society reduced to nothing the official occasions of the Court, except for Sundays and major fêtes, which were reserved as the occasions demanded by etiquette, and consequently occasions of boredom."

But, if Louis tried ineffectively to maintain the solemnity of his Court, he continued also some of the habits of privacy of his grandfather. He also liked to sup in the intimacy of the Petits Cabinets, and it appears that he did himself uncommonly well. "It must be admitted," wrote the marquis de Séguret, "that it would be difficult to carry the art of gastronomy to greater lengths."

Much heart-burning was caused by the exclusiveness of these supper parties. Ladies were informed in advance of their invitation and occupied a special bench in the theatre. After the performance they followed the royal family up to the Petits Cabinets. The men were subjected to more humiliating treatment. A special bench was reserved for those who hoped to be invited. "During the entertainment," wrote the comtesse de Boigne, "the King directed his large opera glasses on these benches and could be seen writing down a certain number of names." The applicants then went to the anteroom of the Cabinets, where the Usher read out the names of those selected. "The lucky chosen one made his reverence to the others and entered the holy of holies." When the last name had been read, the Usher banged the door shut "avec une violence d'étiquette". It took years before Madame de Boigne's mother could persuade her husband to submit to this degrading treatment.

Those not invited to the private suppers had the right to eat at the King's expense at the table d'honneur in the Grand Commun. But to eat here was considered an indignity. "One would have sooner eaten a chicken at the rôtisserie." And yet these dinners at the Grand Commun were, by universal consent, regarded as the best, both for good cheer and for good company, at

Versailles. "Their society was most agreeable and enlightened; one met there artists, men of learning and men of letters; it was highly entertaining. But an *homme de Cour* could not make a practice of going there. My father frequently regretted it." Although the new generation considered itself emancipated, it was still enslaved to this kind of stupid snobbery.

In some respects Louis was more emancipated than they were. He had a great interest in things mechanical and set up a forge in the attics over the Cabinet du Conseil, where he amused himself by learning the art of the locksmith. According to Hézècques, his work showed little evidence of real ability, but it was not unknown for the King to be found on his knees before one of the doors of the palace, picking the lock.

Louis was out of tune with his times; he was out of tune with his courtiers. While they were going into ecstasies over Beaumarchais, he remained faithful to Molière, but his real taste was for tragedy and he knew most of Racine by heart. He was interested in history and geography and science and he was a great reader. It is not inappropriate, therefore, that his most important addition to Versailles should have been a library.

This large and elegant apartment was created on the site of Madame Adélaïde's bedroom. It is an impressive testimony to the versatility of the artists that the Library – the noblest room in the Louis XVI style at Versailles – should have been designed by Gabriel and executed by Antoine Rousseau, who were the two great exponents of the previous style. It was the last work either of them was to do at Versailles.

On 10 June, 1774, only one month after Louis came to the throne, the work was commissioned. It was to be carried out that summer during the Voyage de Compiègne. Gabriel drew up his instructions. "You will need to demolish immediately all the existing panelling and to trace out very carefully on the parquet the plan of the whole so as to establish the thickness of the woodwork, and to trace on the walls all the elevations."

The ornament is restrained and exceedingly subtle. The rounded corners of the room are relieved with drops representing the great diversity of subject matter in the library shelves – globe, telescope, Roman sword, shepherd's hat, the masks of Tragedy and Comedy and books which vary from the *Henriade* to the works of Bossuet, all joined together by a network of flowers and ribbons. Other floral drops, of the most delicate design and the most accomplished workmanship, mark the divisions between the bookcases.

Above the mirrors are bas-reliefs, one of Apollo leaning on his lyre and the other representing France receiving homage from the arts. The greatness of France in the world of art and letters was a fitting subject for the symbolism of Versailles, and Louis peopled his library with statuettes in Sèvres porcelain of the great authors of his country – La Fontaine, La Bruyère, Racine, Boileau.

Here, surrounded by the images of a glorious past, Louis loved to sit at a little table drawn up in the window recess, so that he could look down on the people who came and went about their business in the courtyards of the palace. Behind, the vast mahogany table, its top made from a single piece of wood, was littered with books and papers. It was his favourite room, and still one of the few rooms in the palace which have that lived-in look which distinguishes a house from a museum.

"In viewing the King's apartment," wrote Arthur Young in 1787, "which he had not left a quarter of an hour, with those slight traits of disorder that showed he *lived* in it, it was amusing to see the blackguard figures that were walking uncontrolled about the palace, and even in his bedchamber; men whose rags betrayed them to be in the last stage of poverty . . . One loves the master of the house who would not be hurt or offended at seeing his apartment thus occupied if he returned suddenly. This is certainly a feature of that *good temper* which appears to me so visible everywhere in France. I desired to see the Queen's apartment, but I could not. Is Her Majesty in? No. Why then not see it as well as the King's? *Ma foi, Monsieur, c'est une autre chose!*"

On the other side of the château, in the old State Rooms of Marie-Leczinska, lived the new Queen and her ladies, their towering headdresses and unwieldy trains imposing upon them a stately deportment and an odd, distinctive gait by which a lady of the Court could always be identified. "It was a great art," wrote Madame de la Tour du Pin, "to be able to walk in this vast apartment without catching the train of the lady who preceded you. You had to avoid ever raising the foot, but to let it slide along the parquet flooring, always highly polished, until you had crossed the Salon d'Hercule." Those who were to be presented took special lessons in this and the standard was extremely high. "Les dames avaient en tout cela," admitted Hézècques, "une addresse admirable."

As for the Queen herself, she stood out in clear relief against the already brilliant background of the ladies of the Court "as a great oak in a forest dominates the trees around it". She had been endowed by nature and by her upbringing with "all the royal makings of a Queen".

Edmund Burke describes her in a famous passage: "It is now sixteen years since I saw the Queen of France, then Dauphiness, at Versailles, and surely never lighted on this orb, which she hardly seemed to touch, a more delightful vision. I saw her just above the horizon, decorating and cheering the elevated sphere she just began to move in glittering like the morning star, full of life and splendour and joy. Little did I dream that I should have lived to see disasters fallen upon her in a nation of gallant men, in a nation of men of honour and of cavaliers. I thought ten thousand swords must have leapt from their scabbards to avenge even a look that threatened her with insult. But the age of chivalry is gone. That of the sophisters, economists and calculators had succeeded: and the glory of Europe is extinguished for ever."

But it was the Queen herself who helped to extinguish it. That was the tragedy of Marie-Antoinette: she was of the stuff that Queens are made, but her true qualities were only brought out by the suffering which the Revolution imposed upon her. Roussel d'Epinal records a parade of his regiment before the Tuileries. They halted with his platoon exactly opposite the Queen. She asked who they were. "Your loyal men of Lorraine," he answered. "She thanked me with a bow accompanied by a look which I can still see now, so deeply did it affect me. This look, which was not lost on any of my comrades, was so moving that we would have been ready to carry out any orders that this unhappy couple might have given us at that moment."

But Louis was incapable of giving orders. "If Louis XVI had had the same character as Antoinette, I have not the slightest doubt that he would still be

King of France. She missed no occasion to arouse and to retain the love of her subjects. In the Temple and in the Conciergerie she was seen to tame her farouche guardians and to make devoted servants out of her most mortal enemies."

Roussel was saying the same as Burke. If Marie-Antoinette had maintained a steady contact with a wide cross-section of the public all might have been well. But she did not do so until it was too late. Some fatal influence diverted her attentions from her public duty to a small circle of private friends.

It was partly a personal weakness. The comtesse de Boigne observed that "the Queen liked to be surrounded by the most agreeable young men that the Court could offer; she was far more willing to accept the homage that was offered to her as a woman than that offered to her as a sovereign." Unable for many years to return the ponderous affection of her husband, and doubtless deeply frustrated by his long inability to consummate their marriage, she did not give him then the one support that could have saved him.

The other fatal influence was that of Versailles itself. One of the objects of the old ceremonial had been to present the royal family to their subjects, who had free access to Versailles, in as imposing a light as possible. The people enjoyed the pomp and pageantry of the Court, always provided that there was not a shortage of bread. Although financially the country was ripe for revolution, the royal family had a great deal of prestige to lose. It is strange to read in a publication called *La Maison du Roi* of 1789, of "this attachment which borders on fanaticism which the Frenchman had for his King, of the effect of which all those who did not witness the return of Louis XV after his illness at Metz can form only a very imperfect idea".

It was to match and to maintain this fanaticism that the pomp and ceremonial of the Court had been designed. But the etiquette of a Court is like the ceremonial of a church. The moment it is done for its own sake it is in danger of becoming counter-productive and its greatest enemies are often its most ardent devotees.

Just such an ardent devotee was Arpajon, comtesse de Noailles, *dame d'atours* to Marie-Antoinette from the moment she set foot in France. This lady had much the same effect on Marie-Antoinette as an inflexible and puritanical governess might have on a spirited child; instead of instilling in her excellent principles, she provoked reaction. "She had no outward attraction," wrote Madame Campan; "her deportment was stiff, her look severe; she knew her etiquette backwards." The stately, but seemingly pointless ceremonial of the Court was not enhanced in the Queen's eyes by being associated with this old Gruffanuff – "Madame l'Etiquette", as she called her.

Madame Campan relates a typical example of the Countess's preoccupation with minutiae. "One day the Queen was receiving someone or other – I think they were newly presented – and I was near the bed with the ladies-in-waiting. Everything was in order, or so, at least, I supposed. Suddenly I noticed the eyes of the comtesse de Noailles fixed upon mine. She made a little sign with her head. Her eyebrows were raised, lowered and raised again. Then she began to make little gestures with her hand. I had no doubt from this dumb show that something was not *comme il faut*." Completely mystified, Madame Campan looked about for a possible cause for her discomfiture, but the Countess's consternation only increased. "The Queen noticed all this and looked at me with a smile. I found some of means getting close to her, and she said in a low voice: 'undo your pinners or the Countess will die of it.' All this agitation was caused by two pins which were holding up my pinners. The etiquette of costume prescribed for this occasion 'barbes pendantes'."

Marie-Leczinska had respected requirements of etiquette even in child-birth. This was undoubtedly the worst ordeal which confronted a Queen.

On 11 December, 1778, Marie-Antoinette gave birth to her first child. In the great bedroom a special bed had been prepared near the fire and screens were erected to keep off the multitude of onlookers – "the crowds of sightseers who rushed into the room". They even climbed onto the furniture to have a better view of the proceedings; "one could fancy oneself in a public place," wrote Madame Campan. It was on this occasion that Louis broke open the window "with a force that only his love for the Queen could have given him", for she was in danger of suffocating and the princesse de Lamballe had fainted.

Marie-Antoinette's reaction to this public delivery is not recorded, but there was the added disappointment that the child was a girl. In the eyes of the court the Queen had merely failed to produce an heir to the throne. What is recorded is Marie-Antoinette's reaction to her first-born. "Poor little thing – you are not what was wanted, but you will be no less dear to me. A son would have belonged more particularly to the State. You belong to me; you will have all my care, you will share my happiness and sweeten my sorrows."

Although her tardy motherhood brought Marie-Antoinette to a more responsible outlook on life, it did nothing towards reconciling her to a public existence. Her subsequent children were brought into the world before a small, select audience only, and the family was another pretext for her to live her own life in the Petits Cabinets.

In 1779 Marie-Antoinette began a complete reconstruction and redecor-ation of these rooms. The first to be altered was called the library, but this did not arise from any enthusiasm for reading on the part of the Queen. "Apart from a few novels," wrote Besenval, "she never opens a book." Perhaps on account of her lack of interest in their contents, many of the volumes in her library were false, the Court book-binder, Martial, having provided a selection of decorative backs to ornament the shelves.

The Méridienne, a little octagonal room, was mostly decorated with mirrors, for it was here that Marie-Antoinette came to try out her tall and often preposterous coiffures. A portrait of her in one of these was offered to the Empress Maria-Theresa who sent it straight back with the words: "I have not found in this the portrait of a Queen of France but of an actress." Here also the Queen chose her jewels and the materials for her dresses and held her lengthy conferences with her dressmaker, Rose Bertin. An album was kept with samples of the materials of all her costumes and was brought to her every morning. She marked with a pin the choices for the day, and the dresses were then brought up from the wardrobe.

The decoration of the room was designed by Mique and executed by the brothers Rousseau, sons of old Antoine Rousseau. It recalls their only work at Trianon, the little boudoir behind the Queen's bedroom. The minute detail of the patterns carved out of the solid wood has all the precision of the bronze appliqués on the marble fireplace, they incorporate peacocks and flowers, and dolphins. These owed their inclusion to the fact that since 22 October, 1781, France had an heir to the throne. His birth was the signal for an outbreak of rejoicing which almost restored the waning popularity of the Queen.

In 1783 the largest of the rooms, the Cabinet Intérieur, was redecorated and became known as the Cabinet Doré. The decorations were in the very latest style and would almost pass for Empire if the dates were not fully attested to in the accounts. The eight large panels, which form the greater part of the decorative scheme, are richly embellished with gilded carvings in which figure winged sphinxes, displayed eagles, smoking braziers which were to become so fashionable. Here stood the Queen's harp and harpsichord, used when Marie-Antoinette sang with Grétry and Madame Vigée-Lebrun. Here she held her private audiences, and it was from here, relates Madame Campan, that Lauzun was expelled with an indignant "Sortez, Monsieur!" after which the Queen gave orders that he was never to be admitted again. It was assumed that Lauzun had been over-gallant in his address to the Queen.

Marie-Antoinette had only one affair of the heart and that was with Count Axel Fersen, a Swedish nobleman "beautiful as an angel and very distinguished in all respects". The comtesse de Boigne had little doubt as to the nature of the liaison, which "although suspected, never caused a scandal. If the Queen's friends had been as discreet as Monsieur Fersen, the life of this unhappy Princess would have been exposed to less calumny."

Calumny was to be her undoing. The reputation of Marie-Antoinette received a blow from which it never recovered from the repercussions of the affair of the diamond necklace. The story does not belong here, but the moral does. The comte Beugnot, whose memoirs shed a new light on the whole affair *du côté de chez la Motte*, draws attention to the real offence. It was "that M. and Mme la Motte had dared to pretend that the Queen of France, the wife of the King, had gone by night to one of the bosquets of Versailles, had had an interview with the Cardinal de Rohan, had given him a rose and permitted him to throw himself at her feet; and that for his part a Cardinal, one of the great Officers of the crown, had dared to believe that he had been granted a rendez-vous by the Queen of France, the wife of the King, had kept the appointment, had received a rose from her and had thrown himself at her feet."

That was the cause of the royal indignation, but behind this indignation was the deeply unpalatable fact that such an outrage could be felt to be remotely credible. No one could have possibly imagined concocting such a story about Marie-Leczinska. Caesar's wife must indeed be above suspicion.

The site of this nocturnal interview between the Cardinal and the impostor was the bosquet known as the "Queen's Garden". It occupied the place of Louis XIV's Labyrinthe, which had not only fallen into disrepair but was dangerously out of fashion. "It has never been the King's intention to restore the labyrinth," wrote Angivillier in September 1782; "His Majesty preferred a private garden planted with trees and flowering shrubs, mostly exotic species; this was executed three or four years ago, and is beginning to produce a most agreeable effect."

61 Marie-Antoinette playing the harp. Gautier-Dagoly.

The gardens of Versailles were at this time at their highest moment of perfection. On 15 May, 1770, on the eve of the marriage of the Dauphin and Marie-Antoinette, the duc de Croÿ took a walk right round the gardens to inspect the preparations for the fireworks. It was a glorious day – "le plus beau jour du printemps" – and the woods were resplendent in the fresh and varied greens of early spring. "I could not cease to marvel at the height of the trees, which are too often ignored. These are the tallest oaks I have ever seen, equalling in their height and in the straightness of their shafts and tallest pine trees. Their shade, and the number of birds which they shelter, deserve more praise than they receive, but at that time the English taste for artificially natural prairies meant that one made a point of finding fault with these superb gardens which, although perhaps a little monotonous, are the richest in the world."

The vicomte d'Ermenonville, himself the author of one of the first and finest landscape gardens in France, was the severest critic. "Le Nôtre," he said, "massacred nature; he invented the art of surrounding himself, at great expense, with a belt of boredom."

It is not, however, possible to massacre nature. During the last hundred years nature had been steadily enriching the work of Le Nôtre in her own inimitable manner, giving a grandeur and a nobility to the plantations which were not of man's making. The gardens had become, in the words of the poet Delille:

"Chefs d'oeuvre d'un grand Roi, de Le Nôtre *et des ans*."

On the morning of the marriage the duc de Croÿ mounted by means of the Petits Cabinets onto the roof of the palace. It is by far the best viewpoint from which to enjoy the gardens. "I do not believe anything in the world has equalled the beauty of that sight, the effect of which was greatly enhanced by the freshness of the newborn leaves," he wrote; "c'est de là qu'il faut voir Versailles!"

But it was at this moment of mature perfection that the trees were destined to disappear. Outwardly magnificent, the bosquets of Versailles contained a great deal of dead wood. It was decided that it would be best to cut them all down and start afresh. On 15 December, 1774, the comte d'Angivilliers put the timber up for auction.

The felling of a noble wood is always a profoundly moving spectacle, and the destruction of Le Nôtre's trees made a deep impression on the duc de Croÿ. Few people have ever appreciated the gardens of Versailles more wholeheartedly than he. He knew when and from where to enjoy them best; he was prepared to walk to the far end of the Pièce d'Eau des Suisses, "où le coup d'oeil du fond est admirable", or to get up early to see the sun rise upon this princely scene. Now that the trees were gone he could hardly bear to revisit the place. "I did not dare look that way in the gallery; they had been so beautiful when I last saw them, and my heart bled for them." Nevertheless he was too sincere a critic not to recognise the interest now given to the works of statuary; "all the marbles in the garden being visible at once, a superb ensemble was revealed." The appearance of the park denuded of trees is preserved in two paintings by Hubert Robert, now in the collection at Versailles.

Hubert Robert was given the task of designing a new setting for the groups of statuary originally housed in the Grotte de Thétis. Apart from this one concession to contemporary taste it had been decided that the replantation should respect the lay-out of Le Nôtre. This decision was most gratifying to Cröy. "The fact is that that of Le Nôtre is needed to accompany palaces and for the grand taste, and the English or Chinese taste for rural retreats."

Hubert Robert's design was that of a landscape painter who already saw classical art through the eyes of a romantic. The huge rocky outcrop, sculptured slightly to suggest a Grecian architecture, opens its cavernous mouth to contain the statues, which appear strangely dwarfed by their situation; a cascade finds its inconsequent way down the face of the rock and fills a pool at its foot. There is certainly none of Le Nôtre's formality here, but Hubert Robert has not come appreciably nearer to nature. Nothing could be more patently artificial. "One cannot really imitate rocks," observed Delille, "any more than any of the other great effects of Nature."

It was not at Versailles that the Jardin Anglais was to show its real charms, but at Trianon.

The Petit Trianon

IN 1749 the duc de Luynes noted "the King and Madame de Pompadour have been amusing themselves by collecting pigeons and poultry". They were to be found everywhere, at Fontainebleau, at Compiègne, on the rooftops at Versailles. Now they were to have a home of their own, situated to the north-east of the Jardin du Roi at Trianon. By November the Duke was able to report that the "new menagerie" was almost finished. The "new menagerie" was a somewhat grandiose title for what was little more than a farmyard. The hen-coops and pigeon houses were supplemented by the addition of cow-houses and sheep-pens adjacent to a little garden, the architectural focus of which was a pavilion in the shape of an Irish cross, which was one of Gabriel's most charming inventions.

A rotunda with a frieze of farmyard scenes supported by eight Corinthian columns opens by four tall windows onto the gardens, while between the windows four small doors lead each into a tiny room which forms, on the ground plan, one of the arms of the cross. The rich relief and sculptural effects of the skyline are typical of the period. The large, voluptuous volutes of the keystones and the naked children grouped in pairs upon the balustrade – who are no longer the fat-buttocked babies of van Loo and Boucher but old enough to be a little coquettish – provide a note of exuberance. There is nothing here to suggest the new style which Gabriel was to create, twelve years later, within a hundred yards of this pavilion. "The King was very fond of plans and buildings," wrote the duc de Croÿ; "he took me into his pretty pavilion in the gardens of Trianon and observed that that was the style in which I ought to build . . . He worked on his drawing for a long time with M. Gabriel."

A passing fancy for pigeons was succeeded by a more serious interest in botany, which necessitated a considerable increase in the gardens towards the east. It was not long before the idea occurred to the marquise de Pompadour of building here something more habitable than the Pavillon Français. The earliest designs are dated 1761 and show a building smaller than the one we see today. The three main façades were of only three windows, with an attached portico of coupled columns framing the central door or window.

The idea was there, but the perfection was yet to come. The Seven Years' War had still two years to run. On 10 February, 1763, the Treaty of Paris put an end to the war and on 24 February the duc de Praslin, Ministre des Affaires Etrangères, was ordered to pay 700,000 livres from his budget towards the building of the new house. The total spent on the house alone was 861,456 livres. By July of the following year 120 masons and 75 stone-carvers were at work on the site.

The important carvings were done by Honoré Guibert. He worked mostly in the "Greek" style and his partnership with Gabriel was probably fruitful for both of them. Together they produced a building which, by the simplicity of its conception, the purity of its line and the delicacy of its ornament, is at once the first and finest example of the classical revival, usually labelled "Louis Seize". Within and without, the treatment was entirely new and it is difficult to believe that the Petit Trianon was planned by the same architect who had designed the Pavillon Français.

Simplicity is the keynote of the Petit Trianon, but simplicity is nearly always deceptive. It cannot be achieved without a perfect command of technique. In designing his façades, Gabriel appreciated nicely the variety of texture possible in the fine, honey-coloured stone. A rusticated lower storey, fluted pilasters and a delicately chiselled entablature set off the contrasting smoothness of the undecorated wall surfaces. A subtle use has been made of a drop in the ground level to obtain two façades of two storeys and two of three. The north and west fronts have their basements masked by a terrace or perron, whereby the rooms can be approached directly from the gardens. The more imposing height of the entrance front is balanced by the low buildings which enclose the forecourt. The original orientation being towards the Pavillon Français, the west front is accorded the richest treatment. The east front, which used to overlook the botanical gardens, is the plainest.

The interior reflects in its decoration the original purpose of the building and is derived from the vegetable kingdom. The beautiful lilies in their circular wreaths which adorn the panels of the Salon de Musique, the swagged drops over the mirrors and the bunches of roses in the Cabinet du Roi – later to be the Queen's bedroom – are carved with an accuracy and precision which had to pass the scrutiny of a botanist King. In the festoons of fruit which appropriately adorn the panels and marbles of the dining-room, the strawberry is given a prominent place.

The cultivation of strawberries was one of Louis' particular interests. All the existing sorts were assembled at Trianon and before long Louis was able to offer the results of his researches to his courtiers. "One had to eat them in his presence," noted de la Gorse, "praise them and find them delicious if one desired to pay court to him effectively." In 1750 Claude Richard, described by Linnaeus as "the ablest gardener in Europe", received the title of Jardinier-

Fleuriste to the King, but he imposed one condition – that he was to receive his orders only from the King in person. He was joined later by Bernard Jussieu, "the Newton of Botany". Jussieu was a character calculated to please Louis, for he was utterly indifferent to any consideration of interest which might accrue from his royal connection. Not the least attraction of the new gardens at Trianon was the simple, straightforward manner in which the King could talk to his gardeners, who felt in their turn that they could treat him as a man and not as a King.

Also reflecting the horticultural context of the building were the overdoors in the reception suite. Cochin was ordered by Marigny to select subjects and to designate artists suitable to execute them. "It is in this *maison de plaisance*," he wrote to Marigny, "that the King keeps his most beautiful flowers. I have therefore tried to get subjects for the overdoors into which flowers can be worked."

Not only was the Petit Trianon to be strictly private, but the privacy of its inmates was to be insulated as far as possible from the irksome presence of servants. There was already at Choisy-le-Roi a "table volante" which went down through the dining-room floor into the kitchens to be reloaded for the second course. A similar table was designed for Trianon by Loriot and exhibited in the Louvre in 1769. It appears, however, that it was never actually installed at Trianon.

Madame de Pompadour died before the building was completed and it was Madame du Barry who was to accompany the King on his first visits, but their privacy was respected, even by history.

It was here in the spring of 1774 that Louis began to feel the symptoms of the smallpox which was to bring him to his grave. He did not want to leave his little house, but his physician, La Martinière, insisted that he should be moved to Versailles while it was possible. It was not seemly that a King of France should die at Trianon.

One of the first acts of Louis XVI on ascending the throne was to give the Petit Trianon to the Queen. "Vous aimez les fleurs," he said; "j'ai un bouquet à vous offrir." She was delighted to have a place of her own. The staff were put into her own livery – red and silver – and the orders signed in her own name.

At first the public was pleased to hear of Louis' gift of the Petit Trianon; it was a refreshing novelty to have a King whose only mistress was his wife. It seemed innocent enough. The Empress Maria-Theresa wrote to her daughter: "The generosity of the King over Trianon, which I am told is the most adorable of houses, gives me great pleasure." But her second thoughts were more penetrating: "May this charming first gift of the King not be the occasion of incurring too great an expense, let alone of dissipations."

There was little scope in the actual building for expensive alterations, for it was already perfect. The tiny Boudoir behind the Queen's bedroom, made in 1787, is the only decoration which she added. It was in the gardens that Marie-Antoinette was to realize her mother's worst fears and to earn herself the name of "Madame Déficit".

On 2 July, 1774, Mercy reported to the Empress that the Queen was now wholly occupied with a *jardin à l'anglaise*. A visit to the comte de Caraman, whose garden in Paris was one of the most successful in the new fashion, provided Marie-Antoinette with the adviser that she was looking for; Caraman was duly appointed Directeur des Jardins de la Reine.

On 31 July the King gave orders that "everything that the Queen should desire was to be carried out with all the care and all the diligence possible". The Ministers of the Crown were at first only too happy to oblige. "Si ce que la Reine désire est possible," Calonne assured her, "c'est fait; si c'est impossible cela se fera." In September 1776 Mercy was beginning to change the tune of his letters to Vienna. "At first the public took a favourable view of the King's giving Trianon to the Queen," he wrote; "they are now beginning to be uneasy and alarmed at the expenses which Her Majesty incurs there."

In the same year the duc de Croÿ made his first visit since the death of Louis XV. "I thought I must be mad or dreaming," he wrote; "never have two hectares of land so completely changed their form nor cost so much money."

The ground to the north-east had been cast into a miniature range of hills and a lake had been dug, fed by a cascade which gushed from the mouth of a mysterious grotto. Next to the grotto stood the Belvédère, designed by Mique and remarkable for the exquisite ornament of the carvings without and the delicacy of the painted arabesques within. The frieze was moulded in lead fixed onto the entablature and painted to resemble stone.

East of the lake, through green meadows and loosely-planted groves, wandered a river, now forming a little backwater towards the château, now dividing its stream to leave an island planted with lilac and laburnum from which rose the twelve stately columns of Mique's Temple de l'Amour, carrying their stone cupola over Bouchardon's statue of "Love carving his bow from the club of Hercules". There was a rich variety of trees, many of them species recently acclimatised at Trianon. "The glory of *la petite Trianon* [sic]", wrote Arthur Young, "is the exotic trees and shrubs. The world has been successfully rifled to decorate it. Here are curious and beautiful ones to please the eye of ignorance and to exercise the memory of science. Of the buildings the Temple of Love is truly elegant." They formed the background to this artificial paradise. Only the trickle of water and the song of nightingales could be heard. "One could fancy oneself," wrote the prince de Ligne, "three hundred miles from Court." The truth of that statement is the measure of Marie-Antoinette's success. It was exactly what she wanted to feel.

In 1778 Mique was invited to design a special theatre for Trianon. The *Comédie Intime* was becoming fashionable; it had been introduced to Versailles by the duchesse de Villequier and in due course the duchesse de Villequier invited the Queen. It was not long before Mercy had the delicate task of breaking the news to Vienna that the Queen had started an amateur company of her own.

The Queen's instruction to Mique was that the dimensions of the stage should correspond exactly with those of Fontainebleau and Choisy-le-Roi, so that scenery made for one could be used in the others. Mique produced a design that is almost a miniature of the Opéra at Versailles. The arrangement of the ceiling, with its vault pierced by a ring of occuli windows and its ceiling painted by Lagrené, follows the prototype almost exactly. The colour scheme also, based on the same bright, cold blue, owes much to that of Gabriel.

A private theatre meant an amateur theatrical company and the Queen soon surrounded herself with a small coterie. Dominating this coterie was the comtesse Jules de Polignac. Opinions about her differed. To the comte de Ségur she was a paragon of perfection. "It would be impossible to find anyone who combined in their person a more charming countenance, a more sweet expression, a more delightful voice or more lovable qualities of heart and mind." Mercy merely found her "wanting in sense, judgement, or any quality worthy of the confidence of a great princess". Her husband was a nonentity.

For this woman Marie-Antoinette conceived an extravagant affection. It was extravagant also in the financial sense of the word. "This family," wrote Mercy of the Polignacs, "without any deserts as regards the State, and from pure favouritism had already secured for itself ... something like 500,000 livres of annual revenue." It was when visiting the Polignacs that Marie-Antoinette made the significant remark: "Je ne suis plus la Reine: je suis moi."

The private theatre accentuated this separation between Marie-Antoinette and the Queen. All the theatrical arrangements were in the hands of Monsieur Campan, but the duc de Fronsac, First Gentleman of the Bedchamber, considered that such affairs fell by right within his competence. "You cannot be First Gentleman when we are actors," the Queen wrote to him; "besides, I have already let you know my wishes with regard to Trianon; I have no Court there; I live as a private individual."

This attempt to live as a private individual was innocent enough, but it was extremely ill-advised. The Court was offended and the public scandalized.

Mercy, reporting the matter to Vienna, gave a good appreciation of the situation: "Those who approach sovereigns have always some ambitious plans

63 Petit Trianon
(background) and
Pavillon Français.
Engraving by Née.

in their minds ... and the smaller the number of persons who obtain almost
exclusive access, the more insistent are their intrigues, the more difficult to
clear up and by consequence by far the most dangerous. A great Court ought
to be accessible to a great many people." That was no longer true of Versailles,
and Mercy warned the Empress that "want of occasion to pay one's court
would end by reducing both the habit and the desire". The facts indicate that
he was right. "Versailles," wrote the duc de Lévis, "that theatre of Louis XIV's
magnificence, was no more than a little provincial town to which one only
went with reluctance and from which one made one's escape as quickly as
possible."

But there was a more serious side to it than this. It is necessary to many
people's vanity to be always "in the know". This necessity and this vanity
tend to be increased when the person is a courtier and the subject of the
knowledge the royal family. When such people do not know, they invent,
and when they invent they exaggerate. The little snowball of gossip becomes
the great avalanche of calumny. Calumny, as Dr. Johnson defined it, is a
profession that requires neither labour nor courage. It was the force which was
to destroy Marie-Antoinette.

One example will suffice. There was a performance in the theatre at
Trianon of Marmontel's *Dormeur Réveillé*. The scenery represented the Palace
of the Sun, of which the most conspicuous features were twisted columns of
gold studded with diamonds. Needless to say the diamonds were not real, but

in 1789, when the deputies from the States General inspected Trianon, they came with minds already deeply prejudiced. "The extreme simplicity of this *maison de plaisance*," wrote Madame de Campan, "did not correspond with their preconceptions. Some insisted on being shown into the smallest of cabinets, saying that richly-furnished rooms were being concealed from them. Finally they indicated one which, by their account, should have been studded all over with diamonds and twisted columns with rubies and sapphires."

The performance of the *Dormeur Réveillé* was part of Marie-Antoinette's entertainment of Gustavus III of Sweden in June 1784. The royal family each had a copy of the play specially bound for the performance in red morocco tooled in silver – the Queen's livery – with her own armorial bearings. Another copy, bound in green and gold with the royal arms of Sweden, was offered to her guest. Besides the theatre, Gustavus was treated to an illumination of the gardens. The buildings were lit by the glow of an encircling fire, hidden from the eyes by means of a ditch. Thousands of candles in little pots, some fitted with coloured transparencies, cast a pool of light round every clump of trees and "brought out the different colours in the most charming and agreeable manner".

A series of paintings by the Chevalier de Lespinasse has captured the appearance of the gardens by this floodlighting. Above the waters of the lake the Belvédère shone with a lustre that might have been its own, the great light of the faggots picking out some of the trees with a pale luminosity and casting others into a dark, unnatural relief, whitening the surface of the rocks and accentuating the cavernous recesses of the grotto. On the other side of the château, the Temple de l'Amour was aglow, shining "with a brightness that made it the most brilliant point in the whole garden". 6,400 faggots were employed in the illumination of the Temple alone.

In the same year the English Garden was considerably extended by the laying out, after designs by Mique, of the Hameau. Round the borders of a small lake were disposed a number of rustic houses such as might have formed a tiny village, or the background of a painting by Greuze – a farm with a monumental gateway, several thatched cottages and a mill worked by a rivulet fed from the lake. The trees were so disposed as to permit a view of the Church of Saint-Antoine, giving as it were a background of reality to this artificial scene. Cattle grazed upon the meadows, peasants worked in the gardens and village maidens brought their washing to the mill, to which the cottagers also brought their corn to grind. The whole spectacle was an idealised *tableau vivant* of country life.

In the later years of Louis XVI's reign there was a renewed interest in country life. "The present fashion in France for passing some time in the country," noted Arthur Young, "is new. Everybody that have country seats are at them, and those who have none visit others who have; this remarkable revolution in manners is one of the best customs they have taken from England; and its introduction was effected the easier, being assisted by the magic of Rousseau's writings."

The Queen was no exception to this new fashion for country house life, but with her it had be be a game of make-believe. When she entered the Salon at

Trianon the ladies did not rise from the piano or embroidery frames and the gentlemen did not interrupt their billiards or their tric-trac. The formality of the Court gave place to the ease and freedom of a country house.

The Petit Trianon is not as little as its name suggests. It has a surprising number of rooms upstairs. It should be considered as a small, compact and remarkably exquisite stately home. The main reception rooms are on the first floor. Everything is designed to minister to the refined hedonism of a polite society; nothing anywhere sounds the note of royalty. The often oppressive grandeur of Versailles has been completely left behind.

The pale green of the first anteroom, at the head of the stairs, is cool and refreshing; the ornament, in white, is just enough to preserve the room from dullness. The dining-room is a more formal apartment with an elaborate cornice. This room has recently been very well restored. The walls have recovered their delicate colouring of *vert d'eau*, with the decorations of Guibert in crisp relief against it. The frames of the mirrors and pictures have been reconstructed from designs found pencilled on the plaster.

The Salon de Musique is a very fine room; but we might be in the Grand Salon at Le Marais or Montgeoffroy or one of the beautiful eighteenth-century salons at Le Lude. The tall, rectilinear panels are offset by the richly-carved roundels at their base, and make this an elegant and graceful ensemble.

To pass from here into the tiny Boudoir beyond is to go from the stately to the exquisite. The oak panels are carved with a minute precision which will stand the closest scrutiny and which gives an overall texture to the room, like a covering of lace upon a satin counterpane. It was in this room that the *glaces volantes* were installed. When evening came and the window needed to be obscured, instead of closing the shutters, a mirror could be raised, by means of

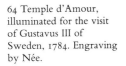

64 Temple d'Amour, illuminated for the visit of Gustavus III of Sweden, 1784. Engraving by Née.

204

a counterpoise, to fill a window recess. Queen Victoria did the same in her drawing-room at Osborne.

With this simplicity and dignity of style came a new dignity and simplicity in dress. The portrait of Marie-Antoinette in a muslin dress and straw hat, exhibited by Madame Vigée-LeBrun in the Salon in 1783, was badly received. The public objected to seeing the Queen clothed "like a chamber maid". But one gentleman from Lorraine, François Cognel, who saw the Queen thus attired at Trianon, declared that "in these modest clothes she looked perhaps even more majestic than in the full dress in which we had seen her at Versailles".

In the last few years before the Revolution a few attempts were made to economise. The first to be hit were the members of the coterie of Trianon. They took it badly. "It is terrible," wrote Besenval, "to live in a country where one cannot be sure of possessing today what one had the day before. That sort of thing only happens in Turkey."

It was only the beginning. In 1789 came the opening of the States General. As the Queen walked in the procession – it was the last occasion on which she appeared in the full majesty of Court dress – she was greeted by cries of "Vive le duc d'Orléans!" The duc d'Orléans – Philippe Egalité as he was to become – was her sworn enemy. In June the Dauphin died at Meudon after his long and harrowing illness. In July the Bastille was stormed and Artois, the Polignacs and a gathering stream of other aristocrats took the road to emigration. In September the King even contemplated abandoning Versailles, and the Marquise de Tourzel, newly appointed Governess of the royal children, was told to keep herself in readiness for instant departure.

On 5 October, Marie-Antoinette returned to Trianon. One place in the gardens corresponded to her mood. There was a wood up behind the Belvédère where a heap of moss-grown boulders overhung a little ravine down which a cascade brought its tumbling waters. Here had been contrived the Grotto. "This grotto," wrote the comte d'Hézècques, "was so dark that the eyes, dazzled before, needed a certain time to be able to discern objects clearly." It was carpeted with moss and cooled by a little stream which flowed through it. The grotto was designed for solitude, and by means of a little crevice it overlooked the meadow before it, and "enabled one to detect from afar anybody who might have wished to approach this mysterious retreat".

It was here that the messenger found the Queen and brought her news that the mob was marching on the palace of Versailles. For years she had played at make-believe in these lovely gardens, vainly pretending to be "an ordinary individual". Now the game was up. There were carriages in readiness that could have taken her to saftey, but she refused them proudly. "Puisqu'il y a du danger," she said, "ma place est auprès du Roi."

The End

SHE FOUND the palace upon tip-toe of expectation. The courtiers, "sous le coup d'une inquiétude mortelle", were thronging the State Apartments, each trying to keep as closely as possible in touch with the course of events. Across the courtyard the iron grilles, some of which "had not turned upon their hinges since the days of Louis XIV", were closed and locked, and the National Guard, whose loyalty was doubtful, was drawn up in front of the main gates. Beyond was a sea of discontented humanity, calling for bread but looking as if they wanted blood. Through the windows came that most terrifying of all sounds, the sullen murmur of an angry mob.

At three o'clock, the King arrived at the gallop from Meudon, where he had been shooting, and omitting in his haste to acknowledge the salute of the Regiment of Flanders. He went straight to his apartment and stayed there in an agony of indecision – now agreeing with Saint-Priest and La Tour du Pin to retreat to Rambouillet – now cancelling the order – always repeating: "I do not want to compromise anyone."

In the Grande Galerie, which had witnessed so many gay and sumptuous occasions of the Court, a tense and anxious silence now prevailed. "On se promenait de long en large," wrote Madame de la Tour du Pin, "sans échanger une parole." As for herself, she admitted: "I was in such a state of agitation that I could not stay one moment in the same place. Again and again I went to the Oeil de Boeuf where I could observe those who came and went from the presence of the King, in the hope of seeing either my husband or my father-in-law and of hearing from them the latest news. The suspense of waiting was unendurable."

Only the Queen's apartment, where a number of her entourage were gathered in the Grand Cabinet, afforded a scene of calm and self-control. Madame de Tourzel was perforce a witness. "Marie-Antoinette," she wrote, "showed on this day that great spirit and great courage which have always characterised her. Her expression was noble, her countenance serene ... no one could have read in it the slightest sign of alarm. She reassured everyone, thought of everything."

She was far from unconscious of the fact that she was the principal target for the malcontents, and for this very reason she gave instructions to Madame de Tourzel that, in the event of an alert, she was to take the Dauphin not to her room but to that of the King. "I would rather," she said, "expose myself to any danger that there may be, and so draw them away from the King's person and from my children."

The marquise de Tourzel is one of the many who have described the events of that night. It is not to be expected that, in the panic and confusion which ensued, the different accounts would be synoptic. The human mind, subjected to such violent emotion, is seldom an infallible recorder. Nevertheless it is possible to follow the course of events through the eyes of those who were actually spectators. The marquise de la Tour du Pin, whose husband was in charge of the Militia, Madame Campan, whose sister was in waiting on the Queen, the comte de Saint-Priest and the comte d'Hézècques, who were in attendance on the King, all tell what is clearly the same story.

Between eleven and twelve o'clock La Fayette arrived in the last stages of exhaustion and was at once admitted to the King's presence. In half an hour he had convinced Louis that there was no immediate danger. A detachment of the Gardes du Corps, which had been drawn up beneath the windows of the Queen's apartment, was sent to Rambouillet; most of the King's attendants were dismissed. At two o'clock the Queen went to bed, insisting that her two ladies-in-waiting did the same. Fortunately for her they decided to keep watch. The Ushers in the Grande Galerie announced that the Queen had retired and everyone departed. "The doors were closed, the candles were extinguished," wrote Madame de la Tour du Pin; "le calme le plus absolu régnait dans Versailles."

At the far end of the Aisle des Princes, in the apartment of the princesse d'Hénin, Madame de la Tour du Pin also retired to rest. Her husband, vigilant as ever, made his round of the sentry posts. Everything was in order. "Not the slightest sound was to be heard, either in the precincts of the palace or in the surrounding streets." Nevertheless he could not, or would not, sleep. He took up his position at an open window in the Aisle des Ministres, the first building on the left as one enters the first courtyard of Versailles. From here he overlooked the narrow courtyard called the Cour des Princes, between the main block and the Aisle des Princes. The entrance to this court was barred by a wrought iron grille and gateway. Once within the court, however, one could pass behind the pillars of the colonnade at the end of the wing and enter the Cour Royale. This passage was guarded by a single sentry. On this fateful night, "by a negligence which would have been unpardonable if it were not actually culpable," the gateway to the Cour des Princes was left unlocked.

At about the break of day, Monsieur de la Tour du Pin, still at his open window, heard the sound of footsteps approaching in large numbers from the direction of the Orangerie. To his horror he saw that this gate, which he had presumed to be locked, was open and an ugly-looking mob was pouring into the Cour des Princes. Conspicuous among them was a hirsute savage armed with an enormous axe. His name was Nicolas Jourdan, but they called him *Coupe-tête*.

At the same time Madame de la Tour du Pin was suddenly awakened by the sound of the tumult in the street below. Above the hubbub she could hear voices crying "A mort! A mort! Tuez les gardes du corps!" Scarcely had she recoiled from the window when her faithful maid Marguerite, panting and pale as death, burst into the room and collapsed into an armchair gasping, "O my God! We are all going to be massacred!" She had decided at daybreak to rejoin her mistress and had walked straight into the mob just in time to see the unfortunate Deshuttes, the sentinel in the Cour des Princes, dragged before Jourdan and brutally beheaded.

More sinister, she had witnessed the arrival of a man whom she was convinced she recognised as the duc d'Orléans.

65 The Salon de'l'Oeil de Boeuf, communicating between the Grande Galerie (left) and the King's Bedroom (right).

In the Queen's apartment the two ladies-in-waiting, Madame Auguier and Madame Thibaut, were keeping their vigil in the Salon next to the Queen's bedroom. At about six they heard the sounds of the mob as it rushed the Escalier de la Reine. Only two rooms separated the Salon from the head of the staircase, the Ante-Room and the Salle des Gardes.

Madame Thibaut ran into the Ante-Room, where she found one of the guards, Miomandre de Sainte-Marie, already trying to barricade the door with his musket. He turned, his face streaming with blood: "Sauvez la Reine!" he shouted, "On vient pour l'assassiner!" Madame Thibaut ran back, bolting the door of the Salon behind her, and burst into the Queen's room. "Sortez du lit, Madame!" she screamed. "Ne vous habillez pas; sauvez-vous, chez le Roi." Hurriedly throwing a skirt over her nightdress, Marie-Antoinette fled by means of a concealed door in the corner of the room, through her Petits Cabinets to the Oeil de Boeuf. The door of the Oeil de Boeuf was bolted on the other side.

The King at this moment, also awakened by the uproar, was hastening by means of a secret passageway contrived in an entresol beneath the Oeil de Boeuf, which afforded a private communication between his bedroom and that of his wife.

208

In the Oeil de Boeuf, Marquant, one of the valets de la garderobe, was aroused by a frantic knocking at the door. "He ran to open it and was astonished to see his Queen, half dressed, flying from the blows of the assassins."

Meanwhile, in the rooms beneath, Madame de Tourzel had been alerted. "I leapt out of bed," she recounts, "and immediately carried the Dauphin to the King's room." Somehow the King and Queen had joined each other there. She found Marie-Antoinette in complete possession of herself. "The danger to which she had just been exposed had in no way affected her courage. Her countenance was sad but calm."

Marie-Antoinette was called upon, during that day, to show a supreme degree of courage. La Fayette insisted on her showing herself to the crowd; it was necessary, he told her, to restore order. Taking her children by the hand, she advanced onto the balcony which overlooks the Cour de Marbre from the King's bedroom. There were muskets levelled in the crowd. She was greeted by a yell of, "No children!" Motioning her children back into the room, she stood for a while alone upon the balcony. The muskets were lowered. For the moment the situation was saved, but the constant clamour of "the King to Paris!" could not be ignored. Finally the order was given for the royal family to return to the capital which it had virtually forsaken since the early days of Louis XIV.

Just before their departure, Madame Campan found the Queen alone in her Petits Cabinets. The pent-up emotion of the last twenty-four hours had finally overtaken her. "She could hardly speak; her face was streaming with tears." In her heart she probably knew that she was leaving Versailles for ever.

As the royal family were getting into the *berline* that was to take them to Paris, Louis turned to the marquis de la Tour du Pin. "You remain in charge here," he said; "try and save me my poor Versailles."

The next day, 7 October, began at Versailles the saddest spectacle that a building can witness; the courtyards rang to the sound of the voices and footsteps of carriers – of furniture being piled into carts, never to return; of windows and shutters being closed, never to be re-opened; of carriages rolling out of the golden gates, never to re-enter.

It was the end. Madame de la Tour du Pin went back to her lodgings in the Aisle des Ministres. "Une affreuse solitude régnait déjà à Versailles."

7

The Château des Tuileries

Before the Revolution

WHILE THE ROYAL family were preparing for their departure from Versailles, a courier had been despatched at the gallop to warn the Governor of the Tuileries that the King and the Court intended to take up residence that day. The prospect of such an invasion must have been appalling. Only six years previously a report had been addressed to the King stating that "the royal apartments no longer really exist; they have been partitioned off; unless something is done about it they will not be able to offer His Majesty's family even a moment's shelter."

Nothing had been done. A miscellaneous medley of retired officials and pensioned-off artists had installed themselves in almost every part of the palace. Not only did all these have to be evicted at a moment's notice, but furniture, fuel, food and other bare necessities of life had to be found for no fewer than 677 persons. According to the comtesse de Rochejacquelin, some two thousand vehicles arrived at the Tuileries during the course of that day.

It was not until ten o'clock that night that the royal family reached the palace, or rather, as d'Hézècques insisted, "this prison disguised under the name of palace". They did not now find "even those little commodities which the meanest bourgeois would have expected in his house". The courtiers spent the first night as best they could, sleeping on sofas or tables or on the benches that lined the anterooms.

"It is all very ugly here," the Dauphin complained to his mother. "My son," she replied, "Louis XIV lived here and found it to his liking; we should not be more difficult than he was."

Louis XIV had made the Tuileries his residence in Paris between 1666 and 1680 when he finally installed himself at Versailles. He had found an unfinished and unsatisfactory suite of buildings which had been started by Catherine de Medici and continued by Henri IV.

The original designs for the Tuileries are only known to us through the drawings of Du Cerceau. As his bird's eye view of the whole does not correspond with his own ground plan, the drawings must be treated with caution. Anthony Blunt has pointed out that many of the features are untypical of Philibert de l'Orme. Philibert de l'Orme, however, gives credit for the overall plan to Catherine de Medici in person, only claiming for

66 Detail of entrance front. Drawing by du Cerceau.

himself the authorship of the architectural detail. Exactly what de l'Orme designed we shall probably never know. Du Cerceau shows us one of those gigantic buildings which the architects of the Renaissance delighted in imagining. In England plans for a Whitehall Palace that would have occupied the whole area between St. James's Park and the Thames, and which no Stuart King could ever have dreamed of being able to afford, resulted in the erection of the tiny portion known as the Banqueting House. Du Cerceau designed the Château de Charleval for Charles IX – an immense compendium of courtyards, one of which could have contained Chambord – but only an insignificant fragment was ever built.

His depiction of the Tuileries shows an architectural extravaganza which would have measured 268 metres by 166 and covered an area ten times that of the Louvre as it then stood. Only some two thirds of the one façade towards the gardens were actually realised.

In January 1570, Philibert de l'Orme died, having built only the central pavilion and its two attendant wings. He was succeeded by Jean Bullant, who added a fourth, rather more massive block at the southern extremity of the building. He then began to erect a symmetrical pavilion to the north, but it never progressed very far. Some authors have stated that all work ceased in August 1572 and suggest a somewhat occult explanation.

The seventeenth-century historian Mézéray records the tradition that Catherine was told by an astrologer that she would meet her death "near Saint-Germain". As the result of this prediction she never revisited the Château de Saint-Germain. But the Tuileries was in the parish of Saint-Germain-l'Auxerrois, and for further security she abandoned that also. In the end the prediction was fulfilled by the priest who brought her extreme unction at Blois: his name was Julien de Saint-Germain.

The claim that Catherine abandoned the Tuileries, however, is not entirely supported by the Inventory of the Queen's Furniture. This unromantic document states that the Queen Mother came here "to walk in the gardens, to dine or to spend the night, which is very seldom indeed". For these purposes "she caused the furniture which she needed to be brought here, which was afterwards removed by her officers". What little had been built of the Tuileries was neither finished, furnished nor inhabited.

Tony Sauval, however, has made a study of the financing of Catherine de Medici's building, which also tells rather a different tale. In spite of frequent grants from her royal sons, she was often in financial straits and had to borrow from financiers. This was not always easy. In February 1571 she had great difficulty in finding anyone who would lend her money "to prevent the ruin of what has already been started in the said palace of the Tuileries".

It looks probable that it was financial necessity rather than superstitious fear which caused the works to be abandoned. But it was not for long. In 1578 and again in 1579 more royal payments were made for the Tuileries "in order that so praiseworthy and necessary an enterprise should be brought to conclusion".

In making the first of these grants, Henri III described the Tuileries as being built "pour accompagner le Louvre". Already the junction of the two buildings was being envisaged. It had occurred to Catherine that a gallery uniting the Tuileries with the Louvre would be of great convenience for her palace. It could provide a covered way for use during inclement weather and a terrace walk above for finer days. Charles IX had even laid the foundation stone on 11 July, 1566, but little progress had been made.

Catherine de Medici died in February 1589. In July of the same year her last son, Henri III, a fugitive from Paris, was assassinated at Saint-Cloud. It was not until Henri IV had taken possession of Paris that any further work on the Tuileries could even have been contemplated.

Between 1595 and 1608 considerable works were undertaken. The Grande Galerie was built joining the Louvre to the Tuileries, and the Tuileries extended to form a junction with this at the Pavillon de Flore. But the block begun by Bullant to the north of de l'Orme's building remained unfinished.

It was just at this time that Thomas Coryat made his visit. "This Palace of the Tuileries," he wrote, "is a most magnificent building, having in it many sumptuous rooms. The Chamber of Presence is exceeding beautiful, whose roof is painted with many antique works, the sides and ends of this chamber are curiously adorned with pictures made in oilwork upon wainscoat, wherein amongst many other things the nine Muses are excellently painted. One of the inner chambers hath an exceeding costly roof gilt, in which chamber there is a table made of so many several colours of marble, and so finely inlaid with ivory that it is thought to be worth above five hundred pounds."

The first real occupant of the Tuileries was Marie-Anne-Louise de Bourbon-Montpensier, "la Grande Mademoiselle", daughter of Gaston d'Orléans the younger brother of Louis XIII. She wrote the first eulogy of the palace. "It was the most agreeable habitation in the world and one which I greatly loved as the place where I had lived since the age of eight days." She took the side of the rebels during the Fronde and ordered the cannons of the Bastille to be fired on the royalist troops. This resulted in her eviction from the Tuileries and banishment to her country estates.

One of the great attractions of the Tuileries was the terrace at first-floor level on either side of the central pavilion. "There is a most pleasant prospect," wrote Coryat, "from that walk into the Tuileries gardens, which is the fairest garden for length of delectable walks that ever I saw." There was one alley 700 feet long, vaulted in trellis work with maples trained up either side so as to meet in the middle; there was "a long and spacious plot full of herbs and knots trimly kept by many persons"; there were "great preparations of conduits of lead" for the unfinished water works. At the bottom of the garden was "an exceeding fine Echo. For I heard a certain Frenchman who sung very melodiously with curious quavers, sing with such admirable art, that upon the resounding of the Echo there seemed three to sound together."

The Tuileries gardens seem rather to have caught the fancy of Englishmen. John Evelyn, visiting Paris in 1644, spent most of 9 February going all over the Louvre. "I finished this day with a walk in the great garden of the Tuileries, rarely contrived for privacy, shade or company, by groves, plantations of tall trees, especially that in the middle, being of elms, the other of mulberries; and that labyrinth of cypresses; not omitting the noble hedges of pomegranates, fountains, fishpools and aviary."

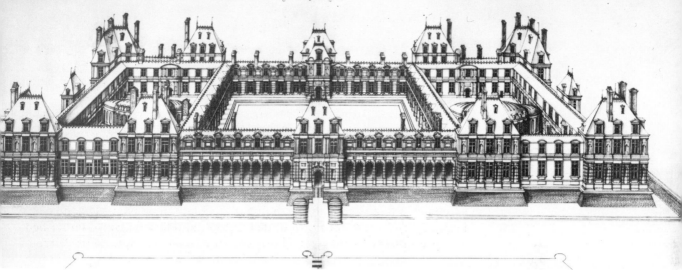

67 Du Cerceau's version
of the original design by
Philibert de l'Orme.

These were the gardens laid out by Claude Mollet. The whole area was
divided into rectangular plots which bore no relationship at all to the façades
of the palace. It was this which was to be rectified by Le Nôtre who redesigned
the gardens in 1664.

There is an excellent drawing by Silvestre of the new gardens of Le Nôtre,
taken from the middle window of the façade. The first and most typical
feature is the great central alley, continued beyond the confines of the garden
by the avenue which is now the Champs-Elysées and vanishing over the
horizon in the direction of Saint-Germain. In 1667 the owners of the land
across which this avenue was to run were warned that they would receive no
compensation for damage to any crops sown on the land on which the King
had determined "to plant avenues of trees from behind his garden of the
Tuileries, as far as the heights of Chaillot".

At the same time the parterres nearest to the palace were being laid out.
They earned the praise of Blondel a century later. "Le Nôtre took good care
only to begin the shady areas of the garden at eighty-two yards from the
façade, and he enriched the ground of this open part with parterres de
broderie, intermixed with strips of lawn, which may be regarded as so many
masterpieces."

They could be looked at both ways. From the first-floor windows and
terraces of the palace they provided, as at Saint-Germain, a decorative
outlook, lying like a great Persian carpet between the palace and the taller
plantations of the lower gardens. But, to anyone walking in these gardens, the
parterres provided a flat foreground which enabled the eye to travel without
interruption over the long expanse of façade.

Once again, it was an Englishman who wrote one of the earliest eulogies on
the work of Le Nôtre. Martin Lister, who came here in 1698, when asked by
"a lady of quality" what had pleased him most in all Paris, replied "the middle
walk of the Tuileries in June, betwixt eight and nine at night. I did not think
there was in the world a more agreeable place than that alley at that hour and
at that time of the year. Nothing can be more pleasant than this garden, where
in the groves of wood ... blackbirds, throstles and nightingales sing most
sweetly."

213

Louis XIV made the Tuileries a palace fit for his own habitation, but in so doing he destroyed the most distinctive features of de l'Orme's architecture – the impressive array of dormer windows and the celebrated oval staircase. The former were to find an admirer in Viollet-le-Duc. "The decoration of the upper storey," he wrote, "which stood out against the dark tones of the roof, crowned the building in the richest possible manner. It was a truly palatial architecture, both in the strength and nobility of its masses and in the refinement of its detail." Blondel, writing with all the self-assurance of an eighteenth-century architect, dismissed the dormers as "the ridiculous decoration of Philibert de l'Orme". He even described his architecture as "semi-Gothic".

The idea, of course, of a steep slate roof against which a series of dormers stood out in brilliant relief was a tradition of French architecture which dated back well into the Middle Ages. The Renaissance had retained the feature while italianising the details. Philibert de l'Orme's rhythmic alternation between tall, pedimented windows and low, pedimented panels seems to take this process a stage further.

But it was the Great Staircase which made de l'Orme's design for the Tuileries justly famous. It was in the centre of the building beneath the dome. Within the rectangular space of the vestibule an oval staircase was fitted by means of *trompes* or squinches which rounded the angles while rising with the stairs. The treads, which were slightly serpentine in contour, projected from the wall with no visible means of support and were enclosed by a bronze handrail.

One of the earliest descriptions of this staircase comes from John Evelyn, who visited the Tuileries – "a princely fabric" – on 9 February, 1644. "The winding geometrical stairs, with the cupola," he wrote, "I take to be as bold and noble a piece of architecture as any in Europe of the kind."

Much later, Sauval described this staircase in his *Antiquités de Paris*: "Every time one looks up at this heavy mass of stone and bronze, made like a snail's shell, which sweeps up between two airy spaces, it seems ready to fall and bury beneath its ruins those who regard it. However, we can mount in safety and in comfort by the curving, spiral steps – not only low and gentle, but separated also by landings for greater facility and seemliness. Nothing of this sort has ever been seen so audacious and so admirable."

Sauval died in 1670. Some eighty years separated his writings from those of Blondel. Blondel admits that this staircase was beautiful; he admits that in it the art of stereotomy was taken to a new degree of perfection; he even goes so far as to use the word "miracle" to describe it. But he insists that Colbert was right in having the staircase destroyed because "the first merit in a building consists in the art of announcing the importance of the interior by means of the exterior". Elsewhere he wrote: "When the exterior has not been made to accord with the interior, there always results an ill-assorted whole." The central pavilion of the Tuileries and its staircase failed to pass this test of classicism and were replaced by a new staircase and a new dome designed by Le Vau and d'Orbay.

These two architects then proceeded to complete the symmetry of the building. The northern end of Philibert de l'Orme's block had been left unfinished by Bullant. This was now completed and the façade extended to what is now the rue de Rivoli. These new buildings contained a Salle de Spectacle reputed to have the largest auditorium, the best scenic machinery and the worst acoustics of any theatre in Europe.

It has to be said that the result was unsatisfactory. Le Vau and d'Orbay destroyed de l'Orme's creation without putting anything distinguished in its place. Henri IV had already committed them to a straight elongation of de l'Orme's work into one immense façade. By adding the Pavillon de Pomone – now Pavillon de Marsan – at the northern extremity of the building they finally achieved the frontage towards the gardens of 340 metres, with fifty-nine windows on each floor.

Blondel was justly critical of the result. "Was it necessary," he asked, "to flank it with two large wings and two pavilions of monstrous size, adorned with a colossal order, which by their gigantic proportions overwhelm those which were executed in the first place?" By recessing the new buildings deeply behind the old, the disparity of proportion could have been offset by the diminishing effect of perspective. It would have been better to have destroyed de l'Orme's work and to have replaced it with a composition "more in conformity with the rules of good taste and more worthy of the splendour of the reign of Louis le Grand".

In 1662, Louis XIV decided to celebrate the birth of his first child by holding a "carrousel" – a sort of tattoo on horseback which gave opportunity for an impressive piece of showing off to a large number of distinguished

68 Garden front as completed by Louis XIV. Drawing by I. Silvestre.

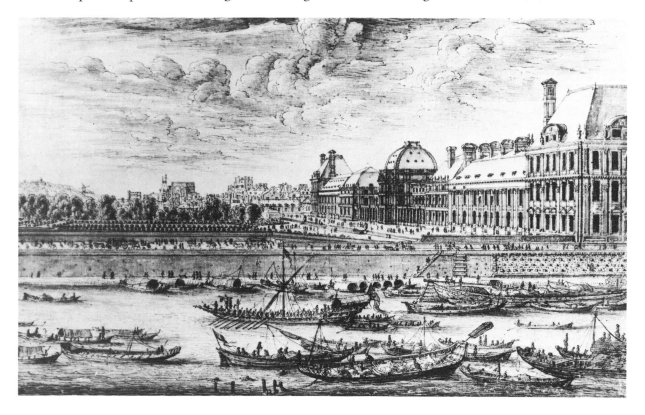

cavaliers. To provide space for this gigantic tournament, Louis had many of the buildings and gardens cleared away between the Louvre and the entrance front of the Tuileries. This area is still called Place du Carrousel.

In 1680 Louis XIV moved to Versailles and the Tuileries was abandoned by the Court. It was gently invaded by a number of minor officials who set up their lodgings among its hall and galleries. It was not until the King's death in 1715 that the palace was to serve again as a royal residence. Its proximity to the Palais Royal – the house of the Regent, the duc d'Orléans – made it an appropriate residence for the young King Louis XV. His rooms gave access to the terrace above Philibert de l'Orme's arcade, to the south of the central Pavillon de L'Horloge. His frequent appearances on this terrace were the delight of the Parisians who frequented the Tuileries gardens. On 14 June, 1722, the Court returned to Versailles. It was the last time a sovereign was to leave the Tuileries of his own free will.

From then until 1789 the palace was chiefly known to the Parisians as a theatre. The great Salle de Spectacle, commonly called the Salle des Machines on account of the elaborate scenic effects made possible by its equipment, was in constant use. First, Servandoni was allowed to produce his pantomimes here; then in 1763, when the Salle de l'Opéra was burnt down, the company moved to the Tuileries. The scenery, in accordance with the topography of the palace, was marked "côté cour" or "côté jardin". Long after the Opéra left the Tuileries, the words "cour" and "jardin" continued to mean right and left in the language of the backstage.

With the sudden arrival of the Royal Family and the Court on 6 October, 1789, the Tuileries became once more the Palace of the King. It had to be furnished at the expense of Versailles. "For several days," wrote Roussel d'Epinal, "there was one long convoy of vehicles loaded with the immense amount of furniture which had been collected in this palace during the course of three reigns."

In a surprisingly short time, the old way of life of the Court was more or less re-established. So deeply was the ceremonial of Versailles ingrained in the ritual that it was found easiest to maintain the nomenclature of the rooms. Thus the second antechamber of the Tuileries became the Salon de l'Oeil de Boeuf although it possessed no oval window by virtue of which it might merit the name.

The Chapel, which was immediately to the north of the Pavillon de l'Horloge, and therefore next to the theatre, was the cause of endless discomfort to the Court. The comte d'Hézècques provides the details: "It was necessary, in order to reach the tribune of the Chapel, to go out onto one of the terraces above the arcades. The greater part of those in attendance were obliged to wait out of doors until the end of the Mass, exposed to the elements. Every time the King and his family went to the Chapel, they were held up on the terrace by the great crowd of spectators in the gardens, who demonstrated to this illustrious but unfortunate family their joy and their enthusiasm by the reiteration of their applause."

It must have recalled to Marie-Antoinette her very first visit to the Tuileries, just after her marriage. What had touched her most, she wrote to her mother, was "the eager affection of the poor people who, in spite of the taxes which cripple them, were in transports of joy on seeing us . . . How lucky we are in our estate to gain the love of the people at such an easy price! There is, however, nothing more precious."

The comte d'Hézècques makes the important observation that "the first part of their time in Paris revealed how much the King was loved by the people, who had not yet been exasperated and alienated by the intrigues of trouble-makers and criminals. The misfortunes of the Royal family, their virtues, their courage during the frightful days of the 5th and 6th of October, had recalled the imbeciles of Paris to that love for the sovereign which is natural to the French."

Again and again there were outbursts of popular enthusiasm. On 14 September, 1791, after Louis had accepted the Constitution, the Royal family were cheered all the way back to the Tuileries. Marie-Antoinette remarked: "Ce n'est plus le même peuple."

More shrewd in her observation, but writing with the hindsight of historical perspective, Pauline de Tourzel, an eye-witness of all these events, wrote: "I have noticed that in times of Revolution there were always moments of calm before the great storms, and it is these which mislead those who are involved in the crises. If these crises developed without these discontinuities, one would stiffen oneself to resist them and one might even finish by triumphing over them."

The decisive turn for the worse in the Revolution was the degradation of the clergy into the paid functionaries of the State who were obliged to take an oath to the State which most Catholic consciences rejected. If anything was needed to determine Louis that he could not co-operate with the Revolution, it was this. The mismanaged flight to Varennes was his ultimate reaction and its failure opened the way to dethronement and to death.

The details of the flight to Varennes do not concern this book. No one was ever more glad to leave the Tuileries than the Royal family and Madame de Tourzel. No one was ever more glad to find themselves outside the city of Paris. There the great travelling *berline* awaited them. It is described in some detail by Roussel d'Epinal. It was immense – "une petite maison ambulante". It was equipped with" a sort of larder; and there you will see a cooker for reheating meat or soup; raise this double floor; it offers you a dining table. In removing the cushion from this seat, you will find a commode; all that it lacks is a bed. Nothing more ingenious could be imagined than this vehicle." But it was heavy and it was slow. The succession of failures during that ill-fated voyage, which led inexorably to the final disaster, were at least partly due to the slowness of the royal family's progress.

The return to the Tuileries, which had been placarded as "Maison à louer" during their absence, was a return to prison. It was more than a year, however, before matters came to a head. On Friday, 10 August, 1792, the Tuileries were sacked and the King was deposed.

The week had begun badly. On Sunday, Madame Campan relates, the Chapel choir, by secret arrangement, "trebled the force of their voices in a terrifying manner when they repeated, in the Magnificat, the words: *Deposuit potentes de sede*". The royal family gave up using the Chapel and the last Masses in the Tuileries were celebrated in the Gallery. By Thursday the 9th it was

clear that a major uprising was to be expected. The events of the next twenty-four hours are chronicled by Madame Campan, Roussel d'Epinal, the marquise de Tourzel, her daughter Pauline and François de la Rochefoucauld, all of them eye-witnesses.

That evening, for the first time ever, the ceremony of the *coucher* was cancelled. To courtiers for whom this ritual was sacrosanct this must indeed have looked bad. The loyal supporters of the King took what rest they could, on the chairs, on the tables and even on the floor, in spite of the insistence on the part of some of the officers of the Royal Household that it was contrary to etiquette to be seated in the King's room. François de la Rochefoucauld was extremely tired – he had been arrested and interrogated twice that week already – but now a new strength was given him: "At such a time, zeal makes good whatever is lacking." Charged with this reserve of energy, the whole palace was in a state of tense and anxious expectation.

Meanwhile, in the room beyond the King's bedroom, the little Dauphin slept. "His calm and peaceful slumber," wrote the marquise de Tourzel, "formed the most striking contrast with the agitation which reigned in every heart." No one else in the Tuileries went to bed; "everyone remained in the royal apartments and awaited anxiously the issue of a day which was ushered in with such baleful auspices."

At about three in the morning, the tocsin started. In tower after tower and steeple after steeple the bells took up the strong, pulsating rhythm – the quickened heartbeat of an over-excited city. Bells that were meant to summon men to prayer now intoxicated them for slaughter.

Within the anxious confines of the palace such preparations as were possible were being made for its defence. The Queen, Roussel d'Epinal recorded, had had a special bullet-proof waistcoat made of nine layers of white satin interlined with horsehair. She urged the King to don this and to put himself at the head of his devoted subjects. "If you are to die," she exhorted him, "let it be with your sword in your hand and defending the Crown, of which you are only the trustee. Be like Henri IV! Arm yourself and fight!"

She must have known that Louis would never have fought against his own subjects, nor was he capable of providing the slightest inspiration to others. At about six in the morning Louis went out to "review" the Guards. La Rochefoucauld went with him. "Although I was very close to his person," he wrote, "I never heard him say a single word to the troops." With so little to encourage them, their failure was a foregone conclusion. General Vioménil, who was in charge of the defence of the Tuileries, admitted to Madame Campan: "Our means of defence are nil. They could only exist in the vigorous action of the King – and that is the only virtue which he lacks."

La Rochefoucauld, together with some two hundred others who had come "to die before the King and at his feet", waited in the apartments. They had themselves announced as "la Noblesse de France!" Madame Campan noticed many among them "who cut a ridiculous figure among what was called the nobility, but whose devotion in this hour ennobled them".

At about half past eight, the comte Roederer, the Attorney General, persuaded the royal family to take refuge in the hall of the National Assembly. The mob, however, had already invaded the Tuileries gardens. At the foot of the terrace the King encountered a furious crowd, hurling insults at him and threatening him with their pikes. "I feared each moment", wrote la Rochefoucauld, "to see him massacred before my eyes and in the middle of his family."

Before leaving the Tuileries, the King had said to his faithful supporters: "I beg you to retire and to give up this useless defence; there is nothing to be done here, neither for me or for you." The inmates of the Palace were left to their fate.

Pauline de Tourzel now takes up the tale. "Soon after the departure of the

70 Mass in the Gallery the week before the sack of the Palace. Hubert Robert.

219

71 Entrance vestibule during the attack of August 10th, 1792.

King, the cannonade against the château started. We heard bullets whistling past in the most terrifying manner. The smashing of glass and breaking of windows made the most appalling row." Together with the princesse de Tarente and a few other ladies, Pauline retreated to one of the ground-floor rooms overlooking the gardens. They had the idea of closing the blinds and lighting all the candles in the hope of dazzling their assailants and thus gaining time to parley. No sooner were the candles lit than they heard terrible cries coming from the next room. "It was all done in a moment; the doors were broken in and men with sabres in their hands and with their eyes starting out of their heads, rushed into the room. They stopped for an instant, astonished at what they saw, and at finding only a dozen women in the room. The lights reflected and repeated in the mirrors made such an impact on the brigands that they stood still stupefied."

One of the ladies was so overcome with fear that she collapsed on her knees and started stammering the words of Absolution. This gave the princesse de Tarente her chance. Turning to a young Marseillais, she asked him to help her conduct the lady to safety. He agreed to see them both, together with Pauline de Tourzel, out of the Tuileries. Pauline and her mother were to have a similar experience at the beginning of the September Massacres, when an unknown Englishman – surely the original of the "Scarlet Pimpernel" – managed to smuggle them safely out of prison. He returned too late to save their companion in prison, the princesse de Lamballe.

The first visitor to record his impressions of the massacre and the pillage was Roussel d'Epinal, who arrived, together with Lord Bedford, upon the scene while the new-spilt blood was still warm upon the ground.

The noise was appalling. Above the "vast and continuous hubbub that came from all the rooms", piercing cries and sudden, strident voices jarred the air. Already intoxicated with the lust for blood, the insurgents were now inflamed with alcohol. "Through the ventilators of the cellar I could see a thousand hands groping in the sand ... the royal wine flows upon the flagstones and parquets of the palace, mingling with the blood of the victims."

On entering the palace, they were aghast: "The Vestibule is awash with blood, still smoking. The smell of it suffocates me. My hair stands on end. I rush headlong up the stairs and into the Chapel. What a spectacle! What pandemonium! Corpses everywhere, horribly disfigured and already the prey to millions of buzzing flies. In the royal tribune a man with a trumpet is performing a parody of the Angel of the Resurrection."

In the State Rooms it was just the same. The floor was strewn with fragments of brightly-coloured porcelain and crystal chandeliers. But the paintings, the Le Bruns and the Veroneses, had survived. So had the splendid curtains 'all sparkling with gold".

"The entrance to the Queen's Apartment is blocked by a pile of corpses ... the women had got into Marie-Antoinette's wardrobe; bonnets, hats, pink skirts, white petticoats, blue petticoats are scattered hither and thither."

In the Queen's Bedroom the sheets were red with blood. One of the Swiss Guards had sought to hide beneath the mattress and might have escaped had not a certain fishwife decided to see what it was like to lie on the Queen's bed. She discovered the fugitive who was promptly pulled out and butchered.

At five o'clock, Roussel d'Epinal and Lord Bedford came down the stairs of the Pavillon de Flore; on every step drunken men were lying side by side with corpses. Outside, in the Place du Carrousel, it appeared to be snowing feathers from the mattresses that had been ripped open, and the Guardrooms were ablaze. "I made my escape in the midst of the crowd and had the good luck to arrive safe and sound in my own home."

It must have been difficult at that moment to imagine the possibility of the Tuileries ever again becoming a royal palace. The National Convention sat in what had been its theatre; the notorious Committee of Public Safety occupied another of its rooms. The people had extinguished monarchy – even to the design of their playing cards and the pieces on their chessboards – everything had been purged of the odious taint.

But it did not last. Deep down, the capacity of the Parisian for devoted affection to a sovereign was still alive.

After the Revolution

NOTHING COULD express more clearly the love-hate relationship which existed between Paris and the Monarchy – whether Royal or Imperial – than the history of the Tuileries since the beginning of the French Revolution. Four times all France went delirious with joy at the birth of an heir – the King of Rome – the duc de Bordeaux – the comte de Paris – the Prince Imperial. Three times the storm centre of a revolution was concentrated round the Parisian palace, which was sacked, desecrated and finally burnt.

The most emotional occasion was the return of the comte d'Artois, harbinger of Louis XVIII, on 12 April, 1814. It was a quarter of a century since he had left France after the fall of the Bastille, and now the Monarchy was to be re-established by the Allied forces. It was a radiant spring morning, and he went first to Notre Dame, where a Te Deum was sung. Then he rode to the Tuileries. As he entered the courtyard of the Carrousel, the white flag of the Bourbons was hoisted over the Pavillon de l'Horloge. It seemed as if the French Revolution had at last been reversed. Artois was so overcome by emotion on re-entering the palace that he had to be assisted up the steps by two Marshals.

The gardens of the Tuileries, in which the hand of Le Nôtre was still to be discerned, were just coming to their annual moment of perfection. "Would you believe it?" Artois demanded of the comte Beugnot; "I heard it said a hundred times at Versailles that it was impossible to do anything with the Tuileries; that it was nothing but a compendium of hovels – but just look at its commodious and magnificent apartments!" This metamorphosis had been the work of Napoleon.

It had been arranged for the First Consul to take up residence in the Tuileries the 2nd Pluvôse in the year VIII (1800). It was pointed out by Monsieur de Benezech, a Conseiller d'Etat, that this, the 21st of January, was the anniversary of the execution of Louis XVI. Napoleon thanked him and postponed his arrival until February.

The decree was that all three Consuls should occupy the Tuileries. Cambacérès, however, preferred the Hôtel d'Elboeuf, on the Place du Carrousel. Lebrun did install himself in the Pavillon de Flore, but only for a short time. Napoleon was soon sole occupant of the former palace of the Bourbons.

After the rough treatment which it had received during the Revolution, the fabric of the Tuileries was in a bad way. It was also in need of modernisation. Under the direction of Etienne-Chérubin Leconte, three thousand workmen laboured night and day, "when the season was at its most rigorous", to effect their transformation. They were given one month: it took them two. Among other things central heating, in the form of "conduits de chaleur", was installed beneath the parquets, while sanitation, in the form of "cabinets d'aisance", was contrived within the thickness of the walls.

On 19 February in the year 1800 Napoleon drove in triumph to the Tuileries. To enter the courtyard from the Carrousel, he had to pass between two Guardrooms. On one of these was written: "Royalty has been abolished in France: it will never raise its head again."

A police report of the time confirms that "the new residence of the Consuls has not caused the Republicans any uneasiness". Madame de Staël thought otherwise. She saw the palace as the pathway to the throne. "All that was necessary was, as it were, to leave it to the walls for everything to be re-established." She noticed a readiness on the part of all those who surrounded Napoleon "to become oriental-type courtiers, which must have convinced him that it was no difficult task to rule the world".

In due course her prophecies were to be fulfilled, but before the new Court of the Tuileries attained its high summer in the brilliance and boredom of the Imperial Court, it was to pass through a springtime of exceptional charm.

One of those who lived at close quarters to Napoleon from her childhood in Corsica until his exile to St. Helena was Laure de Saint-Martin-Permon, wife of Maréchal Junot, duc d'Abrantès. Like her husband she was a devoted admirer of Napoleon. The account which she gives in her *Mémoires* is therefore sympathetic, but she was by no means blinded by her affection and could on occasion be severe in her criticism. As a writer she was a considerable artist with a real gift for capturing the atmosphere of a great occasion. Her picture of the Coronation of Napoleon is a model of carefully-observed detail and vividly-recorded emotion.

No one could convey more convincingly that "first, fine careless rapture" of the Consulate. The painful labour of the Revolution was over and past, and France seemed to have been reborn. "The Consular Court, at the time of my marriage [1800] was at its highest point of perfection. Later on there was a very different atmosphere which all the protocol and the etiquette introduced into the Tuileries."

The simplicity and charm of these early days was reflected in the furnishings, which were accomplished "with taste but with no extravagance, the upholstery and the fringes were of silk, the woodwork mahogany; nowhere was there any gilding." The duchesse d'Abrantès contrasts the "new-born elegance of the Consular Court" with the overpowering magnificence of its Imperial successor. "Already the Consular Court was a cage, but the bars were concealed by flowers: later the flowers became more rare, but the bars were gilded."

At the centre of this new and radiant society was the figure of Joséphine. A few months after her death Napoleon made his last visit to Malmaison with Queen Hortense. Every view, every winding of the path and every delicate embellishment of architecture reminded him of the happy days of the Consulate and spoke of Joséphine. "I keep seeing her," he told Hortense, "appearing at the end of one of these walks and picking one of the roses of which she was so fond. She was the most graceful woman I have ever seen." As the duchesse d'Abrantès affirmed: "I have had the honour of being presented to many 'real' princesses, as they used to say in the Faubourg Saint-Germain, and I have to state in all conscience that I never saw a single one who impressed me more than Joséphine – c'était de l'élégance et de la majesté."

The personnel of her Court was scarcely inferior. "One of the most attractive and wonderful things, which no other Court could offer, was this great throng of good-looking people, of faces that were fresh and charming. The matter is easily understood, for nearly all the Generals and senior officers of the Imperial Guard had married for love."

This was still true after Napoleon took the title of Emperor. "Among the young women who made up the Empress's household it would be difficult to name a single one who was plain." This galaxy of beauties, "this basket of fresh roses", which had been the glory of the Consular Court, had always been dressed "with a taste which seemed to be perfection when compared with the styles which succeeded it". In due course the men succumbed to the pressure and rivalled the ladies in the beauty of their lace, the extravagance of their embroideries and even in the decorative use of diamonds about their persons.

This sartorial splendour was one of the greatest ornaments of the Tuileries. "I recall, with the pleasantness of a memory which is free from all pain, the really fantastic vision presented by the Salle des Maréchaux, when on both sides of the room there were three ranks of ladies, adorned with flowers and diamonds and nodding ostrich plumes; and behind them that solid line formed by the officers of the Imperial Household."

The Salle des Maréchaux, occupying the three upper storeys of the central pavilion, or Pavillon de l'Horloge, was the most magnificent room in the palace.

Overhead, the four facets of the square dome, decorated with paintings by Gérard, converged upon the central aperture from which there hung an enormous crystal chandelier surrounded by four smaller ones. The angles of the dome were filled with gigantic military trophies.

Between the windows of the two main storeys a balcony ran right round the apartment, breaking forward over the south wall into a sort of gallery upheld by caryatids. These were copied from Jean Goujon's figures in the famous Salle des Cariatides of the Louvre.

But it was the pictures which gave the Salle des Maréchaux its real distinction and the particular character which justified its name. Fourteen full-length portraits of Napoleon's Marshals alternated with canvasses depicting the principal battles of his campaigns in Italy and Egypt, and set between them were twenty-two busts of the generals and admirals who had been involved.

Three windows faced east towards the courtyard and the newly-erected triumphal arch of the Carrousel; three windows faced west towards the gardens, the central bay commanding the magnificent perspective right down the middle of the Tuileries Gardens, across the Place de la Concorde and up the Champs-Elysées to the newly-erected Arc de Triomphe of the Etoile.

By now Leconte had been dismissed and replaced by Percier and Fontaine. It was January 1801 – just after the *attentat* of Cadoudal – that Napoleon sent for Pierre Fontaine. "I have no further use for Leconte," he told him; "I put my confidence in you; try not to lose it." In the official decree the name of Percier was coupled with that of Fontaine.

Percier and Fontaine: their names are almost inseparable. Their relationship progressed from that of boyhood friends to that of lifelong partners. It had started at the School of Architecture of M. Peyre, Inspecteur des Bâtiments du Roi, where Percier had gained the coveted Grand Prix.

In 1792, when the Tuileries became the property of the Nation, Percier and Fontaine were put in charge of certain repairs and with them a young cabinetmaker named Jacob. Their instructions were to produce something "*de style républicaine*". What they did is not known, but in after years Fontaine never spoke of the Republic except in terms of contempt and disapproval. What these three men were to create was *le style Empire*, and it was at the Tuileries, where they had made this inauspicious start, that they did some of their most important work.

Percier and Fontaine were both designers of great versatility. Fontaine had been employed on stage scenery for the Opéra in his early days and had retained a sense of theatre which was to be of great use to Napoleon when he abandoned the tasteful simplicity of the Consulate for the glittering splendour

72 Salle du Trône. Napoleon receiving a deputation of the Italian Senate, 1803. I. L. Goubaud.

of the Empire. It was Percier and Fontaine who designed his triumphal arches, decorated the streets of Paris or dressed up Notre-Dame for the sumptuosity of the Sacre.

One of the first indications of the new status was the ordering of a throne for the Tuileries and another for Saint-Cloud. Fontaine's design achieved a combination of richness and distinction while avoiding any vulgarity or ostentation. It consisted of a large corona of gilded laurel leaves, set about with ostrich plumes and surmounted by an imperial helmet with a huge panache. From the corona was suspended a mantle of crimson velvet lined with ermine, looped into a festoon on either side and caught up by two imperial standards from which it hung in theatrical drapes to either side of the throne.

Raised on a dais at the focal point of this sumptuous ensemble, the throne itself was richly worked and rather small. Its circular back was so proportioned as to frame closely the head and shoulders of the Emperor, and the Emperor was a small man.

The painting, now at Versailles, by Innocent-Louis Goubaud, which shows Napoleon receiving a deputation from the Italian Senate in 1803, confirms that Fontaine's design was faithfully executed. It also illustrates the care with which Napoleon's architects preserved what they could of the décor of the Ancien Régime. Above the cornice the stucco bas-reliefs of Lerambert and Girardon dated back to Louis XIV, the tapestries, after designs by De Troy, to the mid-eighteenth century.

It is interesting to see how Napoleon was led by his experience of governing along a path not unlike that trodden by Louis XIV. He came to place more and more importance on the trappings of royalty and on the ceremonial with which it was attended. "A King is not a product of Nature," he reflected in St. Helena; "he is a product of Civilization. He does not exist in a naked condition; he can only exist dressed up." In pursuance of this principle he adopted much the same policy as the Grand Monarque.

But Louis XIV had one advantage which Napoleon could never have. He was of royal lineage. "One of Napoleon's keenest regrets," wrote Prince Metternich, "was that he could not invoke the principle of legitimacy as a foundation for his power. Few men have understood more profoundly than he to what extent authority, deprived of this support, is fragile and precarious, and how much it leaves its flank open to attack."

Napoleon's desire not to appear a parvenu seems to have influenced his attitude to the palaces of the Ancien Régime. Here at least was an element of continuity with royal precedent. The restoration of the Tuileries by Percier and Fontaine was accomplished with a tact unusual for the period, in which a necessary attention to the demands of the present was nicely balanced with a sympathetic respect for the achievements of the past.

The most ubiquitous defect of the palace was lack of light: many of the State Rooms had but a single window. To mitigate the sombreness thus occasioned, the two architects made skilful use of mirrors, sometimes by making dummy windows opposite the genuine apertures, sometimes by placing them on the partition wall and thus contriving "to prolong the perspectives of the gallery". The avoidance of heavy decorations and the employment of bright colouring added to the general effect "to overcome the drawback of the place".

A typical use of this procedure was in the Galerie de Diane. This was the last room in the suite of State Apartments running south from the Pavillon de l'Horloge and overlooking the Carrousel. Percier and Fontaine found it "with its ceilings in ruins but still preserving dilapidated traces of their former painting; one could hardly recognise the different subjects with which they were decorated." The delicate task of restoration was undertaken rather than the sacrifice of the old to anything new. "We carefully conserved all the ornaments and the paintings, which were transferred onto new canvasses. The form and lay-out of the ceiling has not undergone the slightest change."

One of Fontaine's earliest successes had been the library at Malmaison. Here he had divided the long room into three sections by two Doric screens, each in the form of an arch upheld by twin columns on either side. The disposition somewhat resembled that of a Venetian window. It became a recurrent theme in Fontaine's repertoire which received its grandest treatment in the great Salle de Spectacle constructed within the same walls as Le Vau's original Salle des Machines, at the Tuileries.

Here the central opening has been expanded into a great vaulting arch which was reflected in similar container arches above the cornice of the side-walls. The square space thus outlined was roofed with a circular dome. This unit was repeated three times to complete the auditorium, the last of the arches serving as the proscenium. The whole room was inscribed within an Ionic colonnade, which ran right round the perimeter, breaking forward into porch-like projections to support each of the vaulting arches. The end opposite the stage curved into a graceful hemicycle with the Imperial box in the centre.

As at the Opera House at Versailles, the stage could be converted into an extension of the auditorium thus forming an enormous banqueting hall. It was just such an occasion which was so brilliantly caught by Emmanuel Viollet-le-Duc in a watercolour which records an occasion in 1835 of unusual *éclat* for the court of Louis-Philippe. Viollet-le-Duc, father of the famous architect Eugène, was Governor of the Tuileries.

The Salle des Spectacles was Napoleon's most important contribution to the Tuileries. It was used for the banquet following his second marriage to the Archduchess Marie-Louise of Austria, the niece of Marie-Antoinette. It was on such occasions that the Salle de Spectacle really came into its own. "The brilliance created by the light of the chandeliers and girandoles which were hung all round the room," wrote Fontaine, "the freshness and elegance of the decorations and the magnificent and sumptuous display upon the tables defy description."

Fontaine was very ready to praise his own work. On 9 January, 1808, he recorded in his journal the first theatrical performance here. The piece was an Italian opera *Griselda* by Päer. "The audience was brilliant and everything conspired to render more impressive the beautiful proportions of the room. The Emperor is so well pleased that he has charged the Grand Maréchal to convey his satisfaction to his architect."

In the course of these reconstructions the old Chapel – which overlooked the Place du Carrousel – was turned into a new gallery, the Salle de la Paix. A new Chapel was therefore needed. The old Theatre, the Salle des Machines, had occupied a disproportionate amount of the building. The new Salle des Spectacles left room for a Chapel, facing the gardens, and alongside it a new room for the Conseil d'Etat known as the Salle des Travées. It opened by a triple arcade into the upper storey of the Chapel and could be used as an overflow gallery. Its decoration was, however, entirely secular. The flat surface of the ceiling was devoted to an enormous painting of the Battle of Austerlitz enframed by the coved surrounding which was treated as a frieze. Here Gérard painted a series of scenes, done in grisaille with highlights picked out in gold leaf, representing Legislation, Finance, the Navy, the Arts and the Art of War – the normal preoccupations, in fact, of the Conseil d'Etat.

The Chapel itself was a two-storied chamber of superimposed Doric orders, with the imperial gallery at the south end and the altar at the north. The Doric columns divided the lower storey into nave and aisles, and above the aisles were the galleries for the Court. The painting by François-Marius Granet shows a building that was dignified if not distinguished in its architecture.

The Catholic Religion had been restored to France by the Concordat with the Pope of July 1801. The idea had come to Napoleon the year before one Sunday in the gardens of Malmaison. "I was taking a solitary walk there," he told Thibeaudau, "when all of a sudden the sound of the Rueil church bells struck my ear. I felt very moved, so great is the influence of our early habits and our education. I thought 'what an impression these bells must make on simple, credulous people!' Let your philosophers and your ideologists answer that. The people must have religion."

The re-establishment of the Catholic hierarchy paved the way for the spectacular visit, in 1804, of the Pope to assist with the crowning of Napoleon

73 The Chapel built by
Fontaine for Napoleon.
Louis-Philippe presenting
the cardinals' hat to the
Cardinal de Chevreuse.
Painting by Granet.

as Emperor of the French. Pius VII arrived in Paris on 29 November and was lodged in the Pavillon de Flore. These were the rooms which had been used during the Terror by the ill-named Committee of Public Safety, but they had previously been occupied by Madame Elizabeth, the sister of Louis XVI, who had followed her brother to the guillotine. When the Pope was presented, by the Abbé Froyart, with a copy of his book on Madame Louise, the very religious daughter of Louis XV, he exclaimed: "I occupy here the apartment of another Saint."

Great care had been taken to provide accommodation suitable for so eminent a guest. "With the most delicate consideration," wrote Bourienne, "the bedroom of the Holy Father was arranged and furnished in exactly the same manner as that which he occupied in Rome in the Palazzo Monte Cavallo."

The Pope's entry into Notre-Dame was reported by the duchesse d'Abrantès. "It would be impossible to imagine, if one were trying to form the picture of a face which was at once imposing and venerable, a physiognomy other than that of Pius VII. He advanced from the back of the church with an air in which both majesty and humility were combined."

Not so Napoleon; he behaved throughout with a becoming grace, the duchess noted; "only the length of the service seemed to bore him, and several times I saw him stifling a yawn." He submitted to the threefold anointing with oil, but obviously "wanting more than anything else to wipe it off". But, when the Pope took the crown off the altar, Napoleon snatched it from him and placed it himself upon his brow.

From this moment the Consular Court became the Imperial Court. It had all the brilliance of the Court of Louis XIV and, it has to be said, the same belittling effect upon its members. "All that the memoirs of the time record of the fabulous magnificence of Marly and Versailles," wrote the duchesse d'Abrantès, "comes nowhere near, according to their own account, the Court of Napoleon in the winter of 1808 to 1809 . . . All the Princes of the Rhineland, Germany, Russia, Austria, Poland, Italy, Denmark and Spain – the whole of Europe, in fact, England always excepted – sent their richest and most elegant representatives to admire the Emperor and to contribute to the sumptuous cortège which formed his train when he went . . . from the Salle du Trône to the Salle de Spectacle in this same Château des Tuileries."

Of the belittling effect, Madame de Rémusat gives an only too convincing account: "An honest man, a man of reason, often feels ashamed in his own heart of the pleasures and pains which come to him in his condition of courtier, and yet he can hardly escape the one or the other . . . however dissatisfied he may be, he has to stoop with everyone else, and either quit the Court entirely or capitulate in taking seriously all the fatuities which constitute the air which one breathes."

The comte Beugnot makes the same point, and specifically links the new atmosphere to the influence of Marie-Louise. "While Joséphine shared the throne, her presence was enough to maintain the memory of former times, that is to say of an elegant equality. Now it seems that the stiffness of Austria has succeeded to the elegance of France . . . One only goes to the Tuileries from duty, or because it is in one's interest to do so. There is no place now for those who might have gone from inclination or affection."

The fall of the Empire and the restoration of the Monarchy made little difference. Madame, the duchesse d'Angoulême, daughter of Louis XVI and daughter-in-law of Charles X, took her etiquette very seriously. "This rigid preoccupation, at such a moment," wrote the comtesse de Boigne, "with the length of a *barbe* or the height of a *mantille*, seemed to me a puerility hardly worthy of her position." It was, however, typical of the New Régime. Madame even wanted to re-introduce the paniers that had been worn at Versailles twenty-five years previously.

The etiquette of the new Court was largely the accomplishment of the duc de Duras, "plus duc que feu Monsieur de Saint-Simon". He took the opportunity of increasing considerably the gap between the rank of Duke and those beneath it. It chiefly concerned the Duchesses. At a reception in the Tuileries they had extremely privileged treatment. The comtesse de Boigne paints the picture for us in typically vivid detail.

On arrival at the Tuileries, the ladies mounted into the Salle des Maréchaux. From here they passed through the Salon Bleu and into the Salon d'Apollon, both of which were poorly illuminated. Those who were Duchesses, however, proceeded straight into the Salle du Trône, which was brilliantly lit. An Usher stood at the door to forbid entrance to anyone not qualified. "You should have seen the faces of some of the old ladies of the Court!"

The closing of the door indicated the arrival of the King, who spent some time alone with his Duchesses. The door was then opened and the other ladies trooped in, turning immediately to the right and lining the wall north of the Throne Room. If the King spoke to one in ten of these, they were doing well. If he pronounced more than a single sentence to one, they were doing very well.

The audience over, they all went downstairs to Madame. Madame was more generous with her conversation and this caused considerably more hold-ups, with the ladies waiting and jostling outside her doors. From Madame's apartment they proceeded to that of her husband, the duc d'Angoulême, and from his apartment they passed out into the Vestibule of the Pavillon de Flore, which had neither doors nor windows and was exposed to every intemperance of the weather.

They now had to get themselves somehow to the opposite end of the Tuileries, to the Pavillon de Marsan, to pay their court to Monsieur, the comte d'Artois, and his younger son the duc de Berry. They were not allowed to go back through the Apartments. They were not allowed to wear a shawl or a pelisse. In wet or windy weather they actually had to pick up their trains and put them over their heads, "ce qui faisait des figures incroyables".

The comtesse de Boigne had no use at all for these receptions at Court. "One never came away except in a state of boredom, fatigue and annoyance. I was among the favoured ones" (she was a personal friend of the duc de Berry) "and yet I never went with a good grace and I only went as seldom as was possible."

"One had to change the hour of one's dinner; to deck oneself out in a *toilette* that was awkward and useless for other occasions; to be at the Tuileries by seven o'clock; to wait there a whole hour *à voir passer les duchesses*, as we used to say, jostle at Madame's door and catch cold in the external corridors. I must add to these displeasures that of being on one's feet for three hours. That was the price we paid for the honour of standing for ten seconds before the King, one minute before Madame and about the same with each of the princes. It was out of all proportion."

It was not at the Tuileries but at Saint-Cloud that the final scene of the legitimist monarchy was to take place. The popular phrase, in talking of Charles X and his ministers, was: "Ils travaillent à faire le lit des Orléans – they are paving the way for the house of Orleans." In July 1830, the "Ordinances of Saint-Cloud" provoked an uprising in Paris.

The comtesse de Boigne, who was a friend of the Governor of the Tuileries, Monsieur Glandevès, recounts the incredible credulity of Charles X. When, on 29 July, the comte de Broglie arrived at Saint-Cloud, deeply disquieted by what he had seen as he passed through Versailles, the King merely said: "Jules [de Polignac] saw the Virgin Mary again tonight; she ordered him to persevere and promised that all this would soon come to an end." It did indeed all come to an end; the following night the King was obliged to take the road to exile. The descendants of Louis XIV were never again to sit on the throne of France.

The descendants of Louis XIII now had their opportunity. Louis-Philippe d'Orléans was offered and accepted the throne. It was not a wholly welcome windfall. Marie-Amélie, the new Queen, confided to the comtesse de Boigne: "Now that this crown of thorns is upon our brow, we must only lay it down together with our lives."

Madame de Boigne, an intimate and life-long friend of Marie-Amélie, has much to say about the reign in her memoirs. Although the Tuileries remained the central palace of the King, it is surprising how seldom she mentions it. Of course there were the balls, the suppers, the big receptions; but what chiefly comes across from the memoirs is a picture of the domestic life of that large and unusually happy family.

On 4 June, 1837, a few days after the wedding at Fontainebleau, the new duchesse d'Orléans made her entry into Paris. The weather was "fabulously fine; nature seemed to have adorned herself for her reception. The chestnuts in the Tuileries gardens were covered with flowers; the air was embalmed with the perfume of the lilacs ... The cortège was welcomed with the most lively acclamations. It was nothing less than magnificent ... But her intelligence was too solid and too distinguished for her not to have felt, in the middle of this flattering intoxication, a slight shiver on entering this palace, successively occupied by Marie-Antoinette, Marie-Louise and Marie-Caroline [the duchesse de Berry]. They also had been received with lively and passionate acclamations."

But she was never to be Queen. A fatal coincidence of circumstances, each in itself unimportant, seemed to conspire to bring about the untimely death of her husband.

On Wednesday, 13 July, 1842, the duc d'Orléans was to have left Paris for a few weeks at Saint-Omer. He had dined the night before with his mother at the Château de Neuilly. She begged him to lunch with her also on the 13th but he had to give certain audiences at the Tuileries and declined. The Queen, however, was so insistent that at last he consented. On the next day, the audiences over, he sent to the stables for a fast vehicle. But the horses that would normally have been available were absent; some had been sent on to Saint-Omer; some were with the Duchess at Plombières. The Duke's écuyer, Cambis, ordered a very light phaeton and two fiery young horses. The postillion, "one of the best in the stables", protested that these horses were not yet properly broken in. Angry at being criticised by a subordinate, Cambis appointed another, less experienced, postillion. The vehicle was taken round to the courtyard of the Tuileries. On seeing it the Duke immediately ordered it to be changed but, on consulting his watch, counter manded the order. His aide-de-camp was nowhere to be found. He entered the phaeton alone.

At the Etoile the horses began to get excited. At the Porte de Maillot the equippage took the wrong road, the turning for Villiers and not that for Neuilly. The Duke stood up to speak to the postillion and fell backwards out of the carriage, fracturing his skull. He was carried into the back room of a greengrocer's shop and laid on a dirty mattress. Soon the King and Queen and other members of the royal family – the King's sister, Madame Adélaïde, the prince de Joinville, the duc de Montpensier, the duc d'Aumâle, and their sister-in-law the duchesse de Nemours – had gathered in the little back-room. There was nothing to be done. "For more than an hour a funereal silence reigned in this hovel, where only the family remained, the Curé and the two doctors, who had given up trying, when a fearful cry, coming from the Queen, announced to the groups who crowded round the house that that moment, only too expected, had come. She had seen that young head droop; she had drawn near and felt his dying breath upon her face and her mother's heart had responded in that cry of anguish of which all those who were present will retain an ineffaceable memory."

She never recovered. Nor did the popularity of the régime. On 24 February, 1848, Louis-Philippe realised that all was lost. The duc de Montpensier urged immediate action: "Abdiquez, Sire, abdiquez. Vous n'avez pas d'autre moyen de sauver votre famille; nous allons tous être massacrés!" The deed was done. The family crossed the Tuileries gardens to the Place de la Concorde where two small vehicles awaited them. At Saint-Cloud they exchanged these for a large *berline* with no coat of arms and made for Le Havre.

On 3 March, 1848, Louis-Philippe and Marie-Amélie, bearing the unconvincing pseudonyms of Mr. and Mrs. William Smith, arrived in England. His régime had been sufficiently unpopular for the mob to sack the Tuileries and to carry out the throne for ceremonial incineration. "Louis-Philippe had afforded France some of the happiest years of her history," wrote André Maurois; "but the French do not live on happiness. The French thirst for glory and the Bourgeois King had not provided it."

He was succeeded, after a short republic, by Louis-Napoleon, who was certainly the son of Queen Hortense and rather less certainly the son of Louis Bonaparte, King of Holland. In spite of this uncertainty he was regarded as the Napoleonist pretender. By an astute playing of his cards he became "Prince President" as the result of one plebiscite and Emperor as the result of the next. The transition from President to Emperor was marked by his removal from the Palais de l'Elysée to that of the Tuileries.

Just before he became Emperor, Louis-Napoleon fell in love with the beautiful Eugénie de Montijo, comtesse de Téba. On one occasion he had granted privileged seats for a review in the Place du Carrousel to Eugénie and her mother. They were given the balcony of the central window of the Salle des Maréchaux. Anna Bicknell, the American governess to one of the Court officials, recounts that, as the Prince President rode beneath the window, he looked up and asked: "How can I reach you, Mademoiselle?" "By way of the Chapel, Monseigneur," was the quick reply. The Chapel would, in fact, have afforded direct access to the Salle des Maréchaux.

On 30 January, 1853, the wedding took place in Notre-Dame and Eugénie became Impératrice des Français. Two years later she and her husband received a visit from Queen Victoria. The Queen and her family were lodged at Saint-Cloud, but on 22 August they attended a reception at the Tuileries. "All is so beautiful here," wrote Victoria in her journal; "all seems now so prosperous: the Emperor seems so fit for his position, and yet how little security one feels for the future." Of the Tuileries she wrote: "It is a very fine and truly royal palace."

Victoria's appreciation of the architecture was doubtless coloured by her fascination with the Emperor. "From behind the vast solidity of her respectability, her conventionality, her established happiness," wrote Lytton Strachey, "she peeped out with a strange delicious pleasure at that unfamiliar, darkly glittering foreign object, moving so meteorically before her."

She particularly admired the Salle des Maréchaux, "which is splendid and beautifully redecorated by the Emperor". In each room it was the same: "Everything is so truly regal, so large, so grand, so comprehensive; it makes me jealous that our great country, and particularly our great metropolis, should have nothing of the same kind to show." Buckingham Palace, as left by the Prince Regent, was nothing to be ashamed of, but perhaps it did not enjoy such a magnificent outlook. "The view from the middle window of the Salle des Maréchaux, looking right up the garden of the Tuileries to the Place de la Concorde, is very fine indeed. The Emperor thinks that the obelisk spoils the view. Where that obelisk stands, Louis XVI, Marie-Antoinette and so many others were guillotined. What sad reflections does this not give rise to!"

The advent of Eugénie brought a new lustre to the Royal Palaces of France in what was to be their last moment of glory. The Tuileries, Saint-Cloud, Compiègne and Fontainebleau became once more the scene of brilliant receptions and distinguished house parties. Queen Victoria noted that the Imperial Court greatly outshone that of Louis-Philippe.

Both the Tuileries and Saint-Cloud received considerable redecoration and a new style was to be created in the process. Eugène Rouyer insists that there was a genuine *style Napoléon III*. "The generous and active impulse which the Empire managed to give to the different branches of the Arts, the character of greatness which it has impressed upon our modern architecture, will certainly be, in the eyes of posterity, one of the claims to glory of Napoleon III." He might with justice have added the name of Eugénie.

There had been no "style" since that of the first Empire. "Our century has no form," wrote Alfred de Musset in 1836, "neither in our houses, nor in our gardens, nor in anything else. The rooms of the rich have become collections of curios – *des cabinets de curiosités* – in which the antique, the Gothic, the taste of the Renaissance or of Louis XIII – all is jumbled together. We live on the debris of the past, as if the end of the world were approaching." In the same year the *Album de l'Ornemaniste* published by Aimé Chenavard offered to the builder and furnisher an inexhaustible wealth of eclectic ornament. In reaction to the chaste classicism of Percier and Fontaine, Chenavard "left no space in which the eye could find repose in this orgy of decoration". The good taste, for which France had long been so justly famous, was in danger of being crowded out.

It was largely due to Eugénie that this movement was modified. The day after her marriage was marked by an excursion to Versailles and she expressed a desire to see the Petit Trianon. She was deeply moved by the evocation of the life of Marie Antoinette which the place afforded. "The enthusiasm of the Empress for the memory of Marie-Antoinette," wrote Henri Clouzot, "triumphantly imposed the fashion of the eighteenth century." While England progressed largely in the direction of the Gothic Revival, France returned to the elegance of *Louis Seize* – or rather to that interpretation of it which Clouzot christens "*Louis Seize Impératrice*".

Among the various descriptions which have been made of the Tuileries and of the life of the Imperial court, none is so accurate in detail nor so sympathetic in its appreciation as the three volumes of Madame Carette. A granddaughter of Admiral Bouvet, she had attracted the favourable notice of Eugénie and Louis-Napoleon when they made their triumphant tour of Brittany during August of 1858. Six years later, on the death of her father, Mademoiselle Bouvet was summoned by Eugénie to the Tuileries to become a member of her household with the title of "Assistant Reader". The position was more that of companion-secretary. From her observation post in the very centre of the Imperial court, she was well placed to write the chronicle of its life and to record the details of its architectural setting.

Fortunately for posterity she was a gifted writer. Her descriptions of Eugénie are probably the best portraits to have survived, for, as she said herself, none of the paintings of the Empress managed to do her justice. "People have sought in a hundred ways to reproduce the beauty of the Empress: painters, sculptors, engravers – all have tried, but very few succeeded. There was something impossible to capture, a certain animation of the features, a certain fleeting mobility of expression, which defied interpretation."

Her portrayal of the palace in which she spent so much of her time is not less evocative.

"In the magnificent palace of the Tuileries – so vast and so sumptuous – no provision had been made for private living. After 6 October, 1789, when Louis XVI and Marie-Antoinette established themselves here, the disposition of the rooms had been improvised in great haste and naturally they retained certain disadvantages. Apart from the State Rooms, all the interior communications were without daylight and it was necessary, both in winter and in summer, to have lamps continually burning in the little staircases and corridors which became almost unbearable because of their heat and their stuffiness from the first days of spring. Therefore, in spite of the fine vista of chestnut trees in the garden, we welcomed with joy the departure of the Court for Saint-Cloud or Fontainebleau."

Nothing was ever done to remedy this, but in 1858 Louis-Napoleon invited the architect Hector Lefuel to create a suite of private reception rooms for the Empress. This was achieved by filling in the space of Philibert de l'Orme's terrace south of the central pavilion. It removed the last vestige of relief from the long and monotonous façade. Eugène Rouyer, who wrote a description of these rooms in 1867, set them in their context by contrasting them with the State Apartments. In these nothing could be too sumptuous, nothing too rich for the presentation of the Monarch to the public. "The painting of the ceilings and of the walls together with the tapestries, should call to mind the high achievements of his administration, the great men who have won distinction in war, in the sciences and in the arts. The palace thus becomes a gallery of all that has made the reign illustrious; it transmits to posterity the glorious memory of the great men of an era and of their noble deeds."

Not so the Petits Appartements. Here a different style was requisite. "The decoration needs to be delicate and recherché; brilliant but not ostentatious; by the refinement of the paintings it will suggest the ideas of gracefulness and pleasure and all the more elegant aspects of life." Certainly these more feminine adjectives could be applied to the creation of Lefuel.

The Imperial Apartments occupied the whole range of buildings between the central Pavillon de l'Horloge and the Pavillon de Flore. Those on the ground floor facing the gardens were the Emperor's; those facing the Place du Carrousel, the Prince Imperial's. Eugénie's rooms were on the first floor above the Emperor's and therefore also overlooking the gardens. These were backed by the State Reception Rooms, the Galerie d'Apollon, the Salon Louis XIV and the Galerie de Diane, whose windows overlooked the Carrousel.

A large staircase of white marble gave access to a landing on the first floor. To the right, the double doors opened into the great Salle des Maréchaux. To the left, another door gave access to the Empress's suite.

The first room, the Salon des Huissiers, was the domain of the Chief Usher, Monsieur Bignet. "C'était l'homme indispensable: on l'appelait 'la troisième dame du palais'." A man of the utmost discretion, he sometimes revealed by his actions what he would never have disclosed by word of mouth. For instance, whenever Eugénie left Paris she took with her a tea service of enamel with two little salt cellars in the form of silver owls. The moment a journey was decided upon, Monsieur Bignet packed the owls. Their failure to appear on the tea table was often the first intimation to members of the household of an impending voyage. When the Court left the Tuileries for Saint-Cloud, Eugénie supervised in person the placing of dust covers over the furniture and the admirable Bignet marked with chalk on the parquet flooring the exact position of every table, chair or sofa.

The next room was the Salon Vert or Salon des Dames, for here the Ladies-in-Waiting performed the office which their title suggests; they waited to introduce visitors into the royal presence. The walls were decorated in arabesques in different shades of green "which recalled the first foliage of

74 Napoleon III and Eugénie in the Salon d'Apollon. Painting by G. Castiglioni.

235

Spring"; the ceiling was painted with an enormous basket of flowers and the pictures in the overdoors were of brightly-coloured birds "which seemed to fly hither and thither among the greenery and added by their presence to the illusion of springtime". On the inside wall, Miss Bicknell informs us, was fixed "an immense mirror which reflected the whole view of the gardens and of the Champs-Elysées as far as the Arc de l'Etoile".

The furniture, the fireplace and the bronzes were, according to Madame Carette, "in the purest Louis XVI style; the chairs of gilded wood upholstered in very beautiful Gobelin tapestry, each panel centering on a bunch of large flowers against a white background with a thick border of brown patterned with gold". Here the ladies-in-waiting settled with their embroidery, their books or their letters which were kept in a marquetry chest placed between the two windows.

From here the visitor was ushered into the Salon Rose, "which could with justice be called the 'Salon des Fleurs'". There were flowers everywhere; real flowers in great abundance, arranged in huge bouquets in the Sèvres vases and capacious jardinières; painted flowers in the panelling and overdoors, and all culminating in the Triumph of Flora by Chaplin which formed the principal decoration of the ceiling.

Here Eugénie was to make her own contribution to the life of the Tuileries and to the brilliance of the Second Empire, surrounded by her ladies, that galaxy of beauties some of whom are immortalised in the famous painting by Winterhalter – the vicomtesse d'Aguado, the comtesse de Montebello, the baronne de Malaret "de fort belle taille et d'une rare élégance", the marquise de Latour-Maubourg, the baronne de Pierres, "la femme de France qui montait le mieux à cheval", the duchesse de Bassano, dame d'honneur, and the princesse d'Essling, grande Maîtresse "d'un caractère à monter avec dignité sur l'échafaud".

These ladies were with her till the last. On 4 September, 1870, with the news of the total defeat of the Imperial army at Sedan, the revolutionary party took the opportunity of terminating the Empire. Eugénie had been appointed Regent during the absence of her husband. Repeated efforts were made to induce her to escape to safety, but she answered proudly: "I have been placed here by the Emperor; it is here where the danger is, and all the interests of the country are centred on Paris. I shall remain."

Like Marie-Antoinette before her – and the comparison would have been gratifying to her – the position of personal peril enabled her to draw upon a deep fund of courage and heroism. She thought only of France. When the mob invaded the Corps Législatif, a deputation hastened to the Tuileries. They were received in the Salon Bleu. "The pieces of furniture and the curtains," wrote Madame Carette, "were all wrapped in their coverings and the hiding of all this luxury in the dull-coloured dust sheets greatly added to the sadness and solemnity of the occasion."

No means of saving the Government seemed possible. "It is too late," cried Monsieur Buffet, "it only remains now to provide for the Empress's safety." Madame Carette continues: "Then the delegates rose to take their departure, and each one took his leave with a profound bow and a reverent kiss on the hand held out towards him. 'I could not help shedding tears,' admitted

INSURRECTION DE PARIS. — INCENDIE DU PALAIS DES TUILERIES. 635

Monsieur Buffet, 'in the presence of such disinterestedness and greatness of soul.' ''

But events were moving fast. The mob was soon at the gates of the Tuileries and Eugénie was forced to yield.

During all this, the ladies of the Palace had been waiting "calm and determined, aspiring to the honour of being allowed to go with the Empress and share her dangers. Madame d'Aguado summoned them to her presence. 'Come,' she said; 'the Empress wishes to say goodbye.' They all went into the second Salon and the Empress came from her study to meet those who had remained her friends up to the last hour. She walked slowly with her head slightly bent. All were profoundly moved, and there was a moment's interval filled with broken expressions of grief and anguish." Those last farewells were the most painful of all to Eugénie. "Sadly and reluctantly the Empress then quitted the room, turning again and again to take a last look at her friends, and then disappeared."

By now the rioters were filling the Place du Carrousel. Eugénie was forced to seek another exit and took the Grande Galerie which connected the Tuileries with the Louvre as her line of retreat. Accompanied only by Madame Lebreton, Monsieur Nigra and the Prince Metternich, she reached the door beneath the Colonnade that opened into the Place Saint-Germain-

75 The burning of the Tuileries, May 27th, 1871.

237

l'Auxerrois. The mob was here too, but suddenly decided to invade the church. This gave the fugitives their chance. Madame Lebreton managed to summon a cab and finally conveyed her mistress to the house of an American Doctor Evans, who accepted without hesitation the dangerous honour of housing Eugénie until she could be conveyed safely to the coast.

After the burning of the Tuileries, Madame Carette returned to Paris and looked for the last time, with feelings which are better imagined than described, on the ruins of the Palace which she had known so well in its last moment of glory.

"You can just distinguish today, through the great, empty, gaping windows of the burnt-out Tuileries, certain vestiges of painting which neither the flames nor the ravages of time have managed to destroy." There, in the Salon Bleu, Eugénie had had the overdoors painted with portraits of the most beautiful women of her entourage, each personifying one of the great countries of Europe. Princesse Anna Murat, with her "fraîcheur de blonde éblouissante", had typified the English; the duchesse de Malakoff, endowed with "a pure Andalusian beauty", the ladies of Spain; the duchesse de Morny, brought up in the Court of St. Petersburg, represented Holy Russia; the comtesse Waleska the more Latin beauties of Florence. "You can just make out," continues Madame Carette, "in what were the apartments of the Empress, above the crumbling cornices, certain traces of those female profiles. Ghostly shadows, they seemed to uphold, amid those sorry ruins, the traditions of beauty, elegance and grace which had for so many years radiated from the Court of France throughout a charmed and captivated world."

8
The Château de Compiègne

L OUIS-NAPOLEON and Eugénie had brought something new to the Court of France. Queen Victoria noticed the change when she visited them at Saint-Cloud: "Everything magnificent but all very quiet, very different from things in the poor King's time – much more royal." The "poor King", Louis-Philippe, had entertained her at the Château d'Eu.

But the Court of the Second Empire was not only magnificent and royal: it was enjoyable. It is impossible to read the memoirs of the period and not to feel the breath of fresh air. In the long chronicles of Court life, it seems that only Joséphine and Eugénie had the capacity for being royal without in some way ceasing to be human. It may be significant that neither of them was born to the rôle.

The atmosphere of a Court depends largely on its attitude to etiquette. In order to present the sovereign in as imposing a light as possible, the whole huge, cumbersome machinery of etiquette had been built up and set in motion. It produced its effect, but the cost to human happiness, and to human integrity, was high.

In Louis XIV's reign, La Bruyère had perceived the belittling effect. Dufort de Cheverny observed the same under Louis XV. "I have often made the reflexion that the life of an assiduous courtier resembles that of a valet de chambre, in fact of someone in servitude ... the functions of the court are magnificent, but they depend upon the miseries of etiquette, made more for the narrowing than for the nourishing of the mind." What is interesting is that etiquette emerged again under Napoleon, who had the rare opportunity of making a fresh start.

The King and Queen were either voluntary prisoners of this system – like Louis XIV or Marie-Leczinska – or they sought to escape from it – like Louis XV and Marie-Antoinette. Louis-Philippe had made the Court more like a house party: Louis-Napoleon made the house party more like a Court.

It was at Compiègne that the new style of court life was most in evidence. Here, every November, Louis-Napoleon and Eugénie held their famous series of house parties – les Séries de Compiègne. "They made every effort," says Madame Carette, "to make these as enjoyable as possible ... it is difficult to express with what kindness and cordiality one was received."

One of the guests recorded that the Emperor was "so merry and so kind, and is content that everyone should feel absolutely at home, yet no one is ever tempted to show the slightest familiarity with him". This special blend of majesty, accessibility and affability on the part of the host and hostess made an invitation to Compiègne the highest of social ambitions.

Each house party usually numbered about a hundred. Alongside some of the great names of the French aristocracy and of European diplomacy were found those of Pasteur, Verdi, Gounod, Doré, Flaubert, Dumas, Mérimée and Viollet-le-Duc. They were often an oddly assorted lot and not easy to integrate into a house party. "It is the problem of the cabbage, the goat and the wolf," Eugénie admitted, and she allocated the rooms in person.

"Only a woman of the world who had become an Empress,' the princesse de Metternich shrewdly observed, "could have managed to create such a company. No one born a princess could have done it. It required a worldly savoir faire as well as the authority of the throne."

The Imperial family arrived several days before their guests. A letter from General Malherbe, Adjutant-Général du Palais, to the Régisseur announced their arrival and set in motion the preparations. "I invite you to close the palace forthwith to visitors. Would you also have fires lit in the fireplaces and stoves as from Thursday 9th. P.S. Would you also have all the taps in the palace turned on for twenty-four hours at least, and make sure afterwards that the tanks are entirely refilled."

Meanwhile the Grand Chambellan's department were issuing the invitations. The envelope bearing the coveted summons contained a pink card, beautifully engraved and highly glazed. "Par ordre de l'Empereur," it ran, "le Grand Chambellan a l'honneur de prévenir M. . . . qu'il est invité à passer six jours au palais de Compiègne du . . . au . . . novembre. Réponse s'il vous plaît. Signé: Duc de Bassano."

In 1866 an American lady, Mrs. Charles Moulton, and her husband were invited. She has left a fascinating description of the occasion. "I was obliged to have about twenty dresses," she wrote, "eight day costumes (including my travelling suit), the green cloth dress for the hunt, which I was told was absolutely necessary, seven ball dresses and five tea gowns. Such a quantity of boxes and bundles arrived at the house in Paris that Mademoiselle Wissembourg was in a blue fidget. A professional packer came to pack the trunks, of which I had seven" – the princesse de Metternich had fourteen – "and Charles had two; the maid and valet each had one, making altogether quite a formidable pile of luggage."

They travelled of course by special train with six *wagons salons* for the guests and fourteen first-class coaches for the servants.

They were met at Compiègne by the personnel of the Palace in green livery who conducted them to the *chars-à-bancs* which were awaiting them. Madame Carette records the impeccable precision with which the postillions took their vehicles, without slowing down, in a great sweep round the Cour Royale to rein in exactly in front of the main entrance.

"The arrival of all these people," she continues, "was the cause of an indescribable commotion in the town. For twenty-five or thirty ladies there was such an excess of luggage that one might have supposed it to belong to an army on campaign." She used to watch, through the chink of a doorway, the arrival of the guests in the great Vestibule – some happily recognising old friends, some trying not to look ill at ease, some simply overwhelmed by the problems of luggage.

76 A rendez-vous de
chasse at Compiègne
under Louis XV.
Tapestry by J.-B. Oudry.

Each guest was expected to bring a personal domestic, and this was known
to cause embarrassment to those who kept none. Some young men even
brought personal friends disguised as valets de chambre. One of these, Paul
d'Hormoys, has left his own account of the experience. He acted as valet to the
sculptor Caristides. They were met in the Vestibule by a valet de pied from the
Palace staff and conducted down endless corridors to a room hung with grey
chintz and furnished with a bed "as large as that of Louis XIV at Versailles",
and in the capacious hearth there burned a fire "big enough to roast an ox".
Outside the window the Forêt de Compiègne, still glorious in the dying
autumn, extended its golden perspectives as far as the eye could see.

At seven o'clock the guests assembled for dinner. They were not left to find
their own way. The palace, under the Second Empire, was more like a vast
hotel with accommodation for at least a hundred guests. There are 1,300
rooms at Compiègne and they are linked by an immense warren of staircases
and passages known only to the household staff. The rooms and staircases are
all numbered as in a hotel. All the guests were allotted a member of the staff to
conduct them to the right place at the right time. "On leaving our
apartment," wrote Mrs. Moulton, "we found a lackey waiting to show us the
way ... and we followed his plump calves through the long corridors."

They assembled in the Cabinet des Cartes, so named because of the large maps of the forest which hung on its walls. This room is next to the central Salon on the garden front. Here the guests formed a double rank, the men on one side and the ladies on the other.

Louis-Napoleon and Eugénie now made their entry and newcomers were introduced by the Grand Chambellan or the Dame d'Honneur. It was not a formidable ordeal, for both the Emperor and the Empress had a real gift for putting people at ease. Artists were delighted to hear their latest exhibits appraised; ladies were flattered to be asked about the health of some ailing relative. It was clear, without being too transparently obvious, that their Imperial Majesties had done their 'home-work'.

Large dinners were held in the Salle du Bal, where covers could be laid for a hundred, and the great *surtout de table* in Sèvres porcelain set out at full-length the successive stages of a stag hunt. Those who were to sit next to their host or hostess were forewarned; others sat as they chose.

After dinner there was always an entertainment. This might vary from charades to amateur theatricals or to a lecture by Pasteur on the circulation of the blood. Eugénie offered to have her finger pricked on this occasion, but Pasteur assured her that the blood of frogs would do. The next day a sack full of frogs was delivered to his room. Unfortunately there was no further discourse upon the subject and Pasteur left for Paris forgetting his frogs. The next Series was inaugurated dramatically. Piercing screams were heard issuing from the bedroom lately occupied by the great doctor, where a young lady was becoming hysterical on discovering that her room had been "invaded by a horde of jumping frogs".

In the morning breakfast was served to the guests in their rooms. A printed form which they were invited to fill in stated their choice between tea, coffee, chocolate or consommé, together with boiled eggs, cold meat or fruit. They also indicated if they would require luncheon. They were free to amuse themselves as they chose until midday. After luncheon they returned to the Salon and the Empress would propose a visit to Pierrefonds, with Viollet-le-Duc as cicerone, or an outing into the forest.

At half-past five a small number of the guests were invited to take tea with Eugénie in her Petits Appartements. It was an important moment for the gastronomes. "One eats so well at the Palace that tea is an indispensable aid to those stomachs which are incapable of moderation." It was at these tea parties that the art of conversation was brought to its highest pitch. "When a really good talker, like Monsieur de Saulcy, that learned man at once so gay, so polished and so good-humoured, takes charge of the conversation, with Monsieur Mérimée, for example, as his opposite number, then tea with the Empress becomes a real treat."

The Empress's apartments are to a large extent still in the condition in which she left them. Built by Louis XV, decorated by Louis XVI and for the most part redecorated by Napoleon, they regained under Eugénie some of their Louis XVI furniture which she had brought back into fashion.

There are, therefore, three phases in the evolution of Compiègne. The building which we see today was the creation of Ange-Jacques Gabriel. It is true that when he retired in 1775 the château was far from being finished. But

Gabriel was succeeded by Le Dreux de la Châtre, a former pupil of his, and one who seemed more anxious to honour his master's reputation than to promote his own. In 1780 when the palace was nearing completion he wrote in a memoir: "All the building and work that has been done on the Château de Compiègne has been executed in accordance with the general project accepted in 1752, and since that time it has been followed without any changes, except in little points of detail of no consequence and which could in no way conflict with the general disposition . . . an advantage which few great houses enjoy, because the architects who succeed the first one cannot confine themselves, as they ought to do, to the carrying out of another's plans."

The "Grand Projet Gabriel", then, dates from 1752 and was therefore well out of fashion by the time it was actually built. Perhaps this is why Compiègne has not always received the attention which it merits. Fontaine, writing a report on the royal houses for Louis-Philippe, drew his master's attention to the restrictions which the site had imposed upon the architect. "If, instead of placing the new palace upon the foundations of an old building little suited to the taste or requirements of the age; if, instead of enclosing it in a narrow and irregular space; if, in fact, the sums which had to be spent on making commodious a mass of old buildings had been effected to an entirely new structure, the task of the architect would have been more easy to accomplish and the Château de Compiègne, today little regarded, would be cited as a model French residence."

It is an interesting question whether an architect does his best work when the local conditions make no demands upon his ingenuity, or whether such conditions may not call forth his latent abilities. Curiously enough, it was Fontaine himself who, some twenty years earlier, had supported this second argument. It was at Compiègne that Napoleon first entered into discussion with his architects about the project of building a palace for his son, the King of Rome. This was to have stood on the high ground of Chaillot and to have answered the École Militaire across the Seine. One of the plans put forward was little more than a symmetrical version of Compiègne. The office courts to the left of the main entrance had been repeated on the right and the long façade that fronts the gardens set at right angles to the main axis. "This project," wrote Fontaine, "seemed to have lost the charm and the advantages of the original."

Napoleon's reaction had been an outburst. "Are symmetry and good order, then, obstacles to the convenience and well-being of a habitation? Is is necessary, in order to enjoy all the private comforts, to deny oneself those perfections that make a palace famous? Apart from these conditions in architecture, as well as in more important matters, it seems to me that nothing can be beautiful or really imposing." He went on to give his own philosophy of royal or imperial architecture. "The house of the Sovereign should seldom be commodious. There is no ease for the man who constantly appears in public. Majesty and the little comforts of life can only co-exist with difficulty and if, in any circumstances whatever, it was at the expense of the first that the second could be obtained, no, certainly I would never consent to the slightest sacrifice on the first!"

When, in 1751, Ange-Jacques Gabriel was invited to prepare designs for a complete rebuilding of Compiègne, he was set an admittedly difficult task. One cannot but admire the manner in which he resolved it.

The palace, if so grandiose a name can be applied to so meagre a building, was an irregular compendium of lodgings mostly of only one storey with tall roofs and dormer windows. The downward slope of the site meant that these buildings increased in height towards the north, but only in the façade towards the town was there an attempt at architectural design. Here, where the buildings were at their tallest, a narrow gatehouse, flanked by slender turrets capped with sharply-pointed *poivrières*, marked the principal entrance.

Looking at the drawings of this medley of buildings, now preserved in the Archives Nationales, one can appreciate the saying of Louis XIV: "I am housed at Versailles like a King, at Fontainebleau like a Prince and at Compiègne like a peasant." Nevertheless, the proximity of Compiègne to the battlefields of Flanders and the added attraction of possessing the best of all the forests belonging to the Royal Domain brought Louis here no fewer than seventy-five times during the seventy-two years of his reign.

It was Gabriel's task to create upon this rhomboid site a palace worthy of the name and capable of housing the innumerable personnel of the Court of France. The present building is, in all important respects, his answer to the challenge.

"The great skill of the architect," wrote Jean-Marie Moulin, "was to have given all the appearances of a regular plan to a building which had none."

The passage from the rectangular Cour Royal to the obliquely set façade towards the garden was ingeniously contrived. Access to the Royal Apartments was by the great Salle des Colonnes on the ground floor, up the monumental staircase and into the Salle des Gardes on the first floor. From the Salle des Gardes, the visitor passed into an Ante-Room which was common to

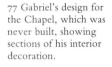

77 Gabriel's design for the Chapel, which was never built, showing sections of his interior decoration.

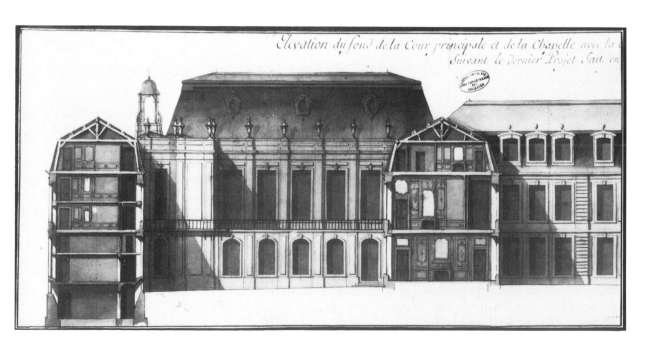

the Apartments of both the King and the Queen. The doors to each of these suites were set in a graceful apse with which Gabriel adorned the southern end of the Ante-Room. It can hardly have occurred to anyone that as he passed from the Cour Royal to the State Apartments he did not make a right-angled turn.

Thus, with one elegant feature, Gabriel made use of a semi-circle to disguise the presence of an acute angle.

His other problem was posed by the lie of the land, which sloped down from the line of the ramparts to the level of the town. Once again his merit was to have made a virtue out of a necessity. He placed his entrance court on the lower ground. It was of course a three-storey structure: the style almost demanded that. It was de rigueur that the State Apartments should be on the first floor and, as we have just seen, they were approached by a suitably sumptuous staircase. It can hardly have occurred to anyone that, as he passed from the Cour Royale to the State Apartments, he no longer had a ground floor beneath him. The Royal Rooms had the added attraction of opening *de plain pied* onto the gardens. Thus Gabriel satisfied the convention that the State Rooms should be on the first floor while giving them the convenience of being on the ground floor towards the gardens.

Gabriel had built, in 1750, the Pavillon Français in the gardens of Trianon. Two years later at Compiègne he was already beginning to develop towards the greater severity of style of his wing at Versailles and the Petit Trianon. The building began with the left range of the Cour Royale, and on 23 February, 1753, it is described as being "wholly built and roofed in". Gabriel wrote to the King: "I hope that His Majesty will be content with the simplicity and nobility of the architecture. The execution of it is good and sound and will serve as a model for the rest of the building."

His claim is justified; the Cour Royale has a nobility imposed by its size and a charm derived from its simplicity. It depends largely for its effect upon the contrast between the plainness of the stone and the patterns formed by the thick white glazing bars of the windows.

On the central façade of the garden front, the windows were renewed, in the nineteenth century, with larger panels of glass and more slender glazing bars. This destroys the balance and is one of the reasons why this side of the palace is less satisfying aesthetically. It is often objected that the façades are too long for their height. It should be remembered, however, that this façade was meant to be seen rising above the massive wall of the former city fortifications. This gave its two storeys the podium which they needed. It was Napoleon who altered this by creating the existing ramp which connects the terrace before the château with its gardens.

In 1755 the work was sufficiently advanced for Marigny to place the orders for the tapestries that were to hang in the King's new apartment, the Cabinet du Conseil and the Cabinet du Jeu. In October of that year Gabriel sent the exact measurements and the details of the lighting.

Two years later the work ceased because of the Seven Years' War and Louis discontinued his visits. At the beginning of 1763 the Contrôleur wrote: "All the Grands Appartements of the King and the royal family, and nearly all the others, have been affected by the long absence of the Court."

78 The entrance court as built by Gabriel and Le Dreux, in the time of the 2nd Empire.

In 1763, after the Peace of Paris, the Voyage de Compiègne was reinstated and Gabriel invited to submit new designs. But in December his original project was once more approved by the King. The only survival of the more grandiose plan was the idea of making a vast Place d'Armes before the château. It was never executed.

In May the following year, Gabriel could report considerable progress. The foundations were laid for the right wing of the Cour Royale; the King's rooms were now "en fort bon état"; the new lay-out of the gardens beyond the terrace was well in hand. This was probably the last Jardin Français to be created. In 1764 2,000 lime trees and 32,000 hornbeam plants for a *charmille* were ordered, but the gardens do not seem to have progressed very far.

If Gabriel was responsible for the external architecture, there is little trace left of his original décor. The château was completely redecorated by Louis XVI between 1782 and 1786. The panelling was painted in plain white. What little gilding there was resulted from pressure by Thierry de la Ville d'Avray, Commissaire-Général du Garde-Meuble. The finest examples of this decoration were in the rooms prepared for Marie-Antoinette. The tragedy is that she never even saw them.

It was at Compiègne, on 13 May, 1770, that Marie-Antoinette first met her future husband and the rest of the royal family.

On 13 May the King set out to meet her at Berneuil, where the road crosses the river Aisne and enters the forest. The duc de Choiseul had already joined her. It was he who had negotiated the Austrian alliance which had culminated in the royal marriage. "I will never forget, Monsieur," said the young

Archduchess, "what you have done for my happiness." "And that of France," replied the Duke.

The first impressions of Marie-Antoinette were wholly favourable. "One could not but admire the airy lightness of her walk," wrote Madame Campan; "one was captivated by a single smile. And in this wholly enchanting creature, in whom there shone all the brilliance and gaiety of the French, with a little touch of august serenity, perhaps also in the slightly proud carriage of her head and shoulders, there could be discerned the daughter of the Caesars." When, a few weeks later, she made her public entry into Paris, she was received with transports of joy. The gardens of the Tuileries were filled with an enthusiastic crowd clamouring for her to appear on the balcony. Seeing so vast a multitude of people, she exclaimed: "Grand Dieu, que de monde!" The duc de Brissac was ready with the gallant reply: "Madame – no offence to the Dauphin – but they are so many lovers."

On 10 May, 1774, Louis XV died and in August the new King and his Queen spent the month at Compiègne. It was not, however, until 1782 that any important changes were envisaged. It was the year after the birth of the first Dauphin. The Queen asked if the "new wing" on the terrace could be affected to her use. These were the rooms at the south end of the garden front and on the right of the Cour Royale as one entered the palace.

Le Dreux replied that these rooms had received as yet no special destination and that her apartment there could be arranged "avec grandeur, dignité et commodité". In fact that they could be as large and convenient as those of the King.

"I am very pleased about it," said the Queen, "because the children are coming and that is the proper place for them." The rooms opened onto the end of the terrace which could be made private to the Queen and her children.

Of all her rooms, the Salon des Jeux is the only one to retain its original appearance. It is a lovely room, cool and spacious. The decorations are in rich relief, but nowhere oppressive. The tall, rectangular panels are left blank. The silk hangings and curtains, recently re-woven at Lyons from a faded remnant, import the freshness of a rose garden – pink and green and slightly out of focus, and even when the curtains are drawn the room retains a delightful luminosity. It must always be remembered that Compiègne was designed as a summer palace.

The original hangings in the Chambre de la Reine were of sky blue embroidered with silver. In a memoir of 24 September, 1784, Thierry de la Ville d'Avray had especially recommended silver "in order to unite in this royal house both magnificence and freshness".

An important feature of these decorations was the set of overdoors painted in trompe l'oeil by Piat Sauvage. They were the first orders which he executed for the King and they are quite remarkable. He was paid 400 livres apiece for them, but in the Chambre du Grand Couvert they were paid at twice that rate. He even went to the length of making a bas-relief model of his composition from which to do his painting. They are so successful that in certain lights it is almost impossible to believe that they are not in three dimensions. It is in this room that the mixture of styles begins. It was Napoleon who had the walls painted to resemble marble of a glowing oyster satin colour which accords beautifully with the paintings by Sauvage.

In 1807 Napoleon decided to add Compiègne to his official residences; the initials of Joséphine are still to be seen on the chairs and cushions of the Grand Salon de l'Impératrice. But he made it over to the exiled King and Queen of Spain until 1810, when he used it for the reception of his second wife. The prospect of such a marriage was one which only her impeccable sense of duty could have enabled Marie-Louise to tolerate; as the baron de Meneval puts it, "she regarded herself almost as a victim sacrificed to the Minotaur". She was only just seventeen, "très simple, très naive et d'une intelligence ordinaire". Her journey from Vienna was a prodigious undertaking and she arrived at Châlons "more tired than it would be possible to express".

Napoleon, meanwhile, having inspected minutely the newly-decorated rooms destined for the Archduchess, was waiting at Compiègne with an impatience which he could hardly master. The most elaborate arrangements had been made for the first meeting in a series of magnificent tents in the neighbourhood of Soissons. But, on the day before, Napoleon suddenly decided to anticipate the ceremony. At ten minutes' notice he took Murat and one valet in a carriage with no livery and, "chuckling like a little boy" at the thought of the escapade, vanished in the direction of Soissons.

At the Relai de Courcelles they met the first outriders of the imperial equipage, and in a few moments the carriage came into view. No sooner had it stopped than Napoleon, opening the door himself, jumped in and greeted his astonished bride with a kiss. His gesture had the desired effect. When Marie-Louise had sufficiently recovered her composure she said, simply and naively, "Sire, your portrait did not flatter you."

A few days later she wrote to her father: "Since my arrival I have been with him all the time and his love for me is very great. I am deeply grateful to him and I respond sincerely to his love. I find that he improves a lot with closer acquaintance."

On 20 March, 1811, Marie-Louise gave birth to a son. The birth was to be announced to all Paris by a cannonade: twenty-one salvoes for a girl, thirty-six for a boy. "The first salvo," wrote the duchesse d'Abrantès, "announced at last that Marie-Louise was a mother. At the first boom everything that was moving came to a halt. Everything. In a second the great city was struck dumb as if by enchantment. Except for the booming of the cannon one could have believed oneself in that city of the Thousand and One Nights petrified by a magic wand. Then the twenty-second salvo sounded in the silence. At that a single cry, a single one but coming from a million throats, echoed through Paris and shook the walls of the very palace where the son of the hero had just been born ... Then hats were thrown in the air, handkerchiefs waved, people ran and embraced each other and repeated to each other the news with laughter and yet with tears, but they were tears of joy."

It was the highest point to which the star of Napoleon was to ascend. In August the Court was back in Compiègne and the Emperor summoned his architects to discuss the building of a palace for the new heir, the Roi de Rome. They found the gardens completely reshaped by Berthaut, with a gently-sloping ramp leading down from the windows of the state apartments and the great *berceaux* of iron trellis to remind the Empress of Schönbrunn.

79 A detail from Marie-Antoinette's Salon de Jeu.

Within the main reception rooms the furniture reflected the new and stricter etiquette of the Imperial Court. "Napoleon having arrived at the summit," wrote Frédéric Masson, "no longer allowed even his family to share it with him. Two armchairs were therefore all that were needed; princesses lost their right to a chair unless they were pregnant. Those who were privileged were accorded a stool. Everybody else remained standing.

The *style Empire* at Compiègne represents the highest moment of Napoleon's pretensions. It is heavily ornate, even in some places gross and overcharged. This is particularly true to Marie-Louise's bedroom, where the bed curtains are held in festoons by posturing angels which are frankly ridiculous. It is referred to in Jacob-Desmalter's *mémoire* as "un lit en acajou, en chaire à prêcher – like a pulpit". Only the quality of the workmanship preserves the décor and the furnishings from the charge of vulgarity. Only in her little Boudoir could Marie-Louise escape this heavy formality of style. It is a circular room, lit from above and hung with white silk lightly decorated in gold, and every piece of furniture is exquisite.

Napoleon had little use for privacy except for work and his Library is the room which most appropriately marks his memory at Compiègne. It is a bold and distinguished piece of architecture. The mahogany shelves and furniture, the gilded calf of the books and the green satin of the upholstery make an impressive colour scheme. Nearly all the furniture at this period was part of the prodigious output of Jacob-Desmalters. In the Library his celebrated "bureau méchanique" still stands. It was made at a cost of 4,000 francs.

Jacob-Desmalters, who at this time was employing no fewer than three hundred and fifty craftsmen in his workshops in the rue Meslée, was by far the most distinguished ébéniste of his day and was later invited by George IV to make an important contribution to the furnishing of Windsor Castle.

Between the years 1810 and 1811, the general inventory of the Garde Meuble Impérial records an expenditure of over thirteen million francs on the furniture of the royal palaces.

In all this redecorating and refurnishing of the eighteenth-century rooms, Napoleon made one important addition: the Salle de Bal. It is a room ornamented with extreme richness and with a delicacy unusual for the period. But it has to be said that its proportions are far from satisfying. It is a building too low for its width; the elaborate and beautifully-carved entablature is too heavy for the columns which support it, and these columns have no podium. The most beautiful thing about the room is the lovely set of chandeliers made under the Empire at the manufacture of Montcenis.

The decorations and furnishings of Napoleon were retained by Louis XVIII. Owing to its geographical situation, Compiègne was the first of the royal palaces to open its doors to the new King at the Restoration.

On 29 April, 1814, Louis XVIII arrived, accompanied by his niece the duchesse d'Angoulême, Madame de Tourzel, the prince de Condé and the duc de Bourbon. His brother, the comte d'Artois, had already gone to the Tuileries and was already compromising his position with rash promises and foolish undertakings. Louis XVIII was more perspicacious. He bided his time and for three days watched the course of events from a safe distance. On 2 May his mind was made up. His proposals for a Constitution – the Declaration of

80 The Salle de Bal
added by Napoleon.

Saint-Ouen – were dated "from the eighteenth year of our reign". In other words he was King, not by virtue of the victorious Allies, not by invitation of the French people, but simply as next in succession to Louis XVII. The principle of heredity was not to be compromised.

The first person whom he received at Compiègne was the Tzar Alexander of Russia. He was received, observed Madame de Boigne, "with a chilly etiquette". He had intended to stay the night, but when he asked to be shown to his apartments "he was taken through three or four magnificently furnished suites. They were designated to him as those of Monsieur [the comte d'Artois], of Monsieur le duc d'Angoulême and Monsieur le duc de Berry, none of whom was present; then, after making him take a veritable journey through corridors and backstairs, they stopped before a little door which gave access to an extremely modest apartment; it was that of the Gouverneur du Château and formed no part of the Grands Appartements. The Tsar turned to his Ambassador, Pozzo di Borgo, and said: "I return to Paris tonight. Have my carriages ready immediately after dinner."

At dinner he fared no better. There was only one armchair at table in which Louis sat. When comments were made abut this, Alexander replied: "What would you expect? The grandson of Catherine [the Great] would perhaps not have enought quarterings to qualify him to ride in the King's coach."

250

The second Empire found Compiègne furnished almost exactly as the first Empire had left it. In course of time, considerable additions were made, mostly in the provision of armchairs, significantly known as "confortables". These began to abound in all the rooms, together with those twin inverted seats with a single S-shaped back known as "confidants" and the triple form of it known as "indiscrets". Compiègne was being adapted to a more enjoyable way of life.

One of the most attractive rooms in the Empress's suite was the Salon des Fleurs. It has been given a pleasing rhythm by the alternation of round arches over the doors and mirrors and rectangular panels with the flower paintings from which it takes its name. These were painted by Louis Dubois from originals by Redouté. In due course it became the bedroom of the Prince Imperial.

Madame Feuillet records having paid a visit to Madame Bizot in the adjoining salon. They could hear the sound of a child's voice and presently that of a saw and hammer. The Emperor was amusing himself by making toys for his son.

On another occasion, Octave Feuillet describes how he was taking tea with the Empress when the Emperor entered and announced: "Eugénie, here is a *valet de chiens* asking for you." "He opened the door and let in the little Prince dressed in a huntsman's coat with knee breeches and white stockings, a large hat and a hunting horn across his shoulder, holding on the leash two pretty white hounds who were pulling him faster than he wanted. He looked ravishing. The Emperor's eyes were moist as he embraced him."

It was the uniform ordained for the royal or imperial hunt at Compiègne. The privilege of wearing the "bouton" – a silver button embossed with the figure of a stag – was accorded to some thirty persons only, who had the right to follow the hounds and to dine at Court whenever there was a hunt. The Prince of Wales enjoyed this distinction, as did the British Ambassador, Lord Cowley. On 21 November, 1868, the Prince of Wales availed himself of this right and hunted at Compiègne. It is recorded that he was thrown from his horse, but without injury.

One of the most dramatic ceremonies of the hunt was the final scene known as the *Curée*, when the remains of the stag were thrown to the pack in the front courtyard of the château. It took place in the evening by the light of flambeaux with the whole Court watching from the first-floor windows. It is described by d'Hormoys. "In the centre of the court is the body of the stag, while the pack, maintained at a distance, are barking furiously, the *piqueurs* sound the *Royale*. Firmin, the *maître d'équipage*, lowers his whip and the pack rushes forward like a cavalry squadron at the gallop, but at one yard from the stag's corpse, it stops, howling and trembling: Firmin has raised his whip again, and they have to go back to the far end of the court and form up again. Twice they rush forward and twice they return in this manner, but the third time the whip remains lowered. The *valet de pied* extricates himself and the howling mass of dogs hurls itself onto its fodder. The *piqueurs* sound *la Vénérie, la Compiègne* and *la Bonaparte*; the windows are closed and the Court retires."

After the fall of the Empire, one of the first acts of the new Government was to order the destruction of every one of the hounds. So closely was the *chasse à course* identified with royalty that this symbolic act of vengeance was wreaked on these innocent creatures.

Towards the end of her long life, Eugénie made what was probably the mistake of returning incognito to the scene of eighteen years' triumphant happiness. Now she was an exile; her husband had died not long after he lost his throne; the Prince Imperial had been killed in the Zulu wars. On entering the Salon Bleu she turned instinctively to the architrave on the right-hand side of the door. There, still pencilled on the woodwork, was a line such as is often drawn on nursery walls to mark the height of a child, with the inscription: "Louis – dix ans." The poor woman burst into tears and it was only then that the guide recognised his former mistress.

9
The Château de Saint-Cloud

ON SATURDAY 18 August, 1855, Queen Victoria, accompanied by Prince Albert, their son Bertie, the Prince of Wales, and their daughter Vicky, arrived in France on a State Visit to Napoleon III. It was an historic occasion. Victoria was the first reigning sovereign of Great Britain to set foot in Paris since the coronation of Henry VI in 1431.

It was a return visit, for Napoleon and Eugénie had been received in April of that year at Windsor Castle. Louis-Napoleon had won the hearts even of the London cockneys. Cries of "Vive le Hemperor!" had been recorded in the royal carriage. But most important of all he had won the heart of the Queen. "She was charmed with the Emperor," wrote Lord Clarendon to Grenville; "he had made love to her, which he did with a tact which proved quite successful. He began this when he was in England and the Queen was evidently mightily tickled with it, for she had never been made love to in her life and had never conversed with a man of the world on the footing of equality."

The success of the imperial visit to Windsor paved the way for the royal visit to Paris. Victoria was, as ever, superlative in her enthusiasm. "Indeed no description can give an idea of the splendour of the whole scene," she wrote; "Paris is the most beautiful and gayest of cities, with its high, handsome houses, in every one of which there is a shop. Imagine all these decorated in the most tasteful manner possible, with banners, flags, arches, flowers, inscriptions and finally illuminations; the windows full of people up to the tops of the houses, which tower storey upon storey, the streets lined with troops ... and everybody most enthusiastic; and yet you will have but a faint notion of this triumph as it was."

The Château de Saint-Cloud had been appointed for the reception of the royal family; it was the Emperor's summer palace. One of Eugénie's ladies, Madame Carette, described it as the most agreeable residence of the Court. "Although large and sumptuous," she wrote, "this palace did not have the immense proportions of Fontainebleau, the solemnity of the Tuileries, the severe and somewhat monotonous lines of Compiègne. Here, more than anywhere, one felt the atmosphere of a *home*."

Set in a garden of cascades and fountains and perched on the high ground across the river from the Bois de Boulogne, Saint-Cloud enjoyed the combined advantages of rural seclusion and proximity to Paris.

It was after dark when the carriages arrived at the foot of the long, oblique

slope which formed the drive, but they did not want for artificial illumination. "In all this blaze of light from lamps, torches, amidst the roar of cannon,
and bands, and drums, and cheers," continues the Queen's journal, "we
reached the Palace. The dear Empress, with Princess Mathilde and the ladies,
received us at the door and took us up a beautiful staircase."

This was the staircase built by the architect Richard Mique for Marie-
Antoinette. In the simplicity of its architecture and in the delicacy of its
ornament, it recalled the prototype of the Petit Trianon. Its landing was
adorned by two large bas-reliefs executed by Deschamps representing "La
course d'Hippolyte et d'Atalante" and "Le Triomphe de Flore". They are
today in the Philadelphia Museum.

It was on 24 October, 1784, that Marie-Antoinette had purchased the
château from the duc d'Orléans. The acquisition of Saint-Cloud had been
connected in the first place with a project for a virtual reconstruction of
Versailles. This would have necessitated the absence of the Court for about ten
years. A complete *déménagement* to the Tuileries would have spelt ruin for the
tradesmen of Versailles, so the plan was for the Government Departments and
some of the offices of the Court, such as the Grande Ecurie, to remain at
Versailles, while the Court itself removed to Saint-Cloud, a distance of some
ten kilometres.

The extravagant projects of Mique, Paris and other architects for bringing
Versailles *au goût du jour* came to nothing, and Marie-Antoinette persuaded the
King to purchase Saint-Cloud in her name. It seemed a good idea. If it were
not the King's House there would be no need for the not inconsiderable
expense of a Gouverneur du Château; as at Trianon the Queen immediately
put the Suisses des Grilles and other domestics into her own livery and posted
notices on the gates about the internal policing which were signed "de par la
Reine".

This action, Madame Campan observed, "caused a great sensation and
produced the most unfortunate results". The matter went as far as the
Parlement, where M. d'Esprémenil denounced it as "equally unwise and
immoral to see palaces belonging to a Queen of France". Had her children
died before her, she could have bequeathed Saint-Cloud to her Austrian
relations.

As at Trianon, the Queen's existence had something in it of a game of
make-believe – the belief that a Queen could behave as an ordinary individual.
"She used to station herself," wrote Soulavie, "for the tournaments and other
sports of the watermen, like an ordinary spectator among the townspeople. It
did not make her any the more popular. Only Monsieur Lenoir knows what it
cost the police to subsidise the common cry of 'Vive la Reine!' The populace
went in shoals to the fêtes at Saint-Cloud, but the words on their lips were
already the significant ones: 'We'll go and see the fountains and the *Austrian
woman.*'"

L'Autrichienne – there was no title that was to do more harm to Marie-
Antoinette. In due course it was to identify her with the enemies of France. A
further and important contribution to the Queen's unpopularity was her
extravagance in building. Trianon had provided the first grounds for
widespread discontent: Saint-Cloud was to furnish the second.

An ambitious project for demolishing the old château and building anew had to be abandoned as too expensive. In the end Mique was commissioned to enlarge the central block by extending it some ten feet towards the west, to reface the two façades which it presented towards the gardens, and to remodel the private apartments in the wing on the south side of the forecourt.

Mique was an architect with a taste for the exquisite. If asked for a design for a garden pavilion or the redecoration of a *petit appartement* he could produce such masterpieces as the Belvédère at Trianon or the Boudoir at Fontainebleau. He was less gifted for large-scale compositions. His project for Versailles was at once grandiose and banal. His refacing of the centre block at Saint-Cloud was banal without being grandiose. The west front was, if possible, duller than the one which it replaced. In the nineteenth century shutters were added to the windows – "as in all châteaux abroad," commented Victoria. If anything was needed to complete the plebeian appearance of the garden front at Saint-Cloud, the shutters provided it.

The most important work at Saint-Cloud was the reshaping of the whole interior of the south wing, known as the Aisle du Fer-à-Cheval. The large state rooms, with ceilings painted by Coypel, Pierre and Nocret, gave place to smaller, more intimate apartments – those of Marie-Antoinette overlooking the Cour d'Honneur; those of Louis XVI facing south over the garden. Central to this suite was the King's Bedroom, the only large room in the new lay-out and later to become Salon de l'Impératrice under Eugénie.

Mique based the rhythm of this room on the fact that in this part of the château the first-floor windows were round-arched. These arches he repeated in false windows, glazed with mirrors, in the inward angles, thus creating a stately alternation between the round arches and the tall, rectangular pier glasses, which reflected each other in endless perspective across the room. The remaining wall spaces were decorated with panels of white and gold in very much the same style as the Méridienne and the Cabinet Intérieur of the Petits Appartements de la Reine at Versailles.

In the middle of the outer wall, on the left of Fournier's watercolour, is a chimney piece, surmounted by a mirror. In the external façade this space was the centre point and it was occupied by a large window beneath the apex of the pediment, which was surmounted by a chimney. The apparent contradiction of having a window and a fireplace with a mirror in the same place is resolved by the Inventory, drawn up in 1792, when Saint-Cloud became the property of the nation: it specifies that in this room a most ingenious device had been contrived. Over the fireplace there was indeed a mirror, but one which could be made to disappear suddenly by the touching of a spring, revealing behind it a window of plate glass through which one could command a magnificent view over the Bassin du Fer-à-Cheval and right down the Allée de la Balustrade towards Sèvres.

The estimate for the work has also survived and is in the Archives Nationales: "Mémoire des ouvrages de serrurerie par Jubault, serrurier à Versailles." He charged nine livres for "a framework to carry a mirror, consisting of two supports ... the said supports made in such a way as to be able to move away or be replaced at will".

The device could not have failed to intrigue so mechanically-minded a man as Louis XVI and would have provided infallible means of astonishing his guests.

Mique's improvements at Saint-Cloud were only finished in 1788. The Queen did not have long in which to enjoy her new creation.

During the Revolution, when the royal family were virtually prisoners in the Tuileries, they were allowed a season of respite at Saint-Cloud. On 29 May, 1790, the Queen wrote to her brother Leopold: "I believe that they will allow us to take advantage of the fine weather by passing several days at Saint-Cloud, which is at the gates of Paris. It is absolutely necessary for our health that we should breathe a purer and a fresher air."

It was not until 4 June – the anniversary of the Dauphin's death at Meudon – that they finally got to Saint-Cloud. With them came the King's two aunts, Mesdames Adélaïde and Victoire, the comte and comtesse de Provence, the marquise de Tourzel and her daughter Pauline, who was allowed – contrary to all etiquette, for she had not even been presented – to eat at the royal table, and Madame Elizabeth, the King's sister, who made the significant comment on the famous view from the terraces: "Paris is beautiful ... *when seen in the distance*."

The royal family's position outside the confines of the capital offered a real opportunity for escape. On one occasion Louis was out riding with the duc de Brissac, the marquis de Tourzel and count Valentin Esterhazy, whose memoirs furnish the record. The Queen and the rest of the royal family were known to have gone out in a calèche. The King prolonged his ride much farther than was his wont, as far, in fact, as Maisons. Brissac and Esterhazy were beginning to entertain hopes that his intention was to cross the Seine and make for Chantilly. They little knew their man. Louis dispelled all their dreams by ordering the relay horses for the Pont du Pecq and returning to Saint-Cloud. But Esterhazy could not put the idea out of his mind. "The more I thought of it," he wrote, "the more I came to believe that such an end would be easily achieved. We could have reached Chantilly before anyone became aware of our flight."

Back at Saint-Cloud he made his ideas known to Marie-Antoinette. "She told me that she thought the same, but that she despaired of ever obtaining the King's consent; that, so far as she was concerned, she was determined never to be separated from him and to accept the lot which destiny was preparing for them." On this, her last visit to Saint-Cloud, the irresponsible hedonism of her former days gave place to the courageous devotion of her final years.

The memory of Marie-Antoinette exerted a fascination over the mind of Eugénie. As she lived in the same rooms and walked in the same gardens as that unhappy Queen, she was subject to premonitions that she would one day share her fate. She collected as much as she could of Marie-Antoinette's furniture. Some of these exquisite pieces were to be seen in her apartments at Saint-Cloud along with the more comfortable upholstery of the Second Empire. "The furniture is so charming and so well stuffed," commented Victoria, "that by lying a little while on the sofa, you are completely rested".

Victoria's first impressions of Saint-Cloud were of the State Apartments along the east front of the Cour d'Honneur. "The saloons are splendid, all *en suite* ... the ceilings are beautifully painted, and the walls hung with

Gobelins." Madame Carette records how she loved to come on hot summer afternoons "and to wander through these great rooms, cool and deserted, filled with masterpieces of art and alive with historical memories." The last room of the suite was the Salon de Mars; "a very fine room" wrote Victoria, "and opens into the fine long gallery called the Salle de Diane in which we dined."

What Victoria called the Salle de Diane was in fact the Galerie d'Apollon. This, together with the Salle de Mars, was one of the most important survivals of the original decorations of Saint-Cloud for Philippe, duc d'Orléans, younger brother of Louis XIV. Dubbed by the Abbé de Choisy as "la plus belle créature de France", Monsieur was effeminate and homosexual. The young Chevalier de Lorraine, "fait comme on peint les anges", ruled his heart and dominated his houschold. As is not infrequently the case, Monsieur combined these traits with a passionate love of the fine arts and a pronounced taste for recherché living. "Il entend l'ajustement d'une maison à merveille," Sophie de Bavière had written of him. The duc de Saint Simon describes with enthusiasm the attractions of Saint-Cloud: "The pleasures of all kinds of games, and the singular beauty of the place ... soft music and good cheer made it a palace of delight, grace and magnificence." To this lyrical passage he added one of his inimitable thumbnail sketches.

"Monsieur was a little round-bellied man, who wore such high-heeled shoes that he seemed mounted always on stilts; was always decked out like a woman, covered everywhere with rings, bracelets and jewels; with a long black wig, powdered and curled in front; with ribbons wherever he could put them, steeped in perfume. He was accused of putting on an imperceptible touch of rouge. He had a long nose, good eyes and mouth, a full but very long face. All his portraits resembled him. I was piqued to see that his features recalled those of Louis XIV."

A large allegorical painting by Nocret, originally at Saint-Cloud but now in the Salon de l'Oeil de Boeuf at Versailles, which shows the royal family in an absurd combination of déshabillé, négligé and butterflies' wings, brings out this resemblance between the two brothers.

Nocret enjoyed the position of Premier Peintre to the duc d'Orléans, and he was given the task of decorating some of the private apartments in the south wing. Most of these were destroyed in the reconstructions of Marie-Antoinette.

It was not, however, Nocret to whom was given the most important contract for the painting at Saint-Cloud, but Pierre Mignard, an artist of sufficiently independent spirit to have set himself up in rivalry to Le Brun. At the beginning of 1677 Philippe d'Orléans visited his studio and what he saw decided him. "Monsieur Mignard," he said as he was leaving, "I am having built at Saint-Cloud a salon, a gallery and a cabinet specially for you to paint them."

This gallery, which formed the north wing to the Cour d'Honneur, was a magnificent apartment. Twenty-three windows – thirteen towards the court and ten towards the gardens – provided an ample illumination for Mignard's paintings.

The theme chosen was almost inevitable – Apollo. Louis XIV had set the fashion with the Galerie d'Apollon at the Louvre; the iconography of Versailles was dictated by it. It must be remembered, however, that Mignard's work at Saint-Cloud preceded that of Le Brun in the Galerie des Glaces. Saint-Cloud was ready for the King's inspection on 10 October, 1678. The Galerie des Glaces was not completed until six years later.

Perhaps the last art historian to study the Gallery at Saint-Cloud while it was still standing was Alexandre Blanc, who published his *Histoire des Peintres* in 1861. "The story of Apollo," he writes, "was the theme chosen by Mignard, and he carried it out with pomp, and with abundance, but with a grace that was wholly French, managing to introduce the most ingenious concepts, with felicitous borrowings from Carracci and Julio Romano, from the Palazzo Farnese and from Mantua. Never did he make use of colours more warm, more clear or more brilliant ... All that poetry, all that fable, all that tradition could provide to grace subjects on which it was so difficult to be original, Mignard conscripted into his service."

In only one respect does Alexandre Blanc reproach his painter; "Mignard was not wholly innocent of courtisanship and painted the sun with the features of Louis XIV."

The paintings of Mignard were destroyed in 1871 when Saint-Cloud was burnt by the Prussians. By a happy chance six of his compositions were used as designs for tapestries, which survive. It was Louvois who, in 1685, placed the order with the Gobelins. He had to do so in his own name because the King could hardly have approved an order so favourable to Mignard under the nose of his Premier Peintre, Le Brun. The death of Le Brun in 1690 must have been a great relief to Louvois, who promptly transferred the order into the King's name. The tapestries are mostly in the Mobilier National today. "The balance and rhythm of their compositions, the beautiful draperies of the figures, the general harmony of the colours," writes Madeleine Jarry, "remain as an incontrovertible testimony to the talent of Mignard."

A secondary theme to these decorations was the series of paintings, set between the windows, of the great houses of France. Along with a view of Versailles – which would have given us a fascinating portrait of the Enveloppe before the final enlargements of Mansart – Clagny, Saint-Germain and Fontainebleau, were the châteaux of some of the King's more opulent subjects – Le Raincy, Sceaux, Maisons and, somewhat daringly, Vaux-le-Vicomte. After the disgrace of Fouquet, that was ground on which most would have felt obliged to tread delicately.

Louis XIV, however, made no comment on this choice of subject. Having completed his inspection he turned to Madame and said: "I very much hope, Madame, that the paintings in my gallery at Versailles will answer the beauty of these."

It was in this gallery that Victoria and Albert dined on their arrival at Saint-Cloud. "The rooms were overpoweringly hot," the Queen complained, "for the table was covered with lights which quite dazzled one; everything magnificent, but all very quiet, very different from things in the poor King's [Louis-Philippe's] time – much more royal."

"Slept very well," continues her journal, "and awoke to admire our lovely room. We have a number of rooms *en suite*, furnished with the greatest taste;

the walls of most of them white and gold; and the ceilings of my sitting and drawing rooms painted to represent the sky. My rooms are a bedroom, and then a little bathroom and dressing room – looking on Paris (the view of which is splendid); a sitting room and drawing room (quite lovely) and two more rooms – all looking out on the gardens." In her bedroom there was a telescope mounted by means of which she could take a closer view of Paris.

She was lodged in the east end of the south wing. Her dressing room, with windows to the east and to the south, was carved out of the original Salon de Madame which had been decorated by Nocret. This would have been an appropriate room for the reception of Victoria, for the ceiling was a vast allegory representing the Alliance of France and England. It referred to Monsieur's first marriage with Princess Henrietta, daughter of Charles I, who had negotiated the secret Treaty of Dover between Louis XIV and Charles II.

"The English Princess," wrote Madame de Motteville, "was a fairly large woman. Her beauty was not of the highest perfection. But she made up for this lack of classical beauty by the delicacy of her complexion, the sparkle of her eyes and the quality of her teeth, which were the finest and whitest that could possibly be desired." She had not married a King, but to make up for this she sought to reign in people's hearts and to cover herself in glory by her charm or by the beauty of her wit. She could not, however, compete with the Chevalier de Lorraine for the heart of her husband.

Whether she was poisoned by her young rival or whether she died of some natural disease is open to question. Madame de Lafayette has recounted the full story of her last moments – how the doctors dismissed her agonizing pain as a simple colic – how her relentless confessor, the Chanoîne Feuillet, pressed home his strictures: "You confess now that there exists a God of whom you have taken very little account during your life" – how she implored Lord Montagu, the English Ambassador, to deny the rumour that she had been poisoned – how Bishop Bossuet, a more merciful pastor "avec un douceur infini lui ouvrait les voies du ciel".

He held a crucifix before her eyes, saying, "Behold our Lord Jesus Christ opening his arms to you." Presently he spoke again: "Madame, you believe in God, you hope in Him, you love Him?" She managed to answer, "With all my heart." They were her last words.

She died on 3 June at three in the morning. On 21 August Bossuet preached her Oraison Funèbre at Saint-Denis. It remains one of the great classics of the French language. "Bossuet's genius had been conspicuous in his funeral oration over the Queen of England," wrote Cardinal de Bausset; "he put forth the whole tenderness of his soul in that spoken over her daughter."

"Woeful night, when like a thunderclap, the startling news was spread abroad – Madame se meurt! Madame est morte!" He dwelt with earnestness upon the vanity, the emptiness of all things mortal, returning again and again to the particular subject of his discourse. "Madame met death gently and sweetly as she had ever met all else." He did not fail to point his moral to his princely congregation: "As you gaze upon these courtly places where she no longer moves, remember that the glories you admire were her greatest dangers in this life."

More secular in her concern, Madame de Sévigné wrote: "With her were lost all the joy, all the charm and all the pleasures of the Court."

Henriette d'Angleterre was succeeded by Liselotte von der Pfalz, a lady of ample proportions and teutonic features who carried beneath her capacious bustle "the imposing rotundity of a part that shall be nameless". The second Madame was no more likely to distract her husband's affections than the first. "Sulky and surly," according to Saint-Simon, "she passed her days in a little cabinet which she had chosen ... gazing perpetually on the portraits of Paladins and other German princes with which she tapestried the walls; and writing every day with her own hand whole volumes of letters of which she always kept autograph copies."

It was Liselotte who bore Philippe d'Orléans his first sons – the duc de Valois in 1673, followed by the duc de Chartres the next year. It may have been this new dimension to his family that caused him to think of seating himself more definitely at Saint-Cloud.

It was not until the 1670s that the first enlargements were made under the first architect, Le Pautre. By 1677 the south wing had been matched to the north by the Galerie d'Apollon. In August of that year Monsieur entered into an agreement with the entrepreneur Jean Girard "for the construction of the great building which H.R.H. desires to have ... in his château of Saint-Cloud between the two existing wings". In the following year Jules-Hardouin Mansart, who had already made his name in the construction of Clagny and was about to embark on the final enlargements of Versailles, put the last touches to the architecture of the Cour d'Honneur.

It has to be said that the result was unsatisfactory. The west front was distinctly dull. An engraving by Aveline shows the monotony of a four-storied façade, with nineteen windows to each floor, unrelieved by any device of architecture. The courtyard had a certain grandeur. Queen Victoria said that it reminded her of Brühl. This merely warns us that she was not an accurate recorder of architecture: the resemblances between Saint-Cloud and Brühl are few and insignificant.

What is interesting about the east front of the main block is that, without its Mansart roof, it would have resembled fairly closely the architecture of the garden front at Versailles as built by Le Vau and before its alteration by Mansart in 1678. The windows of the first floor are rectangular and each surmounted by a panel carved in bas-relief. If this façade had been crowned with a balustrade and trophies, its resemblance to Versailles would have been unmistakable. As it was, the high-pitched Mansart roof gave it the appearance of a rather large *hôtel particulier* of no particular distinction.

In many of the earlier paintings and engravings chimneys – often so impressive a feature of a French château – are conspicuous only by their absence. This absence is explained by Madame in one of her letters to the Raugrave Louise. "Saint-Cloud is a summer palace. Many of my personnel there have rooms without fireplaces; this is not tolerable in winter; it would kill most of them."

The fact that Saint-Cloud was a summer palace made the gardens all-important in the total design. The great bird's eye view, now at Versailles, painted by Etienne Allegrain in about 1677, leaves little or nothing to be desired as a portrait of the palace and its gardens.

81 The Château and garden as finished by Philippe, duc d'Orléans. E. Allegrain.

He has taken his viewpoint from an imaginary height to the south-east, looking northwards over the whole scene towards Mont Valérien. Hervart's wing, incorporating the under-croft of the Maison des Gondi, is that nearest to the spectator, its façade reflected in a large *pièce d'eau* which was later remodelled as the Fer-à-Cheval. To the right of this is the elaborate ensemble of the Grande Cascade.

Since the château occupied the north-east corner of its terrain, it was impossible to make it the focal point of its gardens. In van der Meulen's painting the Cascade appears as the centre of gravity to the lower gardens which bordered the river Seine. On 14 October, 1665, Bernini, who was in France and trying unsuccessfully to interest Louis XIV in his designs for the Louvre, made a visit to Saint-Cloud. He was armed with a ticket from Monsieur without which Billon, the Concierge du Château, was not authorised to turn on the *grandes eaux*. The cascade sprang into movement and life and the great architect exclaimed, "E bella! E bella!" But in private he was less complimentary, saying to Chantelou that it might pass as a marvel in a French garden, but would only just be acceptable in an Italian one. The

261

Cascade did not, however, receive its final form from Le Pautre until 6 May, 1667, when it was officially inaugurated in the presence of the King.

In front of the Cascade, and closely embowered in the trees of a *salle de verdure*, is a square *pièce d'eau* known from its central fountain as the Grand Jet. Thanks to reservoirs up on the high plateau of the park, this column of water could reach a height of forty-two metres. The English traveller Martin Lister, who visited Saint-Cloud in 1698, said that "it threw up a spout of water ninety feet high, and did discharge itself with that force that it made a mist and coolness in the air a great compass round about, and gave now and then cracks like the going off of a pistol".

Answering the Aisle du Fer-à-Cheval on the far side of the courtyard is the north wing containing the Galerie d'Apollon, beyond which an elaborate parterre stretches away to the north. At the far end of this parterre there used to be a "Perspective" – a large trompe l'oeil painting, done by Bon Boulogne, of a Corinthian rotunda representing the Temple of Flora.

To the west of the Jardin d'Apollon the ground rises steeply to the dark evergreen of the Labyrinthe. In 1825 these parterres were replaced by an "English Garden" named after the victory of Trocadero.

Thus, in Allegrain's painting, the gardens follow a main axis north and south, corresponding with the two wings of the forecourt in which Monsieur placed his principal apartments. With the building of the large double *corps de logis* which united these two wings, the need arose to develop the lay-out to the west, and a new axis, designed by Le Nôtre, contrived a further perspective of parterres opening into the long avenue known as the Allée de Marnes which vanished over the horizon.

All that is shown of this in Allegrain's painting is the Parterre de l'Orangerie, nearest to the château. On the far side of the parterre, its windows correctly facing the south, was the Orangerie itself, a fine building, not unlike the one added to Sceaux by Colbert's son, the marquis de Seignelay. On the wall opposite its thirteen windows, Jacques Rousseau painted a vast mural, the design for which is in the Victoria and Albert Museum today.

Rousseau was a Huguenot and it must be remembered that Liselotte von der Pfalz had been of the reformed religion before her marriage to Monsieur. One day in 1681 she entered the Orangerie. "I thought I was alone," she wrote, "and began to sing the sixth psalm [Lutheran]. I had hardly finished the first verse when I heard someone coming down in great haste from the scaffolding. It was Monsieur Rousseau, who threw himself at my feet. I thought he had gone mad.

" 'Good God! Monsieur Rousseau,' I said to him, 'what is the matter with you?'

" 'Is it possible, Madame, that you still remember your psalms and sing them? May the good God bless you and keep you in the right way of thinking.'

"There were tears in his eyes as he spoke. A few days later he ran away. I don't know where he went."

He went, ultimately, to London where, in 1687, he received an important commission from Ralph, Duke of Montagu. Together with Charles la Fosse and Jean-Baptiste Monnoyer, he executed the superb decorations of Montagu

House in Bloomsbury, of which Horace Walpole wrote: "It would be impossible to take the art of painting to greater lengths."

Montagu had been Ambassador to France and had visited Saint-Cloud, where the duc d'Orléans "treated him in the most splendid and magnificent manner at his noble seat of St. Cloud, that Prince doing him the Honour to walk to the end of his whole Garden with him (the most exquisite at that time in France), a favour he was not used to bestow on any, even the Princes of the Blood".

Jacques Rousseau became converted to Rome and returned to finish the Orangerie at Saint-Cloud. Just over a century later, this building was to be the scene of one of the decisive acts of French history, Napoleon's coup d'état of 18 Brumaire, that is to say 9 November, 1799.

The councils of the Directoire were summoned for midday, "les Anciens" in the Galerie d'Apollon and "les cinq Cents" in the Orangerie. The story is told by an anonymous member of the Five Hundred who claims to have been an "impartial eye-witness" of the events.

It was a critical situation. The Directoire had outlived its usefulness and was only able to exercise "la tyrannie de la faiblesse". The Treasury was empty; the situation in the Vendée grew daily more calamitous.

Napoleon first harangued the Anciens. "Let no one look for comparisons with the past," he warned them; "nothing in history can be compared with the end of the eighteenth century; nothing in the late eighteenth century can be compared with the present moment." No one dared to oppose him – "une morne silence fut la réponse qu'on lui fait."

Napoleon then turned his attention to the Five Hundred. The mood in the Orangerie had been more turbulent. As he entered there were cries of "Voilà Cromwell!" "Voilà le tyran!" and "A bas le tyran!" The author testifies that Napoleon was quite unmoved by his hostile reception – "I could not detect the slightest alteration of his countenance."

At the critical moment the doors were flung open and twelve Grenadiers with fixed bayonets entered the Orangerie. Their commander announced: "Those representatives who are friends of order and justice are to stay in their places, or retire to the chamber of les Anciens."

It was enough. The Jacobins were broken. There was a stampede for the windows: "They rush headlong; they crash into one another; they knock each other down; they all imagine that they have already been pierced by a thousand bullets." Down the avenues and alleys of the gardens they fled, discarding as they ran the distinctive clothing and insignia of their position. "The next day some of their costumes were found complete in the dry moats of the park."

It was a total triumph for Napoleon. "The day of 18 Brumaire," concludes the anonymous author, "will always be for me one of those political miracles which change in a single moment the face of empires."

An empire it was to become. On 18 May, 1804, Cambacérès was received by Napoleon in the Galerie d'Apollon at Saint-Cloud and after a short, obsequious speech, claiming that "the imperial crown adds nothing to your glory nor to your rights" he announced: "au nom du Sénat, pour la gloire comme pour la bonheur de la République, je proclame Napoléon Empereur

82 Aisle du fer-à-cheval after Mique's rebuilding. Engraving by Delaporte.

des Français." A contemporary engraving shows Cambacérès with two attendants bearing the imperial crown on a large cushion.

It is extraordinary how the position of Saint-Cloud, overlooking the capital and yet insulated from it by the Seine, made it a vantage point and drew it into the life of the country, so that what was intended for a *maison de plaisance* became the theatre of political events of the first importance. The palace was to be the scene of the downfall of Charles X and the legitimist Bourbon line; it was to witness also the last moments of the imperial dynasty under Napoleon III.

In 1829 the government of Charles X turned reactionary. The Prince de Polignac became first minister. Polignac was a visionary, claiming to receive direct guidance from the Virgin Mary. His appointment was really a gauntlet thrown before liberal opinion. Charles allowed himself to be puffed up by the success of French arms, notably in Algiers, and felt himself secure enough for a trial of strength.

On Sunday, 25 July, 1830, there were issued the four Ordonnances de Saint-Cloud. The secret had been well guarded; no one suspected anything. "Le Château de Saint-Cloud," noted the comte de Fleury, "avait son aspect accoutumé". As the King came out from the Chapel into the Galerie d'Apollon, there was the usual gathering of notables: the Papal Nuncio, Prince Paul of Württemberg, the British, Spanish and Neopolitan Ambassadors among others. At two in the afternoon the Conseil des Ministres met in the Library and the Ordonnances were laid before them. Monsieur Mangin, Préfet de Police, was asked to report on the state of Paris. He was bland in his optimism. "Whatever you do, Paris will not budge."

The King was the only one to show any hesitation. Article 14 of the *Charte*, to which he had sworn allegiance at his coronation, stated that the Head of State could make "les règlements et ordonnances nécessaires pour l'exécution des lois et la sûreté de l'Etat". The public had only the right to publish their opinions "en se conformant aux lois qui doivent reprimer les abus de cette liberté". Charles sat for a moment with his head in his hands; then he took his pen. "The more I think of it, the more I am convinced that it would be impossible to act otherwise."

Monday the 26th dawned warm and sunny. The bombshell of the Ordonnances was published in the *Moniteur*. Charles and the Dauphin went off to hunt in the Forêt de Rambouillet. Before leaving he embraced his grandchildren with an expression of melancholy which did not escape their Governess, the duchesse de Gontaut-Biron. Her memoirs give the most dramatic account of the events of the next four days. With the almost maternal instincts of one who is responsible for children, she had a deep sense of foreboding and tackled the King head on.

He held up a copy of the *Moniteur*. "Read it," he said; "you will find four Ordinances which I signed yesterday." And, counting them on his fingers, he began thus: "The modification of the electoral law; suspension of the constitutional rule; suppression of the liberty of the Press; finally, dissolution of the Chambre."

"The obvious disapproval of the King," continues the Duchess, "could not in any way silence my passionate devotion to the royal children." She asked him point blank if his Ordinances were not in violation of the Charter.

In Paris this was certainly the interpretation at once put upon them. Thiers was commissioned to write a protest in the *National*. "The rule of law has been suspended, the rule of force has started; obedience ceases to be a duty." The sparks were flying in the stubble, but the normal life of Paris continued. That day, it did not budge.

The royal children were expected at an official function at Versailles. The Duchess of course accompanied them. Every mark of loyal affection was showered upon the duc de Bordeaux: "flowers were strewn along the way; the fishwives presented bouquets; young girls presented compliments; the workers disputed the honour of holding him in their arms; he was received like a Prince – ce fut alors, hélas, pour la dernière fois!"

They went on to play in the gardens of the Petit Trianon. Like Marie-Antoinette in those same gardens, when another Revolution was looming on the horizon, they were unconscious of their fate. "On y était gai et heureux dans l'ignorance." The Duchess, however, sent M. Grenier, the drawing master, to see how the situation was at Versailles. He came back with an alarming report. The storm had already broken. It was decided to return immediately to Saint-Cloud. They had to drive back through the very street where, earlier in the day, they had been so spontaneously applauded. The flowers that had strewn the roads were now thrown back at them, mixed with sand and dirt.

Back at Saint-Cloud, the Duchess was prey to the deepest anxiety. "The air was warm," she writes; "I passed several hours of that night at the window of my salon, which commanded the whole of Paris, from which I could see in several places the red glows of what I feared to be fires."

She seems to have been the only person in the château to take the situation seriously. Polignac sent a dispatch on Tuesday saying that the reports were exaggerated and that the disorders were "a mere riot".

The Duchess, however, was better informed. The famous view of Paris from the windows of Saint-Cloud now gave her a front seat. By means of an excellent telescope in her salon she could see the further half of the rue de Rivoli, beyond the Tuileries. "From every house, from every window, men and women were hurling projectiles, pianos, chests of drawers, any furniture in fact that they could lay their hands on, with which to crush the troops concentrated in this street." It was a bright, sunny day and she could see with perfect clarity the towers of Notre-Dame. On the north tower was taking place "an appalling struggle between the rioters, who were raising the tricolor flag and the soldiers trying to remove it. A man was hurled from the top of the tower; I uttered a cry of horror. The ominous sound of the tocsin could be heard all the time, to which that of the cannon was soon joined." The Duchess, who had lived, forty years previously, through the first French Revolution, was in agonies: "L'anxiété de ce moment donnait à mon coeur le supplice du désespoir."

In the State Rooms of the château, however, all was calm. "None of the times, none of the routines was interrupted; the little walk after dinner on the terrace, where the children played ... the game of whist which nothing disturbed", and this in full view of the fires of Paris and to the incessant sound of the tocsin. "Voir les quatre joueurs de whist calme, tout à leur jeu, oserai-je dire le mot? me scandalisait."

On Tuesday the 29th the atmosphere at Saint-Cloud had completely changed. The whist table disappeared. The silence of the Court was only broken by the wounded soldiers who flocked into the courtyard, dying of hunger and crying for bread. The Duchess tried to get them provisions from Boulogne, from Bassy, even from Sèvres. Nothing was to be had. "The royal children, having seen the wretched wounded soldiers in the courtyard and heard them clamouring for food, had the idea of taking them their own dinner. Never will I forget the bright and animated countenance and the heartfelt enthusiasm of Monseigneur as, seizing an immense leg of mutton, he rushed downstairs. Mademoiselle followed him, carrying all she could lay her hands on. On reaching the soldiers these wonderful little royal children cried: 'Prenez, mes amis; c'est notre dîner.' Je les laissai faire; ils furent comblés de bénédictions."

On the night of the 30th General Greisseau arrived from Paris with a report so serious that the Dauphin decided to take the extreme step of waking the King. "Il dormait d'un paisible sommeil, le dernier dans un de ses palais."

The order for the departure was given. It was two in the morning. The duc de Bordeaux's carriage led the way; the Duchess and Mademoiselle followed in the next. "I saw a hand resting on the carriage doorhandle; I leant forward; it was beginning to be daylight; my eyes met those of the King; they were sad but not dejected. He did not speak to me but continued in silence to escort his grandchildren, all that was still precious to him on earth. To leave Saint-Cloud, the Court and all its grandeur had not cost me a sigh, but on seeing the sad, resigned expression of the King, I burst into tears."

Some nine months later, Louis-Philippe d'Orléans, who had accepted the Crown, returned as King to the house of his forefathers. Perhaps the most significant change which he made at Saint-Cloud was to rename the Salle du Trône the Salon de Famille.

He was deposed in 1848 and, after the brief Second Republic, was

83 The Cascade.
Drawing by I. Silvestre.

succeeded in 1852 by Napoleon III, under whom the Court of Saint-Cloud reached a level of brilliance which it had not witnessed since the days of Monsieur. The reign of Louis-Napoleon lasted for eighteen years.

The year 1870 dawned with a profound assurance of tranquillity. "On every side we look," declared the Premier Ministre, Emile Ollivier, "there is an absence of troublesome questions; at no moment has the maintenance of peace in Europe been better secured." He little knew how short was his political sight. On 14 July Bismarck's plans, carefully and methodically laid over a period of years, were detonated by the famous "Ems telegram". Incensed by an imaginary insult, the French were stampeded into a war for which they were utterly unprepared. Once again, Saint-Cloud was to witness the last scene before the downfall of a Sovereign.

On 18 July, the Emperor gave a dinner for the officers of the Guards Light Infantry, who were leaving for the front. The dinner was in the Galerie d'Apollon "splendidement illuminée". When dessert was served, Louis-Napoleon gave the order sotto voce for the band to strike up the "Marseillaise". "He knew well," wrote Fleury, "that it would stir up patriotic vibrations in the hearts of the officers." The success was immediate. They rose to their feet, raised their glasses to the Emperor and shouted, "Vive la France! Vive l'Empereur! A Berlin!"

The following day the Prince Imperial, then aged fourteen, dressed in a top hat and Eton collar, "comme un jeune Anglais", went to see Maréchal

84 Eugénie's Cabinet de
Toilette. Water-colour by
F. Fournier.

Baillehache. "Suddenly he turned towards the Marshal, his eyes dancing with
excitement: "Vous savez, Maréchal du Logis, que je pars aussi, moi!" He
stressed the word *moi* with youthful satisfaction and the Marshal, deeply
moved, replied, "I do know, Monseigneur, and the whole army is proud of
it.""

The next day the Emperor and the Prince left for the front from the little
private railway station in the park of Saint-Cloud known as the Gare de
l'Empereur. Eugénie was of course there to see them off. "Fais ton devoir,
Louis!" were her last words to her son as the train pulled out of the station.
Shaken with sobs, she returned to the bleak emptiness of the château.

The agony did not last long. On 7 August the comte de Cossé-Brissac
brought the Empress a telegram. It announced the disasters of Worth and
Forbach. "L'armée est en déroute," read the message; "il faut élever notre
courage à hauteur des circonstances." Considering the circumstances, the
imperial family were lucky to find themselves before the end of the year safe
in Chislehurst.

The palace of Saint-Cloud was less fortunate. On 17 September the
Régisseur, Schneider, began removing the most valuable works of art. All the
Gobelin tapestries, done from the cartoons of Rubens; twenty-two pieces of
furniture by Boulle, eight paintings by Vernet and four crystal chandeliers
were removed.

On 19 September the Prussians, under General von Kirchbach, took
possession of Saint-Cloud. After a few puerile gestures – such as taking turns
to sit at the Emperor's desk, and a lot of minor acts of pillage – the new
occupants began to settle down. "Un calme rélatif regnait à Saint-Cloud."

On the 27th, with the arrival of Colonel von Flottow, the situation began
to deteriorate. On 13 October the Prussians blew up the Tour de Démosthène,

85 Mique's staircase after the fire.

a lighthouse built by Napoleon at the end of the south alley, thinking it might provide a hostile observatory. This attracted fire from the French batteries of Mont Valérien. Several of the shells fell short and landed on the château.

An ordinary shell does not easily set fire to an ordinary building. It is more probable that the shelling of Saint-Cloud was the pretext for the conflagration rather than its cause and that the Prussians did to the château what they certainly did to the houses of the town. On 28 January, after the truce had been signed, M. Duchain, Inspecteur du Service des Eaux, returned to Saint-Cloud to find German soldiers going round with barrels of paraffin, deliberately setting fire to house after house.

The palace was completely gutted. The Crown Prince expressed a polite regret that it had been impossible to save the painting by Muller of Queen Victoria's visit. Among the many photographs of the ruins, perhaps the most pathetic is one which shows the elegant wrought iron hand-rail of the Escalier de la Reine – the same staircase up which Victoria had been conducted on her first arrival at the château – lying crumpled at the bottom of its well.

269

For twenty years the empty carcase of the château continued to dominate the town. In 1890 there was still enough standing for the English traveller Augustus Hare to admire. "The château is more reddened than blackened by the fire," he wrote; "and the beautiful reliefs of its gables" (he must have meant the pediments), "its statues and the wrought iron grilles of its balconies are still perfect. Grass and even trees grow in its roofless halls, in one of which the marble pillars and sculptured decorations are seen through the gaps where windows once were."

The following year the last remains were cleared away.

The ruins of Saint-Cloud could have been restored. The same is true of the Tuileries. The palace was burnt in 1871, not by the Prussians but by the leaders of a purely Parisian revolution, the Commune.

The first reactions of the Communards after the collapse of the Empire was to take possession of the Tuileries. Popular concerts were given in the State Apartments. But placarded on the walls for all to see was the notice put up by Dr. Ronselle: "People! the gold which glistens on these walls is your sweat. For too long your labour has fed and your blood has watered this insatiable monster, the Monarchy. Today the Revolution sets you free; you enter into possession of yourselves. Remain worthy of that and take good care that the tyrants never come back."

The organisers of the Revolution were determined to stop at nothing. "Paris will be ours or will cease to exist," was their slogan. Bergeret had made the ominous statement: "When I leave the Tuileries they will be a heap of ashes." He and a certain Benot proceeded with deliberate plans for the burning of the palace. On the afternoon of 23 May waggons loaded with gunpowder and paraffin were seen crossing the courtyard between the Louvre and the Tuileries. Benot and his assistants disposed their combustible materials in every room and set light to the fuse.

Bergeret and his "staff" were dining together in the Louvre and mounted onto the leads to watch the conflagration. For three hours the fire raged, bringing beams and ceilings crashing onto the floors below. At eleven o'clock came the *pièce de résistance* – a sudden explosion burst through the dome of the Pavillon de l'Horloge. Their work of devastation was complete.

A week later, Octave Feuillet and his wife returned to Paris and took up residence in the Hôtel de Rivoli. From their balcony they overlooked the ruins of the Tuileries. "All that remained of the Palace of our Kings were the charred walls and gaping windows, through which the moon cast its luminous rays, as if the fire were not yet extinguished. In all this chaos our eyes still sought through their tears the Master and Mistress of the place who had been our friends; sought the spectre of a brilliant past which had been the envy of the world. Nothing was left but a dark abyss which lay beneath the stars. *C'était un monde disparu.*"

Epilogue:

Resurrection

ON 10 June, 1837, the Château de Versailles, restored by Louis-Philippe and reorganised to fit its new role as a museum dedicated "to all the Glories of France", was thrown open to an admiring public. "It was a case of the Palace of Louis XIV being taken by assault by the bourgeoisie," wrote Madame de Boigne.

She had of course been invited to the opening ceremony. A banquet for fourteen hundred people was served in the Galerie des Glaces and its attendant Salons. The Countess noted, with her usual observant eye, that the King was seated immediately beneath Le Brun's allegorical painting: "Le Roi gouverne par lui-même." Returning after coffee in the royal apartments, they found all traces of the banquet removed and the Gallery cleared for the reception.

"The weather was magnificent, and the sun was beginning to sink towards the great basin at the end of the park and darted its beams on the façades of the château." From the windows of the gallery, the King's guests could overlook the alleys and parterres of the restored gardens. "I appreciated in that moment and for the first time the merit of the talent of Le Nôtre. It was in order to be inhabited with this royal splendour that this pompous Versailles had been conceived," wrote Madame de Boigne; "all honour to the King who has found the way to resurrect it as far as circumstances permit. Only the whole nation – a sufficiently 'grande dame' for today – can replace Louis XIV in his palace."

To make room for the new galleries, hundreds of the most beautiful eighteenth-century interiors were swept away and many of those which survived were disfigured by the application of a thick coat of grey paint misnamed "gris Trianon". But, regrettable though some of his actions were, Louis-Philippe deserves the indulgence of posterity; he devoted some twenty-four million livres of his civil list to his new museum and thereby saved Versailles from becoming a barracks – a fate which, for such a building, is simply unthinkable.

Much of the damage was only superficial. Under the grey paint there still lurked the chaste colours of Etienne Martin and the finely-chiselled carvings of Verberckt. Up in the attics, awaiting classification, were stacked the canvasses of Largillière, Boucher and Nattier. Down in the gardens, scarcely visited except when the fountains were playing, the statues remained as Le Brun had placed them. Restoration was still a possibility.

But, before anyone could undertake an accurate restoration, the exact topography of the palace had to be reconstituted. The break with the Ancien Régime had been complete. The naming of the rooms had always been complicated; now it was forgotten. Only by the patient and painstaking classification of the innumerable plans and documents could questions of the authentic decorations be resolved. This great work was the achievement of Pierre de Nolhac.

Parallel with his researchers among the archives went the rediscovery of Versailles itself. One day, finding a door which did not answer to his master key, Nolhac enquired its purpose. It was a closet, he was informed, where the staff kept their cleaning materials. He had the door opened, and penetrated into an obscure chamber whose walls, dimly visible, revealed a strange and fascinating decoration. Scenes of bathing and aquatic sports framed in oval bullrush borders were carved in the centre of each panel, while swans and dolphins, scissors and shaving utensils, formed the unusual adornment of the window recess. The store cupboard of the charwomen was nothing less than the bathroom of Louis XV, the last of his extensive redecorations of the palace. Four shades of gilding – glossy, matt, green and bronze – had been used by Dutems and Brancour to vary the effects of this exotic décor.

By 1925 the researches of Nolhac had made possible a work of accurate restoration. But the First World War had left the fabric of the building in a condition which was approaching ruin. Millions of francs were needed for its repair.

It was just at this time that, by a happy chance, John D. Rockefeller, Jr, chose to spend his honeymoon in France. He and his wife were profoundly moved by the beauty of Versailles and Fontainebleau and by the pitiable condition of Reims Cathedral. He set himself to make a thorough study of the problem.

The result was the creation of the Fondation Rockefeller. In 1925 there was a first donation of 11,000,000 francs, followed two years later by a further grant of 23,000,000.

On 19 September, 1925, Monsieur Albert Bray, Architecte en Chef, addressed the Société des Amis de Fontainebleau and gave them the welcome news of this munificence. He began, of course, by expressing their immense gratitude to "le donateur magnifique et délicat". The words were well-chosen, for while his gift was magnificent, Rockefeller had that delicacy which could recognise that the French, with their great tradition of expertise in the fine arts, would not misuse his gift. "I would consider it a privilege," he said, "if I were allowed to contribute to this cause in placing one million dollars at the distribution of a committee composed of French and American members."

Albert Bray reminded his listeners that the first crisis of this sort at Fontainebleau had been in 1580, under Henri III, when a memoir was drawn up "to avoid and remedy the total and entire ruin of the said château". The main concern was with the roof. The manner in which Fontainebleau had been built, with each generation making its own additions, had played havoc with the roofscape. Valleys had been created between twin roofs without adequate drainage. The importance of these roofs in the silhouette of the château was also stressed. French architecture almost depends upon it. The

Monuments Historiques set up a commission under the chairmanship of Boeswilwald, Paléologue from the Franco-American committee, and the marquise de Ganay, President of the Société des Amis de Fontainebleau, to administer the trust.

At Versailles also the main expenditure was on the roof, but at Rockefeller's particular request the little theatre of Marie-Antoinette at Trianon and the houses of the Hameau were also restored.

The Rockefeller donation is a great landmark in the history of Versailles. It testifies to what Gabriel Hanotaux called "the internationalism of beauty", the recognition by the world that all great works of art are the world's irreplaceable heritage, and an acceptance by the whole of civilisation of responsibility for their preservation. It gave impetus to a movement which is still in process.

But the preservation of the fabric was only the prerequisite for the restoration of the décor and of the furnishings. It is interesting to look back at some of the old guide books of Versailles or Fontainebleau and to compare the denuded aspect of the rooms with their condition today. In the years since the Second World War there has been a steady programme of redecoration and refurnishing; little by little the palaces are regaining their original sumptuosity.

The problem of the furniture was one of the most difficult to resolve. Starting from the year 1685, the 3,600 pages of the *Journal du Garde-Meuble* recorded, in the course of just over a century, the purchase of some nine thousand articles of furniture. Every room in every palace was carpeted with the luxurious pile and colourful designs of the Aubusson and Savonnerie works; the furniture, often specially designed to match the decorations, filled the rooms with the magnificent commodes of Benneman and Riesener and with the elegant chairs and sofas of Foliot and Tilliard. Every detail was exquisite, down to the furniture of the doors and windows and fireplaces in beautifully-worked bronze by Gouthière and Caffieri or the silk hangings and upholsteries woven at Lyons by the houses of Pernon, Gaudin or Baudoin. "No museum in the world," wrote Pierre Verlet, "could give an impression of what were, before 1790, the apartments at Versailles or Compiègne or Fontainebleau. One day, perhaps, it will be understood how desirable it is to reconstitute exactly the magnificence of this or that room in these châteaux; to that which seems to belong to the category of a dream, I would like to give a precise foundation of reality."

It needed his own work, of equal importance in its own field to that of Pierre de Nolhac, of patient research into the archives of the Garde-Meuble, before the secure identification of the pieces of furniture and the rooms to which they belonged could be established.

The dispersal of the furniture had been world-wide. The Revolutionary government, issuing its own money in the form of *assignats*, found other countries reluctant to accept it and used pieces of furniture as items of barter. "It exchanged many lots of furniture," writes Verlet, "of tapestry and of carpets against sacks of coffee or cargoes of corn. The contractors to the Republic, nearly all installed abroad, preferred to these *assignats* the solid values represented by the furniture of the *ci-devant* royal château."

On 25 August, 1793, began the sale of furniture at Versailles. It lasted for a whole year. In 1794 that of Fontainebleau occupied the four months between the end of June and the end of October. Only relatively few items found their way into the national collection at the Louvre.

The recovery of any substantial amount of this must have seemed impossible. But the setting up of the Versailles Foundation, the great work of the Curator Gerald van der Kemp, has already resulted in the redecoration and refurnishing of some of the most important rooms. The work continues under his successor Pierre Lemoine.

This resurrection of the former glories is being achieved in two ways: the recovery of some of the original items and the remaking of others from the original designs. Clearly, when it comes to fabrics, the latter is likely to be the more usual.

One of the most scintillating successes has been the reconstitution of Louis XIV's bedroom. It was decided to recreate the *meuble d'été* of 1723. Two remnants of brocade of very similar design to that described in the inventory served as a model. Fifty-six metres of the material were needed for the bed alone. The houses of Prelle and Tassarini-Chatel at Lyons were able to reweave the fabric. Then came the elaborate embroidery, carried out under the direction of Madame Brocart. It was thanks to donations from Ms. Barbara Hutton and Mr. Arturo Lopez-Willshaw that this reconstruction was made possible.

Together with generous donations of money came equally generous returns of pieces of furniture. In the Queen's bedroom Barbara Hutton presented the original carpet made in 1730 for Marie-Leczinska. The original counterpane was offered by the Kress Foundation, while the silk hangings, authentic in design, were given by the Silk Federation of Lyons.

And so the work continues and will continue. The roll of honour is long and will become longer. It already contains names which range from the present head of the French royal family, the comte de Paris, to the Coca-Cola Company; from the Duke of Buccleuch to Paramount Studios; from the Gaekwar of Baroda to Mitsukoshi-Tokyo.

That all these people should have wished to contribute to such a cause in such a way is one of the most encouraging aspects of the international scene today. "The Arts of Peace" is a phrase which in these days, when peace is so precarious, we need to take seriously to heart. We other countries can freely and generously acknowledge the proper and particular contribution to the artistic achievement of the world made by the creators of the royal palaces of France. "Who could have told," asked Montesquieu in the eighteenth century, "that the late King had established the greatness of France by building Versailles and Marly?"

Bibliography

The Palais de la Cité

Jean Gerout: Le palais de la Cité à Paris des Origines à 1417. In *Mémoires de la Fédération des Sociétés Historiques et Archaeologiques de Paris et de l'Ile de France*, Vols I, II & III. 1952.

Jacques Hillairet: L'Ile de la Cité. 1969.

Henri Stein: Le Palais de Justice et la Sainte-Chapelle de Paris. 1927.

Louis Grodecki: La Sainte-Chapelle. 1975.

Robert Branner: Saint-Louis and the Court Style in Gothic Architecture.

Sauveur-Jérôme Morand: Histoire de la Sainte-Chapelle Royale du Palais. 1790.

J. Spencer: Les Vitraux de la Sainte-Chapelle. In *Bulletin Monumental*. 1932.

The Château de Vincennes

F. de Fossa: Le Château Historique de Vincennes à travers les Ages. 1908.

Ernest Lemarchand: Le Château Royal de Vincennes de son Origine à nos Jours. 1907.

Martial de Pradel de Lamase: Vincennes. 1932.

Jean Cordey: Colbert, Le Vau et la construction du Château de Vincennes. In *Gazette des Beaux Arts*. 1933.

The Château de Fontainebleau

F. Herbert: Le Château de Fontainebleau. 1937.

L. Dimier: Le Château de Fontainebleau. 1949.

Le Père Dan: Trésor des Merveilles de la Maison Royale de Fontainebleau. 1642.

A. Bray: Les Origines de Fontainebleau. Fontainebleau avant François I. In *Bulletin Monumental*. 1935.

A. Chastel and others: La Galerie François I. In *Revue de l'Art*. 1972.

C. & J. P. Samoyault: Le Château de Fontainebleau au XVIe Siècle. In *Petit Journal des Grands Expositions*. 1972.

C. & J. P. Samoyault: Le Château de Fontainebleau sous Henri IV. In *Petit Journal des Grands Expositions*. 1978.

J. Héroard: Journal de Jean Héroard sur l'Enfance et la Jeunesse de Louis XIII. 1868.

J. Ehrmann: La Belle Cheminée de Fontainebleau. In *Actes du Colloque International sur l'Art de France*. 1975.

Y. Bottineau: La Cour de Louis XIV à Fontainebleau. In *Bulletin de la Société de l'Étude du 17e Siècle*. 1954.

Y. Bottineau: Le Château de Fontainebleau sous Louis XV. In *Médecine de France*. December 1972.

Y. Bottineau: Précisions sur le Fontainebleau de Louis XVI. In *Gazette des Beaux Arts*. 1967.

P. Verlet: Le Boudoir de Marie-Antoinette à Fontainebleau. In *Art de France*. 1961.

J. P. Samoyault: Le Château de Fontainebleau sous Napoléon I. In *Médecine de France*. 1974.

J. Aigoin: Fontainebleau sous le Deuxième Empire. 1931.

The Château de Saint Germain

G. Houdard: Les Châteaux Royaux de Saint Germain en Laye. 1911.

R. Berthon: Saint Germain en Laye. 1966.

L. de la Tourasse: Le Château Neuf de Saint Germain, ses Terrasses et ses Grottes. In *Gazette des Beaux Arts*. 1924.

A. Mousset: Les Francines, Créatures des Eaux de Versailles. 1930.

The Château du Louvre

L. de Hautecoeur: Histoire du Louvre. 1942.

L. de Hautecoeur: Le Louvre de Pierre Lescot. In *Gazette des Beaux Arts*

L. de Hautecoeur: Le Louvre et les Tuileries de Louis XIV. 1927.

L. Battifol: Les Travaux du Louvre sous Henri IV. In *Gazette des Beaux Arts*. 1927.

T. Sauvel: Le Mercier et la Construction du Pavillon de l'Horloge. In *Bulletin Monumental*. 1966.

T. Sauvel: Les Auteurs de la Colonnade du Louvre. In *Bulletin Monumental*. 1964.

Versailles. Louis XIV. The Palace

P. de Nolhac: La Création de Versailles. 1925.

P. de Nolhac: Versailles, Résidence de Louis XIV. 1925.

A. Marie: Naissance de Versailles. 1968.

A. Marie: Mansart à Versailles. 1972.

F. Kimball: The Genesis of the Château Neuf at Versailles. In *Gazette des Beaux Arts*. 1949.

L. Lange: La Grotte de Thétis et le Premier Versailles. In *Art de France*. 1961.

I. Murat: Colbert. 1976.

Versailles. Louis XIV. The Gardens

A. Barbet: Les Grandes Eaux de Versailles. 1907.

E. de Ganay: Le Nôtre. 1962.

S. Hoog: Louis XIV. La manière de montrer les jardins de Versailles. 1982.

F. H. Hazelhurst: Gardens of Illusion. The Genius of Le Nôtre. 1980.

Trianon

R. Danis: La Première Maison Royale de Trianon. 1927.

P. de Nolhac: Trianon. 1927.

A. Marie: Trianon de Porcelaine et Grand Trianon. In *Bulletin de l'Histoire de l'Art Français*. 1945.

B. Jestaz: Le Trianon de Marbre ou Louis XIV Architecte. In *Gazette des Beaux Arts*. 1969.

Marly

J. & A. Marie: Marly. 1947.

A. Marie: Marly. Son jeu de construction reconstitué pièce par pièce. In *Connaissance des Arts*. 1972.

Jean Feray: Epaves de Marly. In *Bulletin de la Société de l'Histoire de l'Art Français*. 1979.

The Château de Meudon

P. Biver: Histoire du Château de Meudon. 1923.

F. H. Hazelhurst: Gardens of Illusion. The Genius of Le Nôtre. 1980.

Versailles. Louis XV

P. de Nolhac. Versailles au XVIIIe Siècle. 1926.

I. Dunlop: The Petits Appartements de Louis XV at Versailles. In *Connoisseur Year Book*. 1955.

H. Racinais: La Vie inconnue des Petits Cabinets de Versailles. 1951.

J. Feray, P. Verlet, A. Japay: Opéra de Versailles. In *Les Monuments Historiques de la France*. 1957.

Versailles. Louis XVI

D. Meyer: Quand les Rois régnaient a Versailles. 1982.

M. Jallut: Cabinets Intérieurs et Petits Appartments de Marie-Antoinette. In *Gazette des Beaux Arts*. 1964.

P. Verlet: Le Mobilier Royal Français. 1945.

Versailles. Petit Trianon

G. Desjardins: Le Petit Trianon. 1885.

P. de Nolhac: Trianon. 1927.

The Château des Tuileries I

G. Lenôtre: Les Tuileries. 1933.

J. Hillairet: Le Palais Royal et Impérial des Tuileries et son Jardin. 1965

P. Roussel d'Epinal: Le Château des Tuileries. 1802.

T. Sauvel: Recherches sur les resources dont Catherine de Medicis a disposées pour construire les Tuileries. In *Bulletin de la Sociéte de l'Histoire de l'Art Français*. 1967.

The Château des Tuileries II

F. Boyer: Les Tuileries sous le Directoire. In *Bulletin de la Société de l'Histoire de l'Art Français*. 1934.

M.-L. Biver: Pierre Fontaine. 1964.

E. Bouyer. Les Appartements de S. M.
l'Impératrice au Palais des Tuileries.
1867.

H. Lefuel: Jacob Desmalters. 1955.

The Château de Compiègne

J. Pelassy de l'Ousle: Histoire du Palais de
Compiègne. 1862.

P. Quentin-Bauchart: Chroniques du
Château de Compiègne. 1953.

F. Thiveaud-Henand: La Reconstruction
du Château de Compiègne au XVIIIe
Siècle. 1970.

Comte de Fels: Ange-Jacques Gabriel.
1912.

The Château de Saint-Cloud

Comte de Fleury: Le Palais de Saint-
Cloud, ses Origines, ses Hôtes, ses
Fastes, ses Ruines. 1902.

Queen Victoria: Leaves from a Journal.
1961.

Comte de Fels: Dans les Jardins de Saint-
Cloud. In *Gazette Illustrée des Amateurs
des Jardins*. 1914.

D. Meyer: Les Appartements Royaux du
Château de Saint-Cloud sous Louis
XVI et Marie-Antoinette. In *Gazette
des Beaux Arts*. 1965.

Epilogue (Resurrection)

P. de Nolhac: La Resurrection de Versailles. Souvenirs d'un Conservateur
1887–1920. 1937.

A. Hallays: La Donation de M. Rockefeller 11 à Versailles. In *Journal des
Débats*. 1926.

W. Dawson: Versailles and the Rocke-
fellers. In *Revue des Deux Mondes*.
1954.

A. Bray: Conférence faite par M. Albert
Bray, Architecte en chef du Palais sur
l'emploi du Don Rockefeller. Société
des amis de Fontainebleau. 1925.

Illustration acknowledgements

The colour illustrations are reproduced by the kind permission of the following: 1) Musée de Sceaux/Photo Bulloz; 2) Cliché Flammarion; 3) Musée de Fontainebleau/Cliché des Musées Nationaux; 4) Kunsthistorisches Museum, Vienna; 5) Musée de Fontainebleau/Photographie Giraudon; 6) Musée Carnavalet/Photo Bulloz; 7) By kind permission of Mlle. de Gineste; 8) Reproduced by Gracious Permission of Her Majesty The Queen; 9) Musée de Versailles/Cliché des Musées Nationaux; 10) Musée de Versailles/Photographie Giraudon; 11) Musée de Versailles/Cliché des Musées Nationaux; 12) By kind permission of His Grace The Duke of Devonshire; 13) Reproduced by Gracious Permission of Her Majesty The Queen; 14) Musée des Arts Décoratifs/Photo Sully-Jaulmes; 15) Musée de Compiègne/Photo Hutin; 16) Reproduced by Gracious Permission of Her Majesty The Queen.

The black and white illustrations are reproduced by the kind permission of the following: Reproduced by Gracious Permission of her Majesty The Queen, no. 43; Phot. Bibl. Nat. Paris, nos. 1, 36, 37, 38, 40, 41, 42, 44, 48, 52, 54, 73, 76, 82, 85; British Museum, nos. 32, 34, 35, 66, 67; Musée de Versailles/Cliché des Musées Nationaux, nos. 9, 57, 61, 62, 65, 69, 72, 73, 81; Musée du Louvre/Cliché des Musées Nationaux, nos. 33, 45, 46, 56, 60, 68, 83; Musée du Louvre/Cabinet des Dessins, no. 47; Musée de Compiègne/Cliché des Musées Nationaux, no. 84; Musée Condé/Photographie Giraudon, nos. 7, 31; Musée Carnavalet/Photo Bulloz, no. 29; Collection Viollet, nos. 39, 63, 75; Photo Hutin, nos. 79, 80; Photo Germond, nos. 5, 6; Ian Dunlop, nos. 2, 11, 14, 50, 54; The Metropolitan Museum of Art/Robert Lehman Collection, no. 3; Photographie Giraudon, no. 4; BBC Hulton Picture Library, no. 10; The Mansell Collection, no. 71; Photo Bulloz, no. 70; Archives Nationales, Paris, no. 37; Archives Nationales, Paris/Conway Library, no. 75; National Museum, Stockholm, no. 49; Arch. Phot. Paris/S.P.A.D.E.M., nos. 8, 16, 17, 27; Château de Fontainebleau Service Photographique, nos. 12, 13, 19, 20, 21, 23, 24, 25, 26; Fonds Iconographique sur Saint Germain, 29; Château de Versailles Service Photographique, nos. 58, 59, 65.

INDEX